Gregory Benford

TIME-SCAPE

PUBLISHED BY POCKET BOOKS NEW YORK

POCKET BOOKS, a Simon & Schuster division of
GULF & WESTERN CORPORATION
1230 Avenue of the Americas, New York, N.Y. 10020

ISBN: 0-671-83389-8

First Pocket Books printing July, 1981

10 9 8 7 6 5 4 3 2 1

POCKET and colophon are trademarks of Simon & Schuster.

Also available in Simon and Schuster trade edition.

Printed in the U.S.A.

Special Acknowledgment

I wish to acknowledge warmly the contribution made by my sister-in-law, Hilary Foister Benford, to this book. She contributed significantly to the manuscript, bringing to it her special qualities of interest in people. Certain characters are in part her creation. As a native of England and a graduate of Cambridge University, she gave invaluable help in developing and maintaining a consistent British idiom. Without her contribution this would be a quite different book.

Gregory Benford
Cambridge
August, 1979

Acknowledgments

For technical discussions I am indebted to Doctors Riley Newman, David Book and Sidney Coleman.

Many facets of this work were improved by my wife, Joan Abbe. Her patience and support, as well as that of my children, Alyson and Mark, were invaluable.

For editing and work on the final draft I thank Asenath Hammond. I am indebted to David and Marilee Samuelson, Charles Brown, Malcolm Edwards, Richard Curtis, Lawrence Littenberg and especially David Hartwell for comments on the manuscript.

Many scientific elements in this novel are true. Others are speculative, and thus may well prove false. My aim has been to illuminate some outstanding philosophical difficulties in physics. If the reader emerges with the conviction that time represents a fundamental riddle in modern physics, this book will have served its purpose.

GREGORY BENFORD
Cambridge
August, 1979

to RICHARD CURTIS with thanks

Absolute, true, and mathematical time, of itself and from its own nature, flows equably without relation to anything external.

—NEWTON

•

For us believing physicists the distinction between past, present, and future is only an illusion, even if a stubborn one.

—EINSTEIN, 1955

•

How is it possible to account for the difference between past and future when an examination of the laws of physics reveals only the symmetry of time? . . . present-day physics makes no provision whatever for a flowing time, or for a moving present moment.

—P. C. W. DAVIES
The Physics of Time Asymmetry,
1974

TIME-
SCAPE

chapter one

SPRING, 1998

Remember to smile a lot, John Renfrew thought moodily. People seemed to like that. They never wondered why you kept on smiling, no matter what was said. It was a kind of general sign of good will, he supposed, one of the tricks he could never master.

"Daddy, look—"

"Damn, watch out!" Renfrew cried. "Get that paper out of my porridge, will you? Marjorie, why are the bloody dogs in the kitchen while we're having breakfast?"

Three figures in suspended animation stared at him. Marjorie, turning from the stove with a spatula in her hand. Nicky, raising a spoon to a mouth which formed an O of surprise. Johnny beside him, holding out a school paper, his face beginning to fall. Renfrew knew what was going through his wife's mind. *John must be really upset. He never gets angry.*

Right, he didn't. It was another luxury they couldn't afford.

The still photograph unfroze. Marjorie moved abruptly, shooing the yelping dogs out the back door. Nicky bowed her head to study her cooked cereal. Then Marjorie led Johnny back to his place at the table. Renfrew took a long, rustling breath and bit into his toast.

"Don't bother Daddy today, Johnny. He's got a very important meeting this morning."

A meek nod. "I'm sorry, Daddy."

Daddy. They all called him Daddy. Not Pop, as Renfrew's father had wanted to be called. That was a name for fathers with rough hands, who worked with caps on.

Renfrew looked moodily round the table. Sometimes he felt out of place here, in his own kitchen. That was his son sitting there in a Perse school uniform blazer, speaking in that clear upper-class voice. Renfrew remembered the confusing mixture of contempt and envy he had felt towards such boys when he was Johnny's age. At times he would glance casually at Johnny and the memory of those times would come back. Renfrew would brace himself for that familiar well-bred indifference in his son's face—and be moved to find admiration there instead.

"I'm the one should be sorry, lad. I didn't mean to shout at you like that. It's as your mother said, I'm a bit bothered today. So what's this paper you wanted to show me, eh?"

"Well, they're having this competition for the best paper —" Johnny began shyly "—on how school kids can help clean up the environment and everything and save energy and things. I wanted you to see it before I give it in."

Renfrew bit his lip. "I haven't got time today, Johnny. When does it have to be in? I'll try and read it through tonight if I can. Okay?"

"Okay. Thanks, Daddy. I'll leave it here. I know you're doing frightfully important work. The English master said so."

"Oh, did he? What did he say?"

"Well, actually . . ." The boy hesitated. "He said the scientists got us into this beastly mess in the first place and they're the only ones who can get us out of it now, if anyone can."

"He's not the first one to say that, Johnny. That's a truism."

"Truism? What's a truism, Daddy?"

"*My* form mistress says just the opposite," Nicky came in suddenly. "She says the scientists have caused enough trouble already. She says God is the only one who can get us out of it and He probably won't."

"Oh, lor', another prophet of doom. Well, I suppose that's better than the primmies and their back-to-the-stone-age rubbish. Except that the prophets of doom stay around and depress us all."

"Miss Crenshaw says the primmies won't escape God's judgment *either,* however far they run," Nicky said definitively.

"Marjorie, what's going on in that school? I don't want her filling Nicky's head with ideas like that. The woman sounds unbalanced. Speak to the headmistress about her."

"I doubt that it would do much good," Marjorie replied equably. "There are far more 'prophets of doom,' as you call them, around than anyone else these days."

"Miss Crenshaw says we should all just pray," Nicky went on obstinately. "Miss Crenshaw says it's a *judgment.* And probably the end of the world."

"Well, that's just silly, dear," Marjorie said. "Where would we be if we all just sat about and prayed? You have to get on with things. Speaking of which, you children had better get a move on or you'll be late to school."

"Miss *Crenshaw* says, 'Consider the lilies of the field,'" Nicky muttered as she left the room.

"Well, I'm no bloody lily," Renfrew said, pushing back his chair and rising, "so I'd better go off and toil for another day."

"Leaving me to spin?" Marjorie smiled. "It's the only way, isn't it? Here's your lunch. No meat again this week, but I got a bit of cheese at the farm and I pulled some early carrots. I think we may have some potatoes this year. You'd like that, wouldn't you?" She reached up and kissed him. "I do hope the interview goes well."

"Thanks, luv." He felt the old familiar tightening begin. He had to get that funding. He'd put vast sums of time and thought into this project. He must have the equipment. It had to be tried.

Renfrew left the house and mounted his bicycle Already he was sloughing off the family man, his thoughts reaching ahead to the lab, the day's instructions to the technicians, the coming interview with Peterson.

He pumped along, leaving Grantchester and skirting round Cambridge. It had rained during the night. A slight mist hung low over the ploughed fields, softening the light. Drops clung to the new green leaves on the trees. Moisture glittered on the carpet of bluebells covering the ground in the clearings. The lane here ran alongside a little stream lined by low alder bushes and nettles. On the surface of the stream he could see ripples forming as the bugs called water boatmen jerked themselves along on their oarlike legs. Kingcups were blooming in a sheet of gold along the banks and big soft furry catkins were coming out on the willows. It was a fresh April morning, the kind he had loved as a boy in Yorkshire, watching the mist rise off the moors in the pale morning sun and the hares scurry off at his approach. The lane he was cycling along had sunk deep over the years and his head was nearly level with the tree roots on either side. A smell of damp earth and rain-washed grass came to him, mixed with an acrid tang of coal smoke.

A man and a woman eyed him blankly as he pedaled by. They leaned idly against a sagging wood fence. Renfrew grimaced. Each month more squatters drifted into the area, thinking Cambridge was a rich town. Off to the right was the shambles of an old farmhouse. In the last week the yawning black windows had been blocked in with newspaper, boards, and rags. It was surprising squatters hadn't smelled out the place before.

The last bit of cycling, nipping through the outskirts of Cambridge, was the worst. The streets were difficult to negotiate, with cars parked every which way, abandoned. There had been a national program to recycle them, but all Renfrew had seen come of it was a lot of talk on television. He threaded among the cars, which sat there like eyeless, legless beetles, stripped of all their removable parts. Students were living in some of them. Drowsy faces turned to watch him wobble by.

In front of the Cavendish he locked his bicycle into the rack. One car in the lot, he noticed. Surely that bugger Peterson wasn't here this early? It wasn't yet 8:30. He trotted up the steps and across the entrance hall.

To Renfrew the present complex of three buildings was anonymous. The original Cav, where Rutherford had discovered the nucleus, was an old brick building in the center of Cambridge, a museum. From the Madingley Road two hundred meters away this place could easily be taken for an insurance center or a factory or any business place. When it had opened in the early '70s the "new Cav" had been immaculate, with harmonized color schemes, carpets in the library, and well-stocked shelves. Now the corridors were poorly lit and many laboratories yawned empty, stripped of equipment. Renfrew made his way to his own lab in the Mott building.

"Good morning, Dr. Renfrew."

"Oh, morning, Jason. Has anyone been in?"

"Well, George came in to start the roughing pumps, but—"

"No, no, I mean a visitor. I'm expecting a fellow from London. Peterson's his name."

"Oh, no. No one like that. You want me to get started here, then?"

"Yes, go ahead. How's the apparatus?"

"Fairly good. The vacuum is coming down. We're at ten microns now. We've got a fresh charge of liquid nitrogen and we've checked out the electronics. Looks as if one of the amplifiers is going. We're doing some calibrations and the equipment should be checked out in about an hour."

"Okay. Look here, Jason, this fellow Peterson is coming down from the World Council. He's considering increasing funding. We'll have a run for him, put the apparatus through its paces in a few hours. Try to look lively and spruce the place up a bit, will you?"

"Right. I'll get her running."

Renfrew went down the catwalk to the floor of the laboratory and stepped nimbly over the wires and cables. The room was of bare concrete, outfitted with old-fashioned electrical connections and rather newer cables strewn through the aisles of apparatus. Renfrew greeted each of the technicians as he came to them, asked questions about the running of the ion focusers, and gave his instructions. He knew this warren of equipment well now, had painfully gathered the pieces and designed it himself. The liquid nitrogen went *tick* and burbled in its flask. Powered units hummed in spots where there was a slight voltage mismatch. The oscilloscopes' green faces danced and rippled with smooth yellow curves. He felt at home.

Renfrew seldom noticed the austere walls and blocky angles of his lab; to him it was a comfortable gathering of familiar elements working together. He could not fathom the now-fashionable abhorrence of things mechanical; he suspected it was one side of a coin, the other being awe. But either was nonsense. One might as well feel the same emotions about a skyscraper, for example, yet the building was no greater than a man—men made *it*, not the other way round. The universe of artifacts was a human one. As Renfrew moved through the lanes of bulky electronics, he sometimes seemed to himself a fish swimming in the warm waters of his own ocean, carrying the elaborate scheme of the experiment as a multi-layered diagram in his mind, checking it against the never-perfect reality before him. He loved this thinking, correcting, and searching for the unseen flaw that could destroy the whole effect he wanted.

He had assembled most of this apparatus by scavenging among the other research groups in the Cav. Research had always been a highly visible luxury, easily cut. The past five years had been a disaster. When a group had been shut down, Renfrew had salvaged what he could. He had started out in the nuclear resonance group as a specialist in making beams of high-energy ions. This became important in the discovery of a completely new kind of subatomic particle, the tachyon, which had been theorized about for decades. Renfrew had moved over into that field. He had kept his small crew afloat by adroit grantsmanship and by using the fact that tachyons, as the newest of the new, had a clear intellectual claim to whatever funds remained in the National Research Council. The NRC had dissolved last year, though.

This year research was a puppet whose strings led to the World Council itself. The western nations had pooled their research efforts in a gesture towards economy. The World Council was a political animal. To Renfrew it seemed the Council's policies boiled down to supporting highly visible efforts and little else. The fusion reactor program still got a lion's share, despite no apparent progress. The Cav's best groups, such as radio astronomy, had disbanded last year when the Council decided astronomy as a whole was impractical and such work should be suspended "for the duration." Precisely how long the duration might be was a point the Council neatly dodged.

The idea was that as the present crisis deepened the western nations had to shuck off their research luxuries in favor of sweaty-browed concentration on the ecoproblems and assorted disasters which dominated the newspaper headlines. But one had to sail with whatever wind was blowing, Renfrew knew. He had managed to find a way that tachyons could have a "practical" purpose, and that slant had kept his group afloat so far.

Renfrew finished calibrating some electronics gear—it was always going on the blink these days—and paused for a moment, listening to the preoccupied hum of the lab around him.

"Jason," he called, "I'm off to get coffee. Keep it all going, will you?"

He picked his old corduroy jacket off a hook and stretched mightily, showing crescents of sweat in the cloth around his armpits. In mid-stretch he noticed two men on the platform. One of the technicians was pointing down at Renfrew, talking, and as Renfrew lowered his arms the other man started down the catwalk to the laboratory.

Renfrew had a sudden memory of his college days at Oxford. He had been walking down a corridor which gave back the hollow, ringing echo only stonework can. It was a beautiful October morning and he was brimming with eagerness to begin this new life he had looked forward to, the goal of the long student years. He had known he was bright; here, among his intellectual equals, he would at last find his niche. He had come in on the train from York the night before and now he wanted to get out into the morning sun and take it all in.

There were two of them sauntering towards him down the corridor. They wore their short academic gowns like courtiers' robes and they walked as though they owned the building. They were talking loudly as they approached him and looked him over as if he were an Irishman. As they passed him, one said with a lazy drawl, "Oh, God, another bloody yokel up on a scholarship." It had set the tone of his years at Oxford. He had got a First, of course, and he had made his name now in the physics world. But he had always felt that even if they were wasting their time, they were enjoying life more than he ever could.

The memory of it stung again as he watched Peterson walk towards him. At this distance in time, he could not remember the faces of those two undergraduate snobs and there was probably no physical resemblance, but this man wore the same graceful, arrogant self-assurance. Also, he noticed the way Peterson dressed and he resented noticing another man's clothes. Peterson was tall and lean and dark-haired. At a distance, he gave the impression of a young and athletic dandy. He walked lightly, not like the rugby player that Renfrew had been in his youth, but like a tennis or polo player or perhaps even a javelin thrower. Seen closer, he looked to be in his early forties and was unmistakably a man used to wielding power. He was handsome in a rather severe way. There was no contempt in his expression, but Renfrew thought bitterly that he had probably just learned to hide it in his adult years. *Pull yourself together, John,* he admonished himself silently. *You're the expert, not him. And smile.*

"Good morning, Dr. Renfrew." The smooth voice was just what he had expected.

"Good morning, Mr. Peterson," he murmured, holding out a large square hand. "Pleased to meet you." Damn, why had he said that? It might almost have been his father's voice: "I'm reet pleased to meet ya, lad." He was getting paranoid. There was nothing in Peterson's face to indicate anything but seriousness about his job.

"Is this the experiment?" Peterson looked round with a remote expression.

"Yes, would you like to see it first?"

"Please."

They passed some old gray cabinets of English manufacture and some newer equipment housed in brightly colored compartments from Tektronics, Physics International, and other American firms. These garish red and yellow units came from the small Council appropriation. Renfrew led Peterson to a complex array housed between the poles of a large magnet.

"Superconducting setup, of course. We need the high field strength to get a nice, sharp line during transmission."

Peterson studied the maze of wires and meters. Cabinets housing rank upon rank of electronics towered over them. He pointed out a particular object and asked its function.

"Oh, I didn't think you'd be wanting to know much of the technical side," Renfrew said.

"Try me."

"Well, we've got a large indium antimonide sample in there, see—" Renfrew pointed at the encased volume between the magnet poles. "We hit it with high-energy ions. When the ions strike the indium they give off tachyons. It's a complex, very sensitive ion-nuclei reaction." He glanced at Peterson. "Tachyons are particles that travel faster than light, you know. On the other side—" he pointed around the magnets, leading Peterson to a long blue cylindrical tank that protruded ten meters away from the magnets "—we draw out the tachyons and focus them into a beam. They have a particular energy and spin, so they resonate only with indium nuclei in a strong magnetic field."

"And when they hit something in the way?"

"That's the *point*," Renfrew said sharply. "Tachyons have to strike a nucleus in precisely the correct state of energy and spin before they lose any energy in the process. They pass right through ordinary matter. That's why we can shoot them across light years without having them scattered out of their path."

Peterson said nothing. He scowled at the equipment.

"But when one of our tachyons strikes an indium nucleus in precisely the right state—a situation that doesn't occur naturally very often—it will be absorbed. That tips the spin of the indium nucleus away from wherever it was pointing. Think of the indium nucleus as a little arrow that gets knocked to the side. If all the little arrows were pointing in one direction before the tachyons arrived, then they would get disordered. That would be noticeable and—"

"I see, I see," Peterson said disdainfully. Renfrew wondered if he had overdone that bit about little arrows. It would be fatal if Peterson thought he was talking down to him—which of course he was.

"That's some other fellow's indium, I suppose?"

Renfrew held his breath. This was the tricky part. "Yes. An experiment operating in the year 1963," he said slowly.

Peterson said drily, "I read the preliminary report. These prelims are often deceptive, but I understood that. The technical staff tell me it makes sense, but I can't believe some of the things you've written. This business of altering the past—"

"Look, there's this fellow Markham coming—he'll put you straight on that."

"If he can."

"Right. See, the reason nobody's even tried to send messages back is an obvious one, once you think of it. We can build a transmitter, see, but there's no receiver. Nobody in the past ever built one."

Peterson frowned. "Well, of course—"

Renfrew went on enthusiastically, "*We*'ve built one, naturally, to do our preliminary experiments. But the people back in 1963 didn't know about tachyons. So the trick is to interfere with something they're already doing. That's the ticket."

"Um."

"We try to concentrate bursts of tachyons and aim them just so—"

8

"Hold on," Peterson said, putting up a hand. "Aim for *what?* Where *is* 1963?"

"Quite far away, as it works out. Since 1963, the earth's been going round the sun, while the sun itself is revolving around the hub of the galaxy, and so on. Add that up and you find 1963 is pretty distant."

"Relative to what?"

"Well, relative to the center of mass of the local group of galaxies, of course. Mind, the local group is moving, too, relative to the frame of reference provided by the microwave radiation background, and—"

"Look, skip the jargon, can't you? You're saying 1963 is in the *sky* somewhere?"

"Quite so. We send out a beam of tachyons to hit that spot. We sweep the volume of space occupied by the earth at that particular time."

"Sounds impossible."

Renfrew measured his words. "I think not. The trick is creating tachyons with essentially infinite speed—"

Peterson made a wry, tired smile. "Ah—'essentially infinite'? Comic technical talk."

"I *mean,* with unmeasurably high velocity," Renfrew said precisely. "Sorry for the terminology, if that's what bothers you."

"Well, look, I'm only trying to understand."

"Yes, yes, sorry, I may have jumped the gun there." Renfrew visibly composed himself for a fresh attack. "Mind, the essential trick here is to get these high-velocity tachyons. Then, if we can hit the right spot in space, we can send a message back quite a way."

"These tachyon beams will go straight through a star?"

Renfrew frowned. "We don't know, actually. There's a possibility that other reactions—between these tachyons and other nuclei besides indium—will be fairly strong. There's no data on those cross sections yet. If they are, a planet or a star getting in the way could be trouble."

"But you've tried simpler tests? I read in the report—"

"Yes, yes, they've been very successful."

"Well, still—" Peterson gestured at the maze of equipment. "This strikes me as a fine physics sort of experiment. Commendable. But—" he shook his head "—well, I'm amazed you got the money for this."

Renfrew's face tightened. "It's not all that bloody much."

Peterson sighed. "Look here, Dr. Renfrew, I'll be frank with you. I'm down here to evaluate this for the Council, because some pretty big names have said it makes some sort of sense. I don't feel I have the technical background to evaluate this properly. No one on the Council has. We're ecologists and biologists and systems people for the most part."

"Should be broader based."

"Granted, yes. Our idea in the past has been to bring in specialists as they're needed."

Gruffly: "So reach Davies at King's College in London. He's keen on this and—"

"There isn't time for that. We're looking for emergency measures."

Renfrew said slowly, "It's that bad?"

Peterson paused, as though he had given away too much. "Yes. Looks so."

"I can move fast, if that's your idea," Renfrew said briskly.

"You may have to."

"It would be better if we got a whole new generation of equipment in here," Renfrew took in the lab with a hand wave. "The Americans have developed new electronics gear that would improve matters. To be really sure we got through, we need the Americans to come in. Most of the circuitry I need is being developed in their national labs, Brookhaven and so on."

Peterson nodded. "So your report said. That's why I want this fellow Markham in on this today."

"Has he got the necessary weight to swing it?"

"I think so. He's well thought of, I'm told, and he's an American on the spot. That's what his National Science Foundation needs to cover itself in case—"

"Ah, I see. Well, Markham's due here any time now. Come have some coffee in my office."

Peterson followed him into the cluttered den. Renfrew cleared books and papers off a chair, bustling about in that nervous manner people have when they have suddenly realized, along with a guest, that their office is messy. Peterson sat down, lifting his trousers at the knees and then crossing his legs. Renfrew made more of a business than necessary out of fetching the acrid-smelling coffee, because he wanted time to think. Things were starting badly; Renfrew wondered if the memories from Oxford had soured him automatically on Peterson. Well, there was nothing for it; everyone was fairly edgy these days, anyway. Perhaps Markham could smooth things over when he arrived.

chapter two

Marjorie locked the kitchen door behind her and walked round the side of the house, carrying a bucket of chicken feed. The lawn behind the house was crisply quartered by brick paths, with a sundial at the intersection. From force of habit, she followed the path and did not step on the wet grass. Beyond the lawn was a formal rose garden, her own pet project. As she walked through it, breaking beaded spider webs with her body, she stopped here and there to pinch off a dead bloom or to sniff at a bud. It was early in the year, but a few roses were blossoming already. She talked to each bush as she passed it.

"Charlotte Armstrong, you're doing very well. Look at all those buds. You're going to be absolutely beautiful this summer. Tiffany, how are you? I see some greenfly on you. I'll have to spray you. Good morning, Queen Elizabeth, you're looking very healthy, but you're sticking out rather too far into the path. I should have pruned you more on this side."

Somewhere in the distance she could hear a knocking sound. It alternated with the trill of a blue tit perched on the hedge. With a start she realized that the knocking was coming from her own house. It couldn't be Heather or Linda; they would come round the back. She turned. Raindrops splattered from the leaves as she brushed past the rose bushes. She hurried across the lawn and round the side of the house, setting the bucket down by the kitchen door.

A shabbily dressed woman with a pitcher in her hand was turning away from the front door. She looked as though she had camped all night; her hair was matted and there were smudges on her face. She was about Marjorie's height, but thin and round-shouldered.

Marjorie hesitated. So did the woman. They eyed each other across the U-shaped sweep of the gravel drive. Then Marjorie moved forward.

"Good morning." She was about to say, "Can I do something for you?" but held back, uncertain as to whether she wanted to do anything for this woman or not.

11

"Morning, Miss. Could you lend me a bit o' milk, do you think? I'm all out o' milk and the kids 'aven't 'ad their breakfast yet." Her manner was confident but somehow not cordial.

Marjorie narrowed her eyes. "Where are you from?" she asked.

"We just moved into the old farm down the road. Just a little milk, lady." The woman moved closer to her, holding out the pitcher.

The old farm—but that's derelict, Marjorie thought. *They must be squatters.* Her uneasiness increased.

"Why do you come here? The shops are open at this time of day. There's a farm along the road, you know, where you can buy milk."

"Come on, lady, you wouldn't make me walk miles while the little ones are waiting, would you? I'll let you 'ave it back. Don't you believe me?"

No, Marjorie thought. Why hadn't the woman gone to one of her own kind? There were some little Council houses just a few yards beyond her grounds.

"I'm sorry," she said firmly, "but I haven't got any to spare."

They confronted each other for a moment. Then the woman turned towards the shrubbery.

" 'Ere, Rog," she called. A tall, gaunt man emerged from the rhododendrons, tugging a small boy by the hand. With an effort Marjorie kept herself from showing any alarm. She stood stiffly, her head a little back, trying to look in control of the situation. The man shuffled over to stand next to the woman. Marjorie's nostrils flared slightly as she caught a sour odor of sweat and smoke. He was wearing an assortment of clothes that must have come from many different sources, a cloth cap, a long striped college scarf, woolen gloves with all the fingers unraveled, a pair of jaunty blue espadrilles with one sole flapping, trousers that were several inches too short and too wide, and, incongruously, a lavishly embroidered waistcoat under a dusty old vinyl jacket. He was probably about Marjorie's age but looked at least ten years older. His face was leathery, his eyes deep set, and he had several days' growth of stubble on his chin. She was aware of the contrast she made with them, standing there plump and well-fed, her short hair fluffy from washing, her skin protected by creams and lotions, in what she called her "old" gardening clothes, a soft blue wool skirt, a handknit sweater, and a sheepskin jacket.

"You expect us to believe you don't 'ave no milk in the 'ouse, lady?" the man growled.

"I didn't say that." Marjorie's voice was clipped. "I have enough for my own family but no more. There are plenty of other houses down there you could try, but I suggest you go into the village and buy some. It's only half a mile. I'm sorry I can't help you."

"Like 'ell you are. You just don't want to. Stuck up, like all you rich types. You want to keep it all for yerselves. Look at what you've got—a great big 'ouse just for you, I bet. You dunno 'ow 'ard life is for us. I 'aven't 'ad a job for four years, an' nowhere to live, while you 'ad it soft—"

"Rog," the woman said warningly. She laid a restraining hand on his arm. He shook it off and moved a step closer to Marjorie. She held her ground and anger surged in her. What right did they have to come here and shout at her, damn it, in her own garden?

"I've already *told* you I only have enough for my own family. These are hard times for everyone," she said coldly. *But I would never go begging*, she thought. *No moral backbone, these people.*

The man moved closer. Instinctively she stepped back, maintaining the space between them.

"Hard times for everyone," he said, mimicking her accent. "Just too bad, ain't it? Too bad for everyone else, just so long you 'ave a nice 'ouse and food and maybe a car too and telly." His eyes were raking the house, taking in the garage, the TV antenna on the roof, the windows. Thank God the windows were locked, she thought, and the front door.

"Look, I can't help you. Will you please go?" She turned and started to walk back round the house. The man kept pace with her, the woman and child following silently.

"Yes, that's right, just turn your back on us and go on into your big 'ouse. You won't get rid of us that easy. The day is comin' when you'll 'ave to get down off that bloody 'igh—"

"I'll thank you to—"

" 'At's it, Rog!"

"Your kind 'ave 'ad it all their way. There'll be a revolution and *then* you'll be beggin' for 'elp. And you think you'll get it? Not bloody likely!"

Marjorie increased her pace until it was almost a trot, trying to shake him off before she reached the kitchen door. She was fumbling in her pocket for the key when he came up close behind her. Afraid that he would touch her, she whirled around and faced him.

"Get *out* of here. Go. Don't come bothering me. Go to the authorities. Get off my land!"

The man fell back a step. She seized the bucket of chicken feed, not wanting to leave anything out that he might steal. The key turned easily, *thank God*, and she slammed the door just as he came up on the step. She snapped the lock home. He shouted through the door: "You bleedin' stuck-up tart. Don't fucking care if we *starve*, do you?"

Marjorie began to shake all over, but she shouted back, "I'm going to call the police if you don't leave at once!"

She walked through the house, eying the windows. They would be so easy to break. She felt vulnerable, trapped in her own house. Her breathing was very fast and shallow now. She felt nauseated. The man was still shouting outside, his language becoming more and more obscene.

The phone was on the hall table. She picked it up and held it to her ear. Nothing. She pressed the receiver bar up and down a few times. Nothing. Damn, damn, damn. What a time for it to go out. It happened often, of course. *But not now, please,* she prayed. She shook the phone. Still silence. She was completely cut off. What if the man broke in? Her mind raced over potential weapons, the poker, the kitchen knives—Oh God, no, better not start any violence, there were two of them and the man looked a nasty customer. No, she would go out the back. Through the French windows in the living room. Run to the village for help.

She couldn't hear him shouting any longer, but was afraid to show herself at the window to see if he were still there. She tried the phone again. Still nothing. She slammed it down. She focused her attention on the doors and windows, listening for sounds of a break-in. Then the knocking started again at the front door. It was a relief to know where he was and that he was still outside. She waited, gripping the edge of the hall table. *Go away, damn you,* she willed him. The knocking repeated. After a pause, steps crunched on the gravel. Was he going away at last? Then there was a knock at the kitchen door. Oh Christ! How could she get rid of him?

"Marjorie! Hello, Marjorie, are you there?" A voice hailed her.

Relief flooded her and she felt close to tears. She was too limp to move.

"Marjorie! Where are you?" The voice was moving away. She straightened up and went to the kitchen door and opened it.

Her friend Heather was moving off towards the garden shed. "Heather!" she called. "I'm here."

Heather turned and came back to her. "Whatever's the matter? You look awful," she said.

Marjorie stepped outside and looked around. "Has he gone?" she asked. "There was a dreadful man here."

"A shabby-looking man with a woman and child? They were just leaving when I came. What happened?"

"He wanted to borrow some milk." She started to laugh, a little hysterically. It sounded so ordinary. "Then he got rude and started shouting. They're squatters. Moved into that empty farm down the road last night." She sank into a kitchen chair. "God, that was scary, Heather."

"I believe it. You look quite shaken. Not like you, Marjorie. I thought you could handle anything, even fierce and dangerous squatters." She had adopted a bantering tone and Marjorie responded to it.

"Well, I could, of course. I was going to bash him over the head with the poker and then stick him with a kitchen knife, if he broke in."

She was laughing, but it wasn't funny. Had she actually thought of doing that?

chapter three

FALL, 1962

He *had* to find a way to get rid of the damned noise in the experiment, Gordon thought moodily, picking up his scuffed briefcase. The damned stuff wouldn't go away. If he couldn't find the difficulty and correct it, then the whole experiment ended up sucking wind.

The palm tree still stopped him every time. Each morning, after Gordon Bernstein had slammed the yellow front door of the bungalow a little too loudly, he turned and looked at the palm tree and stopped. The pause was a moment of recognition. He was really here, in California. Not a movie set; the real thing. The palm tree silhouette thrust spearing fronds into a cloudless sky, silently exotic. This matter-of-fact plant was far more impressive than the strangely blank freeways or the unrelentingly balmy weather.

Most evenings, Gordon sat up late with Penny, reading and listening to folk records. Things were exactly like his years at Columbia. He kept the same habits, and very nearly forgot that half a block away was Wind 'n Sea beach with its rolling surf. When he left his windows open, the rumble of the waves seemed like the traffic noise on 2nd Avenue, a distant blur of other people's lives that he had always successfully avoided, there in his apartment. So it came as a small shock each morning when he ventured out, jiggling his car keys nervously, mind mumbling away to itself, and the palm tree yanked him back into this new reality.

Weekends, it was easier to remember that this was California. Then he would wake to see Penny's long blond hair fanned out over the pillow beside him. During the week she had early classes and left while he was still asleep. She moved so lightly and quietly that she never disturbed him. Each morning, it was as though she had never been there. She left nothing lying around. There wasn't even a dent in the bed where she had slept.

Gordon slipped the tinkling keys into his pocket and walked along a bottlebrush hedge and out into the broad boulevards of

La Jolla. This, too, was still a little strange to him. The streets had ample room to park his '58 Chevy and leave immense stretches of concrete for the two center lanes. The streets were as big as the building lots; they seemed to define the landscape, like vast recreation grounds for the dominant species, automobiles. Compared to 2nd Avenue, which was more like a ventilating shaft between slabs of brown brick, this was extravagant excess. In New York, Gordon had always braced himself when he went down the steps, knowing that when he pushed open the front door of wired glass there would be dozens of people within sight. They would be briskly moving along, a churn of lives. He could always count on that press of flesh around him. Here, nothing. Nautilus Street was a flat white plain baking in the morning sun, unpeopled. He climbed into his Chevy and the roar of starting the engine cracked the silence, seeming to conjure up in his rear view mirror a long low Chrysler which came over the rise a block away and went by, making a swishing noise.

On the way to the campus he drove with one hand and spun the radio dial with the other, rummaging through the discordant blocks of sound that passed for pop music out here. He preferred folk music, really, but had an odd affection for some old Buddy Holly songs and lately had found himself humming them in the shower—*Every day it's a-gittin closer . . . Well, that'll be the day . . .* He found a high-pitched Beach Boys number and let the dial rest. The tenor warblings about sand and sun described perfectly the travelogue views that swept by outside. He coasted down La Jolla Boulevard and watched the distant small dots that were riding in on a slowly broadening fan of white surf. Kids, unaccountably not in school, even though classes had started two weeks ago.

He swooped down the hillside and into a pack of slowed cars, mostly big black Lincolns and Cadillacs. He eased down on the brake and noticed new buildings on Mount Soledad. The earth was scraped raw and terraced, trucks climbing over the ruined soil like insects. Gordon smiled tartly, knowing that even if he unsnarled the experiment, and produced a brilliant result, and got tenure, and therefore made a higher salary, he still could not afford the cedar and glass homes that would slant out from that hillside. Not unless he took on a lot of consulting on the side and rose quickly at the University to boot, perhaps wangling his way into a part-time deanship to boost the monthly check. But that was unlikely as hell.

He grimaced behind his thick black beard, shifted the Chevy's gears as the Beach Boys faded into a *Dirt's out, Tide's in* jingle, and the car surged through traffic with a rich, throaty growl, toward the University of California at La Jolla.

•

Gordon tapped absentmindedly on the dewar of liquid nitrogen, trying to think how to say what he wanted, and dimly realized that he just couldn't like Albert Cooper. The guy seemed pleasant enough: sandy-haired, a slow talker who sometimes slurred his words, obviously well muscled from his hobbies of scuba diving and tennis. But Cooper's taciturn calm blunted Gordon's momentum, time and again. His smiling, easygoing manner seemed to reflect some distant, bemused tolerance of Gordon, and Gordon found himself bristling.

"Look, Al," he said, turning rapidly away from the steaming nozzle of the dewar. "You've been with me well over a year, right?"

"Check."

"You were doing pretty well with Professor Lakin, I joined the department, Lakin was too busy, so you shifted over to me. And I took you on." Gordon rocked back on his heels, wedged his hands into his back pockets. "Because Lakin said you were good."

"Sure."

"And now you've been plugging away on this indium antimonide experiment for—what?—a year and a half, easy."

"Right," Cooper said somewhat quizzically.

"I think it's time you canned the bullshit."

Cooper gave no visible reaction. "Ummmm. I don't . . . uh . . . know what you mean."

"I come in here this morning. I ask you about the job I gave you. You tell me you went over every amplifier, every Varian component, the works."

"Uh huh. I did."

"And the noise is still there."

"I checked. Ran the whole sequence."

"That's bullshit."

Cooper sighed elaborately. "So you found out about it, huh?"

Gordon frowned. "Found out what?"

"I know you're a stickler for carrying an experiment through, *A* to *Z*, with no delays, Dr. Bernstein. I know that." Cooper shrugged apologetically. "But I couldn't finish the whole thing last night. So I went out and had a few beers with the guys. Then I came back and did it all over."

Gordon wrinkled his brow. "There's nothing wrong with

18

that. You can always take a break. Just so you keep everything steady, don't let the preamps or the scopes go off their zero adjustments."

"No, they were still okay."

"Then—" Gordon spread his hands, exasperated. "—you have screwed up somewhere. It's not the beer-drinking I care about, it's the *experiment*. Look, the conventional wisdom is that it takes four years minimum to get out. Do you want to make it that fast?"

"Sure."

"Then do what I say and don't slack off."

"But I haven't."

"You must've. You just haven't looked. I can—"

"The noise is still there," Cooper said with a certainty that stopped Gordon in mid-sentence. Gordon abruptly realized that he had been browbeating this man, only three years younger, for no reason whatever, aside from frustration.

"Look, I—" Gordon began, but found the next word catching in his throat. He felt suddenly embarrassed. "Okay, I believe you," he said, making his voice brisk and businesslike. "Let's see the chart recordings you took."

Cooper had been leaning against the blocky magnet that enclosed the kernel of their experiment. He turned and threaded his way through the lanes of cables and microwave guides. The experiment was still running. The silvery flask, suspended between the poles of the magnet and all but obscured by cable lead-ins, had grown a coat of ice. Inside it liquid helium frothed and bubbled, boiling away at temperatures only a few degrees above absolute zero. The ice was water frozen out from the air around the jacket, and it made an occasional *snap* as the equipment expanded and contracted to relieve stress. The brilliantly lit laboratory hummed with electronic life. A few meters away the sheer heat of the banks upon banks of transistorized diagnostics made a warming wall of air. From the helium, though, Gordon could feel a gentle, chilling draft. Despite the coolness Cooper wore a torn T-shirt and blue jeans. Gordon preferred a blue long-sleeve button-down shirt, Oxford broadcloth, with corduroy slacks that belted in the back, and a tweed jacket. He had not yet adjusted to the informality of laboratories here. If it meant going as far downhill as Cooper, he was certain he never would.

"I took a lot of data," Cooper said conversationally, ignoring the tension that had hung in the air only moments before. Gordon moved through the assembly of scopes and wheeled cabinets to where Cooper was methodically laying out the automatically recorded graphs. The paper was gridded in bright red, so that the green jiggling lines of the signal stood out, making the page almost three-dimensional from contrast.

"See?" Cooper's thick fingers traced the green peaks and valleys. "Here's where the indium nuclear resonance should be."

Gordon nodded. "A nice fat peak, that's what we should find," he said. But there was only a chaos of narrow vertical lines, made as the recorder pen had rocked back and forth across the paper, under the action of random nudges.

"Just hash," Cooper murmured.

"Yes," Gordon admitted, feeling the air wheeze out of him as he said it, his shoulders sagging.

"I got these, though." Cooper laid out another green rectangle. It showed a mixed pattern. At the right was a clean peak, its sides smooth and untroubled. But the center and left of the page was a meaningless jumble of scratchings.

"Damn," Gordon whispered to himself. On these graphs the frequency of emissions from the indium antimonide sample increased from left to right. "The noise wipes out the high frequencies."

"Not always."

"Huh?"

"Here's another try. I took it just a few minutes after that one."

Gordon studied the third x-y output sheet. On this one there was a reasonably clear peak on the left side, at low frequencies, and then noise to the right. "I don't get it."

"I sure don't either."

"We've always got flat, constant noise before."

"Yep." Cooper looked at him blankly. Gordon was the professor here; Cooper was tossing the riddle over to him.

Gordon squinted, thinking. "We're getting the peaks, but only part of the time."

"That's what it looks like."

"Time. Time," Gordon muttered distantly. "Hey, the pen takes about, say, thirty seconds to move across the sheet, right?"

"Well, we could change that, if you think—"

"No, no, listen," Gordon said rapidly. "Suppose the noise isn't always there? In this one—" he shuffled back to the second sheet "—there was some source of noise when the pen was recording the low frequencies. About ten seconds later it vanished. Here—" he planted a stubby finger on the third x-y graph

"—the hash started in as the pen reached high frequencies. The noise was returning."

Cooper wrinkled his brow. "But . . . I thought this was a steady state experiment. I mean, nothing changes, that's the whole point. We keep the temperature low but constant. The scopes and amps and rectifiers are all warmed up and holding to pattern. They—"

Gordon waved him into silence. "It's nothing *we* are doing. We've spent weeks checking the electronics; that's not malfunctioning. No, it's something else, that's my point."

"But what?"

"Something from outside. Interference."

"How could—"

"Who knows?" Gordon said with new energy. He began his characteristic nervous pacing. His shoe soles squeaked on the floor at every turn. "What's happening is, there's another source of signal in the indium antimonide. Or else the indium is picking up a time-varying input from outside the lab."

"I don't understand."

"Hell, I don't either. But something's screwing up the nuclear resonance detection. We've got to track it down."

Cooper squinted at the erratic lines, as though measuring in his mind's eye the alterations that had to be made to study the problem further. "How?"

"If we can't remove the noise, study it. Find out what it's coming from. Is it occurring in all the indium antimonide samples? Does it filter in from some other lab here? Or is it something new? That sort of thing."

Cooper nodded slowly. Gordon framed a few quick circuit diagrams on the back of one of the sheets, sketching in the components with a pencil. He could see fresh possibilities now. An adjustment here, a new piece of equipment there. They could borrow some components from Lakin down the hall, and probably talk Feher out of his spectrum analyzer for a day or two. Gordon's pencil made a small scratching sound against the background chugging of roughing pumps and the pervasive hum of the electronics, but he heard nothing. The ideas seemed to come up out of him and squeeze through the pencil onto the page, jotted down almost before he had thought them through, and he felt that he was on the track of something in this noise problem. There might be a new structure hiding behind the data like big game in a dense thicket. He was going to find out; he was sure of that.

chapter four

1998

Gregory Markham cycled past the fragrant buildings devoted to Veterinary Medicine and swooped into the driveway of the Cavendish Laboratory. He liked the soft brush of moist air as he arced around the curves, shifting his weight in a careful rhythm. His aim was to find a minimum curve which would deposit him at the lab entrance, a geodesic for this particular local curvature of space. One last burst of pedaling and he dismounted at a respectable speed, trotting alongside, using the bike's energy to roll it into one of the concrete wheelstands.

He straightened his brown Irish jacket and took the steps two at a time, a habit which gave him the appearance of being always late for something. He absently pushed his glasses back up his nose, where they had worn a red mark, and combed fingers through his beard. It was a well-defined beard, following the conventional course along his sharp jaw from sideburns to moustache, but it seemed to get mussed every hour or so, as did his hair. He was puffing from the bike ride more than usual. Either he had put on some weight in the last week, he deduced, or the simple erosion of age had nicked a little deeper. He was fifty-two and kept in moderately good condition. Medical research had shown enough of a correlation between exercise and long life to keep him at it.

He pushed open the glass doors and headed for Renfrew's laboratory. Every week or so he had come round to peer judiciously at the equipment and nod, but in truth he learned little by the visits. His interests lay in the theory behind the electronic maze. Gingerly he entered the busy ball of sound that was the lab.

He could see Renfrew through the office window—stocky, rumpled as usual, his shirt untucked, his mouse-brown hair falling untidily over his forehead. He was shuffling papers round on his cluttered desk. Markham did not recognize the other man. He assumed it was Peterson and was amused by the contrast between the two. Peterson's dark hair was smoothly in place and he was expensively and elegantly tailored. He looked suave and self-confident and, thought Markham, altogether a tough bastard to deal with. Experience had taught him that it was hard to get through to that type of cool, self-contained Englishman.

He opened the office door, giving it a perfunctory knock as he did so. Both men turned towards him. Renfrew appeared relieved and jumped up, knocking a book off his desk.

"Ah, Markham, here you are," he said unnecessarily. "This is Mr. Peterson from the Council."

Peterson rose smoothly from his chair and extended a hand.

"How do you do, Dr. Markham."

Markham shook his hand vigorously.

"Glad to meet you. Have you looked at John's experiment yet?"

"Yes, just now." Peterson looked faintly perturbed by the speed with which Markham came to the point. "How does the NSF feel about this, do you know?"

"No opinion so far. I haven't reported to them. They asked me only last week to act as liaison. Can we sit down?"

Without waiting for an answer Markham crossed the room, cleared the only other chair, and sat down, putting one ankle up on his knee. The other two men resumed their seats, less casually.

"You're a plasma physicist, is that right, Dr. Markham?"

"Yes. I'm here on sabbatical leave. Most of my work has been in plasmas until the last few years. I wrote a paper on tachyon theory long ago, before they were discovered and became fashionable. I suppose that's why the NSF asked me to be here."

"Did you read the copy of the proposal that I sent you?" Peterson asked.

"Yes, I did. It's good," Markham said decisively. "The theory's fine. I've been working on the ideas behind Renfrew's experiment for some time now."

"You think this experiment will work, then?"

"We know the *technique* works. Whether we can actually communicate with the past—that we don't know."

"And this set-up here—" Peterson swept an arm towards the laboratory bay "—can do that?"

"If we're damned lucky. We know there were similar nuclear resonance experiments at the Cavendish and a few other places, in the States and the Soviet Union, functioning as far back as the 1950s. In principle they could pick up coherent signals induced by tachyons."

"So we can send them telegrams?"

23

"Yes, but that's all. It's a highly restricted form of time travel. This is the only way anyone's figured out how to send messages into the past. We can't transmit objects or people."

Peterson shook his head. "I did a degree involving social issues and computers. Even I—"

"Cambridge?" Markham broke in.

"Yes, King's College." Markham nodded to himself and Peterson hesitated. He disliked the American's obvious placing of him in a category. He did the same thing himself, of course, but certainly with more genuine reason. Slightly irritated, he seized the initiative. "Look, even I know there's a paradox involved here somewhere. The old thing about shooting your grandfather, isn't it? But if he died, you wouldn't exist yourself. Someone on the Council brought that up yesterday. We almost booted the whole idea out because of that."

"A good point. I made the same error in a paper back in 1992. It turns out there are paradoxes and then, if you look at things the right way, paradoxes go away. I could explain, but it would take time."

"Not now, if you don't mind. The whole point, as I understand it, is to send these telegrams and tell somebody back in the 1960s or so about our situation here."

"Well, something like that. Warn them against chlorinated hydrocarbons, sketch in the effects on phytoplankton. Getting a lead on certain kinds of research could give us the edge we need *now* to—"

"Tell me, do you think this experiment might be of any *real* help?"

Renfrew stirred impatiently but said nothing.

"Without being melodramatic," Markham said slowly, "I believe it could save millions of lives. Eventually."

There was a moment's silence. Peterson recrossed his legs and picked an invisible piece of lint from his knee.

"It's a question of priorities, you see," he said at last. "We have to take the large view. The Emergency Council has been in session since nine this morning. There has been another full-scale dieback in North Africa due to drought and lack of food reserves. You'll hear more about it in the news in due course, no doubt. Meanwhile, this and other emergencies have to take priority. North Africa's not the only trouble spot. There's a large diatom bloom off the South American coast, too. Thousands of people are dying in both places. You're asking us to put money into an isolated experiment that may or may not work—one man's theory, essentially—"

Markham interrupted swiftly. "It's more than that. The tachyon theory is not new. There's a group at Caltech right now—the gravitational theory group—working on another angle of the same problem. They're trying to see how tachyons fit into the cosmological questions—you know, the expanding universe picture and all."

Renfrew nodded again. "Yes, there was a paper in the *Physical Review* just recently, on huge density fluctuations."

"They're having their problems in Los Angeles, too," Peterson said, considering. "Mainly the big fire, of course. If the wind changes, that could be disastrous. I don't know what effect these things have on the Caltech people. We can't afford to wait for years."

Renfrew cleared his throat. "I thought funding of scientific experiments was to be given top priority." He sounded slightly petulant.

Peterson's answer held a hint of condescension. "Ah, you're referring to the King's speech on television the other day. Yes, well, of course, he wants to look good in his Coronation year. So he's encouraging funding of scientific experiments—but of course, he knows nothing of science, he's not even a politician. Very well meaning fellow, of course. Our committee advised him to stick to uplifting generalities in future. With a touch of humor. He's good at that. Anyway, the basic fact is that money is short and we have to pick and choose carefully. All I can promise at this stage is that I will make a report to the Council. I'll let you know as soon as I can their decision about granting you emergency priority. Personally, I think it's a bit of a long shot. I don't know if we can afford to take chances."

"We can't afford *not* to," Markham said with sudden energy. "Why keep on plugging the leaks here and there, sinking money into relief funds for drought and dieback? You can slap on patches but the dam's going to burst. Unless—"

"Unless you tinker with the past? Are you *sure* tachyons can reach the past at all?"

Renfrew said, "We've done it. Tried some table-top experiments. They work. It's in the report."

"The tachyons *are* received, then?"

Renfrew nodded briskly. "We can use them to heat up a sample in the past, so we know they've been received."

Peterson arched an eyebrow. "And if, after measuring this heat increase, you decided not to send the tachyons after all?"

Renfrew said, "That option's not really available in these experiments. See, the tachyons have to travel a long way if they're to go far back in time—"

"A moment, please," Peterson murmured. "What has traveling faster than light have to do with time travel?"

Markham stepped toward a blackboard. "It comes straight out of special relativity, see—" and he launched into a description. Markham drew space-time diagrams and told Peterson how to understand them, stressing the choice of slanted coordinates. Peterson kept an intent expression through it all. Markham drew wavy lines to represent tachyons launched from one spot, and showed how, if they were reflected about in the laboratory, they could strike another portion of the lab at an earlier time.

Peterson nodded slowly. "So your point about the experiments you've done is that there's no time to reconsider? You fire the tachyons. They heat up this indium sample of yours, a few nanoseconds or so *before* you triggered the tachyons in the first place."

Renfrew agreed. "Point is, we don't *want* to set up a contradiction, either. Say, if we connected the heat detector to the tachyon switch, so heat coming in would switch off the tachyons."

"The grandfather paradox."

"Right," Markham broke in. "There are some subtle points involved with doing that. We think it leads to a sort of intermediate state, in which a little heat is generated and a few tachyons get launched. But I'm not sure."

"I see . . . ." Peterson struggled with the ideas, scowling. "I'd like to go into that some time later, once I've had a thorough reading of the technical material. Actually, I'm not depending on my own judgment alone in this—" he glanced around at the two intent men beside him "—as you've probably guessed. I got an assessment from Sir Martin at the Council, and from that fellow Davies you mentioned. They say it's the straight stuff."

Markham smiled; Renfrew beamed. Peterson held up a hand. "Hold on, though. I really stopped by here to get the scent of things, not to make the final decision. I've got to make my case to the Council itself. You want electronics flown in from the American labs, and that means wrangling with the NSF."

"Are the Americans thinking along the same lines?" Renfrew asked.

"I don't think so. The Council's attitude is that we must pool our resources. I'm going to urge that you fellows get the backing and the Americans chip in."

"And the Soviets?" Markham asked.

"They say they have nothing along these lines." Peterson sniffed in disdain. "Probably lying again. It's no secret that we

26

English have a big role in the Council only because the Soviets are keeping a low profile."

"Why are they?" Renfrew asked innocently.

"They figure our efforts are going to blow up in our faces," Peterson said. "So they're giving token support and probably hoarding their resources for later."

"Cynical," Markham said.

"Quite so," Peterson agreed. "Look, I must get back to London. I've got a number of other proposals—conventional stuff, mostly—the Council wants a report on. I'll do what I can for you." He shook hands formally. "Dr. Markham, Dr. Renfrew."

"I'll walk out with you," Markham said easily. "John?"

"Of course. Here is a folder of our papers on tachyons, by the way." He handed it to Peterson. "Plus a few ideas about things to transmit, if we're successful."

The three men left the building together and paused in the bare parking lot. Peterson turned towards the car Renfrew had noticed there that morning.

"So that *was* your car," Renfrew blurted out involuntarily. "I didn't think you could have got here that early from London."

Peterson raised an eyebrow. "I stayed the night with an old friend," he said.

The flash of amused reminiscence that touched his eyes for a split second indicated clearly to Markham that the old friend was a woman. Renfrew missed it, being busy putting on his bike clips. Also, Markham suspected, it was not the kind of thought that would occur to Renfrew. A good man, but basically dull. Whereas Peterson, though almost certainly not a good man by anyone's definition, was equally certainly not dull.

chapter five

Marjorie was in her element. The Renfrews did not entertain often and when they did, Marjorie always gave John and their guests the impression of bustling activity and even of domestic disasters narrowly averted. In fact, she was not only an excellent cook but a highly efficient organizer. Every step of this dinner party had been meticulously planned in advance. It was only out of a subconscious feeling that she should not intimidate her guests by being too perfect a hostess that she darted back and forth from the kitchen, chattering constantly, and pushing back her hair as though it were all a bit too much for her.

Heather and James, as their oldest friends, had arrived first. Then the Markhams, a correct ten minutes late. Heather was looking startlingly sophisticated in a low-cut black dress. In heels, she was the same height as James, who was only five feet, six inches and sensitive about it. As usual, he was impeccably dressed.

They were drinking sherry now, except for Greg Markham, who had settled on a Guinness. Marjorie thought that a bit odd right before dinner, but he looked as though he had a large appetite, so it would probably be all right. She found him a little disconcerting. When John had introduced him to her, he had stood just a little too close and stared at her and asked her rather abrupt and unconventional questions. Then, when she had backed away—both physically and from direct answers to his questions—he had appeared to dismiss her. When she had offered him some expensive nuts later, he had scooped up a large handful while continuing to talk and had hardly acknowledged her presence at all.

Marjorie resolved to let nothing disturb her. It was now over a week since the awful incident with the squatters and—she brushed the thought away. She resolutely turned her attention to her bright, fresh party and to Markham's wife, Jan. Jan was quiet, of course—hardly surprising, as her husband had been dominating the conversation ever since they arrived. His technique was to talk very rapidly, skipping from one subject to the next as they came to mind, in a sort of verbal broken-field running. A lot of it was interesting, but Marjorie had no time to think about a subject and work up a comment before the conversation lurched off in another direction. Jan smiled at his verbal leaps, a rather wise smile which Marjorie interpreted as signifying depth of character.

"You sound a little English," Marjorie probed. "Is it rubbing off on you already?"

This served to break them off from the circle of talkers. "My mother's English. She's been in Berkeley for decades, but the accent sticks."

Marjorie nodded receptively and drew her out. It developed that Jan's mother lived in the Arcology being built in the Bay Area. She was able to afford it because she wrote novels.

"What kind of thing does she write?" Heather broke in.

"Gothics. Gothic novels. She writes under the absurd pen name of Cassandra Pye."

"Good heavens," Marjorie said, "I've read a couple of her books. They're jolly good, for that sort of thing. Well, how exciting to think that you're her daughter."

"Her mother's a marvelous old character," Greg interjected. "Not all that old, really. She's—what, Jan?—in her sixties and will probably outlive us all. Healthy as a horse and a little crazy. Big in the Senior Culture Movement. Berkeley's full of them these days and she fits right in. Whizzing around the place on her bike, sleeping with all kinds of people, dabbling in mystical nonsense. Transcendent snake oil. A little over the edge, in fact, isn't she, Jan?"

This was obviously a standing joke between them. Jan laughed easily in response.

"You're such an unrelenting scientist, Greg. You and Mother just don't inhabit the same universe. Just think what a shock you'd get if you were to die and find out that Mother was right all along. Still, I agree that she's become a trifle eccentric lately."

"Like last month," Greg added, "when she decided to give all her worldly possessions to the poor of Mexico."

"Whatever for?" James asked.

"To show support for the Hispanic Regionalist cause," Jan explained. "That's the people who want to make Mexico and the western US a free region, so people can move around as economy dictates."

James scowled. "Won't that simply mean the Mexicans will move north en masse?"

Jan shrugged. "Probably. But the Spanish-speaking lobby in California is so strong maybe they can force it through."

"A strange sort of welfare state," Heather murmured.

"A farewell state is more like it," Greg put in. The chorus of laughter which greeted this remark rather surprised Marjorie. There was a quality of compressed energy being released.

●

A bit later Markham got Renfrew aside and asked about progress in the experiment. "I'm afraid we're pretty limited without better response time," John said.

"The American electronics, yeah." Markham nodded. "Look, I've been doing the calculations we discussed—how to focus the tachyons on 1963 with good reliability, and so on. I think it'll work okay. The constraints aren't as God-awful as we thought."

"Excellent. I hope we have a chance to use the technique."

"I've been doing a little nosing around, too. I know Sir Martin, Peterson's boss, from the days he was at the Institute for Astronomy. I reached him by telephone. He promised me we would hear soon."

Renfrew brightened and for a moment lost his air of the slightly nervous host.

●

"Why don't we take our drinks outside on the terrace? It's a lovely evening, quite warm, and not dark yet."

Marjorie threw open the French windows and gradually managed to herd her guests outside, where the Markhams exclaimed, as she had hoped they would, over her garden. The powerful fragrance of the honeysuckle in the hedge reached them. Footsteps crunched on gravel as they crossed the terrace.

James asked, "California is doing well, I take it?" and Marjorie, listening to others talk as well, caught fragments of Greg Markham's reply. "The governor's keeping the Davis campus open . . . The rest of us—I'm on half salary right now. Only reason I got even that was the labor union . . . leverage . . . professors are allied with the clerical workers now . . . damn students want to take shop courses . . . ." When she next looked his way conversation had trickled away.

Greg slipped away from the group and walked to the edge of the patio, his face clouded. Marjorie followed.

"I had no idea things were being cut back so," she said.

"It's happening everywhere." A resigned, flat tone.

"Well," she said, putting a bright, cheerful lift in her voice, "we here all hope things will straighten up in a short while and the labs will reopen. The colleges are quite optimistic that—"

"If wishes were horses, beggars would ride," he said sourly. Then, glancing at her, he seemed to shake himself free of the mood. "Or, if horses were vicious, rides would go begging." He smiled. "I love transmuted clichés, don't you?"

It was this sort of sudden, darting way of thinking Marjorie had come to associate with a species of scientist, the theoretical types. They were hard to understand, granted, but more interesting than the experimenters, like her John. She smiled back at him. "Surely your year here at Cambridge has taken you away from budget worries?"

"Um. Yes, I suppose it's better to live here in somebody else's past, rather than your own. It's a lovely place to forget the world outside. I've been enjoying the leisure of the theory class."

"In your ivory tower? This is a town of dreaming spires, as I think the poem goes."

"Oxford's the town of dreaming spires," he corrected her. "Cambridge is more like perspiring dreams."

"Scientific ambition?"

He grimaced. "The rule of thumb is that you don't do much first-class work past forty. That's mostly wrong, of course. There are lots of great discoveries made late in life. But on the average, yes, you feel the ability slipping away from you. It's like composers, I guess. Flashes out of nowhere when you're young, and . . . and more a sense of consolidation, layering things on, when you're older."

"This time communication thing you and John are onto certainly seems exciting. A lot of dash *there*."

Greg brightened. "Yes, it's a real chance again. Here's a hot topic and nobody's around to dig in except me. If they hadn't closed most of the Department of Applied Mathematics and Theoretical Physics, there'd be a squad of bright young guys swarming over it."

Marjorie stepped further away from the rest of the party, towards the moist masses of green that regimented their garden. "I've been meaning to ask someone who knows," she began with a touch of uncertainty, "just what this tachyon thing of John's *is*. I mean, he explains it, but not much gets through my arts education, I'm afraid."

Greg clasped his hands behind him in a studied way, staring up into the sky. Marjorie noted yet another sudden shift in him; his expression became remote, as though he were peering at some persistent interior riddle. He gazed up, as if unmindful of the awkwardly stretching silence between them. Above, she saw, an airplane scratched an arc, green wing light winking, and she had a curious, uneasy feeling. Its vapor trail spread, cold silver on a sky of slate.

"I think the hardest thing to see," Greg said, starting as though he were composing an article in his head, "is why particles traveling faster than light should mean anything about time."

"Yes, that's it. John always jumps over that, into a lot of stuff about receivers and focusing."

"The myopia of a man who has to actually make the damned thing work. Understandable. Well look, you remember what Einstein showed a century ago—that light was a kind of speed limit?"

"Yes."

"Well, the mindless, popular description of relativity is—" here he arched his eyebrows, as if to put visible, disdaining quotation marks about the next phrase "—that 'everything is relative.' Meaningless statement, of course. A better shorthand is that there are no privileged observers in the universe."

"Not even physicists are privileged?"

Greg smiled at the jibe. "*Especially* physicists, since we know what's going on. Point is, Einstein showed that two people moving with respect to each other can't agree on whether two events happen at the same time. That's because light takes a finite time to travel from the events to the two people, and that time is different for each person. I can show you that with some simple mathematics—"

"Oh, don't, truly." She laughed.

"Agreed. This *is* a party, after all. Thing is, your husband has gone after some big fish here. His tachyon experiment takes Einstein's ideas a step further, in a way. The discovery of particles traveling faster than light means those two moving observers won't agree about which event came first, either. That is, the sense of time gets scrambled."

"But surely that's merely a difficulty of communication. A problem with the tachyon beams and so on."

"No, dead wrong. It's fundamental. See, the 'light barrier,' as it was called, kept us in a universe which had a disordered sense of what's *simultaneous*. But at least we could tell which way time flowed! Now we can't even do that."

"'Using these particles?'" Marjorie said doubtfully.

"Yes. They rarely occur in nature, we think, so we haven't seen the effects of them before. But now—"

"Wouldn't it be more exciting to build a tachyon spaceship? Go to the stars?"

He shook his head fiercely. "Not at all. All John can make is streams of particles, not solid objects. Anyway, how do you get onto a spaceship moving by you faster than light? The idea's nonsense. No, the real impact here is the signaling, a whole new kind of physics. And I . . . I'm lucky to be in on it."

Marjorie instinctively put her hand out and patted his arm, feeling a burst of quiet joy at this last sentence. It was good to see someone wholly involved with something beyond himself, especially these days. John was the same way, of course, but with John it was somehow different. His emotions were bottled up in an obsession with machinery and with some inner turbulence, almost a defiant anger at the universe for withholding its secrets. Perhaps that was the difference between merely thinking about experiments, as Greg did, and actually having to do them. It must be harder to believe in serene mathematical beauties when you have dirty hands.

James approached. "Greg, have you any information on the political mood in Washington? I was wondering . . . "

Marjorie saw the moment between herself and Greg was broken and she moved off, surveying the geometry of her guests. James and Greg fell to discussing politics. Greg shifted conversational gears immediately. They quickly disposed of the incessant strikes, the Trades Union Council taking most of the blame. James asked when the American government might reopen the stock market. John was hovering rather awkwardly. How odd, Marjorie thought, for a man to be so ill at ease in his own home. She sensed, from the wrinkling of his brow, that he was uncertain whether to join the two men. He knew nothing of the stock market and rather despised it as a form of gambling. She sighed and took pity on him.

"John, come and give me a hand, will you? I'm going to put the first course on the table now."

He turned with relief and followed her into the house. She checked the mottled gray pâté and touched up the plates with carrot curls and lettuce from her vegetable garden. John helped her set out butter pats and Melba toast made from home-baked bread. He gingerly popped open some of her home-made wine.

Marjorie went among the knots of conversing people, shepherding them with little bursts of bright invitation toward the dining table. She felt rather like a sheep dog, doubling back to urge on those who had snagged at a point of interest and had stopped drifting in from the garden. There were murmured comments of appreciation at the table, set with flowers from the garden and individual candles cleverly folded into the napkins. She organized them around the table, Jan next to James as they seemed to be getting on well together. Greg sat by Heather; she seemed a bit nervous about this.

"Marjorie, you're a marvel," Heather declared. "This pâté is delicious—and this is home-made bread, isn't it? However do you manage, with the power rationing and everything?"

"God, yes. Terrible, isn't it?" Greg exclaimed. "I mean the power rationing," he added quickly. "The pâté is excellent. Good bread, too. But to have electricity only four hours a day —incredible. I don't know how you people can live with it," and the table dissolved into "It's an experimental measure, you understand" . . . "think it will last?" . . . "too many inequities" . . . "factories get power, of course" . . . "staggered working hours" . . . "ones who suffer—old codgers like us" . . . "the poor don't care, do they?" . . . "as long as they can open a tin of beans and a pint of beer" . . . "the wealthy who have all the electrical gadgets who" . . . "that's why it'll be thrown straight out" . . . "I just do everything at the same time, laundry and vacuuming and" . . . "between ten and noon and the evening hours" . . . "Next month will be worse, when the hours change round again" . . . "East Anglia gets what the Midlands are getting now, twelve to two and eight to ten"—

John put in, "How long will it be before East Anglia gets this six to eight time slot again? It's good for dinner parties, at least."

"Not until November," Marjorie answered. "Coronation month."

"Ah, yes," Greg murmured. "Dancing in the dank dark."

"Well, they may make an exception," Heather said, somewhat daunted by Greg's wry tone.

"How?"

"By letting the power stay on. So people round the country can all see it."

"Yes," Marjorie said, "London won't need extra power to put it on. Come to think of it, a Coronation is quite ecological."

"You intend 'ecological' to mean 'virtuous,' don't you?" Greg asked.

"We-e-ell." Marjorie drew out the word while she tried to judge just what Greg meant. "I know that's a misuse of the word, but really, at a Coronation they always use horse-drawn coaches and the Abbey will be lit by candles. And they don't need any heat there with all the peers in their furred robes."

"Yes, I love to see them," Jan said. "So colorful."

"Quite public-minded, too, the peers," James stated judiciously. "They've been very helpful to the government. Getting legislation through speedily and so on."

"Oh, yes." Greg smiled. "They'll do anything for the worker, except become one."

To a chorus of agreeing chuckles, Heather added, "Well, yes, anyone would rather talk than work. The peers just fill the air with their speeches."

"And from what I've seen, vice versa," Greg responded.

James' face stiffened. Marjorie suddenly remembered that he had an influential relative in the House of Lords. She stood quickly and murmured something about fetching the chicken. As she left, Markham started a sentence about the American view of the opposition party and James' thin-lipped mouth relaxed. One end of the table focused on Greg's political stilettos and at the other James asked, "It still seems strange saying 'the King' after a whole lifetime of 'the Queen,' doesn't it?"

Marjorie returned with a large casserole of chicken in cream sauce with spring vegetables and a rice pilaff. Appreciative murmurs greeted the wash of steamy aroma that rose when she lifted the lid. As she served the chicken, the conversation fragmented, James and Greg talking about the labor laws, the others talking of the forthcoming Coronation. Queen Elizabeth had abdicated in favor of her eldest son the previous Christmas and he had chosen to be crowned on his fiftieth birthday, in November.

John had gone to get more wine, a home-made hock this time.

"I think it's a *terrible* waste of money," Heather declared. "There are so many *better* things we could spend the money on than a Coronation. What about *cancer* for instance? The statistics are horrifying. One in four, is it now?" She abruptly fell silent.

Marjorie knew the cause, and yet it seemed pointless to smooth over it. She leaned forward. "How is your mother?"

Heather did not hesitate to take up the topic; Marjorie realized she needed to talk about it. "Mummy's doing fine, all things considered. I mean, she's deteriorating, of course, but she really seems to have accepted it. She was dreadfully afraid of being doped up at the end, you know."

"She's not going to be?" John asked.

"No, the doctors say not. There is this new electronic anaesthetic thing."

"They simply tap into the superficial brain centers," James added. "It blocks the perception of pain. Much less risky than chemical anaesthetics."

"Less addictive, too, I suppose?" Greg asked.

Heather blinked. "I hadn't thought of that. Could you get addicted?"

"Maybe not, if they simply turn off the pain," Jan said. "But what if they find a way to stimulate the pleasure centers as well?"

"They already have," Greg murmured.

"Really?" Marjorie said. "Are they using that, too?"

"They don't dare." James spoke with an air of finality.

"Well, in any case," Heather continued, "it's all quite beside the point for Mummy. The doctors haven't a clue how to stop the cancer she has."

Before interest could center on details of the prognosis, Marjorie steered talk to other subjects.

●

When the telephone rang John answered. A reedy voice identified itself as Peterson.

"I wanted to let you know before I packed it in for the night," he said. "I'm in London; the Council's European meeting just broke up. I think I've got what you need, or at least part of it."

"Tremendous," John said rapidly. "Bloody good."

"I say 'part' because I'm not sure the Americans will send everything you need. They say there are other uses they have in mind. Uses aside from this tachyon business, I mean."

"Could I get a list of what they have?"

"I'm working on it. Listen, I must ring off. Wanted to let you know."

"Right. Fine. And, and thanks!"

The news changed the tenor of the party. Heather and James knew nothing of John's experiment, so there was much explaining to do before they could understand the import of the telephone call. Renfrew and Markham took turns explaining the basic idea, skipping over the complicated matter of Lorentz transformations and how tachyons could propagate backward in time; they would have needed a blackboard to make the attempt. Marjorie came in from the kitchen, wiping her hands on an apron. The men's voices were authoritative, booming in the small dining room. Candlelight bathed the faces around the table in a pale yellow glow. The women spoke with rising inflections, questioning.

"It seems strange to think of the people in one's own past as real," Marjorie said distantly. Heads turned towards her. "That is, to imagine them as, as still alive and changeable in some sense . . ."

The company sat silent for a moment. Several frowned. Marjorie's way of putting the issue had caught them off balance. They had spoken often this evening of things changing in the future. To imagine the past as alive, too, as a moving and flexing thing—

The moment passed, and Marjorie returned to the kitchen. She came back with not one but three desserts. When she set them down, the *pièce de résistance*—a meringue confection with early raspberries and whipped cream—created the wave of *ahs* she had anticipated. She followed this in short order with pots of strawberry mousse and a large glass bowl of carefully decorated sherry trifle.

"Marjorie, you're too much," James protested.

John sat and beamed silently as the guests heaped praises on his wife. Even Jan managed two helpings, though she refused the trifle.

"I think," Greg commented, "that sweets must be the English substitute for sex."

After dessert the party moved near the fireplace as Greg and John cleared away the dessert plates. Marjorie felt a warm relaxation seeping through her as she brought in the tea things. The room had taken on a chill as darkness deepened; she added a small, glimmering candle heater to warm the cups. The fire crackled and shot an orange spark onto the worn carpet.

"I know coffee is supposed to be bad for you but I must say it goes better with liqueurs," Marjorie observed. "Would anyone like some? We've got Drambuie, Cointreau, and Grand Marnier. *Not* home-made."

She felt a relaxed sense of accomplishment now that the meal was over. Her duties ended with handing out the cups. Outside, a wind was getting up. The curtains were open and she could see the silhouetted pine branches tossing outside the windows. The living room was an oasis of light and peace and stability.

As if reading her thoughts, Jan quoted softly: "Stands the church clock at ten to three? And is there honey still for tea?"

They all exaggerated, Marjorie thought, especially the press. History was a series of crises, after all, and they'd all survived so far. John worried about it, she knew, but really, things hadn't changed all that much.

chapter six

SEPTEMBER 25, 1962

Gordon Bernstein put down his pencil with deliberate slowness. He held it between thumb and forefinger and watched the tip tremble in the air. It was an infallible test; as he brought the pencil lead near the formica table top, the jittering of his hand made a *tick-tick-tick* rhythm. No matter how strongly he willed the hand to be still, the ticking continued. As he listened it seemed to swell and become louder than the muted chugging of the roughing pumps around him.

Abruptly Gordon smashed the pencil down, gouging a black hole in the table, snapping off the lead, splintering the wood and yellow paint.

"Hey, ah—"

Gordon's head jerked up. Albert Cooper was standing beside him. How long had he been there?

"I, ah, checked with Doctor Grundkind," Cooper said, looking away from the pencil. "Their whole rig is off the air."

"You looked it over yourself?" Gordon's voice came out thin and wheezing, overcontrolled.

"Yeah, well, they're kinda gettin' tired of me coming around," Cooper said sheepishly. "This time they unplugged all their stuff from the wall outlets, even."

Gordon nodded silently.

"Well, I guess that's it."

"What do you mean?" Gordon said evenly.

"Look, we've been working on this for—what?—four days."

"So?"

"We're at a dead end."

"Why?"

"Grundkind's low-temperature group was the last candidate on our list. We've got everybody in the building shut down."

"Right."

"So this noise—it can't be spillover from them."

"Uh huh."

"And we *know* it isn't leaking in from outside."

"The chicken wire we wrapped around the apparatus proves that," Gordon agreed, nodding at the metal cage now embracing the entire magnet assembly. "It *should* shield out stray signals."

"Yeah. So it has to be some screwup in our electronics."

"Nope."

"Why not?" Cooper demanded impatiently. "Hell, maybe Hewlett-Packard is shittin' us on the specs, how do we know?"

"We've checked the rig ourselves."

"But that's *got* to be it."

"*No,*" Gordon said with compressed energy. "No, there's something else." His hand shot out and seized a stack of *x-y* recorder plots. "I've been taking these for two hours. Look."

Cooper paged through the red-gridded sheets. "Well, it looks a little less noisy. I mean, the noise has got some regular spikes in it."

"I tuned it in. Improved the resolution."

"So? It's still noise," Cooper said irritably.

"No, it isn't."

"Huh? Of course it is."

"Look at those spikes I brought up out of the hash. Look at their spacing."

Cooper fanned the sheets out on the formica table top. After a moment he said, "I'm just eyeballing it, but . . . well, looks like they come at only two different intervals."

Gordon nodded energetically. "Correct. That's what I noticed. What we're seeing here is a lot of background noise—damned if I know where that's coming from—with some regular stuff on top."

"How'd you get these plots?"

"Used the lock-in correlator, to cull out the genuine noise. This structure, this spacing—it's there, probably been there all the time."

"We just never looked closely enough."

"We 'knew' it was garbage, and why study garbage? Stupid." Gordon shook his head, smiling wryly at himself.

Cooper's forehead wrinkled as he stared off into space. "I don't get it. What've these pulses got to do with the nuclear resonance?"

"I don't know. Maybe nothing."

"But, hell, that's what this experiment *is*. I'm measuring the big nuclear resonance spike, when we flip the spins of the atomic nuclei. These pulses—"

"They're not resonances. Not as I understand a simple resonance, anyway. Something's tipping over those nuclear spins, all right, but . . . wait a sec.''

Gordon stared down at the x-y graphs. His left hand twitched absently at a button on his rumpled blue shirt. ''I don't think this is any sort of frequency-dependent effect.''

''But that's what we're *plotting*. The intensity of the signal received, versus the frequency we see it at.''

''Yes, but that assumes everything's steady.''

''Well, it is.''

''Who says? Suppose the noise comes in bursts?''

''Why should it?''

''Damn it!'' Gordon slammed a fist down, sending the snapped pencil skittering off the table. ''Try the idea on for *size!* Why is it every student wants things spelled out for him?''

''Well, okay.'' Cooper earnestly knitted his forehead into a worried expression. Gordon could see the man was obviously too tired to do any real thinking. For that matter, so was he. They'd been hammering away at this nightmare problem for days, sleeping a minimal amount and going out for meals in greasy fast-food franchises. Hell, he hadn't even got down to the beach to do any jogging. And Penny—Christ, he'd hardly caught a glimpse of her. She'd said something abrupt and feisty to him last night, just before he fell asleep, and it hadn't registered with him until he was getting dressed, alone, this morning. So there was some patching-up to do there, when he got home. If he *ever* got home, he added, because he was damned if he'd give up on this puzzle until . . .

''Hey, try this,'' Cooper said, jarring Gordon out of his musing. ''Suppose we're seeing a time-varying input here, the way you said it was, you know, days ago—when we started searching for outside noise sources. Our transcribing pen is moving at a constant rate across the paper, right?'' Gordon nodded. ''So these spikes here are spaced about a centimeter apart, and then two spaced half a centimeter. Then a one centimeter interval, three half-centimeters, and so on.''

Gordon suddenly saw what he was driving at, but he let Cooper finish.

''That's the way the signal came in, spaced out in *time*. Not frequency, time.''

Gordon nodded. It was obvious, now that he stared at the wiggles and peaks of the recording pen. ''Something coming in bursts, all across the frequency spectrum we're studying.'' He pursed his lips. ''Bursts with long intervals between them, then some with shorter intervals.''

"Right." Cooper nodded enthusiastically. "That's it."

"Short ones, long ones . . . Short, long, short, short. Like . . ."

"Like a goddamned code," Cooper finished.

Cooper wiped at his mouth and stared at the x-y recordings.

"Do you know Morse code?" Gordon asked him quietly. "I don't."

"Well, yeah. I did when I was a kid, anyway."

"Let's lay out these sheets, in the order I took the data." Gordon stood up with renewed energy. He picked the broken pencil off the floor and inserted it in a pencil sharpener and started turning the handle. It made a raw, grinding noise.

●

When Isaac Lakin came into the nuclear resonance laboratory anyone, even a casual visitor, could tell it was his. Of course, the National Science Foundation paid for essentially all of it, except the war surplus electronics gear acquired from the Navy, and the University of California owned the immense pancake magnets under a Grantor's Assignment, but in any useful sense of the term the laboratory belonged to Isaac Lakin. He had established his reputation at MIT in a decade of sound work, research occasionally flecked by the sparkle of real brilliance. From there he had gone to General Electric and Bell Labs, each step taking him higher. When the University of California began building a new campus around the Scripps Institute of Oceanography, Lakin became one of their first "finds." He had the contacts in Washington and brought a big chunk of money with him, money that translated into gear and lab space and slots for junior faculty. Gordon had been one of the first to fill those slots, but from the beginning he and Lakin had failed to hit it off. When Lakin came into Gordon's lab he usually found something out of place, a snarl of wires that almost tripped him, a dewar poorly secured, something that soured his mood.

Lakin nodded to Cooper and murmured a hello to Gordon, his eyes scanning the lab. Gordon quickly led Lakin through a summary of their process of elimination. Lakin nodded, smiling faintly, as Cooper then detailed the weeks he had spent checking and rechecking the rig. As Cooper went on Lakin drifted away, thumbing a knob here, studying a circuit there.

"These leads are reversed," he declared, holding up wiring with alligator clips attached.

"That unit we aren't using anyway," Gordon replied mildly. Lakin studied Cooper's circuitry, made a remark about assembling it better, and moved on. Cooper's voice followed him around the large laboratory bay. To Cooper, describing an experiment was like field-stripping a rifle, each part in its place and as necessary as any other. He was good and he was careful, but he hadn't the experience to go for the throat of a problem, Gordon saw, to give only the essentials. Well, that was why Cooper was a student and Lakin a full professor.

Lakin flipped a switch, studied the dancing face of an oscilloscope, and said, "Something's out of alignment."

Cooper scurried into action. He tracked down the snag, setting it right in a few moments. Lakin nodded in approval. Gordon felt a curious tightness in his chest ease, as though it had been himself being tested, not Cooper.

"Very well, then," Lakin said finally. "Your results?"

Now it was Gordon's turn to perform. He chalk-talked his way through their ideas, followed them up with the data displays. He gave Cooper credit for guessing there was a coded message in the noise. He picked up a recorder sheet and showed it to Lakin, pointing out the spacings and how they were always close to either one centimeter or 0.5 centimeters, never anything else.

Lakin studied the jittery lines with their occasional sharp points, like towers jutting up through a fog-shrouded cityscape. Impassively he said, "Nonsense."

Gordon paused. "I thought so, too, at first. Then we decoded the thing, assigning the 0.5 centimeter intervals as 'short' and one centimeter as 'long' in Morse code."

"This is pointless. There is no physical effect which could produce data like these." Lakin glanced around at Cooper, clearly exasperated.

"But look at a translation from the Morse," Gordon said, scribbling on the blackboard. ENZYME INHIBITED B.

Lakin squinted at the letters. "This is from one sheet of recorder paper?"

"Well, no. Three together."

"Where were the breaks?"

"ENZYM on the first, E INHIB on the second, ITED B on the third."

"So you haven't got a complete word at all."

"Well, they *are* serial. I took them one after the other, with just a quick pause to change paper."

"How long?"

"Oh . . . twenty seconds."

"Time enough for several of your 'letters' to go by undetected."

"Well, maybe. But the structure—"

"There is no structure here, merely guesswork."

Gordon frowned. "The chances of getting a set of words out of random noise, arranged this way—"

"How do you space the words?" Lakin said. "Even in Morse code there's an interval, to tell you where one word stops and another begins."

"Doctor Lakin, that's just what we've found. There are two-centimeter intervals on the recordings between each word. That fits—"

"I see." Lakin took all this stoically. "Quite convenient. Are there other . . . messages?"

"Some," Gordon said evenly. "They don't make a great deal of sense."

"I suspected as much."

"Oh, there are words. 'This' and 'saturate'—what are the odds against getting an eight-letter word like that, offset on each side with two-centimeter spacings?"

"Ummm," Lakin said, shrugging. Gordon always had the feeling that at such moments Lakin had some expression in his native language, Hungarian, but couldn't translate it into English. "I still believe it to be . . . nonsense. There is no physical effect such as this. Interference from outside, yes. I can believe that. But this, this James Bond Morse code—no."

With that Lakin shook his head quickly, as though erasing the matter, and ran a hand through his thinning hair. "I think you have wasted your time here."

"I don't really—"

"My advice to you is to focus on your true problem. That is to find the source of noise in your electronics. I fail to understand why you cannot seek it out." Lakin turned, nodded to Cooper curtly, and was gone.

•

An hour after Lakin had left, after the equipment was turned off or cycled down, the data collected, the lab books compiled and details filled in, Gordon waved goodbye to Cooper and walked out into the long corridor leading to the outside. He was surprised; the glass doors showed gathering gloom, and Jupiter rising. Gordon had assumed it was still late afternoon. The frosted glass in each office door was black; everyone had gone home, even Shelly, whom he'd counted on talking to.

Well then, tomorrow. There was always time tomorrow, Gordon thought. He walked down the corridor woodenly, lurching to the side as his briefcase banged against a knee. The labs were in the basement of the new physics building. Because of the slope of the shoreline hills, this end of the building gave out onto flat land. Beyond the glass doors at the end of the corridor night crouched, a black square. Gordon felt that the telescoping hallway was swimming past him, and realized that he was more tired than he thought. He really ought to get more exercise, stay in shape.

As he watched, Penny stepped into the framed darkness and pushed through.

"Oh," he said, staring at her blankly. He remembered that he had mumbled a promise this morning to come home early and make supper. "Oh damn."

"Yes. I finally got tired of waiting."

"God, I'm sorry, I, I just . . ." He made a gawky gesture. The plain fact was that he had completely forgotten, but it didn't seem wise to say that.

"Honey, you get too wrapped up." Her voice softened as she studied his face.

"Well, I know, I . . . I'm really sorry, God I am . . ." He thought, self-accusingly, *I can't even get started on an apology.* He stared at her and marveled at this compact, well-designed creation, womanly and slight, making him feel bulky and awkward. He really ought to explain how it was with him, how the problems took up all the space inside him while he was working on them, leaving room for nothing else—not even for her, in a sense. It sounded harsh but it was the truth and he tried to think of a way to tell her that without . . .

"Sometimes I wonder how I can love such a dope," she said, shaking her head, a small smile beginning.

"Well, I *am* sorry, but . . . let me tell you about the set-to we had with Lakin."

"Yeah, do tell." She bent over to pick up his briefcase. She was wiry and she lifted the bulging case without difficulty, shifting her hips. Despite his fatigue, Gordon found himself studying the motion. The tightening of her skirt made her thighs leap into outline beneath the fabric. "C'mon, what you need is food." He began his story. She nodded at his words and led the way out the back and around the liquid nitrogen filling station and down into the small parking lot, where safety lamps cast shadows of the guard railings, making a stretched and warped fretwork on the fresh blacktop.

chapter seven

Penny turned the ignition key and the radio came alive, blaring a shrill, *"Pepsi Cola hits the spot! Twelve full ounces, that's a lot—"* Gordon reached over and clicked it off.

Penny pulled out of the parking lot and onto the boulevard. Cool night air fanned her hair. The strands were mousy brown at the scalp but then lightened into blond, bleached by sun and the chlorine of swimming pools. A sea tang thickened the soft breeze.

"Your mother called," Penny said carefully.

"Oh. You told her I'd call back?" Gordon hoped this would chop off the subject.

"She's flying out soon to visit you."

"What? Goddamn, why?"

"She says you're not writing her at all any more and she wants to see what the west coast is like, anyhow. She's thinking of moving out here." Penny kept her voice calm and flat and drove with quick, precise movements.

"Oh, Christ." He had a sudden mental picture of his mother in a black dress, walking down Girard Avenue in the yellow sunlight, peering in the windows of the shops, a full head shorter than everyone else going by. She would be as out of place as a nun in a nudist colony.

"She didn't know who I was."

"Huh?" The image of his mother frowning at the thinly clad girls on Girard distracted him.

"She asked if I was the cleaning lady."

"Oh."

"You haven't told her we're living together, have you?"

A pause. "I will."

Penny made a humorless smile. "Why haven't you already?"

He looked out the side window, which was smeared with oil where he had been leaning his head against it, and studied the scattering of jewellike lights. La Jolla, the jewel. They were running down the bumpy canyon route and the fresh, minty scent of the eucalyptus stands filled the car. He tried to place himself back in Manhattan and look on things from that angle, to anticipate what his mother would think of all this, and found it impossible.

"Is it because I'm not Jewish?"

"Good God, no."

"But if you had told her that, she'd be out here in a flash, right?"

He nodded ruefully. "Uh huh."

"You going to tell her before she arrives?"

"Look," he said with sudden energy, turning in the bucket seat to face her, "I don't want to tell her *any*thing. I don't want her butting into my life. Our life."

"She's going to ask questions, Gordon."

"Let her ask."

"You won't answer?"

"Look, she's not going to stay in our apartment, she doesn't have to know you live there, too."

Penny rolled her eyes. "Oh, *I* get it. Just before she gets here, you'll start hinting that maybe I should pick up a few of my things that are lying around the apartment? Maybe take my face cream and birth control pills out of the medicine chest? Just a few subtle touches?"

He wilted under her withering tone. He hadn't thought that clearly, but yes, some idea like that had been floating around in his mind. The old game: defend what you have to, but hide the rest. How long ago had he gotten into that pattern with his mother? Since Dad died? Christ, when was he going to stop being a kid?

"I'm sorry, I . . . ."

"Oh, don't be a retard. It was just a joke."

They both knew it wasn't a joke, but instead hung somewhere in that space between fantasy and a reality about to materialize, and that if she had said nothing he would have stumbled his way into the suggestion eventually. It was this uncanny way she had of seeing his mind working on a problem with its blunt tools, and then leaping ahead to the spot he would reach, that endeared her to him at the most unlikely of moments. By tipping over the rock and exposing the worms underneath she had made it easy for him; there was no alternative but to be honest. "God damn, I love you," he said, suddenly grinning.

Her smile took on a wry cast. Beneath the flickering street lights she kept her eyes intently on the road. "That's the trouble with going domestic. You move in with a man and pretty soon, when he says he loves you, you hear underneath it that he's thanking you. So, you're welcome."

"What's that, WASP wisdom?"

"Just making an observation."

"How do you girls on the west coast get so smart so fast?" He leaned forward, as if questioning the California landscape outside.

"Getting laid early helps a lot," she said, grinning.

This was another sore point with him. She had been the first girl he had slept with and when he told her that, at first she wouldn't believe it. When she made a joke about giving lessons to a professor he had felt his veneer of eastern sophistication shucked away. He had begun to suspect, then, that he used that intellectual carapace to protect himself from rubbing against the uncertainties of life, and particularly from the spikes of sensuality. As he watched the stucco beach cottages go by, Gordon thought, a bit grimly, that merely acknowledging a flaw didn't mean you had overcome it. He still felt a certain uneasiness at Penny's direct, straightforward approach. Maybe that was why he couldn't think of her and his mother in the same world together, much less their meeting in his apartment, with Penny's clothes in the closet as silent testimonial.

He impulsively reached out and switched on the radio. Its tinny voice sang, "Big gurrls don't cry—" and he snapped it off.

"Let it play," Penny said.

"It's junk."

"Fills up the air," she said meaningfully.

He turned it back on with a grimace. Over the refrain of "Biig gurrls?" he said, "Hey, it's the 25th, isn't it?" She nodded. "The Liston-Patterson fight's on. Wait a sec." He thumbed the dial and found a staccato announcer filling in pre-fight statistics. "Here. They're not televising it. Look, drive on into Pacific Beach. We'll eat out. I want to hear this." Penny nodded silently and Gordon felt an odd sensation of relief. Yeah, it was good to get away from your own problems and listen to two guys pound each other to a pulp. He had picked up the habit of following the fights from his dad around the age of ten. They would sit in the overstuffed chairs of the living room and listen to the excited voices coming from the big brown old-fashioned Motorola in the corner. His father's eyes jerked back and forth, blank, seeing the punches and feints described from a thousand miles away. Dad had been overweight even then and when he unconsciously threw an imaginary punch, jerking his right elbow forward, the fat flapped on his upper arm. Gordon could see the flesh move even through his father's white shirt, and watched to see if the ash on his cigar would jerk off and crumble into a gray stain on the carpet. It always did, at least once, and his mother would come in on the middle of the fight and cluck-cluck about it and go out to get the dust pan. Dad would wink at him when there was a good punch or somebody went down, and Gordon would grin. He remembered it now as always happening in the summer, so that a traffic hum drifted up from 12th Street and 2nd Avenue, and his father always had damp crescents under his armpits when the fight was over. They drank cokes afterward. It had been a good time.

•

As they entered the Limehouse, Gordon pointed to a far table and said, "Say, there are the Carroways. What does that make our average?"

"Seven out of twelve," Penny pronounced.

The Carroways were prominent astronomers, an English couple recently recruited into the Physics Department faculty. They were working at the forefront of the field, struggling with the recent discovery of the quasi-stellar sources. Elizabeth was the observer of the pair, and spent a good deal of time nearby at Palomar, taking deep plates of the sky and searching for more reddened points of light. The red shifts indicated that the sources were very far away and thus incredibly luminous. Bernard, the theoretician, thought it pretty likely that they were not distant galaxies at all. He was working on a model which regarded the sources as expelled lumps from our own galaxy, all rushing away from us at very nearly the speed of light and thus red-shifted. Either way, neither had the time to cook, and they seemed to prefer the same restaurants Gordon and Penny frequented. Gordon had noticed the correlation and Penny was keeping track of the statistics.

"The resonant effect seems to be holding up," Gordon said to Bernard as they walked by. Elizabeth laughed, and introduced them to the third member of their party, a compact man with a piercing way of looking straight at people as he talked. Bernard asked them to sit at their table and soon the conversation turned to astrophysics and the red shift controversy. Partway through it they ordered the most exotic items they could find on the menu. The Limehouse was a rather second-rate Chinese restaurant, but it was the only one in town and the scientists were all confirmed in the belief that even second-level Chinese was preferable to first-level American. Gordon was wondering idly if this was an outcome of the internationalism of science when he suddenly realized that he hadn't caught the other man's name correctly. It was John Boyle, the famous astrophysicist who had a long string of successes to his credit. It was surprises like this, meeting the very best of the scientific community, that made La Jolla what it was. He was very pleased when Penny made a few funny remarks and Boyle laughed, his eyes studying her. This was the kind of thing, meeting the great, that would impress his mother; for this reason he instantly decided not to tell her. Gordon listened to the ebb and flow of the conversation carefully, trying to detect what quality made these colleagues stand out from the rest. There was a quickness of mind, certainly, and a lighthearted skepticism about politics and the way the world was run. Beyond that they seemed pretty much like everybody else. He decided to try a feeler of a different sort.

"What did you think of Liston knocking out Patterson?"

Blank stares.

"He decked him in only two minutes of the first round."

"Sorry, don't follow that sort of thing," Boyle said. "I should imagine the spectators would be rather miffed if they paid very much for seats."

"A hundred dollars for a ringside seat," Gordon said.

"Almost a dollar a second," Bernard chuckled, and that got them off on a comparison of time per dollar of all human events, considered as a class. Boyle tried to find the most expensive of all and Penny topped him with sex itself; five minutes of pleasure and an entire costly child to bring up if you weren't careful. Boyle's eyes twinkled and he said to her, "Five minutes? Not a great advertisement for you, Gordon."

In the quick bubble of laughter no one noticed Gordon's jaw muscles clench. He was mildly shocked that Boyle would assume they were sleeping together, and then make a joke about it. Damned irritating. But talk moved on to other subjects and the knotting tension eased away.

Food arrived and Penny continued to inject witty asides, plainly charming Boyle. Gordon admired her in silence, marveling that she could move so easily through such deep waters. He, on the other hand, found himself thinking of something original to say a minute or two after the conversation had passed on to something else. Penny noticed this and drew him in, feeding him a line to which she knew he already had a funny reply. The Limehouse swelled with the hum of talk, the tang of sauces. When Boyle produced from his coat pocket a notebook and made an entry in it, Gordon described how a physicist at a Princeton party was writing in his notebook, and Einstein, sitting next to him, asked why. "Whenever I have a good idea, I make sure I don't forget it," the man said. "Perhaps you'd like to try it—it's handy." Einstein shook his head sadly and said, "I doubt it. I have only had two or three good ideas in my life."

This got a good laugh. Gordon beamed at Penny. She had drawn him out and now he was fitting in well.

After dinner the five of them debated going to a movie together. Penny wanted *Last Year at Marienbad* and Boyle favored *Lawrence of Arabia,* contending that since he only saw one film a year he might as well take in the best. They voted in favor of *Lawrence,* four to one. As they left the restaurant Gordon hugged Penny in the parking lot outside, thinking, as he leaned to kiss her, of the smell of her in bed. "I love you," he said.

"You're welcome," she replied, smiling.

•

It seemed afterward, as he lay beside her, that he had turned her on the lathe of the light slanting in from the window, re-forming her in an image that was fresh each time. He shaped her with his hands and tongue. She, in turn, guided and molded him. He thought he could sense in her sure moves and choices, first this way and then that, past imprints of the lovers she had known before. Strangely, the thought did not bother him, thought he felt that in some way it should. Echoes of other men came from her. But they were gone now and he was here; it seemed enough.

He panted slightly, reminding himself that he ought to get down to the beach and run more often, and studied her face in the dim gray street light that leaked into their bedroom. The lines of her face were straight, without strategies, the only curves a few matted damp strands of hair across her cheek. Graduate student in literature, dutiful daughter to an Oakland investor, by turns lyrical and practical, with a political compass that saw virtues in both Kennedy and Goldwater. At times brazen, then timid, then wanton, appalled at his sensual ignorance, reassuringly startled by his sudden bursts of sweaty energy, and then soothing with a fluid grace as he collapsed, blood thickening, beside her.

Somewhere, someone was playing a thin song, Peter, Paul, and Mary's "Lemon Tree."

"Goddam, you're good," Penny said. "On a scale of one to ten, you get eleven."

He frowned, thinking, weighing this new hypothesis. "No, it's *we* who are good. You can't separate the performance from the players."

"Oh, you're so analytical."

He frowned. He knew that with the conflicted girls back east it would have been different. Oral sex would have been an elaborate matter, requiring much prior negotiation and false starts and words that didn't fit but would have to do: "What about if we, well . . ." and "If, you know, that's what you want . . ."—all leading to a blunt incident, all elbows and uncomfortable positions that, once assumed, you feared to change out of sheer unspoken embarrassment. With the intense girls he had known, all that would have had to happen. With Penny, no.

He looked at her and then at the wooden walls beyond. A puzzled concern flickered across his face. He knew this was where he should be urbane and casual, but it seemed more important now to get it right. "No, it's not me or you," he repeated. "It's us."

She laughed and poked him.

chapter eight

OCTOBER 14, 1962

Gordon thumbed through the stack of mail in his slot. An ad for a new musical, *Stop the World—I Want to Get Off,* forwarded by his mother. Not likely he'd be making it to the fall openings on Broadway this year; he dropped the ad in the trash. Something called the Citizens for Decent Literature had sent him a gaudy booklet, detailing the excesses of *The Carpetbaggers* and Miller's *Tropic of Capricorn*. Gordon read the excerpts with interest. In this forest of parting thighs, wracking orgasms, and straightforward gymnastics he could see nothing that would corrupt the body politic. But General Edwin Walker thought so, and Barry Goldwater made a cameo appearance as savant with a carefully worded warning about the erosion of public will through private vice. There was the usual guff about the analogy between the US and the decline of the Roman Empire. Gordon chuckled and threw it away. It was another civilization entirely, out here in the west. No censorship group would ever solicit university staff for contributions on the east coast; they'd know it was futile, a waste of postage. Maybe out here these simpletons thought the Roman Empire line would appeal even to scholars. Gordon glanced through the latest *Physical Review,* ticking off papers he would read later. Claudia Zinnes had some interesting stuff about nuclear resonances, with clean-looking data; the old group at Columbia was keeping up their reputation.

Gordon sighed. Maybe he should have stayed on at Columbia on a postdoc, instead of taking the leap into an Assistant Professorship so early. La Jolla was a high-powered, competitive place, hungry for fame and "eminence." A local magazine ran a monthly feature titled *A University on Its Way to Greatness,* full of hoopla and photos of professors peering at complicated instruments, or ruminating over an equation. California goes to the stars, California leaps ahead, California trades bucks for brains. They'd gotten Herb York, who used to be Deputy Director of the Defense Department, to come in as the first Chancellor of the campus. Harold Urey came, and the Mayers, then

Keith Brueckner in nuclear theory, a trickle of talent that was now turning into a steady stream. In such waters a fresh Assistant Professor had all the job security of live bait.

Gordon walked down the third floor hallways, looking at the names on the doors. Rosenbluth, the plasma theorist some thought was the best in the world. Matthias, the artist of low temperatures, the man who held the record for the superconductor with the highest operating temperature. Kroll and Suhl and Piccioni and Feher, each name summoning up at least one incisive insight, or brilliant calculation, or remarkable experiment. And here, at the end of the fluorescent and tiled sameness of the corridor: Lakin.

"Ah, you received my note," Lakin said when he answered Gordon's knock. "Good. We have decisions to make."

Gordon said, "Oh? Why?" and sat down across the desk from Lakin, next to the window. Outside, bulldozers were knocking over some of the eucalyptus trees in preparation for the chemistry building, grunting mechanically.

"My NSF grant is coming up for renewal," Lakin said significantly.

Gordon noticed that Lakin did not say "our" NSF grant, even though he and Shelly and Gordon were all investigators on the grant. Lakin was the man who okayed the checks, the P.I. as the secretaries always put it—Principal Investigator. It made a difference. "The renewal proposal isn't due in until around Christmas," Gordon said. "Should we start writing it this early?"

"It's not writing I'm talking about. What are we to write *about?*"

"Your localized spin experiments—"

Lakin shook his head, a scowl flickering across his face. "They are still at an exploratory stage. I cannot use them as the staple item."

"Shelly's results—"

"Yes, they are promising. Good work. But they are still conventional, just linear projections of earlier work."

"That leaves me."

"Yes. You." Lakin steepled his hands before him on the desk. His desk top was conspicuously neat, every sheet of paper aligned with the edge, pencils laid out in parallel.

"I haven't got anything clear yet."

"I gave you the nuclear resonance problem, plus an excellent student—Cooper—to speed things up. I expected a full set of data by now."

"You know the trouble we're having with noise."

"Gordon, I didn't give you that problem by accident," Lakin said, smiling slightly. His high forehead wrinkled in an expression of concerned friendliness. "I thought it would be a valuable boost to your career. I admit, it is not precisely the sort of apparatus you are accustomed to. Your thesis problem was more straightforward. But a clean result would clearly be publishable in *Phys Rev Letters,* and that could not fail to help us with our renewal. And you, with your position in the department."

Gordon looked out the window at the machines chewing up the landscape, and then back at Lakin. *Physical Review Letters* was the prestige journal of physics now, the place where the hottest results were published in a matter of weeks, rather than having to wait at *Physical Review* or, worse, some other physics journal, for month after month. The flood of information was forcing the working scientist to narrow his reading to a few journals, since each one was getting thicker and thicker. It was like trying to drink from a fire hose. To save time you began to rely on quick summaries in *Physical Review Letters* and promised yourself you would get around to reading the longer journals when there was more time.

"That's all true," Gordon said mildly. "But I don't have a result to publish."

"Ah, but you do," Lakin murmured warmly. "This noise effect. It is most interesting."

Gordon frowned. "A few days ago you were saying it was just bad technique."

"I was a bit temperamental that day. I did not fully appreciate your difficulties." He combed long fingers through his thinning hair, sweeping it back to reveal white scalp that contrasted strongly with his deep tan. "The noise you have found, Gordon, is not a simple aggravation. I believe, after some thought, that it must be a new physical effect."

Gordon gazed at him in disbelief. "What kind of effect?" he said slowly.

"I do not know. Certainly something is disturbing the usual nuclear resonance process. I suggest we call it 'spontaneous resonance' just to have a working name." He smiled. "Later, if it proves as important as I suspect, the effect may be named for you, Gordon—who knows?"

"But Isaac, we don't understand it! How can we call it a name like that? 'Spontaneous resonance' means something inside the crystal is causing the magnetic spins to flip back and forth."

"Yes, it does."

"But we don't *know* that's what's happening!"

"It is the only possible mechanism," Lakin said coolly.

"Maybe."

"You do not still treasure that signal business of yours, do you?" Lakin said sarcastically.

"We're studying it. Cooper is taking more data right now."

"That is nonsense. You are wasting that student's time."

"Not in my judgment."

"I fear your 'judgment' is not the only factor at work here," Lakin said, giving him a stony look.

"What does that mean?"

"You are inexperienced at these matters. We are working under a deadline. The NSF renewal is more important than your objections. I dislike putting it so bluntly, but—"

"Yes, yes, you have the best interests of the entire group in mind."

"I do not believe I need my sentences finished for me."

Gordon blinked and looked out the window. "Sorry."

There was a silence into which the grating of the bulldozers intruded, breaking Gordon's concentration. He glanced into the stand of jacaranda trees further away and saw a mechanical claw rip apart a rotten wooden fence. It looked like a corral, an aged artifact of a western past now fading. On the other hand it was more probably a remnant of the Marine land the University had acquired. Camp Matthews, where foot soldiers were pounded into shape for Korea. So one training center was knocked down and another reared up in its place. Gordon wondered what he was being trained to fight for here. Science? Or funding?

"Gordon," Lakin began, his voice reduced to a calming murmur, "I don't think you fully appreciate the significance of this 'noise problem' you're having. Remember, you do not have to understand everything about a new effect to discover it. Goodyear found how to make tough rubber accidentally by dropping India rubber mixed with sulfur on a hot stove. Roentgen found x-rays while he was fumbling around with a gas-filled electrical discharge experiment."

Gordon grimaced. "That doesn't mean everything we don't understand is important, though."

"Of course not. But trust my judgment in this case. This is exactly the sort of mystery that *Phys Rev Letters* will publish. And it will bolster our NSF profile."

Gordon shook his head. "I think it's a signal."

"Gordon, you will come up for review of your position this year. We can advance you to a higher grade of Assistant

Professor. We could even conceivably promote you to tenure.''

"So?" Lakin hadn't mentioned that they could also, as the bureaucratese went, give him a "terminal appointment."

"A solid paper in *Phys Rev Letters* carries much weight."

"Uh huh."

"And if your experiment continues to yield nothing, I am afraid I will, regretfully, not have very much evidence to present in support of you."

Gordon studied Lakin, knowing there wasn't anything more to say. The lines were drawn. Lakin sat back in his executive chair, bobbing with controlled energy, watching the impact of his own words. His Ban-Lon shirt encased an athletic chest, his knit slacks clung to muscled legs. He had adapted well to California, getting out into the welcoming sun and improving his backhand. It was a long way from the cramped, shadowy labs at MIT. Lakin liked it here and he wanted to enjoy the luxury of living in a rich man's town. He would hustle to maintain his position; he wanted to stay.

"I'll think it over," Gordon said in a flat voice. Beside Lakin's sturdy frame he felt overweight, pale, awkward. "And I'll keep taking data," he finished.

•

On the drive back from Lindbergh Field Gordon kept the conversation on safely neutral ground. His mother rattled on about neighbors on 12th Street whose names he didn't remember, much less their intricate family squabbles, their marriages, births, and deaths. His mother assumed he would instantly catch the significance of the Goldbergs buying a place in Miami at last, and understand why their son Jeremy went to NYU rather than Yeshiva. It was all part of the vast soap opera of life. Each segment had meaning. Some would get their come-uppance. Others would receive, after much suffering, their final reward. In his mother's case he was plainly reward enough, at least in this life. She *oohed* at each marvel that loomed up in the fading twilight, as they zoomed along Route 1 toward La Jolla. Palm trees just growing by the roadside, without help. The white sand of Mission Bay, unpeopled and unlittered. No Coney Island, here. No cluttered sidewalks, no press of people. An ocean view from Mount Soledad that went on into blue infinity, instead of a gray vista that terminated in the jumble of New Jersey. She was impressed with everything; it reminded her of what people said about Israel. His father had been a fervent Zionist, plunking down coin regularly to insure the homeland. Gordon was sure she still gave, though she never implored him to; maybe she felt he needed all his *gelt* to keep up with the professoring image. Well, it was true. La Jolla was expensive. But Gordon doubted if he would give anything for the traditional Jewish causes now. The move from New York had severed his connection to all that mumbo jumbo of dietary laws and Talmudic truths. Penny told him he didn't seem very Jewish to her, but he knew she was simply ignorant. The WASPland she'd grown up in had taught her none of the small giveaway clues. Still, most people in California were probably equally oblivious, and that suited Gordon. He didn't like having strangers make assumptions about him before they'd shaken his hand. Getting free of New York's claustrophobic Jewish ambience was one of the reasons for coming to La Jolla in the first place.

They were nearly home, swinging onto Nautilus Street, when his mother said too casually, "This Penny, you should tell me something about her before I meet her, Gordon."

"What's to tell? She's a California girl."

"Which means?"

"She plays tennis, hikes in the mountains, has been to Mexico five times but no farther east than Las Vegas. She even goes surfing. She's tried to get me to do it, but I want to get in better shape first. I'm doing my Canadian Air Force exercises."

"That sounds very nice," she said doubtfully.

Gordon checked her into the Surfside Motel two blocks from his apartment and then drove her over to his apartment. They walked into a room full of the smell of a Cuban casserole dish Penny had learned to make when she was rooming with a Latin American girl. She came out of the kitchen, untying an apron and looking more domestic than Gordon could remember her ever being. So Penny was putting on a bit of a show, despite her objections. His mother was effusive and enthusiastic. She bustled into the kitchen to help with the salad, inspecting Penny's recipe and banging pots around. Gordon busied himself with the wine ritual, which he was just learning. Until California he had seldom had anything that didn't taste of Concord grape. Now he kept a stock of Krug and Martini in a closet and could understand the jargon about big noses and full body, though in truth he wasn't sure what all the terms meant.

His mother came out of the kitchen, set the table with quick, clattering efficiency, and asked where the bathroom was. Gordon told her. As he turned back to the uncorking Penny caught his eye and grinned. He grinned back. Let her Enovid be a flag of independence.

Mrs. Bernstein was subdued when she returned. She walked with more of a waddle than Gordon remembered, her invariable black dress bunching as her slight wobble carried her across the room. She had a distracted look. Dinner began and progressed with only minor newsy conversation. Cousin Irv was going into drygoods somewhere in Massachusetts, Uncle Herb was making money hand over fist as usual, and his sister—here his mother paused, as though suddenly remembering this was a subject she should not bring up—was still running around with some crazies in the Village. Gordon smiled; his sister, two years older and a whole lot bolder, was looking after herself. He made a remark about her art, and how it took time to come to terms with that, and his mother turned to Penny and said, "I suppose you are interested in the arts, too?"

"Oh yes," Penny said. "European literature."

"And what did you think of Mr. Roth's new book?"

"Oh," Penny said, plainly stalling for time. "I don't believe I've finished reading it."

"You should. It would help you understand Gordon so much more."

"Huh?" Gordon said. "What do you mean?"

"Well, dear," Mrs. Bernstein said with a slow, sympathetic tone, "it could give her some idea about . . . well . . . I think Mr. Roth is—you agree, Penny?—is a very deep writer."

Gordon smiled, wondering if he could allow himself an outright laugh. But before he could say anything Penny murmured, "Considering that Faulkner died in July, and Hemingway last year, I guess that puts Roth somewhere in the best hundred American novelists, but—"

"Oh, but they were writing about the *past*, Penny," Mrs. Bernstein said adamantly. "His new one, *Letting Go*, is full of—"

At this point Gordon sat back and let his mind drift. His mother was onto her theory about the rise and preeminence of Jewish literature, and Penny was responding precisely as he could have predicted. His mother's theories rapidly became confused in her mind with revealed facts. In Penny she had a stubborn opponent, however, who wouldn't knuckle under to keep the peace. He could feel the tension rising between them. There was nothing he could do to stop it. The issue wasn't literary theory at all, it was *shiksa* versus mother's love. He watched his mother's face as it tightened up. Her laugh lines, which actually came from squinting, grew deeper. He could break in but he knew how it would go then: his voice would slide up in pitch without his noticing it, until suddenly he was talking with the whine of the teenager barely past Bar Mitzvah. His mother always brought that out in him, a triggered response. Well, this time he would avoid that trap.

Their voices got louder. Penny cited books, authors; his mother pooh-poohed them, confidently assured that a few courses at night school entitled her to strong opinions. Gordon finished his food, savored the wine slowly, looked at the ceiling, and finally broke in with, "Mom, it must be getting late for you, with the time difference and all."

Mrs. Bernstein paused in mid-sentence and looked at him blankly, as if coming out of a trance. "We were simply having a discussion, dear, you don't need to get all flustered." She smiled. Penny managed a matching wan stretching of the face. Mrs. Bernstein poked at her beehive hairdo, a castle of hair that resisted change. Penny got up and removed plates with a clatter. The pressing silence between them grew. "C'mon, Mom. Best to go."

"Dishes." She began gathering cutlery.

"Penny'll."

"Oh, then."

She rose, brushed her shiny black dress free of invisible crumbs, fetched her bag. She went down the outside steps with a hastening step, *clump clump,* more rapid at the bottom, as though fleeing an undecided battle. They took an alleyway shortcut he knew, their footsteps echoing. Waves muttered at the shoreline a block away. Fog fingers drifted and curled under street lamps.

"Well, she is different, isn't she?" Mrs. Bernstein said.

"How?"

"Well."

"No, really." Though he knew.

"You're—" she made a sign, not trusting the words: crooking her longest finger over the index to make an entwined pair —"like that, yes?"

"Is that different?"

"Where we live it is."

"I'm older now."

"You could've said. Warned your mother."

"Rather you met her first."

"You, a scholar."

She sighed. Her bag swung in long arcs as she waddled along, the slant of street lamps stretching her shadow. He decided she was resigned to it.

But no: "You don't know any Jewish girls in California?"

"Come on, Mom."

"I'm not talking about you taking rumba classes or something." She stopped dead. "This is your whole life."

He shrugged. "First time. I'll learn."

"Learn what? To be a something-else?"

"Isn't it a little obvious to be so hostile to my girl friends? Not much analysis needed to understand that."

"Your Uncle Herb would say—"

"Screw Uncle Herb. Hustler philosophy."

"Such language. If I should tell him what you said—"

"Tell him I have money in the bank. He'll understand."

"Your sister, at least your sister's close to home."

"Only geographically."

"You don't know."

"She's slapping oil on canvas to cure her psychosis. Yeah. Psycho Sis."

"Don't."

"It's true."

"You're living with her, yes?"

"Sure. I need the practice."

"Since your father died . . . "

"Don't start with that." A cutting-off chop with his hand. "Listen, you've seen how it is. That's the way it'll stay."

"For your father's sake, God rest his soul . . . "

"You can't—" He was going to finish *push me around with a ghost* and that was the way he felt, but he said, "know what I'm like now."

"A mother doesn't know?"

"Right, sometimes not."

"I tell you, I ask you, don't break your mother's heart."

"I'll do as I like. She's fine for me."

"She is . . . a girl who would do this, live with you without marriage—"

"I'm not sure what I want yet."

"And she wants what?"

"Look, we're finding out. Be reasonable, Mom."

"You throw up to me reasonable? That I should lie down and die and say nothing? I can't stay here and watch you two love birds cooing to each other."

"So don't watch. You have to learn who I am, Mom."

"Your father would—" but she didn't finish. In the cool wan light she jerked erect. "Leave her." Her face was rigid.

"No."

"Then walk me to my bed."

•

When he returned to their bungalow Penny was reading *Time* and eating cashews. "How'd it go?" She tugged her mouth to one side wryly, wearily.

"You're not going to win the Susie Semite contest."

"I didn't think I would. Jesus, I've seen stereotypes before but . . ."

"Yeah. That dumb stuff of hers about Roth."

"That wasn't what it was about."

"No, it wasn't," he agreed.

The next morning his mother phoned him from her motel. She was planning on spending the day walking around town, seeing the sights. She said she did not want to take up his time at the University, so she would do it on her own. Gordon agreed that was probably best, since he had a busy day ahead; a lecture, a seminar, taking the seminar speaker to lunch, two committee meetings in the afternoon, and a conference with Cooper.

He returned to the apartment later than usual that evening. He called her motel, but there was no answer. Penny came home and they made supper together. She was having some problems with her course work and needed to get in some reading. By nine o'clock they finished cleaning up and Gordon spread some of his lecture materials out on the dining room table to do some overdue grading. Around eleven he finished, entered the grades in his book, and only then remembered his mother. He called the motel. They said she had a "do not disturb" sign out and wanted no calls put through. Gordon thought of walking over and knocking on her door. He was tired, though, and resolved to see her first thing in the morning.

He woke late. He had a bowl of shredded wheat while he looked over his lecture notes in Classical Mechanics, reviewing the steps in some of the sample problems he would work for the class. He was putting the papers away in his briefcase when he thought of calling the motel. Again, she was out.

By mid-afternoon his conscience was nagging him. He came home early and walked over to the motel first thing. There was no answer to his knock. He went around to ask at the desk and the clerk looked in the little mail slot under her room number. The man fished out a white envelope and handed it to Gordon. "Dr. Bernstein? Yes. She left this for you, sir. She's checked out."

Gordon tore it open, feeling numb. Inside was a long letter, repeating the themes of the alleyway in more detail. She could not understand how a son, once so devoted, could hurt his mother this way. She was mortified. It was morally wrong, what he was doing. Getting involved with a girl so different, living like that—a terrible mistake. And to do that for such a girl, such a *shtunk* of a girl! His mother was weeping, his mother was filled with worry for him. But his mother knew what sort of a boy he was. He would not change his mind easily. So she was going to leave him alone. She was going to let him come to his senses on his own. She would be all right. She was going up to Los Angeles to see her cousin Hazel, Hazel who had three fine children and who she hadn't seen in seven years. From Los Angeles she would fly back to New York. Maybe in a few months she could come and visit again. Better, he should come home for a time. See his friends at Columbia. Come visit people in the neighborhood; they would be overjoyed to see him, the big success of the block. Until then, she would be writing him and hoping. A mother always hopes.

Gordon put the letter in his pocket and walked home. He showed it to Penny and they talked about it for a while and then he resolved to put it in the back of his mind, to deal with his mother later. These things usually cured themselves, given time.

chapter nine

1998

"Well, where the hell *is* he?" Renfrew exploded. He paced up and down his office, five steps each way.

Gregory Markham sat quietly, watching Renfrew. He had meditated for half an hour this morning and felt relaxed and centered. He looked beyond Renfrew, out the big windows the Cav sported as the prime luxury item in its construction. The broad fields beyond lay flat and still, impossibly green in the first rush of summer. Cyclists glided silently along the Coton footpath, bundles perched on their rear decks. The morning air was already warm and lay like a weight. Blue shrouded the distant spires of Cambridge and ringed the yellow sun that squatted over the town. This was the blissful fraction of the day when there seemed an infinite span of time before you, Markham thought, as though anything could be accomplished in the sea of hushed minutes that stretched ahead.

Renfrew was still pacing. Markham stirred himself to say, "What time did he say he'd be here?"

"Ten, damn it. He set out hours ago. I had to call his office about something and I asked if he was still there. They told me he'd left very early in the morning, before the rush hour. So where is he?"

"It's only ten past," Markham pointed out reasonably.

"Yes, but hell, I can't get started until he gets here. I've got the technicians standing by. We're all set. He's wasting everybody's time. He doesn't care for this experiment and he's making it hard on us."

"You got the funding, didn't you? And that equipment from Brookhaven."

"Limited funds. Enough to keep going, but only just. We'll need more. They're strangling us. You know and I know that this may be the only chance of pulling us out of the hole. What do they do?—make me run the experiment on a shoestring and *then* that sod doesn't even care enough to show up on time to watch it."

"He's an administrator, not a scientist. Sure, the funding

policy does seem short-sighted. But look, the NSF won't send anything more without more pressure. They're probably using it for something else. You can't expect Peterson to work miracles."

Renfrew stopped his pacing and stared at him. "I suppose I have made it rather obvious that I don't like him. I hope Peterson himself isn't aware of it or it might turn him against the experiment."

Markham shrugged. "I'm sure he knows. It's clear to anyone you two have different personality types, and Peterson's no fool. Look, I can talk to him, if you want—I will, in fact. As to you turning him off the experiment—tripe. He must be used to being disliked. I don't suppose it bothers him at all. No, I think you can count on his support. But only partial support. He's trying to cover all his bets and that means spreading support pretty thin."

Renfrew sat down in his swivel chair. "Sorry if I'm a bit tense this morning, Greg." He ran thick fingers through his hair. "I've been working evenings as well as days—may as well use the light—and I'm probably tired. But mainly I'm frustrated. I keep getting noise and it scrambles up the signals."

A sudden flurry of subdued activity in the lab caught their attention. The technicians who had been casually chatting a minute before were now looking purposeful and prepared. Peterson was threading his way across the lab floor. He came to the door of Renfrew's office and nodded curtly to the two men.

"Sorry I'm late, Dr. Renfrew," he said, offering no explanation. "Shall we start on it right away?"

As Peterson turned towards the lab again, Markham noticed with mild surprise the caked mud on his elegant shoes, as though he had been walking in ploughed fields.

•

It was 10:47 a.m. Renfrew began tapping slowly on the signal key. Markham and Peterson stood behind him. Technicians monitored other output from the experiment and made adjustments.

"It's this easy to send a message?" Peterson asked.

"Simple Morse," Markham said.

"I see, to maximize the chances of its being decoded."

"Damn!" Renfrew suddenly stood up. "Noise level has increased again."

Markham leaned over and looked at the oscilloscope face. The trace danced and jiggled, a scattered random field. "How

can there be that much noise in a chilled indium sample?"
Markham asked.

"Christ, I don't know. We've had trouble like this all along."

"It can't be thermal."

"Transmission is impossible with this going on?" Peterson put in.

"Of course," Renfrew said irritably. "Broadens the tachyon resonance line and muddles up the signal."

"Then the experiment can't work?"

"Bloody hell, I didn't say that. There's just a holdup. I'm sure I can find the problem."

A technician called down from the platform above. "Mr. Peterson? Telephone call, says it's urgent."

"Oh, all right." Peterson hastened up the metal stairway and was gone. Renfew conferred with some technicians, checked readings himself, and fretted away several minutes. Markham stood peering at the oscilloscope trace.

"Any idea what it could be?" he called to Renfrew.

"Heat leak, possibly. Maybe the sample isn't well insulated from shocks, either."

"You mean people walking around the room, that sort of thing?"

Renfrew shrugged and went on with his work. Greg rubbed a thumbnail against his lower lip and studied the yellow noise spectrum on the green oscilloscope screen. After a moment he asked, "Have you got a correlator you could use on this rig?"

Renfrew stopped for a moment, thinking. "No, none here. We have no use for one."

"I'd like to see if there is any structure we could bring out of that noise."

"Well, I suppose we could do that. Take a while to scrounge up something suitable."

Peterson appeared overhead. "Sorry, I'm going to have to go to a secured telephone. Something's come up." Renfrew turned without saying anything. Markham climbed the stairway.

"I think there will be a delay in the experiment, anyway."

"Ah, good. I don't want to return to London just yet, without seeing it through. But I'll have to talk to some people on a confidential telephone line. There's one in Cambridge. It will probably take an hour or so."

"Things are that bad?"

"Seems so. That large diatom bloom off the South American coast, Atlantic side, appears to be expanding out of control."

"Bloom?"

"Biologist's word. It means the phytoplankton are coming to

terms with the chlorinated hydrocarbons we've been using in fertilizer. But there's something more to this one. The technical people are scrambling to find out how this case differs from the earlier, smaller effects on the ocean food chain.''

"I see. Can we do anything about it?"

"I don't know. The Americans have some controlled experiments in the Indian Ocean, but I gather progress is slow."

"Well, I won't keep you from the telephone. I've got something to work on, an idea about John's experiment. Say, do you know the Whim?"

"Yes, it's in Trinity Street. Near Bowes & Bowes."

"I'll probably need a drink and some food in an hour or so. Why don't we meet there?"

"Good idea. See you round midday."

●

The Whim was packed with undergraduates. Ian Peterson pushed his way through a crowd near the door and stood for a moment trying to get his bearings. The students near him were passing jugs of beer back over each other's heads and some spilled on him. Peterson took out a handkerchief and wiped it off with distaste. The students had not noticed. It was the end of the academic year and they were in boisterous spirits. A few were already drunk. They were talking loudly in dog Latin, a parody of some official function they had just attended.

"Eduardus, dona mihi plus beerus!" shouted one.

"*Beerus?* O Deus, quid dicit? Ecce sanguinus barbarus!" another declaimed.

"Mea culpa, mea maxima culpa!" the first speaker responded in mock contrition. "But what's beer in bloody Latin?"

Several voices answered. "Alum!" "Vinum barbaricum!" "Imbibius hopius!" There were shouts of laughter. They thought they were being very witty. One of them, hiccuping, slid gently to the floor and passed out. The second speaker raised his arm above him and solemnly intoned. "Requiescat in pace. Et lux perpetua something or other."

Peterson moved clear of them. His eyes were becoming accustomed to the comparative gloom after the brightness of Trinity. On the wall a yellowed poster announced that some menu items were discontinued—temporarily, of course. In the center of the pub a large coal range popped and hissed. An harassed cook presided over it, shifting pans from smaller rings to larger ones and back. Whenever he lifted a pan from one of the rings, a glow of light from inside the range momentarily lit his hands and perspiring face, so he abruptly loomed like an earnest, orange ghost. Students at tables around the stove called encouragement to him.

Peterson made his way across the crowded eating section, through blue curls of pipe smoke layering the air. The acrid tang of marijuana reached him, mingled with the odors of tobacco, cooking oil, beer and sweat. Someone called his name. He peered around until he saw Markham in a side booth.

"It's chancy finding anyone here, isn't it?" Peterson said as he sat down.

"I was just ordering. Lots of salads, aren't there? And plates full of crappy carbohydrates. There doesn't seem to be much worth eating these days."

Peterson studied the menu. "I think I may have the tongue, though it's incredibly expensive. Any kind of meat is just impossible."

"Yes, isn't it." He grimaced. "I don't see how you can eat tongue, knowing it came out of some animal's mouth."

"Have an egg, instead?"

Markham laughed. "I suppose there's no way to turn. But I think I'll splurge and have the sausages. That should do up my budget pretty nicely."

The waiter brought Peterson's ale and Markham's Mackeson stout. Peterson took a big swallow.

"They allow marijuana here, then?"

Markham looked around and sniffed the air. "Dope? Sure. All the mild euphorics are legal here, aren't they?"

"They have been for a year or two. But I thought by social convention, if there's any of that left, one didn't smoke it in public places."

"This is a university town. I expect the students were smoking it in public long before it was legalized. Anyway, if the government wants to distract people from the news, there's no point in requiring them to do it only at home," Markham said mildly.

"Ummm," Peterson murmured.

Markham stopped his Mackeson stout short of his mouth and looked at him. "You're being noncommittal. I guessed right, then? The government had that in mind?"

"Let's say it was brought up."

"What's the Liberal government going to do about these drugs that increase human intelligence, then?"

"Since I moved up to the Council I haven't had a great deal of contact with those problems."

"There's a rumor the Chinese are way ahead on them."

"Oh? Well, I can scotch that one. The Council had an intelligence report on precisely that point last month."

"They gather intelligence on their own members?"

"The Chinese are formal members, but—well, look, the problems of the last few years have been technical. Peking has enough on its hands without meddling into subjects where they have no research capability."

"I thought they were doing well."

Peterson shrugged. "As well as anyone can with a billion souls to care for. They're less concerned with foreign matters these days. They're trying to slice up precisely equal portions of an ever-diminishing pie."

"Pure communism at last."

"Not so pure. Equal slices keeps down unrest due to inequality. They're reviving terraced farming, even though it's labor-intensive, to get food production up. The opiate of the masses in China is groceries. Always has been. They're stopping use of energy-intensive chemicals in farming, too. I think they're afraid of side effects."

"Such as the South American bloom?"

"Dead on." Peterson grimaced. "Who could've foreseen—?"

From the crowd there came a sudden, rattling cry. A woman surged up from a nearby table, clutching at her throat. She was trying to say something. Another woman with her asked, "Elinor, what is it? Your throat? Something caught?"

The woman gasped, a rasping cough. She clutched at a chair. Heads turned. Her hands went to her belly and her face pinched with a rush of pain. "I—it *hurts* so—" Abruptly she vomited over the table. She jerked forward, hands clutching at herself. A stream of bile spattered over the plates of food. Nearby patrons, frozen until this moment, frantically spilled from chairs and backed away. The woman tried to cry out and instead vomited again. Glasses smashed to the floor; the crowd moved back. "He—elp!" the woman cried. A convulsion shook her. She tried to stand and vomited over herself. She turned to her companion, who had retreated to the next table. She looked down at herself, eyes glazed, and pressed her palms to her belly. Hesitantly she stepped back from the table. She slipped suddenly and crashed to the floor.

Peterson had been shocked into immobility, as had Markham. As she fell he leaped to his feet and dashed forward. The crowd muttered and did not move. He leaned over the woman. Her scarf was tangled about her neck. It was twisted and sour with puke. He yanked at it, using both hands. The fabric ripped. The woman gasped. Peterson fanned the air around her, creating a breeze. She sucked in air. Her eyes fluttered. She stared up at him. "It . . . it hurts . . . so . . ."

Peterson scowled up at the surrounding crowd. "Call a doctor, will you? Bloody hell!"

•

The ambulance had departed. The Whim staff were busy mopping up. Most of the patrons were gone, driven off by the stench. Peterson came back from the ambulance, where he had followed, making sure the attendants had a sample of her food.

"What did they say it was?" Markham asked.

"No idea. I gave them the sausage she'd been eating. The medic said something about food poisoning, but those weren't any poisoning symptoms I've ever heard about."

"All we've been hearing about is impurities—"

"Maybe." Peterson dismissed the idea with a wave of his hand. "Could be anything, these days."

Markham sipped meditatively on his stout. A waiter approached bearing their food. "Tongue for you, sir," he said to Peterson, placing a platter. "And sausage here."

Both men stared at their meals. "I think . . ." Markham began slowly.

"I agree," Peterson followed up briskly. "I believe we'll be skipping these. Could you fetch me a salad?"

The waiter looked dubiously at the plates. "You ordered this."

"So we did. Surely you don't expect us to choke it down after what's just happened, do you? In a restaurant like this?"

"Well, I dunno, the manager, he says—"

"Tell your manager to watch his raw materials or I'll bloody well have this place closed down. Follow me?"

"Christ, no reason to—"

"Just tell him that. And bring my friend here another stout."

When the waiter had backed away, obviously unwilling to confront either Peterson or the manager, Markham murmured, "Great. How'd you know I'd prefer another stout?"

"Intuition," he said with weary camaraderie.

•

They had both had more drinks when Peterson said, "Look, it's Sir Martin who's really the technical type on the British delegation. I'm a nonspecialist, as they call it. What I want to know is, how in hell do you get around this grandfather paradox bit? That fellow Davies explained about the discovery of tachyons right enough, and I accept that they can travel into our past, but I still can't see how one can logically *change* the past."

Markham sighed. "Until tachyons were discovered, everybody thought communication with the past was impossible. The incredible thing is that the physics of time communication had been worked out earlier, almost by accident, as far back as the 1940s. Two physicists named John Wheeler and Richard Feynmann worked out the correct description of light itself, and showed that there were *two* waves launched whenever you tried to make a radio wave, say."

"Two?"

"Right. One of them we receive on our radio sets. The other travels backward in time—the 'advanced wave,' as Wheeler and Feynmann called it."

"But we don't receive any message before it's sent."

Markham nodded. "True—but the advanced wave is *there*, in the mathematics. There's no way around it. The equations of physics are all time-symmetric. That's one of the riddles of modern physics. How is it that we perceive time passing, and yet all the equations of physics say that time can run either way, forward or backward?"

"The equations are wrong, then?"

"No, they're not. They can predict anything we can measure —but *only* as long as we use the 'retarded wave,' as Wheeler and Feynmann called it. That's the one that you hear through your radio set."

"Well, look, surely there's a way to change the equation round until you get only the retarded part."

"No, there isn't. If you do that to the equations, there's no way to keep the retarded wave the same. You *must* have the advanced wave."

"All right, where *are* those backward-in-time radio shows? How come I can't tune into the news from the next century?"

"Wheeler and Feynmann showed that it can't get here."

"Can't get into this year? I mean, into our present time?"

"Right. See, the advanced wave can interact with the whole universe—it's moving back, into our past, so it eventually hits all the matter that's ever been. Thing is, the advanced wave strikes all that matter before the signal was sent."

"Yes, surely." Peterson reflected on the fact that he was now, for the sake of argument, accepting the "advanced wave" he would have rejected only a few moments before.

"So the wave hits all that matter, and the electrons inside it jiggle around in *anticipation* of what the radio station will send."

"Effect preceding a cause?"

"Exactly. Seems contrary to experience, doesn't it?"

"Definitely."

"But the vibration of those electrons in the whole rest of the universe has to be taken into account. *They* in turn send out both advanced and retarded waves. It's like dropping two rocks into a pond. They both send out waves. But the two waves don't just add up in a simple way."

"They don't? Why not?"

"They interfere with each other. They make a criss-cross network of local peaks and troughs. Where the peaks and troughs from the separate patterns coincide, they reinforce each other. But where the peaks of the first stone meet the troughs of the second, they cancel. The water doesn't move."

"Oh. All right, then."

"What Wheeler and Feynmann showed was that the rest of the universe, when it's hit by an advanced wave, acts like a whole lot of rocks dropped into that pond. The advanced wave goes back in time, makes all these other waves. They interfere with each other and the result is zero. Nothing."

"Ah. In the end the advanced wave cancels itself out."

Suddenly music blared over the Whim's stereo: "An' de Devil, he do de dance *whump whump* with Joan de Arc—"

Peterson shouted, "Turn that down, will you?"

The music faded. He leaned forward. "Very well. You've shown me why the advanced wave doesn't work. Time communication is impossible."

Markham grinned. "Every theory has a hidden assumption. The trouble with the Wheeler and Feynmann model was that all those jiggling electrons in the universe in the past might *not* send back just the right waves. For radio signals, they do. For tachyons they don't. Wheeler and Feynmann didn't know about tachyons; they weren't even thought of until the middle '60s. Tachyons aren't absorbed the right way. They don't interact with matter the way radio waves do."

"Why not?"

"They're different kinds of particles. Some guys named Feinberg and Sudarshan imagined tachyons decades ago, but nobody could find them. Seemed too unlikely. They have imaginary mass, for one thing."

"*Imaginary* mass?"

"Yes, but don't take it too seriously."

"Seems a serious difficulty."

"Not really. The mass of these particles isn't what we'd call an observable. That means we can't bring a tachyon to rest, since it must always travel faster than light. So, if we can't bring it to a stop in our lab, we can't measure its mass at rest. The only definition of mass is what you can put on the scales and weigh—which you can't do, if it's moving. With tachyons, all you can measure is momentum—that is, impact."

"You have a complaint about the food, sir? I am the manager."

Peterson looked up to find a tall man in a conservative gray suit standing over their table, hands clasped behind him military style. "Yes, I did. Mostly I preferred not to eat it, in view of what it did to that lady a short while ago."

"I do not know what the lady was eating, sir, but I should think your—"

"Well, I do, you see. It was certainly close enough to what my friend here ordered to make him uncomfortable."

The manager bridled slightly at Peterson's manner. He was sweating slightly and had a harried look. "I fail to see why a similar type of food should—"

"I can see it quite plainly. A pity you can't."

"I am afraid we shall have to charge you for—"

"Have you read the recent Home Office directives on imported meats? I had a hand in writing them." Peterson gave the manager the full benefit of his assessing gaze. "I would say you probably get much of your imported meat from a local supplier, correct?"

"Well, of course, but—"

"Then you presumably know that there is a severe restriction on how long it can be kept before use?"

"Yes, I'm sure . . ." the manager began, but then hesitated when he saw the look on Peterson's face. "Well, actually I haven't read much of those lately because—"

"I think I would take more care in future."

"I am not sure the lady actually ate any imported meat whatever—"

"I would look into it, if I were you."

Abruptly the man lost some of his military bearing. Peterson looked at him with assurance.

"Well, I think we can forget the misunderstanding, sir, in light of—"

"Indeed." Peterson nodded, dismissing him. He turned back to Markham. "You still haven't got round the grandfather thing. If tachyons can carry a message back to the past, how do you avoid paradoxes?" Peterson did not mention that he had gone through a discussion with Paul Davies at King's about this, but understood none of it. He was by no means assured that the ideas made any sense.

Markham grimaced. "It's not easy to explain. The key was suspected decades ago, but nobody worked it out into a concrete physical theory. There's even a sentence in the original Wheeler-Feynmann paper—'It is only required that the description should be logically self-consistent.' By that they meant that our sense of the flow of time, always going in one direction, is a bias. The equations of physics don't share our prejudice—they're time-symmetric. The only standard we can impose on an experiment is whether it's *logically* consistent."

"But it's certainly illogical that you can be alive even after you've knocked off your own grandfather. Killed him before he produced your father, I mean."

"The problem is, we're used to thinking of these things as though there was some sort of switch involved, that only had two settings. I mean, that your grandfather is either dead or he isn't."

"Well, *that's* certainly true."

Markham shook his head. "Not really. What if he's wounded, but recovers? Then if he gets out of the hospital in time, he can meet your grandmother. It depends on your aim."

"I don't see—"

"Think about sending messages, instead of shotgunning grandfathers. Everybody assumes the receiver—back there in the past—can be attached to a switch, say. If a signal from the future comes in, the switch is programmed to turn off the transmitter—*before* the signal was sent. There's the paradox."

"Right." Peterson leaned forward, finding himself engrossed despite his doubts. There was something he liked about the way scientists had of setting up problems as neat little thought experiments, making a clean and sure world. Social issues were always messier and less satisfying. Perhaps that was why they were seldom solved.

"Trouble is, there's no switch that has two settings—on and off—with nothing in between."

"Come now. What about the toggle I flip to turn on the lights?"

"Okay, so you flip it. There's a time when that switch is hanging in between, neither off nor on."

"I can make that a very short time."

"Sure, but you can't reduce it to zero. And also, there's a certain impulse you have to give that switch to make it jump from off to on. In fact, it's possible to hit the switch just hard

73

enough to make it go halfway—try it. That must've happened to you sometime. The switch sticks, balanced halfway between."

"All right, granted," Peterson said impatiently. "But what's the connection to tachyons? I mean, what's *new* about all this?"

"What's new is thinking of these events—sending and receiving—as related in a chain, a *loop*. Say, we send back an instruction saying, 'Turn off the transmitter.' Think of the switch moving over to 'off.' This event is like a wave moving from the past to the future. The transmitter is changing from 'on' to 'off.' Now, that—well, let's call it a wave of information—moves forward in time. So the original signal doesn't get sent."

"Right. Paradox."

Markham smiled and held up a finger. He was enjoying this. "But wait! Think of all these times being in a kind of loop. Cause and effect mean nothing in this loop. There are only *events*. Now as the switch moves towards 'off,' information propagates forward into the future. Think of it as the transmitter getting weaker and weaker as that switch nears the 'off' position. Then the tachyon beam that transmitter is sending out gets weaker."

"Ah!" Peterson suddenly saw it. "So the receiver in turn gets a weaker signal from the future. The switch isn't hit so hard because the backward-in-time signal is weaker. So it doesn't move so quickly toward the 'off' mark."

"That's it. The closer it gets to 'off,' the slower it goes. There's an information wave traveling forward into the future, and—like a reflection—the tachyon beam comes back into the past."

"What does the experiment *do* then?"

"Well, say the switch gets near 'off,' and then the tachyon beam gets weak. The switch doesn't make it all the way to 'off' and—like that toggle controlling the lights—it starts to fall back toward 'on.' But the nearer it gets to 'on,' the stronger the transmitter gets in the future."

"So the *tachyon* beam gets stronger," Peterson finished for him. "That in turn drives the switch away from 'on' and back towards 'off.' The switch is hung up in the middle."

Markham leaned back and drained his stout. His tan, weakened by the dim Cambridge winter, crinkled with the lines of his wry smile. "It flutters around there in the middle."

"No paradox."

"Well . . ." Markham shrugged imperceptibly. "No logical contradictions, yes. But we still don't actually know what that intermediate, hung-up state means. It *does* avoid the paradoxes, though. There's a lot of quantum-mechanical formalism you can apply to it, but I'm not sure what a genuine experiment will give."

"Why not?"

Markham shrugged again. "No experiments. Renfrew hasn't had the time to do them, or the money."

Peterson ignored the implied criticism; or was that his imagination? It was obvious that work in these fields had been cut back for years now. Markham was simply stating a fact. He had to remember that a scientist might be more prone simply to state things as they were, without calculating a statement's impact. To change the subject Peterson asked, "Won't that stuck-in-the-middle effect prevent your sending information back to 1963?"

"Look, the point here is that our distinctions between cause and effect are an illusion. This little experiment we've been discussing is a causal *loop*—no beginning, no end. That's what Wheeler and Feynmann meant by requiring only that our description be logically consistent. *Logic* rules in physics, not the myth of cause and effect. Imposing an order to events is *our* point of view. A quaintly human view, I suppose. The laws of physics don't care. That's the new concept of time we have now—as a set of completely interrelated events, linked self-consistently. *We* think we're moving along in time, but that's just a bias."

"But we know things happen *now,* not in the past or future."

"When is 'now'? Saying that 'now' is 'this instant' is going around in circles. Every instant is 'now' when it 'happens.' The point is, how do you measure the rate of moving from one instant to the next? And the answer is, you can't. What's the rate of the passage of time?"

"Well, it's—" Peterson stopped, thinking.

"How can time move? The rate is one second of movement per second! There's no conceivable coordinate system in physics from which we can measure time passing. So there isn't any. Time is frozen, as far as the universe is concerned."

"Then . . ." Peterson raised a finger to cover his confusion, frowning. The manager appeared as though out of nowhere.

"Yes sir?" the man said with extreme politeness.

"Ah, another round."

"Yes *sir.*" He hustled off to fill the order himself. Peterson took a small pleasure in this little play. To get such a response with a minimum display of power was an old game with him, but still satisfying.

"But you *still* believe," Peterson said, turning back to Markham, "that Renfrew's experiment makes sense? All this talk of loops and not being able to close switches . . ."

"Sure it'll work." Markham accepted a glass dark with the thick stout. The manager placed Peterson's ale carefully before him and began, "Sir, I want to apol—"

Peterson waved him into silence, impatient to hear Markham. "Perfectly all right," he said quickly.

Markham eyed the manager's retreating back. "Very effective. Do they teach that in the best schools?"

Peterson smiled. "Of course. There's lecture, then field trips to representative restaurants. You have to get the wrist action just right."

Markham saluted with the stout. After this silent toast he said, "Oh yes, Renfrew. What Wheeler and Feynmann didn't notice was that if you send a message back which has nothing to do with shutting off the transmitter, there's no problem. Say I want to place a bet on a horse race. I've resolved that I'll send the results of the race back in time to a friend. I do. In the past, my friend places a bet and makes money. That doesn't change the outcome of the race. Afterward, my friend gives me some of the winnings. His handing over the money won't stop me from sending the information—in fact, I can easily arrange it so I only get the money *after* I've sent the message."

"No paradox."

"Right. So you *can* change the past, but only if you *don't* try to make a paradox. If you try, the experiment hangs up in that stuck-in-between state."

Peterson frowned. "But what's it like? I mean, what does the world seem like if you can change it round?"

Markham said lightly, "Nobody knows. Nobody's ever tried it before."

"There were no tachyon transmitters until now."

"And no reason to try to reach the past, either."

"Let me get this straight. How's Renfrew going to avoid creating a paradox? If he gives them a lot of information, they'll solve the problem and there'll be no reason for him to send the message."

"That's the trick. Avoid the paradox, or you'll get a stuck switch. So Renfrew will send a *piece* of the vital information—enough to get research started, but not enough to solve the problem utterly."

"But what'll it be like for us? The world will change round us?"

Markham chewed at his lower lip. "I think so. We'll be in a different state. The problem will be reduced, the oceans not so badly off."

"But what is *this* state? I mean, us sitting here? We know the oceans are in trouble."

"Do we? How do we know this *isn't* the result of the experiment we're about to do? That is, if Renfrew hadn't existed and thought of this idea, maybe we'd be *worse* off. The problem with causal loops is that our notion of time doesn't accept them. But think of that stuck switch again."

Peterson shook his head as though to clear it. "It's hard to think about."

"Like tying time in knots," Markham conceded. "What I've given you is an interpretation of the mathematics. We *know* tachyons are real; what we don't know is what they imply."

Peterson looked around at the Whim, now mostly deserted. "Strange, to think of this as being an outcome of what we haven't done yet. All looped together, like a hooked rug." He blinked, thinking of the past, when he had eaten here. "That coal stove—how long have they had that?"

"Years, I suppose. Seems like a sort of trademark. Keeps the place warm in winter, and it's cheaper than gas or electricity. Besides, they can cook at any time of day, not just the power hours. And it gives the customers something to watch while they're waiting for their orders."

"Yes, coal's the long-term fuel for old England," Peterson murmured, apparently more to himself than Markham. "Bulky though."

"When were you a student here?"

"In the '70s. I haven't been back very often."

"Have things changed much?"

Peterson smiled reminiscently. "I dare say my rooms haven't changed much. Picturesque view of the river and all my clothes get moldy from the damp . . ." He shook off his mood. "I'll have to be getting back to London soon."

They elbowed through the students to the door and out into the street. The June sunshine was dazzling after the pub's dark interior. They stood for a moment, blinking, on the narrow sidewalk. Pedestrians stepped off into the street to walk past them and cyclists swerved around the pedestrians with a trilling of bells. They turned left and strolled back towards King's Parade. On the corner opposite the church, they paused to look in the windows of Bowes & Bowes bookstore.

"Do you mind if I go in for a minute?" Peterson asked. "There's something I want to look for."

"Sure. I'll come in, too. I'm a bookstore freak; never pass one by."

Bowes & Bowes was almost as crowded as the Whim had been earlier, but the voices here were subdued. They edged cautiously between the knots of students in black gowns and pyramids of books on display. Peterson pointed out one on a less conspicuous table towards the back of the store.

"Have you seen this?" he asked, picking up a copy and handing it to Markham.

"Holdren's book? No, I haven't read it yet, though I talked to him about it. Is it good?" Markham looked at the title, stamped in red on a black cover—*The Geography of Calamity: Geopolitics of Human Dieback* by John Holdren. In the bottom right corner was a small reproduction of a medieval engraving of a grinning skeleton with a scythe. He thumbed through it, paused, began to read. "Look at this," he said, holding the book out to Peterson. Peterson ran his eyes over the chart and nodded.

		Attributable Deaths (estimated)
1984–96	Java	8,750,000
1986	Malawi	2,300,000
1987	Philippines	1,600,000
1987–present	Congo	3,700,000
1989–present	India	68,000,000
1990–present	Colombia, Ecuador, Honduras	1,600,000
1991–present	Dominican Republic	750,000
1991–present	Egypt, Pakistan	3,800,000
1993–present	General Southeast Asia	113,500,000

Markham whistled softly. "Is it accurate?"

"Oh, yes. Underestimated, if anything."

Peterson moved towards the back of the store. A girl was perched on a high stool adding a column of figures into an autoaccountant. Her fair hair hung forward, hiding her face. Peterson studied her covertly while leafing through some of the books in front of him. Nice legs. Fashionably dressed in some frilly peasant style he disliked. A blue Liberty scarf artfully arranged at her neck. Slim now, but not for many more years, probably. She looked about nineteen. As though aware of his gaze, she looked up straight at him. He continued to stare at her. Yes, nineteen and very pretty and very aware of it, too.

She slid from her stool and, clutching papers defensively to her chest, came over to him.

"May I help you?"

"I don't know," he said with a slight smile. "Maybe. I'll let you know if you can."

She took this as a flirtatious overture and responded with a routine which probably, he reflected, was a knock-out with the local boys. She turned away from him and looked back over her shoulder, saying huskily, "Let me know then." She gave him a long look from under her lashes, then grinned cheekily and flaunted her way towards the front of the store. He was amused. At first, he had really thought that she intended her coquettish routine seriously, which would have been ludicrous if she hadn't been so pretty. Her grin showed that she was playacting. Peterson felt suddenly in very good spirits and almost immediately noticed the book he had been looking for.

He picked it up and went to look for Markham. The girl was with two others, her back to him. Her companions were laughing and staring. They obviously told her he was watching them, because she turned to look at him. She really was exceptionally pretty. He made a sudden decision. Markham was browsing through the science fiction selection.

"I have a couple of errands," Peterson said. "Why don't you go on ahead and tell Renfrew I'll be there in half an hour?"

"Okay, fine," Markham said. Peterson watched him as he strode out the door, moving athletically, and disappeared into the alley behind the building known as Schools.

Peterson looked for the girl again. She was serving someone else, a student. He watched as she went through another routine, leaning forward more than was necessary to write a receipt, quite enough to enable the student to look down the front of her blouse. Then she straightened up and looked quite offhand as she gave him his book in a white paper bag. The student went out, with a disconcerted look on his face. Peterson caught her eye and lifted the book in his hand. She slammed the cash register shut and came over to him.

"Yes?" she asked. "Have you made up your mind?"

"I think so. I'll take this book. And maybe you could help me with something else. You live in Cambridge, do you?"

"Yes. You don't?"

"No, I'm from London. I'm on the Council." He despised himself immediately. Like shooting a rabbit with a cannon. No artistry at all. Anyway, he had all her attention now, so he might as well take advantage of it. "I wondered if you could recommend any good restaurants around here to me?"

"Well, there's the Blue Boar. And there's a French one in Grantchester that's supposed to be good, Le Marquis. And a new Italian one, Il Pavone."

"Have you eaten at any of them?"

"Well, no . . ." She blushed slightly and he knew she regretted appearing at a disadvantage. He was well aware that she had named the three most expensive restaurants. His own favorite had not been mentioned; it was less showy and less expensive, but the food was excellent.

"If you could choose, which one would you go to?"

"Oh, Le Marquis. It looks a lovely place."

"The next time I'm up from London, if you're not doing anything, I would count it as a great favor if you would have dinner there with me." He smiled intimately at her. "It gets pretty dull, traveling alone, eating alone."

"Really?" she gasped. "Oh, I mean . . ." She struggled furiously to repress her triumphant excitement. "Yes, I'd like that very much."

"Fine. If I could have your telephone number . . ."

She hesitated and Peterson guessed she had no telephone. "Or if you'd rather, I can simply stop by this shop early on."

"Oh yes, that would be best," she said, seizing on this graceful out.

"I'll look forward to it."

They walked forward to the front desk, where he paid for his book. When he left Bowes & Bowes, he turned the corner towards Market Square. Through the side windows of the bookstore he could see her in consultation with her two friends. Well, that was easy, he thought. Good God, I don't even know her name.

He crossed the square and walked through Petty Cury with its bustling throng of shoppers, coming out opposite Christ's. Through its open gate the green lawn in its quad was visible and behind that, the vivid colors of a herbaceous border against the gray wall of the Master's Lodge. In the gateway the porter sat reading a paper. A knot of students stood studying some lists on the bulletin board. Peterson kept on going and turned into Hobson's Alley. He finally found the place he was looking for: Foster and Jagg, coal merchants.

chapter ten

John Renfrew spent Saturday morning putting up new shelving on the long wall in their kitchen. Marjorie had been after him for months to do it. Her bland asides about where the planes of wood should go "when you get around to it" had slowly accreted into a pressing weight, an agreed duty, unavoidable. The markets were open only a few days each week—"to avoid fluctuations in supply" was the common explanation, rendered on the nightly news—and with the power cuts, refrigerating was impossible. Marjorie had turned to putting up vegetables and was amassing a throng of thick-lipped jars. They waited in cardboard boxes for the promised shelving.

Renfrew assembled his tools systematically, with as much care as he took in the laboratory. Their house was old and leaned slightly, as though blown by an unfelt wind. Renfrew found that his plumb line, nailed to the wainscotting, weaved a full three inches out from the scuffed molding. The floor sagged with an easy fatigue, like a well-used mattress. He stepped back from the tilting walls, squinted, and saw that the lines of his home were askew. You put down the money on a place, he reflected, and you get a maze of jambs and beams and cornices, all pushed slightly out of true by history. A bit of settling in that corner, a diagonal misaimed there. He had a sudden memory of when he had been a boy, looking up from a stone floor at his father, who squinted at the plaster ceiling as if to judge whether the roof would fall.

As he studied the problem his own children caromed through the house. Their feet thumped on the margins of polished wood that framed the thin rugs. They reached the front door and ricocheted outside in a game of tag. He realized that to them he probably had that same earnest wrenched look of his father, face skewed in concentration.

He arrayed his tools and began to work. The piles of lumber on the back porch gradually dwindled as he cut them into a suitable lattice. To fit the thin planks at the roof he had to make oblique cuts with a rip saw. The wood splintered under his lunging thrusts, but kept to line. Johnny appeared, tired of tag with his older sister. Renfrew set him to work fetching tools as they were needed. Through the window a tinny radio announced that Argentina had joined the nuclear club. "What's a nuclear club, Daddy?" Johnny asked, eyes big. "People who can drop bombs." Johnny fingered a wood file, frowning at the fine lines that rubbed his thumb. "Can I join?" Renfrew paused, licked his lips, peered into a sky of carbon blue. "Only fools get to join," he said, and set back to work.

The radio detailed a Brazilian rejection of preferential trade agreements, which would have established a Greater American Zone with the US. There were reports that the Americans had tied the favor of cheaper imports to their aid on the southern Atlantic bloom problem. "A bloom, Daddy? How can the ocean do like a flower?" Renfrew said gruffly, "A different kind of bloom." He hoisted boards under his arm and took them inside.

He was sanding down the ripped edges when Marjorie came in from the garden for inspection. She had mercifully taken the battery-operated radio into the garden with her. "Why's it jut out at the base?" she asked by way of greeting. She put the radio on the kitchen table. It seemed to go with her everywhere these days, Renfrew noted, as though she could not bear to be alone with a bit of quiet.

"The shelves are straight. It's the walls that are tilted."

"They look odd. Are you sure . . . ?"

"Have a go." He handed her his carpenter's level. She put it gingerly on a rough-cut board. The bubble bobbed precisely into the place between the two defining lines. "See? Dead level."

"Well, I suppose," Marjorie reluctantly conceded.

"Worry not, your jars aren't going to topple off." He put several jars on a shelf. This ritual act completed the job. The boxy frame stood out, functional pine against aged oak paneling. Johnny stroked the sheets of wood tentatively, as though awed that he had had a hand in making this wood lattice.

"Think I'll be off to the lab for a bit," Renfrew said, collecting his rip saw and chisels.

"Steady on, there's more fathering needs doing. You're to take Johnny on the mercury hunt."

"Oh *hell*, I forgot. Look, I'd thought—"

"You'd put in an afternoon tinkering," Marjorie finished for him with mild reproof. " 'Fraid not."

"Well look, I'll just go round to pick up some notes, then, on Markham's work."

"Best make it on the way with Johnny. Can't you leave off for a weekend, though? I thought you had settled things yesterday."

"We worked out a message with Peterson. Ocean stuff, for the most part. We're letting pass the lot on mass fermentation of sugar cane for fuel."

"What's wrong with that? Burning alcohol is cleaner than that wretched petrol they're selling now."

Renfrew scrubbed his hands in the washbasin. "True enough. The snag is that the Brazilians cut back so much of their jungle for the sugar cane fields. That lowers the number of plants which can absorb carbon dioxide from the air. Trace that effect round a bit and it explains the shifts in the world climate, greenhouse effect and rainfall and so on."

"The Council decided that?"

"No, no, research teams worldwide did. The Council simply make policy to offset problems. The UN mandate, extraordinary powers, and all that."

"Your Mr. Peterson must be a very influential man."

Renfrew shrugged. "He says it's pure luck the United Kingdom has a strong voice. The only reason we do is that we've still got research teams working on highly visible problems. Otherwise, we'd have a seat appropriate to Nigeria or the Viet Union or some other swacking nobody."

"What *you're* doing is—what did you say, 'visible,' isn't it?"

Renfrew chuckled. "No, it's bloody transparent. Peterson's deflected some help my way, but he's doing it as sort of a personal lark, I'll wager."

"That's very nice of him."

"Nice?" Renfrew dried his hands, meditating. "He's interested intellectually, I can tell that, though he's no sort of intellectual in my book. It's a fair trade, I'd say. He's getting some amusement from it, and I'm getting his pound notes."

"But he must think you'll succeed."

"Must he? Maybe. I'm not sure I do myself."

Marjorie seemed shocked. "Then why do it?"

"It's good physics. *I* don't know if we can alter the past. No one does. Physics is in chaos about this thing. If there weren't a virtually complete shutdown of research, chaps would be swarming over the problem. I've got a chance here to do the definitive experiments. *That's* the reason. Science, luv."

Marjorie frowned at this but said nothing. Renfrew surveyed his handiwork. She began busily ranking jars on the shelves. Each had a rubber collar and metal sealing clamps. Inside swam vague blobs of vegetables. Renfrew found the sight distinctly unappetizing.

Marjorie abruptly turned from her work, her face knitted with concern, and said, "You're deceiving him, aren't you?"

"Na, luv, I'm—what's the phrase?—keeping his expectations high."

"He *expects*—"

"Look, Peterson's interested in the problem. *I'm* not responsible for guessing his true motivations. Christ, you'll have him on the couch babbling about his early childhood next."

"I've never met the man," she said stiffly.

"Right, see, this conversation has no basis."

"It's *you* we're properly talking about. You—"

"Hold on. The thing you don't realize, Marj old lass, is that nobody really knows *any*thing about these experiments. You can't accuse me of false adverts yet. And for that matter, Peterson seemed as concerned as I was with the interference we're getting, so maybe I misread him."

"Someone's interfering?"

"No, no, some*thing* is. A lot of incoming noise. I'll filter it out, though. I planned to work on that very point this afternoon."

Marjorie said firmly, "The mercury hunt."

She clicked on the radio, which blared to a jingle, "*Your honey is mo-ney, in the new job-sharing plan! That's right, a couple splitting one job can help the current—*"

Renfrew switched it off. "Be good to get out of the house," he said pointedly.

•

He pedaled up to the Cav with Johnny. They passed farm buildings taken over by squatters and Renfrew grimaced to himself. He had gone round to several, trying to find the couple who had frightened Marjorie. They'd given him a surly look and a rude off-wi'-ya. The constable was no help either.

As he passed the slumped walls of a barn Renfrew smelled the sour tang of coal smoke. Someone inside was burning the outlawed low-quality grade, but there was no bluish plume for the constable to trace. That was fairly typical. They'd spend good money on a device to suppress the visible emission, then quickly make up the cost in cheap fuel. Renfrew had heard otherwise respectable people bragging about doing precisely that, like children getting away with some delicious vice their parents had forbidden. They were the sort who threw their bottles and tins into great ruddy heaps down the woods, too, rather than trouble to recycle. He sometimes thought that the only people who obeyed the regs were the dwindling middle classes.

At the Cav, Johnny wandered the shadowy corridors while Renfrew picked up some notes. Johnny prevailed on him to take a quick ride up to the Institute for Astronomy, just across the Madingley Road. The boy had played there often and now that it was closed seldom saw it. There were big potholes in the Madingley where the tanks had come in to quell the riot in '96. Renfrew tipped into one and got a stain of mud on his trouser leg. They pedaled by the long low office building of the Institute, with its outsized yawning windows, a once popular American style from an oil-rich era. They pumped up to the main building, a nineteenth-century pile of tan sandstone with its antiquated astronomical dome atop floors housing the library, offices, and the star chart bays. They glided by the little 36-incher dome on the way and then past the machine shop sheds, where the windows had been starred by the occasional passing sod. Their tires spat gravel as they wheeled up the long driveway. The bright white casements of the windows framed a black interior. Renfrew was turning in the circular drive to go back down the slope to Madingley when the big front doors lurched open. A short man peered out. He was wearing a formal suit with waistcoat and regimental tie, well knotted. He was sixtyish and studied them over bifocals. "You're not the constable," the man said in reedy surprise.

Renfrew, thinking this point obvious, stopped but said nothing. "Mr. Frost!" Johnny cried. "Remember me?"

Frost frowned, then brightened. "Johnny, yes, haven't seen you for years. You came to our Observer's Night regular as the stars."

"Until you stopped giving them," the boy accused.

"The Institute closed," Frost said apologetically, bending over at the waist to bring his face to Johnny's level. "There was no money."

"*You*'re still here."

"So I am. Our electricity is cut off, however, and you can't have the public in where they could fall in the dark."

Renfrew broke in with, "I'm John Renfrew, by the way— Johnny's dad."

"Yes. I thought you might be the constable. I sent word this morning," Frost said, pointing at a nearby window. The frame was smashed. "They simply kicked it in."

"They get anything?"

"A great lot. I tried to have those replaced, back when we

put in the wire mesh on the corridor inside. I *told* them the library was an open invitation. But would they listen to me, the mere curator? No, silly, of course not."

"Did they take the telescope?" Johnny asked.

"No, that's worthless, very nearly. They nicked the books."

"Then I can still look through the telescope?"

"What books?" Renfrew could not imagine that academic references were of much value now.

"The collector's items, of course," Frost said with the proper pride of a curator. "Took a second edition Kepler, a second Copernicus, the original of the seventeenth-century astrometrical atlas—the lot, really. They were specialists, they were. Skipped the newer tomes. They also knew the fifth editions from the third, without taking them out of their protective sleeves. Not so easily done, when you're working in a dead hurry and with a pocket torch."

Renfrew was impressed, not the least because this was the first time he had ever heard anyone use the word "tomes" in conversation. "Why were they in a hurry?"

"Because they knew I would return. I had gone out at dusk for my evening constitutional, to the war cemetery and back."

"You live here?"

"When the Institute closed I had nowhere to go." Frost drew himself up primly. "There are several of us. Old astronomers, mostly, turned out by their colleges. They live down the other building—it's warmer in winter. These bricks hold the chill. I tell you, there was a time when the colleges cared for their old Fellows. When Boyle founded the Institute we had everything. Now it's into the dustbin with the lot, never mind the past, it's the current crisis that matters and—"

"I say, that's the constable coming there." Renfrew pointed, seizing on the distant figure on a bicycle to cut off the stream of academic lament. He had heard much the same lines so often over the last few years that they had ceased to have any effect aside from boredom. The arrival of the constable, puffing and drawn, led Frost to produce the one volume the thieves hadn't made off with, a late edition Kepler. Renfrew studied the book for a moment while Frost went on to the constable, demanding a general alert to catch the thieves on the roads if possible. The pages were dry and brittle, crackling as Renfrew turned them. From long exposure to the new methods of making books he had forgotten how a line of type could raise an impression on the other side of the page, as if the press of history was behind each word. The heavily leaded letters were broad and the ink a deep black. The ample margins, the precise celestial drawings, the heft of the volume in his hands, all seemed to speak of a time when the making of books was a signpost in an assumed march forward, a pressure on the future.

●

The crowd of fathers had a holiday air, chattering and laughing. A few kicked a soccer ball on the gray cobblestones. This was a lark, an event to raise money for the hobbling city government of Cambridge. An official had read about such a search in American cities, and last month London had staged one.

Into the sewers they descended, bright electric torches spiking through the murk. Beneath the scientific laboratories and industrial sites of town the stonework passages were large enough for a man to walk upright. Renfrew tugged the airmask tight against his face, smiling at Johnny through the transparent molded cup. Spring rains had swept clean; there was little stench. Their fellow hunters spilled past, buzzing with excitement.

Mercury was now exceedingly rare, commanding a thousand New Pounds per kilogram. In the gaudy mid-century times, commercial grade mercury had been poured down sinks and drains. It was cheaper then to throw out dirtied mercury and buy a fresh supply. The heaviest metal, it sought the lowest spots in the sewer system and pooled there. Even a liter recovered would justify the trouble.

They soon worked their way into the more narrow pipes, slipping away from the crowd. Their torches cast sparkling reflections from the wrinkled skin of the water caught in pools. "Hey, this way, Dad," Johnny called. The acoustics of the tunnels gave each word a hollow center. Renfrew turned and abruptly slipped. He spilled into the scum of a standing pond, cursing. Johnny bent down. The torch's cone caught a seam of tarnished quicksilver. Renfrew's boot had snagged at a crack where two pipes butted unevenly. Mercury glowed as if alive beneath the filmed water. It gave off a warm, smudged glitter, a thin trapped snake worth a hundred guineas.

"A find! A find!" Johnny chanted. They sucked the metal into pressure bottles. Finding the luminous metal lifted their spirits; Renfrew laughed with gusty good humor. They walked on, discovering unexplored caves and dark secrets in the warrens, fanning the curving walls with yellow beams. Johnny discovered a high niche, scooped out and furnished with a moldy mattress. "Home of some layabout, I expect," Renfrew murmured. They found candle stubs and frayed paperbacks. "Hey, this one's from 1968, Dad," Johnny said. It looked porno-graphic to Renfrew; he tossed it face down on the mattress. "Should be getting back," he said.

They found an iron ladder, using the map provided. Johnny wriggled out, blinking in the late afternoon sunlight. They queued up to turn in their pint of the silvery stuff to the Hunt Facilitator. In line with current theory, Renfrew noted, social groupings were now facilitated, not led. Renfrew stood and watched Johnny talk and scuffle and go through the tentative approaching rituals with two other boys nearby in line. Already Johnny was getting beyond the age when parents deeply influenced him. From now on it was peer pressure and the universals: swacking the ball about in the approved manner; showing proper disdain for girls; establishing one's buffer state role between the natural bullies and the naturally bullied; faking a certain coarse but necessarily vague familiarity with sex and the workings of those mysterious gummy organs, seldom seen but deeply sensed. Soon he would face the consuming problem of adolescence—how to have it off with some girl and thus pass through the flame into manhood, and yet avoid the traps that society laid in the way. Or perhaps this rather cynical view was outdated now. Maybe the wave of sexual freedom that had washed over earlier generations had made things easier. Some-how, though, Renfrew suspected otherwise. What was worse, he could think of nothing very straightforward he himself could hope to do about the matter. Perhaps relying on the intuition of the boy himself was the best path. So what guidance could he give Johnny? "See here, son, remember one thing—don't take any advice." He could see Johnny's eyes widen and the boy reply, "But that's silly, Daddy. If I take your advice, I'm doing the opposite of what you say." Renfrew smiled. Paradoxes sprouted everywhere.

A small student band made a great noisy thing of the an-nounced total, several kilograms in all. Boys cheered. A man nearby muttered, "Livin' off a yes'day," and Renfrew said drily, "Frapping right." There was a feeling here of salvaging the lore and ore of the past, not making anything new. *Like the country itself*, he thought.

Bicycling home, Johnny wanted to stop and see the Bluebell Country Club, an unbearably cute name for an eighteenth-cen-tury stone cottage near the Cam. In it a Miss Bell kept a cat hotel, for owners who were away. Once Marjorie had adopted a disagreeable cat which Renfrew had finally lodged there per-manently, not having the heart to simply throw the bugger in the Cam. Miss Bell's rooms stank of cat piss and perpetual tubercular-class dampness. "No time," Renfrew shouted to Johnny's question and they pedaled on past the cat citadel. Afterward, Johnny was a bit slower than before, his face blank. Renfrew was at once sorry he had been gruff. He was having such moments more often lately, he realized. Perhaps in part his absence from home, working at the lab, made him acutely sensitive to lapsed closeness with Marjorie and the kids. Or perhaps there was a time in life when you realized dimly that you had become rather like your own parents, and that your reactions were not wholly original. The genes and environment had their own momentum.

Renfrew caught sight of an odd yellow cloud squatting on the horizon and remembered the summer afternoons he and Johnny had spent watching the cloud sculptors work above London. "Look there!" he called, pointing. Johnny dutifully gave the yellow cloud a glance. "Angels getting ready to piss," Renfrew explained, "as m'old man used to say." Bucked up by this bit of family history, they both smiled.

They stopped at a bakery in King's Parade, Fitzbillies. Johnny became a starving English schoolboy bravely carrying on. Renfrew allowed as how he could have two, no more. The newsagent's a door down proclaimed on a chalkboard the dreadful news that *The Times Literary Supplement* had gone belly-up, an incoming datum which Renfrew found only slightly less interesting than the banana production of Borneo. The headlines gave no clue as to whether financial strains had caused the foldup, or—what seemed more likely to Renfrew by a long measure—whether it was the dearth of worthwhile books.

●

Johnny banged into the house, provoking an answering cry from his sister. Renfrew followed, feeling a bit clapped out from the cycling, and strangely depressed. He sat in his living room for a moment trying for once to think of nothing whatever, and failing. Half the room seemed totally unfamiliar to him. Antique glass paperweight, suspiciously tarnished candlestick, frilly lampshade with flower on it, Gauguin reprint, whimsical striped china pig on the hearth, brass rubbing of a medieval lady, beige china cat ashtray with poetic quotation written in flowing script round the rim. Hardly a square centimeter hadn't been made sodding *nice*. About the time these registered, the persistent small tinny voice of Marjorie's marauding radio got through to him, on again about the Nicaragua thing. The Americans were again trying to get approval from the motley crew of neighboring governments for a sea-level canal. To compete with the Panamanian one would seem dead easy, considering it was jammed up half the year. Renfrew remembered a BBC interview on just this subject, in which the sod from Argentina or somewhere had gone on at the American ambassador about why the Americans were called the Americans and those south of the USA not. The logic gradually unfurled to include the assumption that since the USAians had appropriated the American name, they would thus appropriate any new canal. The ambassador, not wise to the ways of the telly, had replied with a rational explanation. He noted that no South American nation included the word "America" in its name, and thus had no strong claim to it. The triviality of this point in the face of an avalanche of psychic energy from the Argentinian had put the ambassador far down in total points by the time the viewers phoned in their opinions of the discussion. Why, the ambassador fellow had scarcely smiled or mugged at the camera, or smacked a fist onto the table before him. How could he expect to have any media impact whatever?

He went in to find Marjorie rearranging the preserve jars for what appeared to be a third time. "Somehow, you know, it doesn't look *square*," she said to him with a distracted irritation. He sat at the kitchen table and poured himself some coffee, which, as expected, tasted rather like dog's fur. It always did lately. "I'm sure it's true," he murmured. But then he studied her bustling form as she hoisted the cylinders of pale amber, and indeed, the shelves did seem at a tilt. He had made them on a precise radial line extending dead to the center of the planet, geometrically impeccable and absolutely rational and quite beside the point. Their home was warped and swayed by the times it had passed through. Science came to nought in these days. This kitchen was the true local reference frame, the Galilean invariant. Yes. Watching his wife turn and mix the jars, Prussian rigidities standing on slabs of pine, he saw that it was the shelves which stood aslant now; the walls were right.

chapter eleven

Peterson awoke and looked out of the window. The pilot had looped around to come in to San Diego from the ocean side. From this height most of the coastline north to Los Angeles was visible. That city was cloaked in its permanent haze; otherwise the day was clear and bright. The sun sparked flashes of brilliance from the windows of high-rise office blocks. Peterson stared vacantly at the sea. Tiny puckered lines of waves crawled imperceptibly toward the shore. Here and there, as the plane swung lower, he could see curves of white froth against the blue, vastly different from the ocean he had flown over the day before.

He had taken a commercial flight. From the air, the diatom bloom on the Atlantic had been horribly visible. It now extended over a hundred-kilometer diameter. Bloom was a good word for it, he thought wryly. It had looked like some giant flower, a scarlet camellia blossoming far off the shores of Brazil. His fellow passengers had been excited by the vision, stampeding from window to window to get a better view, asking agitated questions. Interesting, he observed, how red, the color of blood, spelled danger to the human mind. It had been eerie to look down and see that still, wounded ocean, the fringe of pink surf.

His mind had distanced itself from the reality below, turning it into a surrealistic work of art. Add purple jaguars and yellow trees: a Jesse Allen. And orange fishes in the air above . . .

How did that Bottomley poem go? The second stanza— something about forcing the birds to wing too high—*where your unnatural vapors creep; Surely the living rocks shall die when birds no rightful distance keep*. Nineteenth-century doggerel. How one clutched at the shreds of civilization.

There had been rioting in Rio. Standard political stuff, pop Marxism and local gripes touched off by the bloom. A waiting helicopter had whisked him from the airport to a secret rendezvous on a large yacht, anchored offshore north of the city. The Brazilian President was there, with his Cabinet. McKerrow from Washington, and Jean-Claude Rollet, a colleague of Peterson's on the Council. They had conferred from 10 a.m. until late afternoon, having lunch brought in to them. Measures would be taken to contain the bloom, if possible. The crucial thing was to reverse the process; experiments were being conducted in the Indian Ocean and in control tanks in Southern California. Some emergency supplies were voted to Brazil, to compensate for the disruption in fishing. The Brazilian President was to play down the significance of this, avoid wholesale panic. Fingers-in-the-dike, fragile buttresses against the weight of the sickened sea around them, and so on. When they disbanded, Rollet had gone to report directly to the Council.

Peterson had had to step lively to avoid getting loaded up with errand-running, interference-blocking, and other jobs. Lubricating a crisis like this one took a lot of skillful footwork. There were the individual nations to soothe, England's own interests to look out for (though that was not his prime official task), and of course the ever-present snout of the media pig. Peterson had argued successfully that someone needed to give an official beady eye to the California experiments. One had not only to do the right thing, one must above all be seen doing it. This got him the time he needed. His true purpose was a little experiment he'd thought of himself.

•

Straightaway after touchdown canned music came on and chaps began hauling out their carry-ons for the rush. Peterson found this the worst part of commercial travel and wished again he had pressed Sir Martin for authority to have his own executive jet on this trip. They were expensive, wasteful, etc. etc., but a bloody sight better than going in a cattle-car with wings. The standard argument, that private transport let one rest and thus saved the valuable executive's energies, hadn't held up well in the era of dwindling budgets.

He left the plane before anyone else, through the forward door, as per plan. There was a gratifyingly large security guard, decked out in leather boots and helmets. By now he was used to the openly worn automatic pistols.

His limo contained a protocol officer who babbled on to no consequence, but Peterson turned him off early on and enjoyed the ride. The security car behind stayed quite close, he noted. There seemed no sign of the recent "unpleasantness." A few burned-out blocks of buildings, to be sure, and a freeway underpass on Route 5 pocked by heavy-caliber fire, but no air of lingering tension. The streets were fairly clear and the freeway was virtually deserted. Since the Mexican fields had petered out far ahead of notoriously optimistic schedules, California had ceased to be an automobile-worshiping paradise. That, plus the political pressure from the Mexicans to make good the high-flown promises of economic uplift, had mixed in with the rest of the political brew here and led to the "unrest."

•

The usual ceremonies sopped up minimal time. The Scripps Institute of Oceanography had a weathered but solid look to it, blue tiles and salty smell and all that. The staff were by now used to dignitaries trotting through. The TV johnnies got their footage—only it wasn't called that anymore, Peterson reminded himself, the mysterious term "dexers" having materialized in its place—and were duly ushered away. Peterson smiled, shook hands, made bland small talk. The package Markham had asked for from Caltech appeared and Peterson tucked it into his carrying case. Markham had requested this material, said it related to the tachyon business, and Peterson had agreed to use his good offices to extract it from the Americans. The work wasn't publishable yet, a familiar ruse to avoid giving away anything, but a bit of footwork had got round that one.

The morning went by as planned. A general survey by an oceanographer, slides and viewgraphs before an audience of twenty. Then a reprise, more frank and far more pessimistic, with an audience of five. Then Alex Kiefer, head of the thing, in private.

"Don't you want to take your coat off? It's pretty warm today. Great day, in fact." Kiefer spoke fast, almost nervously, and blinked as he spoke. Free of the mob now, Kiefer seemed to have an excess of energy. He walked quickly, bouncing forward on his toes, and looked around him constantly, jerkily saluting the few people they passed. He ushered Peterson into his office.

"Come in, come in," he said, rubbing his hands. "Take a seat. Let me take your jacket. No? Yes, beautiful view, isn't it? Beautiful."

This latter was in response to a comment Peterson had not in fact made, although he had automatically crossed to the large corner windows, drawn by the shimmering expanse of the Pacific below. "Yes," he said now, making the expected remark. "It's a magnificent view. Doesn't it distract you?"

The wide sandy beach stretched toward La Jolla and then curved out, broken up by rocks and coves, to a promontory surrounded by paradise palms. Out on the ocean, lines of surfers in wet suits sat bobbing patiently on their boards like large black sea birds.

Kiefer laughed. "If I find I can't concentrate, I just put on a wet suit and go out and swim. Clears the mind. I try to swim every day. Matter of fact, hardly need a wet suit these days. Water's already pretty warm. Those youngsters out there think it's cold." He indicated the surfers, most of whom were now on their knees, paddling before a good-sized wave. "In the old days it used to get real cold. Before they put those multi-gigawatt nuclear plants at San Onofre, y'know. Well, I'm sure *you* know. That kind of thing is your business, isn't it? Anyway, it's raised the water temperature slightly, just along this section of the coast. Interesting. So far it seems to have stimulated aquatic life. We're watching it carefully here, of course. In fact, it's one of our chief studies. If it gets higher, it could alter some cycles, but as far as we know, it's peaked. There's been no increase for several years now."

Kiefer's movements and speech became less jerky as he began to talk about his work. Peterson guessed him to be in his late forties. There were lines about his eyes and his wiry black hair was gray at the sides but he looked fit and lean. He had the look of an ascetic, but his office belied it. Peterson had already noted, with that mixture of envy and contempt he often felt in America, Kiefer's perks: deep pile of the fitted olive-green carpet, sleek expanse of rosewood desk top, moist hanging ferns and spider plants, Japanese prints on the walls, glossy magazines on the tile-topped coffee table, and of course the vast tinted windows with their Pacific view. He had a momentary vision of Renfrew's cluttered cubbyhole in Cambridge. Apart from the view, however, Kiefer showed no pride or even awareness of his surroundings. They sat down, not at his desk, but in comfortable chairs by the coffee table. Peterson calculated that quite enough had been done along the lines of intimidate-the-visitor and decided a gesture of indifference was needed.

"Do you mind if I smoke?" he asked, producing a cigar and gold lighter.

"Oh . . . I . . . well, sure." Kiefer appeared momentarily flustered. "Yes, yes, of course." He got up and slid the large window partly open, then crossed to his desk and spoke into the intercom. "Carrie? Would you bring in an ashtray, please?"

"I'm sorry," Peterson said. "I seem to have violated a taboo. I thought smoking was allowed in private offices."

"Oh, it is, it is," Kiefer assured him. "It's quite all right. It's just that I'm a nonsmoker myself and pretty much try to discourage others." He flashed Peterson a sudden crooked and disarming grin. "Hopefully, you'll see the light soon. I'd appreciate it if you'd stay rather downwind of me, so to speak." Peterson judged the "rather" was the usual American attempt at speaking English-English, the effect in any case spoiled by the grammatical error in the sentence before it.

The door opened and Kiefer's secretary came in with an ashtray which she set before Peterson. Peterson thanked her, abstractedly tabulating her physical characteristics and giving her a good 8 out of 10. He realized with relish that only his status as a member of the Council had overridden Kiefer's ban on smoking in his office.

Kiefer perched on the edge of the chair facing him. "So . . . tell me how you found the situation in South America." He rubbed his hands together eagerly.

Peterson exhaled luxuriously. "It's bad. Not desperate yet but very serious. Brazil has become more dependent on fishing lately thanks to their shortsighted slash-and-burn policy of a decade or two ago—and of course this bloom seriously affects fishing."

Kiefer leaned forward even more, as eager for details as any gossiping housewife, and at this point Peterson put himself on automatic. He revealed what he had to and extracted from Kiefer a few technical points worth remembering. He knew more biology than physics, so he did a better job than with Renfrew and Markham. Kiefer went into their funding situation—bleak, of course; one never heard any other tune—and Peterson guided him back onto useful stuff.

"We believe the whole food chain may be threatened," Kiefer said. "The phytoplankton are succumbing to the chlorinated hydrocarbons—the kind used in fertilizer." Kiefer leafed through the reports. "Manodrin, specifically."

"Manodrin?"

"Manodrin is a chlorinated hydrocarbon used in insecticides. It has opened a new life niche among the microscopic algae. A new variety of diatom has evolved. It uses an enzyme which breaks down manodrin. The diatom silica also excrete a breakdown product which interrupts transmission of nerve impulses in animals. Dendritic connections fail. But they must have gone into all this at the conference."

"It was mostly at the political level, what steps to be taken to meet the immediate crisis and so on."

"What is going to be done about it?"

"They're going to try to shift resources from the Indian

Ocean experiments to contain the bloom, but I don't know if it'll work. They haven't completed their tests yet."

Kiefer drummed his fingers on the ceramic tiles. He asked abruptly, "Did you see the bloom yourself?"

"I flew over it," Peterson answered. "It's ugly as sin. The color terrifies the fishing villages."

"I think I'll go down there myself," Kiefer muttered, more to himself than to Peterson. He got up and began to pace the room. "Still, y'know, I keep feeling there's something else . . ."

"Yes?"

"One of my lab types thinks there's something special going on here, a way the process can kinda alter itself." Kiefer waved a hand in dismissal. "All hypothetical, though. I'll keep you informed if any of it pans out."

"Pans out?"

"Works, I mean."

"Oh. Do."

•

Peterson got away from Scripps later than he'd planned. He accepted an invitation to dinner at Kiefer's to keep things going on the good-fellow front, always a wise idea. It was harder for a sod to cross you when he's drunk some and told a joke and devoured a casserole in your company, however boring the conversation had been.

Peterson's limo and tag-along security detail took him into La Jolla center for the appointment at San Diego First Federal Savings. It was a bulky squarish building, set dead among a brace of tedious stores of the shoppe variety. He thought of getting something as a traveler-home-from-the-wars gift, something he'd done more often when younger, but dismissed the idea after three seconds of deliberation. The shops were of the semi-infinite markup species and despite the rickety dollar, the pound was worse. All that would be quite to the side if the shops had been interesting, but instead they sported knick-knacks and ornate lamps and gaudy ashtrays. He grimaced and went into the bank.

The bank manager met them at the door, primed by the sight of the security force. Yes, he had been advised of Mr. Peterson's arrival, yes, they had searched the bank records. Once inside the manager's office Peterson asked brusquely, "Well, then?"

"Ah, sir, it was a surprise to us, let me tell you," the thin man said seriously. "A safety deposit box with the fees arranged for decades ago. Not your typical situation."

"Quite so."

"I . . . I was told you would not have the key?" The man obviously hoped Peterson would have it, though, and save him a lot of explaining to his superiors afterward.

"Right, I don't. But didn't you find the box was registered in my name?"

"Yes, we did. I don't understand . . ."

"Let us simply say this is a matter of, ah, national security."

"Still, without a key, the owner—"

"National security. Time is important here. I believe you take my meaning?" Peterson gave the man his best distant smile.

"Well, the undersecretary did explain part of it on the phone, and I have checked with my immediate superior, but—"

"Well, then, I'm happy to see things have worked out so quickly. I congratulate you on your speed. Always good to see an efficient operation."

"Well, we do—"

"I would like to have a quick look at it now," Peterson said with a certain undertone of firmness.

"Well, ah, this, this way . . ."

They went through a pointless ritual of signing in and stamping the precise time and passing through the buzzing gate. The huge steel doors were opened to reveal a gleaming wall array of boxes. The manager nervously fished appropriate keys from his vest pocket. He found the right box and slid it out. There was a moment's hesitation before he surrendered it. "Thanks, yes," Peterson murmured politely, and went directly to the small room nearby for privacy.

He'd had this idea on his own and rather liked it. If what Markham said was right, it was possible to reach someone in the past and change the present. But precisely how this action affected the present wasn't clear. Since the past viewed now might well be the one Renfrew had created, how could they tell it from some other past that never happened, but might have? This whole way of looking at it was a mistake, Markham said, since once you passed a tachyon beam between two times they were forever linked, a closed loop. But to Peterson it seemed essential to know if you had in fact got through. In Markham's idealized experiments, with flipping light switches and toggles moving back and forth between pegs and all, the whole question was confused. So Peterson had proposed a check, of sorts.

True enough, you had to send back the preliminary ocean data and so on. But you could also ask the past to set aside some kind of road marker. One clear sign that the signals had been received—that would be enough to convince Peterson that these ideas weren't drivel. So two days before leaving London he'd called Renfrew and given him a specific message to send. Markham had a list of the experimental groups who could conceivably receive a tachyon message on their nuclear magnetic resonance devices. A message was addressed to each site— New York, La Jolla, Moscow. Each was requested to establish a clearly labeled safety deposit box in Peterson's name with a note inside. That should be enough.

Peterson couldn't reach Moscow without explaining to Sir Martin why he wanted to go. New York was out of the question, temporarily, because of the terrorists. That left La Jolla.

Peterson felt his pulse quicken as the catch on the safety deposit box came free with a click. When the lid of the box tilted back he saw only a sheet of yellow paper folded in thirds. He picked it up and carefully flattened the creases. It crackled with age.

MESSAGE RECEIVED LA JOLLA

That was all. It was quite enough. Instantly Peterson felt two conflicting emotions: elation, and a sudden disappointment that he had not asked for more. Who had written the note? What else did they receive? He realized ruefully that he had assumed the sod getting the signal would obey the instruction and then go on and tell how he got it, what he thought it meant, or at least who he buggering well was.

But no, no, he thought, sitting back. This was enough. This proved the whole colossal business was right. Incredible, but right. The implications beyond that were unclear, granted—but this much was certain.

And as well, he thought with a touch of pride, he had done it all himself. He wondered for a moment if this was what it was like to be a scientist, to make a discovery, to see the world unlocked if only for an instant.

Then the bank manager knocked hesitantly on the door, the mood was lost, and Peterson pocketed the sheet of yellow.

•

He stayed at the Valencia Hotel in a suite overlooking the cove. The park below was part gnawed away by the encroaching surf, as evidenced by the sudden termination of some walkways. All along the coast the waves had undercut the conglomerate soil. Shelves stuck out above the surf, ready to topple. No one seemed to notice.

He told his security men and limo to clear off for the night. They made him conspicuous and he had been under the limelight quite enough for one day. His mind was churning with the success at the bank. He dissipated some of the energy with thirty laps in the hotel pool, and then with unsuccessful forays into the shops near the hotel. The clothing stores interested him most, but they were the sort which could not simply display their wares and stand aside, but set them in scenes of English manor houses or French chateaux. There was still money here, though most of it seemed misdirected. The people were bright and clean and glossy. At least being prosperous set one apart in England; here it guaranteed nothing, not even taste.

The sidewalks thronged with old people, some quite rude if you didn't step aside for them. The younger men, though, were bright and athletic. The women interested him more, crisply fashionable, immaculately groomed. There was a certain blandness to them, though, an indefinable stamp of prosperous neutrality. Part of him envied this life. He knew that these people striding so confidently along Girard were hemmed in by as many restrictions as the English—Southern California was a mass of limits on immigration, buying houses, water use, changing jobs, automobiles, everything—but they looked free. There was still not much of the worldweariness here which Europeans often equated with maturity. He had always missed a certain complexity among the women, as well. They seemed interchangeable, their faces carefully smooth and open. Sex with them was healthy, competent, and matter-of-fact. If one propositioned them, they were never surprised or shocked. Their no meant no and their yes meant yes. He missed the challenge of the no that meant maybe, the elegant game of seduction. These Americans didn't play games; they were energetic and skillful but never devious or secret or subtle. They preferred direct questions, gave direct answers. They liked to be on top.

At this point in his musings, he stopped before a wine store, and decided to see if he could get a few cases of good California wine flown back to England. One never knew when the chance would come again.

He was waiting in the bar for Kiefer when the thought struck him. What if he'd simply sent a letter to Renfrew, with the message inside? Given the post these days, it might not have even reached him by now, never mind being acted upon. In that case, after he'd got the yellow paper today, he could've rung up Renfrew and ordered him not to send the message. What would Markham make of that?

He finished his gin and then remembered the business about the loops. Yes, the scheme he'd just devised would have thrown everything into an indeterminate state. That was the answer. But what kind of answer was that?

●

"Damn streets," Kiefer complained. "Getting like a slum." He wrenched the steering wheel around a sharp curve. Tires howled.

For Peterson this change of topic was a decided improvement. Kiefer had been reciting the virtues and benefits of eating fresh vegetables brought in at something approximating the speed of light from "the valley," a cornucopia needing no further name.

To encourage this new line of discussion Peterson ventured mildly, "It all looks very prosperous to me."

"Yes, well, of course, you don't see it if you keep to the avenues. But it's getting harder to maintain standards. Look around you here, for instance. Notice anything?"

They were high in the hills now, on winding narrow roads that afforded glimpses of the ocean between Spanish ranches and miniature French chateaux.

"See how they're walled in? When we first came here, oh, almost twenty years ago now, they were all open. Great views from every house. Now you can't even call on your neighbor without standing out in the street pushing buttons and talking into an intercom. And frap, you should see the antiburglar networks! Electronics worth a hundred German shepherds. Backup batteries for brownouts, too."

"The crime rate is bad, then?" Peterson asked.

"Terrible. Illegal aliens, too many people, not enough jobs. Everybody feels he has a right to a life of luxury—or at least comfort—so there's a lot of frustration and resentment when the dream craps out."

Peterson began to replan his schedule. He would leave time to find the best electronic security system he could. Stupid of him, not to think of it before. That sort of thing was precisely where the Americans excelled. He would have use for a good system, adaptable and rugged. If possible, he would carry it back with him on the plane. Again he wished for a private jet.

"The town is getting carved up into sealed-off enclaves," Kiefer went on. "Oldsters, mostly."

Peterson nodded as Kiefer cited statistics for California, which was second only to Florida in percentage of old people. Since the foldup of the Social Security system, the Senior Movement lobby had been pressuring even harder for special privileges, tax breaks, and extra favors. Peterson was sure he knew more of the demographics than Kiefer; the Council had got a worldwide picture on them two years ago, including some confidential projections. Attaining the zero-population-growth birth rate had left the US and Europe with a bulge in the population curve, now hitting retirement age. They expected hefty monthly checks, which had to come from the reduced ranks of younger people through taxes. It led to an "entitlement syndrome." The old felt they'd paid heavy taxes all along and then been put on the shelf before they could earn the immense salaries now going to junior executives. They were "entitled," the Senior Movement argued, and society had damned well better cough up. The oldsters voted more often and with a sharper eye for self-interest. They had power. In California a gray head had become a symbol of political activism.

"—they don't come out for *weeks,* with the spiffy televideo systems they buy. Saves 'em shopping or going to the bank or seeing anybody under sixty. They just do it all electronically. Kills the town, though. The oldest movie theater in La Jolla, the Unicorn, closed last month. Damned shame."

Peterson nodded with a show of interest, still thinking about rearranging his schedule. The car swung into a steep driveway as the gate opened before it. They climbed up towards a long white house. Bastard Spanish, Peterson classified silently. Expensive, but without style. Kiefer parked in the carport and Peterson noticed bicycles and a wagon. Christ, children. If he had to share the dinner table with a crew of American brats—

It looked as though his fears were going to be realized when they were met at the door by two young boys jumping at Kiefer and both talking at once. Kiefer managed to quiet them down long enough to introduce them to Peterson. Both children then trained their attention on him. The older boy dispensed with preliminaries and asked directly, "Are you a scientist like my dad?" The younger fixed him with an unwinking stare, shifting from foot to foot in an irritating way. Of the two, he was potentially the noisier and more troublesome, Peterson decided. He knew the older boy's type—earnest, talkative, opinionated, and nearly uncrushable.

"Not exactly," he began, but was interrupted.

"My dad is studying diatoms in the ocean," the boy said, dismissing Peterson. "It's very important. I'm going to be a scientist too when I grow up but maybe an astronomer and David's going to be an astronaut but he's only five so he doesn't really know. Would you like to see the model of the solar system I made for our science project?"

"No, no, Bill," Kiefer answered hastily. "I know it's very nice but Mr. Peterson doesn't want to be bothered now. We're going to have a drink and talk about grown-up things." He led the way to the living room, followed by Peterson and the two boys. Kiefer would be the sort of parent who called adults "grown-ups," Peterson thought drily.

"I can talk about grown-up things *too*," Bill said indignantly.

"Yes, yes, of course you can. What I meant was, we're going to talk about things that wouldn't interest you. What'll you have to drink? Can I offer you a whisky and soda, wine, tequila . . . ?"

"How do you know they wouldn't interest me, lots of things interest me," the child persisted, before Peterson could answer. The situation was saved by a light, firm voice calling from another room. "Boys! Come here at once, please!" The two vanished without argument. Peterson stored for future use the verbal backhand he had been about to deal the older boy.

"I see you have some Pernod there. Could I have a Pernod and tequila, with a dash of lemon, if you please?"

"Jeez, what a mixture. Is it good? I don't often drink hard liquor myself. Liver, y'know. Sit down, I'm pretty sure we have some lemon juice. My wife will know. Does that drink have a name or did you invent it?" Kiefer was acting erratically again.

"I believe it's called a macho," Peterson said wryly.

He looked around the room. It was simple and elegant, totally white except for a few Oriental pieces. An exquisite screen stood against the far wall. To the right of the fireplace was a Japanese scroll, and a flower arrangement sat in an alcove. Opposite the fireplace, uncurtained picture windows looked over roofs and treetops towards the Pacific. The ocean was a black blanket beside lights that glittered everywhere else, up and down the coast, as far as Peterson could see. He chose a seat on a low white sofa, sitting sideways at the end of it so he could see both the room and the view. In spite of little heaps of muddled papers here and there, obviously Kiefer's, the room exuded a certain serenity.

"I hope this is right. Equal amounts of Pernod and tequila, is that it? I'll go and check on the lemon juice. Oh, here's my wife now."

Peterson turned toward the doorway, looked and looked

again. He rose slowly to his feet. Kiefer's wife stunned him. Japanese, young, slender, and very beautiful. Not taking his eyes from her, he tried to sort out his first disoriented impressions. In her late twenties, he decided, which explained Kiefer's having such young children. A second marriage for him, no doubt. She was dressed in white Levis and a high-necked white top of some slithery material. Nothing under it, he noted with approval. Her hair fell smooth and straight, almost to her waist, so black it seemed to have a blue sheen. But it was her eyes that riveted his attention. Seeing her all in white in this dimly lit white room, he had the eerie sensation that her head was floating by itself. She had paused in the doorway, not deliberately for effect, Peterson thought, but her appearance was dramatic. He felt unable to move until she did. Kiefer darted nervously forward.

"Mitsuoko, my dear, come in, come in. I want you to meet our guest, Ian Peterson. Peterson, this is my wife, Mitsuoko." He looked eagerly from one to the other like a child bringing home a prize.

She came forward into the room, moving with a fluid grace that delighted Peterson. She held out her hand to him: cool and smooth.

"Hello," she said. For once Peterson felt he could use the standard American greeting "Glad to meet you" with sincerity.

He murmured "How do you do?" narrowing his eyes slightly to communicate what his formal greeting lacked. The merest hint of a smile lifted the corners of her lips at his unspoken message. Their gazes held fractionally longer than convention dictated. Then she withdrew her hand from his and went over to sit on we sofa.

"Do we have any lemon juice, honey?" Kiefer was rubbing his hands together again in his awkward way. "And what about you? Will you have something to drink?"

"Yes to both questions," she answered. "There's some lemon juice in the fridge and I'll have a little white wine." She turned to Peterson with a smile. "I can't drink much at all. It goes straight to my head."

Kiefer left the room in search of lemon juice.

"How are things in England, Mr. Peterson?" she asked, tilting her head back slightly. "It sounds grim in the news here."

"It *is* bad, although a lot of people don't yet realize how bad," he replied. "Do you know England?"

"I was there for a year a while back. I'm very fond of England."

"Oh? Were you working there?"

"I was on a postdoc at Imperial College in London. I'm a mathematician. I teach at UCSD now." She was smiling as she watched him, expecting a reaction of surprise. Peterson did not show it. "I can see you expected something like a philosophy degree."

"Oh, no, nothing so conventional," he said smoothly, smiling back at her. He thought of philosophers as people who spent great swaths of time on questions of no more true depth than "If there is no God, then who pulls up the next Kleenex?" He was about to form this into an epigram when Kiefer came back into the room with a glass of wine and a small bottle.

"Here's your wine, love. And some lemon juice"—this to Peterson. "How much, just a dash?"

"That's splendid, thank you."

Kiefer sat down and turned to Peterson. "Did Mitsuoko tell you that she spent a year at London University? She's a brilliant woman, my wife. Ph.D. at twenty-five. Brilliant and beautiful too. I'm a lucky man." He beamed proudly at her.

"Alex, don't do that." The words were sharp but her affectionate smile took the edge off them. She shrugged deprecatingly towards Peterson. "It's embarrassing. Alex is always boasting about me to his friends."

"I can understand why." Behind Peterson's blandly smiling exterior he calculated. He had only one evening. Did they have an open marriage? How direct an approach would she tolerate? How to broach the subject with Kiefer there? "Your husband tells me that things are pretty bad here too, although it doesn't look that way to a visitor."

What did her smile mean? It was almost as though they shared a secret. Was she in fact reading his thoughts? Was she merely flirting? Or could it be—the thought flashed upon him —that she was nervous? She was certainly sending him signals.

"There's a psychological inability to give up luxury standards," Kiefer was saying. "People won't give up a life style that they think is, ah, uniquely American."

"Is that a current catch phrase?" Peterson asked. "I saw it used in a couple of magazines I read on the plane."

Kiefer gave this hypothesis his best concerned frown. "Um, 'uniquely American'? Yeah, I suppose it is. Saw an editorial about something like that this week. Oh, say, excuse me, I'll go check the boys."

Kiefer left the room in his eager-terrier style. In a moment Peterson could hear him talking mildly but firmly to the boys somewhere down the hall. They regularly interrupted him with tenor bright-boy-aware-that-he-is-being-bright backtalk. Peterson took a pull on his drink and reflected on the wisdom of proceeding further with Mitsuoko. Kiefer was a link in Peterson's information-gathering chain, the most essential part of an executive's working machinery. This was indeed California, notorious California, and the date was well advanced beyond the nineteenth century, but one could never be sure how a husband would react to these things, never mind what they said in theory about the whole matter. But beyond such calculations was the fact that the man irritated him with his fanaticism about health foods and nonsmoking and undignified devotion to those decidedly unpleasant children.

Well, executives were supposed to be able to make quick, incisive decisions, correct? Correct.

He turned to Mitsuoko, seeking the best way to use these moments alone. She was staring out at the view, which she must have memorized ages ago.

Before he could formulate an opening she asked, not looking at him, "Where are you staying, Mr. Peterson?"

"La Valencia. And the name is Ian."

"Ah, yes. There's a nice strip of beach there, south of the cove. I often take a walk there in the evenings." She looked directly at him. "About ten o'clock."

"I see," Peterson replied. He felt a pulse beating in his neck. It was the only outward sign of excitement. By God, she had done it. She had made an assignation with him almost under her husband's nose. Christ, what a woman.

Kiefer came back into the room. "There's a growing crisis here," he said.

Peterson gave a snort of laughter which he deftly turned into a cough.

"I think you're right," he managed drily. He dared not look at Mitsuoko.

•

On the long flight over the pole Peterson had time to browse through the file from Caltech. He felt relaxed and pleasantly dissipated, with the slack sensation one gets when he knows he has done quite as much as could be expected along the lines of self-indulgence. No regrets, that was the ticket; it meant one had passed up nothing. To reach the grave with that assurance would surely be at least comforting.

Mitsuoko had rather lived up to the subliminal advanced billing. She had cleared off after three hours, presumably with some solid story, or better, a tacit agreement of no questions from Kiefer. A suitable topping off for a wearing trip.

The Caltech file was something else. There were some grimly detailed internal reports, all a tangle of words and mathematical symbols to him. Markham could frolic in it, if he liked. There were signs that the file hadn't been freely given over. A Xerox of an official letter, Peterson-inspired, backgrounding for the Council, had scrawled at the bottom *Stall them—let's not get scooped*. Surely the author of the note would have lifted that out before making it semipublic. The explanation was obvious. The American government had quite effective internal security people. Rather than trade letters with Caltech, they'd clandestinely photographed whatever they could turn up. Peterson sighed. A dicey method, but then again, not his problem.

The only intelligible portion of the file was a personal letter, presumably stuck in because of key words.

Dear Jeff,

I'm not going to make it down for Easter; there's just too much to do here at Caltech. The last few weeks have been extremely exciting. I'm working with a couple of other people and we really don't want to break off our calculations, even for a holiday in Baja. I'm really sorry about it as I was looking forward to getting together with you both again (if you take my meaning!). I shall miss the prickly cactus and the delicious dry heat, too. Sorry, and maybe next time. Tell Linda I'll call her for a chat in the next few days if I can find time. Any chance of you people coming up here for a day (or better yet, a night)?

After breaking a promise like this I suppose I ought to tell you what's stirred me up so. Probably a marine biologist like you won't think this is of such great concern—cosmology doesn't count for a lot in the world of enzymes and titrated solutions and all that, I suppose—but to those of us working in the gravitational theory group it looks as though there's a genuine revolution around the corner. Or maybe it's already arrived.

It's related to a problem that's been hanging around astrophysics for a long time. If there is a certain quantity of matter in the universe, then it has a closed geometry—which means it will eventually stop expanding and begin to contract, pulled back together by gravitational attraction. So people in our line of work have been wondering for some time if there is enough matter in our universe to close off the geometry. So far, direct measurements of the matter in our universe have been inconclusive.

Just counting the luminous stars in the universe gives a small quantity of matter, not enough to close off space-time. But there's undoubtedly a lot of unseen mass such as dust, dead stars, and black holes.

We're pretty sure that most galaxies have large black holes at their centers. That accounts for enough missing matter to close off our universe. What's new is the recent data on how distant galaxies are bunched up together. These galactic-scale clumps mean there are large fluctuations in matter density throughout our universe. If galaxies bunch up together somewhere in our universe, and their density gets high enough, their local space-time geometry could wrap around on itself, in the same way that our universe might be closed.

We now have enough evidence to believe Tommy Gold's old idea—that there are parts of our universe which have enough clustered galaxies to form their own closed geometry. They won't look like much to us—just small areas with weak red light coming out of them. The red is from matter still falling into those clumps. The shocker here is that these local density fluctuations qualify as independent universes. The time for forming a separate universe is independent of the size. It goes like the square root of Gn, where G is the gravitational constant and n the density of the contracting region. So it's independent of the size of the miniuniverse. A small universe will close itself off just as fast as a large one. This means all the various-sized universes have been around for the same amount of "time." (Defining just what time is in this problem will drive you to drink, if you're not a mathematician—maybe if you are, too.)

The point here is that there may be closed-off universes inside our own. In fact, it would be a remarkable coincidence if our universe was the largest of all. We may be a local lump inside somebody else's universe. Remember the old cartoon of a little fish being swallowed by a slightly larger one, in turn about to be swallowed by another bigger one, and so on, ad infinitum? Well, we may be one of those fishes.

The last few weeks I've been working on the problem of getting information about—or out of—these universes inside our own. Clearly, light can't get out of one universe into the next. Neither can matter. That's what a closed geometry means. The only possibility might be some type of particle that doesn't fit into the constraints set by Einstein's theory. There are several candidates like this, but Thorne (the grand old man around here) doesn't want to get into that morass. Too messy, he says.

I think tachyons are the answer. They can escape from smaller "universes" inside our own. So the recent discovery of tachyons has enormous implications for cosmology. It's hard to detect tachyons, so we don't know much about them. They *give us a direct link to the sealed-off space-times inside our universe, though, which is why I'm working so hard on the problem. There's a chance of a first-class discovery in this. We've had the devil of a time pursuing things, with the food strike and the big fire in LA. Probably nobody will give much of a damn, with the world in its present state. But that's what the academic life is for.*

I'm sorry I've gone on about this at such length and probably made no sense, but the whole thing is tremendously exciting to me and I tend to get carried away. Anyway, I'm sorry about Baja. Hope to see you both soon.

> *Love,*
> *Cathy*

Peterson felt a momentary twinge of guilt at reading a private letter. The Council used such methods routinely now, of course, to get quickly round the recalcitrant interests who had not accepted the necessity for quick action. Still, he was a gentleman and a gentleman does not read another's mail. His reluctance soon submerged beneath his interest in the implications of what was said by "Cathy." Subuniverses? Incredible. The landscape of the scientist was ultimately unreal.

Peterson leaned back in his seat and studied Canadian wastes slipping by below. Yes, perhaps that was it. For decades now the picture of the world painted by the scientists had become strange, distant, unbelievable. Far easier, then, to ignore it than try to understand. Things were too complicated. Why bother? Turn on the telly, luv. Right.

chapter twelve

DECEMBER 3, 1962

Cooper laid the red-gridded sheets out in a long line across the lab countertop. He stood back, balancing on his toes like a sprinter preparing to go the distance, and surveyed his work. The subdued hum of the laboratory underlined the expectation in the air. "That's it," Cooper said slowly. "They're in the right order."

"That's our best data?" Gordon murmured.

"Best *I'll* ever get," Cooper said, frowning at something in Gordon's voice. He turned, hands on hips. "It's all consecutive, too. Three hours worth."

"It looks good and clean," Gordon said in a conciliatory tone. "Sharp."

"Yeah," Cooper admitted. "Nothing funny about this. If there was a clear resonance there, I'd see it."

Gordon traced his finger along the green data lines. There were no standard resonances at all. Inside their sample, cooled down to 3 degrees absolute in the bubbling helium, were atomic nuclei. Each was a tiny magnet. They tended to line up along the magnetic field Cooper had applied to the sample. The standard experiment was simple: apply a brief electromagnetic pulse, which tipped the nuclear magnets away from the magnetic field. In time, the nuclei would line up with the field again. This nuclear relaxation process could tell the experimenter much about the environment inside the solid. It was a relatively simple way to learn about microscopic features of the complex solid structure. Gordon liked the work for its clarity and directness, aside from any applications to transistors or infrared detectors it might eventually have. This branch of solid state physics didn't have the high visibility of things like quasars or high-energy particle research but it was clean and had a kind of simple beauty.

The jagged traces before him, though, were neither simple nor beautiful. Here and there were fragments of what they should be getting: nuclear resonance curves, smooth and meaningful. But in most of the gridded traces there were sudden jagged lines bursts of electromagnetic noise, appearing abruptly for an instant, then disappearing just as suddenly.

"The same spacings," Gordon murmured.

"Yeah," Cooper said. "The one-centimeter ones—" he pointed "—and the shorter ones, half a centimeter. Regular as hell."

Both men looked at each other, then back at the data. Each had hoped for a different result. They had done these experiments over again and again, eliminating all possible sources of noise. The ragged bursts would not vanish.

"It's a goddam message," Cooper said. "Must be."

Gordon nodded, fatigue seeping through him. "There's no avoiding it," he said. "We've got hours of signal here. Can't be coincidence, not this much."

"No."

"Okay then," Gordon said, summoning up optimism in his voice. "Let's decode the fucking thing."

•

REDUCTION OF OXYGEN CONTENT TO BELOW TWO PARTS PER MILLION WITHIN FIFTY KILOMETER RADIUS OF SOURCE AFTER DIATOM BLOOM MANIFESTS AEMRUDYCO PEZQEASKL MINOR POLLUTANTS PRESENT IN DEITRICH POLYXTROPE 174A ONE SEVEN FOUR A COMBINES IN LATTITINE CHAIN WITH HERBICIDES SPRINGFIELD AD45 AD FOUR FIVE OR DU PONT ANALAGAN 58 FIVE EIGHT EMITTING FROM REPEATED AGRICULTURAL USE AMAZON BASIN OTHER SITES OTHER LONG CHAIN MOLECULAR SYNERGISTS POSSIBLE IN TROPICAL ENVIRONS OXYGEN COLUMN SUBJECT TO CONVECTIVE SPREADING RATE ALZSNRUD ASMA WSUEXIO 829 CMXDROQ VIRUS IMPRINTING STAGE RESULTS 3 THREE WEEK DELAY IF DENSITY OF SPRINGFIELD AD45 AD FOUR FIVE EXCEEDS 158 ONE FIVE EIGHT PARTS PER MILLION THEN ENTERS MOLECULAR SIMULATION REGIME BEGINS IMITATING HOST CAN THEN CONVERT PLANKTON NEURO JACKET INTO ITS OWN CHEMICAL FORM USING AMBIENT OXYGEN CONTENT UNTIL OXYGEN LEVEL FALLS TO VALUES FATAL TO MOST OF THE HIGHER FOOD CHAIN WTESJDKU AGAIN AMMA YS ACTION OF ULTRAVIOLET SUNLIGHT ON CHAINS APPEARS TO RETARD DIFFUSION IN SURFACE LAYERS OF THE OCEAN BUT GROWTH CONTINUES LOWER DOWN DESPITE CONVECTIVE CELLS FORMING WHICH TEND TO MIX LAYERS IN XMC AHSU URGENT MADUDLO 374 ONLY SEGMENT AMZLSOUDP ALYN YOU MUST STOP ABOVE NAMED SUBSTANCES FROM ENTERING OCEAN LIFE CHAIN AMZSUY RDUCDK BY PROHIBITIONS OF FOLLOWING SUBSTANCES CALLANAN B471 FOUR SEVEN ONE

MESTOFITE SALEN MARINE COMPOUND ALPHA THROUGH
DELTA YDEMCLW URGENT YXU CONDUCT TITRATION ANALY-
SIS ON METASTABLE INGREDIENTS PWMXSJR ALSUDNCH

•

    Gordon had no chance to think about the message until
the afternoon. His morning was filled out by a lecture and then
a committee meeting on graduate student admissions. There
were top-flight students applying from all over—Chicago, Caltech, Berkeley, Columbia, MIT, Cornell, Princeton, Stanford.
The canonical seats of wisdom. A few unusual cases—two odd
ones from Oklahoma who might be promising, a gifted and quiet
fellow from Long Beach State—were put aside for study. It
was plain that La Jolla's fame was spreading rapidly. In part it
was the continuing heady rush of the Sputnik phenomenon.
Gordon was riding that wave himself, and he knew it; these
were ripe times for science. He wondered, though, about the
students just now coming into physics. Some of them seemed
like the same sort that went into law or medicine—not because
it was a fascinating subject, but because it promised big bucks.
Gordon wondered privately whether Cooper had elements of
that; the man showed sparks of the old flame, but it lay hidden
beneath a blanket of mellow relaxation, an aura of physical
assurance. Even the message, the very existence of a message,
struck Cooper as a little funny but basically acceptable, an odd
effect, soon to be explained. Gordon could not tell whether this
was a pose or genuine serenity; either way, it was unsettling.
Gordon was used to a more intense style. He envied the physicists who had made the great discoveries when quantum mechanics was unfolding, when the nucleus first shattered. The
older members of the department, Eckart and Lieberman,
talked of those days sometimes. Before the 1940s, a degree in
physics was a solid basis for a career in electrical engineering,
period. The bomb had changed all that. In the avalanche of
gaudy weapons, new fields of study, increased budgets, and
expanding horizons, everyone discovered suddenly a national
thirst for physicists. In the years following Hiroshima a newspaper story referring to a physicist invariably called him "the
brilliant nuclear physicist," as though there could be no other
kind. Physics got fatter. Even so, physicists were still relatively
poorly paid; Gordon could remember a visiting professor at
Columbia borrowing money to attend the Friday "Chinese
lunch" Lee and Yang had started up. The lunches met in one of
the excellent Chinese restaurants ringing the campus, and it
was there that new results often surfaced first. Attendance was

a good idea if you wanted to keep up. So the visiting scholar had scrounged enough to go, and paid it back within a week. Such days seemed distant to Gordon now, though they must loom large in the minds of the older physicists, he realized. Some, like Lakin, carried an air of uneasy waiting, as though the bubble would soon burst. The dazed public, with its short attention span, would be distracted by the cornucopia of tail fins and ranch-style tract homes, and forget about science. The easy equation—science equals engineering equals consumer yummies—would fade. Physics had spent more time at the bottom of the S curve than chemistry—World War I was the flush time for them—and now was enjoying the steep climb. But a plateau had to follow. The S curve had to curl over.

Gordon mulled this over as he made his way from the laboratory up the outside stairs to Lakin's office. The lab notebooks were carefully organized and he had checked over the decoding of the message repeatedly. Still, he was of half a mind to turn around and avoid seeing Lakin at all.

He was only a few sentences into his presentation when Lakin said, "Really, Gordon, I had trusted you would fix this trouble by now."

"Isaac, these are the facts."

"No." The trimly built man got up from behind his desk and began to pace. "I have looked into your experiment in detail. I read your notes—Cooper showed me where they were."

Gordon frowned. "Why not ask me for them?"

"You were in class. And—I speak frankly—I wanted to see Cooper's own entries, in his own hand."

"Why?"

"You admit you did not take all the data by yourself."

"No, of course not. He's got to do something for a thesis."

"And he is behind schedule, yes. Significantly behind." Lakin stopped and made one of his characteristic movements, dipping his head slightly and raising his eyebrows as he looked at Gordon, as though gazing over the rims of nonexistent eyeglasses. Gordon supposed this was a glance meant to convey something unprovable but obvious, an unspoken understanding between colleagues.

"I don't think he's faking it, if that's what you mean," he said very steadily, keeping inflection out of his voice with some effort.

"How could you tell?"

"The data I took fits in with the syntax of the rest of the message."

"That could be a deliberate effect, somehow cooked up by

Cooper." Lakin turned toward the window, hands clasped behind his back, his voice now carrying a shade of hesitation.

"Come *on*, Isaac."

Lakin suddenly rounded on him. "Very *well*. You tell *me*, then, what is going on," he said crisply.

"We have an effect, but no explanation. That's what's going on. Nothing more." He waved the page of decoded message in the air, slicing blades of sunlight descending from the windows.

"Then we are agreed." Lakin smiled. "A very strange effect. Something makes the nuclear spins relax, *bing*, like that. Spontaneous resonance."

"That's crap." Gordon had thought they were really homing in on the point, and now this old song and dance came up.

"It is a simple statement of what we know."

"How do you explain *this?*" He waved the message again.

"I do not." Lakin shrugged elaborately. "I would not even mention it, if I were you."

"Until we understand it—"

"No. We do understand enough. Enough to talk in public about spontaneous resonance." Lakin began a technical summary, ticking off the points on his fingers with a precise gesture. Gordon could see he had grilled Cooper thoroughly. Lakin knew how to present the data, which quantities to plot, how the figures in a paper could build a very convincing case. "Spontaneous resonance" would make an interesting paper. No, an exciting one.

When Lakin was finished, and had sketched out the scientific arguments, Gordon said casually, "Half a true story can still be a lie, you know."

Lakin grimaced. "I've humored you quite a bit, Gordon. For months. It is time to admit the truth."

"Uh huh. What is it?"

"That your techniques are still faulty."

"How?"

"I do not know." He shrugged, dipping his head and raising his eyebrows again. "I cannot be in the laboratory constantly."

"We have been able to array the resonance signals—"

"So they seem to say something." Lakin smiled tolerantly. "They could say *anything*, Gordon, if you fool with them enough. Look—" He spread his hands. "You remember, from astronomy, the fellow Lowell?"

"Yes," Gordon said suspiciously.

"He 'discovered' the canals on Mars. Saw them for years, decades. Other people reported seeing them. Lowell had his own observatory built in the desert, he was a rich man. He had excellent seeing conditions there. The man had time and fine eyesight. So he discovered evidence of intelligence."

"Yeah, but—" Gordon began.

"The only mistake was that he had the wrong conclusion. The intelligent life was on *his* side of the telescope, not the Mars end. His mind—" Lakin jabbed a forefinger at his own temple "—saw a flickering image and then imposed order on it. His own intelligence was tricking him."

"Yeah, yeah," Gordon said sourly. He couldn't think of a counterargument. Lakin was better at these things, knew more stories, had a subtle instinct for maneuver.

"I propose that we not turn ourselves into Lowells."

"Publish the spontaneous resonance stuff right away," Gordon said, trying to think.

"Yes. We have to finish the NSF proposal this week. We can feature the spontaneous resonance material. I can write it up from the notebooks, in such a way that we can use the same manuscript for a paper to *Physical Review Letters*."

"What good will it do to send it to PRL?" Gordon asked, trying to decide what his reaction was.

"In our NSF proposal we can list the paper in the reference page as 'submitted to PRL.' That puts an earmark on it, says it is work of foremost quality. In fact . . ." he pursed his lips, judging, peering over imaginary hornrims, ". . . why not say 'to be published in PRL'? I am certain they will accept it, and 'to be published' carries more weight."

"It's not true."

"It soon will be." Lakin sat down behind his desk and leaned forward on it, hands clasped together. "And I tell you frankly that without something interesting, something new, the grant is in trouble."

Gordon looked at him steadily for a long moment. Lakin got up and resumed pacing. "No, of course, it was only a thought. We will say 'submitted to' and that will have to do it." He circumnavigated the office with a measured step, thinking. He stopped before the blackboard with its crude sketches of the data. "A very odd effect, and a credit to its discoverer—you."

"Isaac," Gordon said carefully, "I'm not going to drop this."

"Fine, fine," Lakin said, taking Gordon's arm. "Throw yourself into it. I'm sure the business with Cooper will resolve itself in time. You should arrange the date of his doctoral candidacy exam, you know."

Gordon nodded absently. To set out on a full research program for the thesis, a student had to pass the two-hour oral candidacy examination. Cooper would need some coaching; he tended to freeze up if more than two faculty members were within earshot, a remarkably common effect among students.

"I'm glad we have this settled," Lakin murmured. "I'll show you a draft of the PRL paper on Monday. Meanwhile—" he glanced at his watch—"the Colloquium is starting."

•

Gordon tried to concentrate on the Colloquium lecture but somehow the thread of the argument kept eluding him. Only a few rows away Murray Gell-Mann was explaining the "Eight-Fold Way" scheme for understanding the basic particles of all matter. Gordon knew he should be following the discussion closely, for here was a genuinely fundamental question. The particle theorists already said Gell-Mann should get the Nobel for this work. He frowned and shifted forward in his seat, peering at Gell-Mann's equations. Someone in the audience asked a skeptical question and Gell-Mann turned, always smooth and unperturbed, to counter it. The audience followed the exchange with interest. Gordon remembered his senior year at Columbia, when he had first begun attending the Physics Department Colloquia. He had noticed an obvious feature of the weekly meetings, one he never heard talked about. Anyone could ask a question, and when he did all attention of the audience turned to him. If there were several exchanges between lecturer and questioner, all the better. And a questioner who caught the speaker in an error was rewarded with nodding heads and smiles from those around him. All this was clear, and it was doubly clear that no one in the audience prepared for the Colloquia, no one studied for them.

The Colloquium topic was announced a week in advance. Gordon began reading up on the topic and taking down a few notes. He would look up the speaker's papers, with special attention to the Conclusions section, where authors usually speculated a bit, threw out "blue sky" ideas, and occasionally took indirect slams at their competitors. Then he would read the competitors' papers as well. This always generated several good questions. Occasionally such a question, innocently asked, could puncture a speaker's ideas like a stiletto. This would create a murmur of interest in the audience, and inquiring glances toward Gordon. Even an ordinary question, if well delivered, created the impression of deep understanding. Gordon began by calling out questions from near the back. After a few weeks he moved forward. The senior professors in the department always took the first-row seats, and soon he was sitting only two rows behind them. They began turning in their seats to watch as he asked a question. Within a few more weeks he was in the second row. Full professors began to nod to him as they took their seats before Colloquium began. By Christmas Gordon was known to most of the department. He had felt a slight tug of guilt about it ever since, but, after all, he hadn't done anything except show a keen and systematic interest. If it benefited him, so much the better. He had been a demon for physics and mathematics then, more interested in watching a lecturer pull an analytic rabbit out of a higher mathematical hat than in a Broadway show. Once he spent a whole week trying to crack Fermat's Last Theorem, skipping lectures to scribble away. Somewhere around 1650, Pierre de Fermat jotted the equation $x^n + y^n = z^n$ in the margin of his copy of Diophantus' *Arithmetic*. Fermat wrote that if x, y, z, and n were positive integers, there were no solutions to the equation for n greater than two. "The proof is too long to write in this margin," Fermat scribbled. In the 300 years since, no one had been able to prove it. Was Fermat bluffing? Maybe there wasn't a proof. Anyone who could decide the issue with a mathematical demonstration would be famous. Gordon struggled with the riddle and then, falling behind in classes, gave it up: But he swore that some day he would get back to it.

The Last Theorem had a lot of mathematical beauty in it, but that wasn't why he had attacked it. He liked solving problems, simply because they were there. Most scientists did; they were early chess players and puzzle solvers. That, and ambition, were the two traits scientists truly had in common, it seemed to him. Gordon mused for a moment on how different he and Lakin were, despite their common scientific interests—and then suddenly sat upright. Heads nearby turned at this quick movement. Gordon ran the conversation with Lakin through his mind, remembering how his talk about the message had been neatly deflected, first into a dodge about Cooper, then the Lowell story, followed by Lakin's seeming to back down on the "to be published in PRL" business. Lakin got the PRL he wanted, with Gordon and Cooper as coauthors, and Gordon had nothing more than the typescript of his message.

Gell-Mann was describing, in his precise way, a detailed pyramid of particles arranged by mass, spin, and various quantum numbers. It was all a meaningless jumble to Gordon. He reached into his vest pocket—he always put on a jacket for Colloquium, if not a tie as well—and brought out the message. He stared at it a moment and stood up. The audience for Gell-Mann was huge, the biggest draw of the year. They all seemed to be watching him as he worked his way through the forest of knees to the aisle. He walked out of the Colloquium a little unsteadily, the message paper twisted in his hand. Eyes followed him as he went out a side door.

•

"Does it make sense?" Gordon said intensely to the sandy-haired man across the desk from him.

"Well, yeah, sort of."

"The chemistry is legitimate?"

Michael Ramsey spread his palms upward. "Sure, as much as I can follow. These industrial names—'Springfield AD45, Du Pont Analagan 58'—don't mean anything to me. Maybe they're still under development."

"What it says about the ocean, and this stuff reacting together—"

Ramsey shrugged. "Who knows? We're babes in the woods about a lot of this long-chain molecule stuff. Just because we can make plastic raincoats, don't think we're wizards."

"Look, I came over to Chemistry to get help in understanding that message. Who would know more about it?"

Ramsey sat back in his reclining office chair, squinting unconsciously at Gordon, plainly trying to assess the situation. After a moment he said quietly, "Where'd you get this information?"

Gordon shifted uneasily in his chair. "I'm . . . look, keep this quiet."

"Sure. Sure."

"I've been getting some . . . strange . . . signals in an experiment of mine. Signals where there shouldn't be any."

Ramsey squinted again. "Uh huh."

"Look, I know this stuff isn't very clear. Just fragments of sentences."

"That's what you'd expect, isn't it?"

"Expect? From what?"

"An intercepted message, picked up by one of our listening stations in Turkey." Ramsey smiled with a touch of glee, his skin around the blue eyes crinkling so that his freckles folded together.

Gordon fingered the tip of his button-down collar, opened his mouth and then closed it.

"Oh, come on," Ramsey said, cheerful now that he had penetrated an obvious cover story. "I know about all that tip-top secret stuff. Lots of guys try their hand at it. Government can't get enough qualified people to pick over this stuff, so they ring in a consultant."

"I'm not working for the government. I mean, outside of NSF—"

"Sure, I'm not saying you are. There's that working panel Department of Defense has, what do they call it? Jason, yeah. A lot of bright guys in there. Hal Lewis up at Santa Barbara, Rosenbluth from here, sharp people. Did you do any of that ICBM reentry work for DOD?"

"Can't say as I did," Gordon said with deliberate mildness. *Which is precisely the truth,* he thought.

"Ha! Good phrase. Can't *say,* not that you didn't *do.* What was it Mayor Daley said? 'Coming clean isn't the same as taking a bath.' I won't ask you to give away your sources."

Gordon found himself fingering his collar again and discovered the button was nearly twisted off. In the New York days his mother had had to sew one back on every week or so. Lately his rate had gotten lower, but today—

"I'm surprised the Soviets are talking about this sort of thing, though," Ramsey murmured, thinking to himself. The narrowing around his eyes had relaxed and he slipped back into the mold of experimental organic chemist pondering a problem. "They're not very far along in these directions. In fact, at the last Moscow meeting I attended I could've sworn they were way behind us. They've pushed fertilizer for that five-year plan of theirs. Nothing of *this* complexity."

"Why the American and English brand names?" Gordon said intently, leaning forward in his chair. "Dupont and Springfield. And this—'emitting from repeated agricultural use Amazon basin other sites' and so on."

"Yeah," Ramsey allowed, "Seems funny. Don't suppose it's got anything to do with Cuba, do you? That's the only place the Russians are monkeying around in South America."

"Ummm." Gordon frowned, nodding to himself.

Ramsey studied Gordon's face. "Ah, maybe that makes sense. Some kind of Castro side action in the Amazon? A little under-the-counter aid to the backwoods people, to make the guerrillas more popular? Might make sense."

"That seems a little complicated, doesn't it? I mean, the other parts about the plankton neurojacket and so on."

"Yeah, I don't understand that. Maybe it's not even part of the same transmission." He looked up. "Can't you get a better transcription than this? Those radio eavesdroppers—"

"I'm afraid that's the best I can do. You understand," he added significantly.

Ramsey pursed his lips and nodded. "If DOD is so interested

they'd farm out info like this . . . Tantalizing, isn't it? Must be something to it.''

Gordon shrugged. He didn't dare say anything more. This was a delicate game, letting Ramsey talk himself into a cloak-and-dagger explanation, without actually telling him anything that was an outright lie. He had come over to the Chemistry Department prepared to lay things on the line, but he now realized that would have got him nowhere. Better to play it this way.

"I like it," Ramsey said decisively. He slapped his palm with a *whack* onto a pile of examinations on his desk. "I like it a lot. Damned funny puzzle, and DOD interested. Bound to be something in it. Think we can get funding?"

This took Gordon aback. "Well, I don't . . . I hadn't thought . . ."

Ramsey nodded again. "Right, I get it. DOD isn't going to pony up for every blue-sky idea that floats by. They want some backup work."

"A down payment."

"Yeah. Some preliminary data. That'll make a better case for pursuing the idea." He paused, as though juggling schedules in his mind. "I have some idea how we could start. Can't do it right away, you understand. Lots of other work under way here." He relaxed, leaned back in his swivel chair, grinned. "Send me a Xerox of it and let me mull it over, huh? I like a puzzle like this. Puts a little zip in things. I appreciate your bringing it by, letting me in."

"And I'm happy you're interested," Gordon murmured. His smile had a wry and distant quality.

chapter thirteen

JANUARY 14, 1963

He picked his way along Pearl Street, hitting the brakes every moment or two as ruby tail lights winked in warning ahead. Traffic was getting thicker almost daily. Gordon felt for the first time the irritation at others moving in, gobbling up the landscape, crowding this slice of paradise, elbowing him. It seemed pointless, now that he was settled in, to develop this land any further. He smiled wanly as the thought struck him that he had now joined the legion of the genuinely transplanted; California was now *here*, other people were from *there*. New York was more a different idea than a different place.

Penny wasn't at the bungalow. He had told her he would be late because of a recruiting cocktail party at Lakin's house, and had half expected she would have a light supper ready. He prowled the apartment, wondering what to do next, feeling light and restless after three glasses of white wine. He found a can of peanuts and munched them. Penny's papers from the composition class she taught were arranged neatly on the dining table, as though she had left in a hurry without putting them away. He frowned; that was unlike her. The papers were covered with her neat, curling handwriting, labeling paragraphs "tepid" or "arguable," block letters shouting "SEN FRAG" or simply "AG"—failure of agreement between subject and predicate, she had explained to him, not a howl of anguish. At the top of one student essay on *Kafka and Christ* she had written "King Kong died for our sins?" Gordon wondered what it meant.

He decided to go out and buy some wine and nibble food. He certainly wasn't going to wait around the apartment for her. On his way out the door he noticed a duffel bag leaning against the overstuffed armchair he usually sat in. He pulled at the sealing cord until the mouth sagged open. Inside was a man's clothing. He frowned.

Full of a curious jangling energy, he delayed getting back in the Chevy and walked the half block down to Wind 'n Sea beach instead. Big combers battered at the smooth fingers of rock that stretched into the sea. He wondered how long these rocks could stand the constant gnawing of the surf, booming in great bursts over them. To the south a few teenagers, brown as Indians, lounged around the small municipal water station pump house. They studied the tumbling surf in a languid stupor, some of them puffing on short cigarettes. Gordon had never been able to get more than three words out of them, no matter what he asked. *Inscrutable natives,* he thought, and turned away. Returning to his car along Nautilus he passed under Torrey pine trees that had ruptured the sidewalk, the concrete breaking on the hard and heavy bark like frozen waves.

He drove a winding route along the narrow back streets near the ocean. Tiny houses, almost doll-sized, crowded each other. Many were gingerbreaded or sported needless cupolas. Curls and latticework elbowed a neighbor's elephant-eared begonias. Roses rubbed stands of lush bamboo. Filaments of every architectural style seemed to have splashed over the houses and clung, dripping. The streets were straight and silent, regimenting the babble of cultures and pasts that had washed up on this vest pocket village. La Jolla was a place where everything came together in a way unlike New York, with an odd and waiting energy. Gordon liked it. He took a swing around to 6005 Camino de la Costa on an impulse. It was a minor shrine now, the place where Raymond Chandler lived and worked in the '40s and '50s, with a flagstoned courtyard and a jumbled rock garden that spread up the hill behind it. He had read every Chandler novel, immediately after seeing Bogart in *The Big Sleep* for the first time; Penny had said it was one way of finding out what California was about.

He bought food at Albertson's and a case of various white wines at a liquor store near Wall Street. The parquet floors of the store hoarded the slackening dry heat of the day. A burly, tanned man eyed Gordon's button-down shirt with a distant amusement as he sacked the bottles. Coming out of the store, Gordon saw Lakin getting out of an Austin-Healey down the street. He turned away quickly and walked down Prospect; in the dim twilight Lakin had probably missed seeing him. The paper on spontaneous resonance had sailed through *Physical Review Letters* with ease, as Lakin predicted. The entire incident now seemed closed to Lakin, but Gordon still felt the unease of a man who is passing checks but knows his account is overdrawn. He put the bottles, clanking together, in the trunk of the Chevy, and then walked by the Valencia Hotel. There were no gaudy electrical apparitions yelling out their advertisements in La Jolla, no factories, pool halls, smokestacks, graveyards, railroad stations, or cheap diners to besmirch the ambience. The Valencia announced itself with a modestly lettered sign. On the veranda two middle-aged women were playing canasta and chattering with zest. They wore elaborate print dresses bunched at the waist, heavy metallic necklaces, and their hands sported at least three rings apiece. The two men playing with them looked older and tired. *Probably worn out from signing checks,* Gordon thought, and walked past them into the lobby. The hotel bar gave off a buzz of conversation. He made his way along ranks of rattan couches to the rear sitting room of the lobby; he liked to look down from here at the cove below. Ellen Browning Scripps had seen what the land-gobblers were doing to the town and set aside a smooth green lawn around the cove, so that somebody besides the rich could watch the lazy swells roll in. As Gordon watched, the floodlights came on, making the white walls of churning water leap out of the sea's darkness, chewing the land. Gordon's few expeditions into the Pacific had been launched from the half-moon beaches below. Offshore there was a rock where you could stand and rise out of the lapping troughs of waves. It was slippery footing, but he liked to look back at the land, crusted with impermanent stucco and wood and whitewash, as though at this remove he could judge it, get a firm perspective. Chandler had said it was a town full of old people and their parents, but somehow he had never mentioned the sea and the remorseless, roaring breakers that punctuated the long rambling sentences of waves, always gnawing at the shore. It was as though some unnoticed force came over the horizon, all the way from Asia, and chipped away at this cozy pocket of Americana. Stubby breakwaters tried to blunt the effect, but Gordon could not understand how they could last. Time would eat all this away; it had to.

When he went back through the lobby, the bar's murmur was about one drink louder than before. A blonde gave him a look of appraisal and then, realizing he was no prospect, her face turned soft as sidewalk and she looked back down at her copy of *Life*. He stopped by the tobacco shop on Girard and bought a paperback for 35¢, fanning the pages to his nose as he left; they always carried the sweet humus smell of a pipe pouch.

He opened the door of their bungalow with his key. A man sat on the couch pouring some bourbon into a water glass.

"Oh, Gordon," Penny said, her voice lilting as she got up from her seat next to the stranger. "This is Clifford Brock."

The man rose. He was wearing khaki slacks and a brown wool shirt with pockets that buttoned. His feet were bare and Gordon could see a pair of zori lying beside the duffel bag by the couch. Clifford Brock was tall and chunky, with a slow grin that crinkled his eyes as he said, "Glad t'meet ya. Nice place you got here."

Gordon murmured a greeting. "Cliff is an old high school buddy of mine," Penny said merrily. "He's the one took me to Stockton that time for the races."

"Oh," Gordon said, as though this explained a great deal.

"Like some Old Granddad?" Cliff offered the open bottle on the coffee table, still giving off his fixed grin.

"No, no thanks. I just went out to buy some wine."

"I got some, too," Cliff said. He fished a gallon jug from under the coffee table.

"I went out with him to get some stuff to drink," Penny volunteered. Her forehead was lightly beaded with perspiration. Gordon looked at the gallon jug. It was a Brookside red, wine they usually used for cooking.

"Wait'll I bring in the rest from the car," he said to sidestep Cliff's proffered jug. He went out into the cooling evening and brought in the other bottles, storing some in a cabinet and the rest in the refrigerator. He corkscrewed one open, even though it wasn't chilled, and poured himself a glass. In the living room Penny busied herself setting out Fritos and a bean dip and listening to Cliff's slow drawl.

"You stayed late at the Lakin party?" Penny asked, as Gordon settled into their Boston rocker.

"No, I just stopped off to buy some things. Wine. The party was just another back-slapping thing." The image of Roger Isaacs or Herb York slapping a venerated philosopher on the back, like Shriners on a binge, didn't really fit, but Gordon let it go.

"Who was it?" Penny said, showing dutiful interest. "Who were they recruiting?"

"A Marxist critic, somebody said. He mumbled a lot and I couldn't make out much of it. Something about capitalism repressing us and not letting us unleash our true creative energies."

"Universities are great for hiring Reds," Cliff said, blinking owlishly.

"I think he's more of a theoretical communist," Gordon temporized, not really wanting to defend the point.

"Do you think you'll hire him?" Penny asked, obviously steering the conversation.

"*I* don't have any say. That's the Humanities people. Everybody was being very respectful, except for Feher. This guy was saying that under capitalism, man exploits man. Feher poked a finger at him and said, yeah, and under communism, it's vice versa. That got a good laugh. Popkin didn't like it, though.''

"Don't need Reds to teach you anything you can't learn in Laos," Cliff said.

"What did he say about Cuba?" Penny persisted.

"The missile crisis? Nothing."

"*Hum*," Penny said triumphantly. "What's he written, this guy, anyway?"

"There was a little stack of his publications. *One-Dimensional Man* one of them was, and—"

"Marcuse. That was Marcuse," Penny said flatly.

"Who's he?" Cliff murmured, pouring himself some Brookside into another glass.

"Not a bad thinker," Penny admitted with a shrug. "I read that book. He—"

"Learn more about Reds in Laos," Cliff said, hefting the gallon jug so he could pour by resting it on his shoulder. "Filling 'em up here?" he invited, looking at their glasses.

"I'll pass," Gordon said, holding his palm over his glass mouth, as though Cliff would pour into it anyway. "You've been in Laos?"

"Sure." Cliff drank with relish. "I know this stuff isn't up to that of yours—" gesture with glass, a ruby red sloshing—"but it's one damn sight better'n stuff over there, I'll tell you."

"What were you doing?"

He looked at Gordon blankly. "Special Forces."

Gordon nodded silently, a bit uneasily. He had gone through graduate school with a student deferment. "What's it like over there?" he asked lamely.

"Shitty."

"What did the military people think about the Cuban missile settlement?" Penny asked seriously.

"Ol' Jack earned his money that week." Cliff took a long pull of the wine.

"Cliff is back for good," Penny told Gordon.

"Right," Cliff said. "R 'n R forever. Flew me into El Toro. I knew ol' Penny was around here somewhere so I called up her old man and he gave me her address. Caught a bus down." He waved a hand airily, a shift of mood. "I mean, it's okay, man, I'm just an ol' friend. Nothing big. Right, Penny?"

She nodded. "Cliff took me to the senior prom."

"Yeah, and did she look *great*. Ridin' shotgun in a pink evenin' gown in my T-bird." Abruptly he began to sing "When I Waltz Again with You" in a high, wavering voice. "Boy, what crap. Teresa Brewer."

Gordon said sourly, "I hated that stuff. All that high school hotshot business."

Cliff said levelly, "I'll bet you did. You from back east?"

"Yes."

"Marlon Brando, *On the Waterfront*, all that? Boy, it's a mess back there."

"It's not that bad," Gordon murmured. Somehow Cliff had hit upon a precise similarity. Gordon had kept pigeons on the roof for a time, just like Brando, and had gone up there to talk to them on Saturday nights when he didn't have a date, which was pretty often. After a while he had convinced himself that dating on Saturday night didn't have to be the center of a teenage life and then sometime after that he had got rid of the pigeons. They were filthy, anyway.

Gordon excused himself to get some more wine. When he came back with a glass for Penny the two of them were remembering old times. Ivy League styles; hot-wiring cars; the *Ted Mack Variety Hour;* the irritating retort "That's for me to know and you to find out"; Sealtest ice cream; *Ozzie and Harriet; Father Knows Best;* duckass haircuts; the senior class repainting the water tower overnight; girls who popped bubble gum in class and left, pregnant, in their junior year; *My Little Margie;* the dipshit president of the senior class; strapless evening gowns that had to be wired to stay up; penny loafers; circle pins; Eloise, who ruined her crinolines falling in the pool at the all-night party; getting served in bars where they didn't give a damn about your age; girls in straight skirts so tight they had to get on a bus stepping up sideways; the fire in the chem lab; beltless pants; and a parade of other things that Gordon had disliked at the time as he burrowed into his books and planned for Columbia, and saw no reason why he should be nostalgic about now. Penny and Cliff remembered it as dumb and pointless, too, but with a differently soft and fond contempt Gordon could not summon up.

"Sounds like some kind of country club." He kept his voice light but he meant it. Cliff caught the disapproval.

"We were just havin' fun, man. Before, you know, the roof caved in."

"Things look okay to me."

"Yeah, well they're not. Get over there, in mud up to your ass, and you'll find out. The Chinks are nibblin' away at us. Cuba gets all the newspaper space, but where it's really happenin' is over there." He finished his wine, poured another.

"I see," Gordon said stonily.

"Cliff," Penny said brightly, "tell him about the dead rabbit in Mrs. Hoskins' class. Gordon, Cliff took—"

"Look, man," Cliff said slowly, peering at Gordon as though he were nearsighted and waving a finger erratically in the air, "you just don't—"

The telephone rang.

Gordon got up gratefully and answered it. Cliff began mumbling something in a low voice to Penny as Gordon left the room but he couldn't make it out.

He put the receiver to his ear and heard among the hiss of static his mother's voice say, "Gordon? That's you?"

"Uh, yes." He glanced toward the living room and lowered his voice. "Where are you?"

"At home, 2nd Avenue. Where should I be?"

"Well . . . I just wondered . . ."

"If I was back in California again, to see you?" his mother said with irritating perception.

"No, no," he paused a fraction of a second, about to call her Mom and suddenly not wanting to, with Special Forces Cliff within earshot, "I didn't think that at all, you've got it all wrong."

"She's there with you?" Her voice warbled high and faint, as though the connection were getting weak.

"Sure. Sure she's here. What do you expect?"

"Who knows what to expect these days, my son."

Whenever she called him "son" he knew there was a lecture on the way.

"You shouldn't have left like that. With no word."

"I know, I know." Her voice weakened again. "My cousin Hazel said I was wrong to do that."

"We had things to do, places we'd planned to take you," he lied.

"I was so . . ." She couldn't find the word.

"We could have talked about . . . things. You know."

"We will. I'm not feeling so good right now but I hope I can come out there again soon."

"Not so good? What do you mean, Mom, not so good?"

"A little pleurisy, it's nothing. I threw away money on a doctor and some tests. Everything is fine now."

"Oh, good. You take care of yourself, now."

"It's nothing worse than that strep throat you had, remember? I know these things, Gordon. Your sister was over for dinner yesterday and we remembered how—" and she was off in her usual tone of voice, recounting the events of the weeks, tracing an implied return to the fold of the wandering sister, of

126

making cabbage soup and kugel and flanken and tongue with the famous Hungarian raisin sauce, all for one dinner. And after, the "thee-yater," the two of them taking in Osborne's *Luther* ("Such a fuss about things!"). She had never budged his father downtown to lay out his good hard money for such things, but now the process of reclaiming her children justified such small luxuries. He smiled fondly, listening to the easy flow of words from another, earlier life three thousand miles away, and wondered if Philip Roth had heard of Laos yet.

He had a picture in his head of her at the other end of the long copper cord, her hand at first clenched white around the telephone receiver. As her voice softened he could sense the hand relax, the knuckles not so pale now. He was feeling good as the call ended. He hung the heavy black receiver back into its wall mount and only then recognized the choking gasp of repressed crying coming from the living room.

Penny was sitting on the couch beside Cliff, holding him as he sobbed into his cupped hands. "I didn't . . . We was goin' across this paddy, followin' a bunch of Pathet Lao from 'Nam back to where we knew they were runnin', toward the Plain of Jars. I was with this asshole platoon of 'Nam regulars, me and Bernie—Bernie from our class, Penny—and . . . this AR opened up right on us, an' Bernie's head jerked . . . He sat down in the mud an' his helmet fell into his hands, he was reachin' up for his face, an' he started to pick somethin' up out of the helmet and he fell over sideways. I was down behind him with the AR fire goin' right over us. I crawled up to him an' the water was all pink aroun' him and that's when I knew. I looked in the helmet and what he was tryin' to get out was part of his scalp, the hair still stuck in it, the round musta run up inside there an' gone in his brain after it smashed his jaw." Cliff was speaking more clearly now, heaving great sighs as the words tumbled out and his palms worked in the sockets of his eyes. Penny hugged him and murmured something. She reached over his broad shoulders and kissed him on the cheek with a sad, vacant gesture. Gordon saw with a sudden, gnawing shock that she had slept with him somewhere back in those rosy high school days. There was an old intimacy between them.

Cliff looked up and saw Gordon. He stiffened slightly and then shook his head, his mouth a blur. He sniffed. "It started to goddamn rain," he said clearly, as if resolved to go on and tell the rest of it no matter who was there. "They couldn't get any choppers in to us. Those pissass 'Nam pilots won't come in under fire. We was stuck in this little grove of bamboo, where we pulled back to. Pathet Lao and Cong had boxed us in. Me and Bernie were advisors, not supposed to give orders, they'd put us in with this platoon 'cause we weren't s'posed to make contact at all. Ever'body thought with the rainy season comin' on they'd pull out.''

He hoisted the Brookside jug and poured himself another glass. Penny sat beside him, hands folded demurely in her lap, eyes glistening. Gordon realized he was standing rigid, halfway between kitchen and living room, arms stiff. He made himself sit in the Boston rocker.

Cliff drank half the glass and rubbed his eyes on his sleeve, sighing. The emotion ebbed from him now and there was a settled fatigue about the way he went on, as though the words drained away the small drops of feeling as they emerged. ''This ARVN platoon leader went spastic on me. Didn't know which way was up, wanted to move out that night. The mist came in across the paddies. He wanted I should go out with ten 'Nams, reconnoiter. So I did, these little guys carryin' M-1's and scared shitless. We didn't get a hunnert yards before the point man rammed a punji up his boot. Started screamin'. AR fire comes in, we waddle our way back to the bamboo.''

Cliff leaned back in the couch and casually draped his arm around Penny, staring blankly at the Brookside jug. ''The rain feeds fungus that grows in your socks. Your feet get all white. I was tryin' to sleep with that, your feet so cold you think they're gone. An' I woke up with a leech on my tongue.'' He sat silently for a moment. Penny's mouth sagged open but she said nothing. Gordon found he was rocking energetically and consciously slowed the rhythm.

''Thought it was a leaf or somethin' at first. Couldn't get it off. One of the 'Nams got me to lie down—I was runnin' around, screamin'. The pissass platoon leader thought we was *in*filtrated. So this 'Nam puts boot cream on my tongue and I wait lyin' there in the mud an' he just picks this leech out of my mouth, a little furry thing. All the next day I taste that boot cream and it makes me shiver. Relief battalion drove off the Cong around noon.'' He looked at Gordon. ''Wasn't till I got back to base that I thought about Bernie again.''

•

Cliff stayed until late, his stories about advising the ARVN becoming almost nostalgic as he drank more of the sweet wine. Penny sat with her legs tucked under her, arm cocked against the couch back and supporting her occasionally nodding head, a distant look on her face. Gordon supplied short questions, nods of agreement, murmurs of approval to Cliff's stories, not really listening to them all that closely, watching Penny.

As he was leaving Cliff suddenly turned manically gay, wobbling from the wine, face bright and sweating slightly. He lurched toward Gordon, held up a finger with a wise wink, and said, "'Take the prisoner to the deepest dungeon,' he said condescendingly."

Gordon frowned, puzzled, sure the wine had scrambled the man's brains.

Penny volunteered, "It's a Tom Swiftie."

"What?" Gordon rasped impatiently. Cliff nodded sagely.

"A, well, a joke. A pun," she replied, imploring Gordon with her eyes to go along, to let the evening end on a happy note. "You're supposed to top it."

"Uh . . ." Gordon felt uncomfortable, hot. "I can't . . ."

"My turn." Penny patted Cliff's shoulder, in part as though to steady him. "How about 'I learned a lot about women in Paris,' said Tom indifferently?"

Cliff barked with laughter, gave her a good-humored slap on the rear, and shuffled to the door. "You can keep the wine, Gordie," he said. Penny followed him outside. Gordon leaned on the door frame. In the wan yellow glow of the outdoor lamp he saw her kiss him goodbye. Cliff grinned and was gone.

●

He put the Brookside jug in the trash and rinsed out the glasses. Penny rolled up the mouth of the Fritos bag. He said, "I don't want you bringing any more of your old boy friends by here from now on."

She whirled toward him, eyes widening. *"What?"*

"You heard what I said."

"Why?"

"I don't like it."

"Uh huh. And *why* don't you like it?"

"You're with me now. I don't want you starting up anything with anybody else."

"Christ, I'm not 'starting up' with Cliff. I mean, he just came by. I haven't seen him in years."

"You didn't have to kiss him so much."

She rolled her eyes. "Oh God."

He felt hot and suddenly uncertain. How much had he drunk? No, not much, it couldn't be that. "I mean it. I don't like that kind of stuff. He's going to get the wrong idea. You talking about your old high school days, arm wrapped around him—"

"Jee-sus, 'get the wrong idea.' *That's* a Harry Highschool phrase. That's where you're *stuck,* Gordon."

"You were leading him on."

"*Fuck* I was. That man is walking wounded, Gordon. I was comforting him. Listening to him. From the moment he knocked on the door I knew he had something inside, something those rah-rah types in the Army hadn't let him get out. He almost died over there, Gordon. And Bernie, his best friend—"

"Yeah, well, I still don't like it." His momentum blunted, he grasped for some other way he could prove the point. But what *was* the point? He had felt threatened by Cliff from the moment he saw him. If his mother had been able to see through that telephone, she'd have known quite well what to call the way Penny behaved. She'd have—

He stopped, avoiding Penny's hostile, rigid face, and looked down at the Brookside jug waiting forlornly in the trash for its destruction, incompletely used. He had seen Penny and Cliff with his mother's eyes, his New York imprinting, and he knew that he *had* missed the whole point. The war talk had put him off balance, unsure of how to react, and now in some odd way he was taking it all out on Penny.

"Look," he began, "I'm sorry, I . . . ." He brought his hands halfway up into the space between them and then let them drop. "I want to go for a walk."

Penny shrugged. He shouldered past her.

Outside, in the cool and salty air, fog shrouded the tops of the crusty old live oaks. He marched through this La Jolla of the night, his face a sheen of sudden sweat.

Two blocks over, on Fern Glen, a figure emerging from a house distracted him from the jumble of his thoughts. It was Lakin. The man glanced to each side, seemed satisfied, and slipped quickly into his Austin-Healey. In the house Lakin had left, venetian blinds fluttered at a window, momentarily silhouetting a woman's body in the light that seeped from behind her. Gordon recognized the place; it was where two women graduate students from Humanities 'lived. He smiled to himself as Lakin's Healey purred away. Somehow this small evidence of human frailty cheered him.

He walked a long way, past sealed-up summer cottages with yellowed newspapers on their doorsteps, occasionally passing by huge homes still ablaze with light. Cliff and Laos and the sense in Cliff's words of things real and important, muddy and grim—the thoughts chewed at him, all churned together in the layered fog with Penny and his distant, inevitable mother. Experimental physics seemed a toy, no better than a crossword puzzle, beside these things. A distant war could roll across an ocean and crash on this shore. He thought muzzily of Scripps Pier, which jutted out below the campus, used as a loading dock for men and tanks and munitions. But then he snorted to himself, sure the drink was now fuzzing his mind. Around him the tight pocket of La Jolla could not be threatened by a bunch of little guys running around in black pajamas, trying to topple the Diem government. It didn't make any goddamn sense.

He turned back toward home and Penny. It was easy to get overexcited about threats—Cliff, the Cong, Lakin. Waves could batter down a coastline overnight. And dim ideas about Cubans dumping fertilizer into the Atlantic and killing the life there—yeah, it was all too unlikely, more of his paranoia, yeah, he was sure of that tonight.

chapter fourteen

MARCH 22, 1963

Gordon opened the *San Diego Union* and spread it out on the lab workbench. He wished immediately that he had taken the trouble to find a copy of the *Los Angeles Times*, because the *Union* in its usual country-bumpkin manner devoted a lot of space to the wedding between Hope Cooke, the recent Sarah Lawrence graduate, and Crown Prince Palden Thonup Namgyal of Sikkim. The *Union* seemed all a-twitter that an American girl would marry a man who would become a maharajah, just any day now. The real news appeared only as a minor article on the front page: Davey Moore was dead. Gordon thumbed impatiently back to the sports page and was mollified to find a longer story. Sugar Ramos had knocked out Moore in the tenth round of their bout for the featherweight title, in Los Angeles. Gordon wished again that he had got tickets; the press of classes and research had made it slip his mind until they were all sold out. So Moore had died of a cerebral hemorrhage without regaining consciousness; another blot on boxing. Gordon sighed. There were the predictable comments from the predictable people, calling for an end to the whole sport. He wondered for a moment if they might be right.

"Here's the new stuff," Cooper said at his elbow.

Gordon took the data sheets. "More signal?"

"Yep," Cooper said flatly. "I've been getting good resonance curves for weeks now, and all of a sudden—whacko."

"You decoded it?"

"Sure. A lot of repetition in it, for some reason."

Gordon followed Cooper over to Cooper's working area, where the lab notebooks were spread out. He found himself hoping the results would be nonsense, simply interference. It would be much easier that way. He wouldn't have to worry about any messages, Cooper could proceed on his thesis, Lakin would be happy. His life didn't need any complication right now, and he had hoped the whole spontaneous resonance effect would go away. Their *Physical Review Letters* note had aroused interest and nobody in the field had criticized the work; maybe it was best to leave matters that way.

His hopes faded as he studied Cooper's blocky printing.

TRANSWBPRY 7 FROM CL998 CAMBE19983ZX
RA 18 5 36 DEC 30 29.2
RA 18 5 36 DEC 30 29.2
RA 18 5 36 DEC 30 29.2

The mystifying chant of letters and numbers ran on for three pages. Then it abruptly stopped and there followed:

SHOULD APPEAR AS POINT SOURCE IN TACHYON SPECTRUM 263 KEV PEAK CAN VERIFY WITH NMR DIRECTIONALITY MEASURE-MENT FOLLOWS ZPASUZC AKSOWLP BREAKDOWN IN RECTAN-GULAR COORDMZALS SMISSION FROM 19BD 1998COORGHQE

After this came nothing sensible. Gordon studied Cooper's data. "The rest of this stuff looks like simple on and off. No code to it." Cooper nodded, and scratched his leg beneath his cutaway jeans shorts. "Just dots and dashes," Gordon muttered to himself. "Funny." Cooper nodded again. Gordon had noticed lately that Cooper now confined himself to taking the data and venturing no opinions. Perhaps the clash with Lakin had taught him that an agnostic posture was safer. Cooper seemed happy enough when he was getting conventional resonance signals; they were the field stones which would build his thesis.

"This earlier stuff—RA and DEC." Gordon stroked his chin. "Something astronomical about that . . ."

"Ummmm," Cooper volunteered. "Maybe so."

"Yes—Right Ascension and Declination. These are *coordinates*, fixing a point in space."

"Huh. Could be."

Gordon glanced at Cooper irritably. There was such a thing as playing cards too close to your vest. "Look, I want to look into this. Just keep on taking measurements."

Cooper nodded and turned away, obviously relieved to be rid of the perplexing data. Gordon left the lab and went up two floors to 317, Bernard Carroway's office. There was no answer to his knock. He went by the department office, leaned in and called, "Joyce, where is Dr. Carroway?" By convention, office personnel were called by their first names, while faculty always had a title. Gordon had always felt slightly uncomfortable about going along with the practice.

"The big one or the little one?" the dark-haired department secretary said, raising her eyebrows; she scarcely ever let them rest.

"Big one. In mass, not height."

"Astrophysics seminar. It should be nearly over."

He slipped quietly into the seminar as John Boyle was finishing a lecture; the green blackboards were covered with differential equations from Boyle's new gravitation theory. Boyle finished with a flourish, mixing in a Scotsman's joke, and the seminar broke up into rivulets of conversation. Bernard Carroway heaved himself up and led a discussion between Boyle and a third man Gordon didn't know. He leaned over and asked Bob Gould, "Who's that?" Gordon nodded at the tall, curly-haired man.

"Him? Saul Shriffer, from Yale. He and Frank Drake did that Project Ozma thing, listening for radio signals from other civilizations."

"Oh." Gordon leaned back and watched Shriffer argue with Boyle over a technical point. He felt a humming energy in himself, the scent of the hunt. He had put aside the whole matter of the messages for several months, in the face of Lakin's indifference and the disappearance of the effect. But now it was back and he was suddenly sure he should press the issue.

Boyle and Shriffer were arguing over the validity of an approximation John had made to simplify an equation. Gordon watched with interest. It wasn't a cool intellectual discourse between men of reason, as the layman so often pictured. It was a warming argument, with muted shouts and gestures. They were arguing over ideas, but beneath the surface personalities clashed. Shriffer was much the noisier of the two. He pressed down hard with the chalk, snapping it in two. He flapped his arms, shrugged, frowned. He wrote and talked rapidly, frequently refuting what he himself had been saying only moments before. He made careless mistakes in the calculation, repairing them as he went with swipes of an eraser. The trivial errors weren't important—he was trying to capture the essence of the problem. The exact solution could come later. His hasty scrawl covered the board.

Boyle was totally different. He spoke with an even, almost monotonous voice, in contrast to the quick, jabbing tone Gordon remembered from the Limehouse. This was his scientific persona. Occasionally his voice was pitched so low Gordon had to strain to hear him. Those nearby would have to stop their side-talk to listen—a neat tactic to insure their attention. He never interrupted Shriffer. He began his sentences with "I think if we try this . . ." or "Saul, don't you see what will happen if . . ." A form of oneupmanship. He never made a forceful, positive assertion; he was the dispassionate seeker of truth. But gradually the effort of sticking to this low-key role showed. He couldn't prove rigorously that his approximation was justified, so he was reduced to a holding action. In sum his approach amounted to a repeated invitation to "prove that I'm wrong." Gradually, his voice rose. His face tightened into stubbornness.

Suddenly Saul claimed he knew how to refute John's approximation. His idea was to solve a particularly simple test problem where they already knew what the answer should be. Saul zoomed through the calculation. Only for one narrow range of physical conditions did the approximation give the right answer. "There! See—it's no good."

John shook his head. "Bugger off—it works precisely for the most interesting case."

Saul seethed. "Nonsense! You've thrown all the long wave lengths out of the problem."

But heads nodded around them. John had won. Since the embattled approximation was not totally useless, it was acceptable. Saul grudgingly agreed and a moment later was smiling and discussing something else, the issue forgotten. There was no point in remaining excited about an issue where something could be proved. Gordon grinned. It was an example of what he thought of as the Law of Controversy: Passion was inversely proportional to the amount of real information available.

He approached Carroway and held out the coordinates from his message. "Bernard, do you have any idea where this is in the sky?"

Carroway blinked owlishly at the numbers. "No, no, I never remember such details. Saul?" He pointed at the paper.

"Near Vega," Saul said. "I'll look it up for you, if you want."

•

After his lecture on Classical Electrodynamics Gordon intended to search out Saul Shriffer, but when he dropped by his office to leave off his lecture notes someone was waiting. It was Ramsey, the chemist.

"Say, thought I'd zip by and update you," Ramsey said. "I looked into that little riddle you gave me."

"Oh?"

"I think there's some real meat there. We're a long way from understanding much about long-chain molecules, y'know, but I'm interested in that puzzle. The part where it says, 'enters molecular simulation regime begins imitating host.' That sounds like a self-replicating mechanism we don't know beans about."

"Does that happen with the molecular forms you know?"

Ramsey's brow wrinkled. "Nope. But I've been studying the special fertilizing forms some of the companies are experimenting with, and . . . well, it's too early to say. Just a hunch, really. What I came to tell you is that I haven't forgotten about the thing. Classes and my regular grants, y'know—they stack up on you. But I'll keep nudging along at it. Might go down and bug Walter Munk about the oceanography connection. Anyway—" he stood, giving a mock salute of goodbye—"I appreciate the info. Might be a good lead. Gratz a lots."

"Huh?"

"Gratz—gracias. Spanish."

"Oh. Sure." The cavalier Californian appropriation of Spanish slang seemed apt for Ramsey. Yet beneath the used-car salesman manner a quick mind worked. Gordon was glad the man was looking into the first message and hadn't let it fall into a crack. This seemed to be a lucky day; threads were weaving together. Yes, a lucky day. "I'd give it an A plus so far," Gordon mused to himself, and went looking for Shriffer.

●

"I nailed it for you," Saul said decisively, finger arrowing down at a speck on a star chart. It's a point very close to a normal F7 star, named 99 Hercules."

"But not smack on it?"

"No, but very close. What's behind all this, anyway? What's a solid state physicist need a star position for?"

Gordon told him about the persistent signals and showed him Cooper's recent decoding. Saul quickly became excited. He and a Russian, Kadarsky, were writing a paper together on the detection of extraterrestrial civilizations. Their operating assumption was that radio signals were the natural choice. But if Gordon's signals were indeed unexplainable in terms of earthly transmissions, Saul suggested, why not consider the hypothesis of extraterrestrial origin? The coordinates clearly pointed that way.

"See—Right Ascension is 18 hours, 5 minutes, 36 seconds. Now, 99 Hercules is this dot at 18 hours, 5 minutes, 8 seconds, a little off. Declination of your signal is 30 degrees, 29.2 minutes. That fits."

"So? They don't agree exactly."

"But they're damned close!" Saul waved his hands. "A few seconds difference is nothing."

"How in hell does an extraterrestrial know our system of astronomical measurements?" Gordon said skeptically.

"How do they know our *language?* By listening to our old radio programs, of course. Look—parallax for 99 Hercules is 0.06. That means it's over sixteen parsecs away."

"What's that?"

"Oh, about 51 light years."

"How could they be signaling, then? Radio came in about sixty years ago. There hasn't been time for light to go the round trip—it would take over a century. So they can't be answering our own radio stations."

"True." Saul appeared momentarily deflated. "You say there's some more to the message?" He brightened. "Let me see."

After a moment he stabbed the printed message and exclaimed, "Right! That's it. See this word?"

"Which?"

"Tachyon. Greek origin. Means 'fast one,' I'll bet. That means they're using some faster-than-light transmission."

"Oh, come on."

"Gordon, use your imagination. It *fits,* damn it!"

"Nothing travels faster than light."

"This message says something does."

"Crap. Just crap."

"Okay, how do you explain this? 'Should appear as point source in tachyon spectrum 263 KEV peak.' KEV—kilovolts. They're using tachyons, whatever they are, of energy 263 kilovolts."

"Doubtful," Gordon said severely.

"What about the rest? 'Can verify with NMR directionality. Measurement follows.' NMR—Nuclear Magnetic Resonance. Then garbage, a few more words, then garbage again. SMISSION FROM 19BD 1998COORGHQE and so on."

"Not all garbage. See—the rest is simple dots and dashes."

"Hummm." Saul peered at the pattern. "Interesting."

"Look, Saul, I appreciate the—"

"Wait a sec. 99 Hercules isn't just any star, you know. I looked it up. It fits into the kind of star class we think might support life."

Gordon pursed his lips and looked dubious.

"Right, it's an F7. Slightly heavier than our sun—more massive, I mean—and with a big region around it capable of supporting life. It's a binary star—wait, wait, I know what you're going to say," Saul said dramatically, pushing his open, upright palm toward Gordon, who had no idea what he was going to say. "Binary stars can't have livable planets around them, right?"

"Uh, why not?"

"Because the planets get perturbed. Only 99 Hercules doesn't *have* that problem. The two stars circle each other only every 54.7 years. They're far apart, with livable spaces around each of them."

"Both are F7s?"

"As far as we can tell, the bigger one is. You only need one," he added lamely.

Gordon shook his head. "Saul, I appreciate—"

"Gordon, let me have a look at that message. The dots and dashes, I mean."

"Sure, okay."

"Do me a favor. I think there's something big here. Maybe our ideas about radio communication and the 21-centimeter line of hydrogen being the natural choice—maybe they're all wrong. I want to check this message of yours out. Just don't make up your mind. Okay?"

"Okay," Gordon said reluctantly.

●

When Gordon lugged his briefcase into his office the next morning, Saul was waiting for him. The sight of Saul's eager face, with brown eyes that danced as he spoke, filled him with a premonition.

"I cracked it," Saul said tersely. "The message."

"What . . . ?"

"The dots and dashes at the end? That spelled no words? They aren't *words*—they're a picture!"

Gordon gave him a skeptical look and put down his briefcase.

"I counted the dashes in that long transmission. 'Noise,' you said. There were 1537 dashes."

"So?"

"Frank Drake and I and a lot of other people have been thinking of ways to transfer pictures by simple on-off signals. It's simple—send a rectangular grid."

"That scrambled part of the message? RECTANGULAR COORDMZALS and so on."

"Correct. To lay out a grid you need to know how many lines to take on each axis. I tried a bunch of combinations that multiply out to 1537. All gave a mess, *except* a 29-by-53 grid. Laying the dashes out on that scheme gave a picture. *And* 29 and 53 are both prime numbers—the obvious choice, when you think about it. There is only that one way to break 1537 down into a product of primes."

"Ummm. Very clever. And this is the picture?"

Saul handed Gordon a sheet of graph paper with a point filled in for each dash in the transmission. It showed a complex interweaving set of curves moving from right to left. Each curve was made of clusters of dots, arranged in a regular but complicated pattern. "What is it?" Gordon asked.

"I don't know. All the practice problems Frank and I made up gave pictures showing solar systems, with one planet picked out—things like that. This one doesn't look anything like that."

Gordon tossed the drawing on his desk. "Then what use is it?"

"Well—hell! An *immense* amount of good, once we figure it out."

"Well . . ."

"What's the matter? You think this is wrong?"

"Saul, I know you've got a reputation for thinking about —what's that Hermann Kahn calls it?—the unthinkable. But this—!"

"You think I'm making all this up?"

"Me? *Me?* Saul, *I* detected this message. *I* showed it to *you.* But your explanation—! Faster-than-light telegraph signals from another star. But the coordinates don't quite fit! A picture coming out of the noise. But the picture makes no sense! Come on, Saul."

Saul's face reddened and he stepped back, hands on hips. "You're blind, you know that? Blind."

"Let's say . . . skeptical."

"Gordon, you're not giving me a break."

"Break? I admit you've got some sort of case. But until we understand that picture of yours, it doesn't hold water."

"Okay. O-kay," Saul said dramatically, smacking a fist into his left palm. "I'll find out what that drawing means. We'll have to go to the whole academic community to solve the riddle."

"What's that mean?"

"We'll have to go public."

"Ask around?"

"Ask who? What specialty? Astrophysics? Biology? When you don't know, you have to keep your mind open."

"Yes . . . but . . ." Gordon suddenly remembered Ramsey. "Saul, there's another message."

"What?"

"I got it months ago. Here." He rummaged through his desk drawers and found the transcript. "Try that on for size."

Saul studied the long typed lines. "I don't understand."

"Neither do I."

"You're sure this is valid?"

"As sure as I am of what you've already deciphered."

"*Shit.*" Saul collapsed into a chair. "This really confuses things."

"Yes, it does, doesn't it?"

"Gordon, it makes no *sense*."

"Neither does your picture."

"Look, maybe you're getting conflicting messages. When you tune into different radio stations, you get music on one, sports on another, current events on a third. Maybe you've got a receiver here that just scoops up everything."

"Um."

Saul leaned forward in his chair and pressed his palms against his temples. Gordon realized the man was tired. He had probably stayed up all night working on the breakdown of the picture. He felt a sudden burst of sympathy for him. Saul was already known as a proponent of the interstellar communication idea, and a lot of astronomers thought he was too wild, too speculative, too young and impulsive. Well, so what—that didn't mean he was wrong.

"Okay, Saul, I'll accept the picture idea—provisionally. It can't be an accident. So—what is it? We have to find out." He told Saul about Ramsey. That merely complicated matters, but he felt Saul had a right to know.

"Gordon, I still think we've got something here."

"So do I."

"I think we ought to go public."

"With the biochemistry, too? The first message?"

"No . . ." Saul thought. "No, just with this second message. It's clear. It repeats itself for *pages*. How often did you get that first signal?"

"Once."

"That's all?"

"That's all."

"Then let's forget it."

"Why?"

"It might be a decoding error."

Gordon remembered Lakin's story about Lowell. "Well . . ."

"Look, I've got a lot more experience with these things than you do. I know what people will say. If you muddy the water around a subject, nobody jumps in."

"We'd be withholding information."

"Withholding, yes. But not forever. Just until we find out what the picture means."

"I don't like it."

"We'll give them only one problem at a time." Saul raised a finger. "One problem. Later, we'll tell the whole story."

"I don't like it."

"Gordon, look. I think this is the way to do it. Will you take my advice?"

"Maybe."

"I'll take it, go public. I'm known. I'm a crazy guy who fools around with interstellar radio signals and all that stuff. A certified authority on a nonexistent subject. I can get the attention of the academic community."

"Yeah, but . . ."

"One problem at a time, Gordon!"

"Well . . ."

"First, the picture. Later, the rest."

"Well . . ." Gordon had a class coming up. Saul had a hypnotic quality about him, the ability to make notions seem plausible and even obvious. But, Gordon thought, a sow's ear with a ribbon around it was still a sow's ear. Still . . . "Okay. You get into the ring. I'm staying out."

"Hey, *thanks*." Suddenly Saul was shaking his hand. "I appreciate that. I really do. It's a *great* break."

"Yeah," Gordon said. But he felt no elation.

•

The *CBS Evening News* with Walter Cronkite came on as Gordon and Penny were finishing dinner. She had made a soufflé and Gordon had uncorked a white Beaujolais; both were feeling quite flush. They moved into the living room to watch. Penny took off her blouse, revealing small well-shaped breasts with large nipples.

"How do you know it'll be on?" she asked lazily.

"Saul called this afternoon. He did an interview in Boston this morning. The local CBS station did the work, but he said the national network picked it up. Maybe there isn't much else going on." He glanced around to be sure the curtains were drawn.

"Ummm. Looks that way." There was one big story—the nuclear powered submarine *Thresher* had gone down in the

Atlantic without a single cry for help. They had been on a test dive. The Navy said that probably a system failure created progressive flooding. The interference with electrical circuits caused loss of power and the sub plunged to deeper waters, finally imploding. There were 129 men aboard.

Other than this depressing news there was very little. A follow-up on the *Mona Lisa* exhibit which toured New York and Washington, D.C. A preview of the launch of Major L. Gordon Cooper, Jr., who was to be launched on a 22-orbit, two-day trip around the earth in *Faith 7*, the final flight of Project Mercury. A statement by the White House that aid to South Vietnam would continue and that the war might be won by the end of 1965 if the political crisis there did not significantly affect the military effort. Generals grinned at the camera, promising a firm effort by the ARVN and a short mop-up operation in the delta region. In New York, efforts to save Pennsylvania Station had failed, and the classic edifice began to fall to the wrecker's ball to make way for the new Madison Square Garden. The Pan Am Building, dedicated a month earlier, seemed the wave of the urban-blighted future. On camera, a critic decried the fall of Penn Station and declared the Pan Am an architectural atrocity, contributing to congestion in an already crowded area. Gordon agreed. The critic closed with a wistful remark that meeting beneath the clock at the Biltmore hotel, just across the street from the Pan Am, wasn't going to be much of a joy any more. Gordon laughed to himself without quite understanding why. His sympathies suddenly reversed. He had never met a girl at the Biltmore; that was the sort of empty WASP ritual open to Yalies and kids who identified with *The Catcher in the Rye*. That wasn't his world and never had been. "If that's the past, fuck it," he muttered under his breath. Penny gave him a questioning glance but said nothing. He grunted impatiently. Maybe the wine was getting to him.

Then Saul came on.

"From Yale University this evening, a startling announcement," Cronkite began. "Professor Saul Shriffer, an astrophysicist, says that there is a possibility that recent experiments have detected a message from a civilization beyond our Earth."

They switched to a shot of Saul pointing to a speck on a star chart. "The signals appear to come from the star 99 Hercules, similar to our own sun. 99 Hercules is 51 light years away. A light year is the distance—"

"They're giving it so much *time*," Penny said wonderingly.

"Shhh!"

"—light travels in a year, at a speed of 186,000 miles per second." A shot of Saul standing beside a small telescope. "The possible message was detected in a way astronomers had not anticipated—in an experiment by Professor Gordon Bernstein—"

"Oh, Jesus," Gordon groaned.

"—at the University of California at La Jolla. The experiment involved a low-temperature measurement of how atoms line up in a magnetic field. The Bernstein experiments are still being studied—it is not certain that they are, in fact, picking up some signal from a distant civilization. But Professor Shriffer, a collaborator with Bernstein who broke the code in the signal, says he wants to alert the scientific community." A picture of Saul writing equations at the blackboard. "There is a puzzling part of the message. A picture—"

A well-drawn version of the interweaving curves. Saul stood in front of it, speaking into a hand-held microphone. "Understand," he said, "we make no specific claims at this time. But we would like the help of the scientific community in unraveling what this might mean." Some brief talk about the decoding followed.

Back to Cronkite. "Several astronomers *CBS News* asked today for opinions expressed skepticism. If Professor Shriffer proves correct, though, it could mean very big news, indeed." Cronkite made his reassuring smile. "And that's the way it is, April the twelfth—"

Gordon clicked Cronkite off. "God*damn*," he said, still stunned.

"I thought it was very well done," Penny said judiciously.

"Well *done?* He wasn't supposed to use my name at all!"

"Why, don't you want any credit?"

"Credit? Christ—!" Gordon slammed a fist against the gray plaster wall with a resounding thump. "He did it all wrong, don't you see that? I had this sinking feeling when he told me, and sure enough—there's my name, tied to his crackpot theory!"

"But it's *your* measurement—"

"I told him, keep my name *out*."

"Well, it was Walter Cronkite who gave your name. Not Saul."

"Who cares who said it? I'm in it with Saul, now."

"Why didn't they have *you* on TV?" Penny asked innocently, clearly unable to see what all the fuss was about. "It was just a lot of pictures of *Saul*."

Gordon grimaced. "That's his strong suit. Simplify science down to a few sentences, screw it up any way you want, pander to the lowest common denominator—but be sure Saul Shriffer's name is in lights. Big, gaudy neon lights. *Crap*. Just—''

''He sort of hogged the credit, didn't he?''

Gordon looked at her, puzzled. ''Credit . . . ?'' He stopped pacing the room. He saw that she honestly thought his anger was over not getting his face on TV. ''Good grief.'' He felt suddenly hot and flushed. He began unbuttoning his blue broadcloth shirt and thought about what to do. No point in talking to Penny—she was light years away from understanding how scientists felt about something like this.

He rolled up the sleeves of his shirt, puffing, and walked into the kitchen, where the telephone was.

•

Gordon began with, ''Saul, I'm mad as hell.''

''Ah . . .'' Gordon could picture Saul selecting just the right words. He was good at that, but it wasn't going to do him any good this time. ''Well, I know how you feel, Gordon, I really do. I saw the network show two hours ago and it was just as much a surprise to me as it was to you. The local Boston footage was clean, no mention of your name explicitly, the way you wanted it. I called them right away after I saw the Cronkite thing and they said it got all changed around up at the network level.''

''How did the network people *know*, Saul, if you didn't—''

''Well, look, I had to tell the local people. For background info, y'know.''

''You said it wouldn't get on.''

''I did what I could, Gordon. I was going to call you.''

''Why didn't you? Why let me see it without—''

''I thought maybe you wouldn't mind so much, after seeing how much time we got.'' Saul's voice changed tone. ''It's a big *play*, Gordon! People are going to sit up and take notice.''

Gordon said sourly, ''Yeah, notice.''

''We'll get some action on that picture. We'll *crack* this thing.''

''It'll crack *us*, more likely. Saul, I said I didn't want to get dragged in. *You* said—''

''Don't you see that was unrealistic?'' Saul's voice was calm and reasonable. ''I humored you, sure, but it was bound to come out.''

''Not *this* way.''

''Believe me, this is how things *work*, Gordon. You weren't getting anywhere before, were you? Admit it.''

He took a deep breath. ''If anybody asks me, Saul, I'm going to say I don't know where the signals are coming from. That's the plain truth."

"But that's not the *whole* truth."

"*You* are talking to *me* about the whole truth? You, Saul? You, who talked me into withholding the first message?"

"That was different. I wanted to clarify the issue—"

"The issue, shit! Listen, anybody asks me, I say I don't agree with your interpretation."

"You'll release the first message?"

"I . . ." Gordon hesitated. "No, I don't want to stir things up any more." He wondered if Ramsey would continue to work on the experiments if he made the message public. Hell, for all he knew there really was some sort of national security element mixed up in this. Gordon knew he didn't want any part of that. No, it was better to drop it.

"Gordon, I can understand your feelings." The voice warmed. "All I ask is that you don't hinder what I'm trying to do. I won't get in your way, you don't get in mine."

"Well . . ." Gordon paused, his momentum blunted.

"And I truly am sorry about Cronkite and your name getting into it and all that. Okay?"

"I . . . okay," Gordon muttered, not really knowing what he was agreeing with.

chapter fifteen

1998

Gregory Markham stood with his hands behind his back, the gray of his temples giving him a remote, solemn air. The muted humming of the laboratory seemed to him a warming sound, a preoccupied buzzing of instruments which, if only in their unpredictable failures and idiosyncrasies, often resembled busy mortal workers. The laboratory was an island of sound in the hushed husk of the Cavendish, commanding all remaining resources. The Cav had ushered in the modern age, using the work of Faraday and Maxwell to create the tamed miracle of electricity. Now, Markham mused, at its center, a few men remained, trying to reach backward, swimmers against the stream.

Renfrew moved among the banks and lanes of instruments, darting from one trouble spot to another. Markham smiled at the man's energy. In part it arose from the quiet presence of Ian Peterson, who lounged back in a chair and studied the oscilloscope face where the main signal was displayed. Renfrew fretted, aware that beneath Peterson's veiled calm the man never lost his assessing eye.

Renfrew came stamping back to the central oscilloscope and glanced at the dancing jumble of noise. "Damn!" he said vehemently. "Bloody stuff won't go away."

Peterson volunteered, "Well, it's not absolutely necessary for you to send the new signals while I watch. I simply stopped by to check up on matters."

"No, no." Renfrew shifted his shoulders awkwardly under his brown jacket. Markham noted the jacket pockets were crammed with electronics parts, apparently stuck there and forgotten. "I got a good run yesterday. No reason why I shouldn't today. I transmitted that astronomical part steadily for three hours."

"I must say I don't see the necessity for that," Peterson said, "considering the difficulty in sending the truly important—"

"It's to help anyone receiving on the other end," Markham said, stepping forward. He made his face resolutely neutral, though in fact he was rather distantly amused by the way the two other men seemed to immediately hit upon an area of disagreement, as though drawn to it. "John here thinks it might help them to know when our beam will be easiest to detect. The astronomical coordinates—"

"I fully understand," Peterson cut him off. "What I *don't* understand is why you don't devote your quiet periods to the essential material."

"Such as?" Markham asked quickly.

"Tell them what we're doing, and repeat the ocean material, and—"

"We've *done* all that to *death*," Renfrew blurted. "But if they can't *receive* it, what bloody—"

"Look, look," Markham said mildly, "there's time enough to do it all, right? Agreed? When the noise goes down, the first priority should be sending that bank message of yours, and then John here can—"

"You didn't send it right away?" Peterson cried with surprise.

Renfrew said, "Ah, no, I hadn't finished the other material and—"

"Well!" Peterson seemed excited by this; he stood up quickly and paced energetically in the small space before the towering grey cabinets. "I told you about finding the note—quite surprising, I must admit."

"Yes," Markham admitted. There had been considerable agitation when Peterson appeared this morning, bearing the yellow paper. Suddenly the entire thing had seemed real to them all.

"Well," Peterson went on, "I was thinking about your trying to, ah, extend the experiment."

"Extend?" Renfrew asked.

"Yes. Don't send my message."

"Good grief," was all Markham could say.

"But, but don't you see that . . ." Renfrew's voice trailed off.

"I thought it would be an interesting experiment."

Markham said, "Sure. Very interesting. But it will set up a paradox."

"That was my idea," Peterson said swiftly.

"But a paradox is what we *don't* want," Renfrew said. "It'll bugger the whole *idea*."

"I explained that to you," Markham said to Peterson. "The switch being hung up between on and off, remember?"

"Yes, I understand that perfectly well, but—"

"Then don't suggest rubbish!" Renfrew cried. "If you want to reach the past and *know* you have done it, then leave hands off."

Peterson said with glacial calm, "The only reason you do know is that *I* went to the bank in La Jolla. The way I see the matter is that *I* have confirmed your success."

There was an awkward silence. "Ah . . . yes," Markham put in to fill the pause. He had to admit Peterson was right. It was precisely the kind of simple check he or Renfrew should have tried. But they were schooled in thinking of mechanical experiments, full of devices which operated without human intervention. The notion of asking for a confirming sign simply had not occurred to them. And now Peterson, the know-nothing administrator, had proved the whole scheme was right, and he had done it without any sophisticated thinking at all.

Markham took a deep breath. It was heady, realizing that you were doing something never accomplished before, something beyond your own understanding, but undeniably real. It had often been said that science at times put you into a kind of contact with the world that nothing else could. This morning, and Peterson's single sheet, had done that, but in a strangely different way. The triumph of an experiment was when you reached a fresh plateau of knowledge. With tachyons, though, they had no true understanding. There was only the simple note on a scrap of yellow.

"Ian, I know how you feel. It would be damned interesting to omit your message. But no one knows what that would mean. It might prevent us from doing what you want—namely convey the ocean information."

Renfrew underlined these sentiments with a "Damned right!" and turned back to the apparatus.

Peterson's eyelids lowered, as though he was deep in thought. "A good point. You know, for a moment there I thought there could be some way of finding out more that way."

"We could," Markham agreed. "But unless we do only what we understand . . ."

"Right," Peterson said. "We rule out paradoxes, agreed. But later . . ." He had a wistful look.

"Later, sure," Markham murmured. It was odd, he thought, how the players had reversed roles here. Peterson was supposedly the can-do administrator, pressing for results above all else. Yet now Peterson wanted to push the parameters of the experiment and find out some new physics.

And opposing this were Renfrew and himself, suddenly uncertain of what a paradox might produce. Ironies abounded.

•

An hour later the fine points of logic had faded, as they so often did, before the gritty details of the experiment itself. Noise smeared the flat face of the oscilloscope. Despite earnest work from the technicians the jitter in the experiment would not diminish. Unless it did, the tachyon beam would be uselessly diffuse and weak.

"Y'know," Markham murmured, leaning back in his wooden lab chair, "I think your Caltech stuff may bear on this, Ian."

Peterson looked up from reading the file with a red CONFIDENTIAL stamped across it. During the lulls he had been steadily working his way through a briefcase of paperwork. "Oh? How?"

"Those cosmological calculations—good work. Brilliant, in fact. Clustered universes. Now, suppose someone inside them is sending out tachyon signals. The tachyons can burrow right out of those smaller universes. All the tachyons have to do is pass through the event horizon of the closed-off microgeometry. Then they're free. They escape from the gravitational singularities and we can pick them up."

Peterson frowned. "These . . . microuniverses . . . are other . . . other places to live? They might be inhabited?"

Markham grinned. "Sure." He had the serene confidence of a man who has worked through the mathematics and seen the solutions. There was a blithe certainty that came from first comprehending the full Einstein field equations, arabesques of Greek letters clinging tenuously to the page, a gossamer web. They seemed insubstantial when you first saw them, a string of squiggles. Yet to follow the delicate tensors as they contracted, as the superscripts paired with subscripts, collapsing mathematically into concrete classical entities—potential; mass; forces vectoring in a curved geometry—that was a sublime experience. The iron fist of the real, inside the velvet glove of airy mathematics. Markham saw in Peterson's face the hesitant puzzlement that swam over people when they struggled to visualize ideas beyond the comforting three dimensions and Euclidean certainties which framed their world. Behind the equations were immensities of space and dust, dead but furious matter bending to the geometric will of gravity, stars like match heads exploding in a vast night, orange sparks that lit only a thin ring of child planets. The mathematics was what made it all; the pictures men carried inside their heads were useful but clumsy, cartoons of a world that was as subtle as silk, infinitely smooth and varied. After you had seen that, really seen it, the fact that worlds could exist within worlds, that universes could thrive within our own, was not so huge a riddle. The mathematics buoyed you.

Markham said, "I think that may be an explanation for the anomalous noise level. It's not thermally generated at all, if I'm right. Instead, the noise comes from tachyons. The indium antimonide sample isn't just *transmitting* tachyons, it's *receiving* them. There's a tachyon background we've neglected."

"A background?" Renfrew asked. "From what?"

"Let's see. Try the correlator."

Renfrew made a few adjustments and stepped back from the oscilloscope. "That should do it."

"Do what?" Peterson demanded.

"This is a lock-in coherence analyzer," Markham explained. "It culls out the genuine noise in the indium sample—sound wave noise, that is—and brings up any signals out of the random noise background."

Renfrew stared intently at the oscilloscope face. A complex wave form wavered across the scale. "It seems to be a series of pulses strung out at regular intervals," he said. "But the signal decays in time." He pointed at a fluid line which faded into the noise level as it neared the right side of the screen.

"Quite regular, yes," Markham said. "Here's one peak, then a pause, then two peaks together, then nothing again, then four nearly on top of each other, then nothing. Strange."

"What do you think it is?" Peterson asked.

"Not ordinary background, that's clear," Renfrew answered.

Markham said, "It's coherent, can't be natural."

Renfrew: "No. More like . . ."

"A code," Markham finished. "Let's take some of this down." He began writing on a clip-board. "Is this a real-time display?"

"No, I just rigged it to take a sample of the noise for a hundred-microsecond interval." Renfrew reached for the oscilloscope dials. "Would you like another interval?"

"Wait till I copy this."

Peterson asked, "Why don't you just photograph it?"

Renfrew looked at him significantly. "We have no film.

There's a shortage and priority doesn't go to laboratories these days, you know.''

"Ian, take this down," Markham interrupted.

•

Within an hour the results were obvious. The noise was in fact a sum of many signals, each overlaid on the rest. Occasionally a short stuttering group of pulses would appear, only to be swallowed in a storm of rapid jiggling.

"Why are there so many competing signals?" Peterson asked.

Markham shrugged. He wrinkled his nose in an unconscious effort to work his glasses back up. It gave him an unintentional expression of sudden, vast distaste. "I suppose it's possible they're from the far future. But the vest pocket universe sounds good to me, too.''

Renfrew said, "I wouldn't put much weight on a new astrophysical theory. Those fellows speculate in ideas like stock brokers.''

Markham nodded. "Granted, they often take a grain of truth and blow it up into a kind of intellectual puffed rice. But this time they have a point. There are unexplained sources of infrared emission, far out among the galaxies. The microuniverses would look like that.'' He made a tent of his fingers and smiled into it, his favorite academic gesture. At times like these it was comforting to have a touch of ritual to get you through. "That scope of yours shows a hundred times the ordinary noise you expected, John. I like the notion that we're not unique, and there is a background of tachyon signals. Signals from different times, yes. And from those microscopic universes, too.''

"It comes and goes, though," Renfrew observed. "I can still transmit a fraction of the time.''

"Good," Peterson said. He had not spoken for some while. "Keep on with it, then.''

Renfrew said, "I hope the fellows back in 1963 haven't got the detector sensitivity to study this noise. If they stick to our signals—which should stand out above this background, when we're transmitting properly—they'll be all right.''

"Greg," Peterson mused, his eyes remote, "there's another point.''

"Oh? What?''

"You keep talking about the small universes inside ours and how we're overhearing their tachyon messages.''

"Right.''

"Isn't that a bit self-centered? How do we know we, in turn, are not a vest pocket universe inside somebody else's?"

●

Gregory Markham slipped away from the Cav in early afternoon. Peterson and Renfrew were still unable to resist sniping at each other. Peterson was obviously drawn to the experiment, despite his automatic habit of distancing himself. Renfrew appreciated Peterson's support, but kept pushing for more. Markham found the ornate dance between the two men comic, all the more so because it was virtually unconscious. With their class-calibrated speech patterns, the two men had squared off at the first differing vowel. If Renfrew had stayed a laborer's son he would have got along smoothly with Peterson, each knowing his time-ordained role. As a man swimming in exotic academic waters, however, Renfrew had no referents. Science had a way of bringing about such conflicts. You could come out of nowhere and make your mark, without having learned any new social mannerisms. Fred Hoyle's stay at Cambridge had been a case in point. Hoyle had been an astronomer in the old mold of eccentric-seeker-after-truth, advancing controversial theories and sweeping aside the cool, rational mannerisms when they didn't suit his mood. Renfrew might well prove as remarkable as Hoyle, a working-class salmon swimming upstream all the way, if this experiment went through. Most rising scientists from obscure backgrounds nowadays kept a neutral, bland exterior; it was safer. Renfrew didn't. The big modern research teams depended for progress on well-organized, smooth-running, large-scale operations, whose stability demanded a minimum of upsetting—what was the jargon— "interpersonal relationships." Renfrew was a loner with a sandpaper psyche. The odd point was that Renfrew was quite civil towards most people; only the deliberate flaunting of class symbols by such as Peterson set him off. Markham had watched class friction worsen in England for decades, catching glimpses on his occasional visits. Time seemed to strengthen the ties of class, much to the confusion of the condescending Marxists who tended the lumbering government programs. The explanation seemed clear to Markham: in the steepening economic slide, following on the rich years of North Sea oil, people stressed differences, in order to keep alive their sense of self-worth. *Us* against *Them* stirred the blood. Better to play that distracting, antique game than to face the gray grip of a closing future.

Markham shrugged, mulling this over, and walked along the Coton footpath back toward the solemn spires of town. He was an American and thus exempt from the subtle class rituals, a visitor given a temporary passport. A year here had accustomed him to the language differences; now phrases like "the committee are" and "the government have" didn't cause a stumble as the eye slid through a sentence. He now recognized Peterson's skeptical arch of the eyebrow and rising, dry, "Hmmmm?" as a well-honed social weapon. The graceful, adroit sound of Peterson's "lehzure" and "shedule" were certainly far better than the mechanical quack-quack of American administrators, who would call any information an "input," were always "addressing a problem," submitted proposals as a "package" but didn't always "buy it," and who engaged in "dialogue" with audiences; if you objected to such deliberately clanky talk, they answered that this was "only semantics."

Markham thrust his hands into his jacket pockets and tramped on. He had been irked by a balky calculation in mathematical physics for days now, and wanted a long, solitary walk to help sweep his irritation away. He passed a construction site, where overalled chimps carried stonework and did the odd heavy job. Remarkable, what the tinkering with the DNA had done in the last few years.

As he approached a bus queue something caught his attention. A black man in tennis shoes was standing at the end of the line, eyes dancing, his head jerking as if on wires. Markham came up close to him and muttered, "Bobby round the corner," and moved on. The man froze. "Huh? Wha?" He looked wildly around. He eyed Markham. A hesitation, then he decided—he raced off in the opposite direction. Markham smiled. The standard tactic was to wait until the bus hauled up and the queue's attention was focused on getting aboard. Then you grabbed purses away from a few women and left in high gear. Before the crowd could redirect its attention you were streets away. Markham had seen the same maneuver in Los Angeles. He realized, a bit ruefully, that he might not have recognized the setup if the man hadn't been black.

He strolled down the High Street. Beggars' hands appeared magically when they saw his American jacket, and then disappeared quickly as he scowled. On the corner of St. Andrews and Market streets was Barrett's barber shop, a faded sign proclaiming, "Barrett is willing to shave all, and only, men unwilling to shave themselves." Markham laughed. This was a Cambridge insiders' joke, a reference to the local logical trickery of Bertrand Russell and the mathematicians of a century ago. It yanked him back towards the problem that was bothering him, the tangle of reason surrounding Renfrew's experiments.

The obvious question was, "But what about Barrett? Who can shave poor old Barrett?" If Barrett were willing to shave himself, and if the sign were true, then he was *not* willing to shave himself. And if Barrett wouldn't shave himself, then according to his sign he *was* willing to shave himself. Russell had devised this paradox, and tried to solve it by inventing what he called a "meta-sign" which said, "Barrett shall be excluded from the class of all men to whom the first sign refers." That sewed up the problem nicely for Barrett, but in the real world things weren't so easy. Peterson's suggestion this morning, about not sending the message about the bank, had disturbed Markham more than he had wanted to show. The trouble with the whole tachyon theory was that the causal loop idea didn't fit our own perception of time as moving forward. What if they *didn't* send the bank message? The neat little loop, with arrows passing from future to past and back again, was flawed. It didn't have any human beings in it. The aim of a modern physical theory was to talk about reality as independent of the observer —at least, as long as quantum mechanics was left out. But if Peterson was in the causal loop, he had the ability to change his mind at any time, and change the whole damn thing. *Or did he?* Markham paused, looking through the filmed glass at a boy getting his amber hair cut. Where was human free will in this puzzle?

The equations were mute. If Renfrew succeeded, how would the things around them change? Markham had a sudden, sinking vision of a world in which the ocean bloom simply had not happened. He and Renfrew and Peterson would emerge from the Cav to find that no one knew what they were babbling about. *Ocean bloom? We solved that ages ago.* So they would be madmen, a curious trio sharing a common delusion. Yet to be consistent, the equations said that sending the message *couldn't* have too great an effect. It couldn't cut off the very reason for sending the tachyons in the first place. So there had to be some self-consistent picture, in which Renfrew still got his initial idea, and approached the World Council, and yet . . .

Markham shook himself out of the mood, feeling an odd chill run through him. There was something deeper here, some crucial missing physics.

He walked rapidly away, disturbed. A cricket game lazily wound through the afternoon on the large pie-shaped ground known as Parker's Piece. The mathematician G. H. Hardy had watched games there a century before, Markham mused, and often lazed away the afternoon just as he was doing now. Markham could understand the motivation of the game, but not the details. He had never got straight the cricket jargon—square leg, silly mid-on, silly mid-off, cover point, short extra cover—and still never quite knew when a good play was made. He walked behind the ranks of spectators, who were slumped in their canvas chairs, and wondered what the cricket watchers of a century ago would've thought of the England of now. He suspected, though, that like most people even today, they assumed that tomorrow would be pretty much the same as the present.

Markham angled down Regent Street and past the University Botanic Garden. Beyond lay a boys' school. *Dispensing the norms and graces of the upper classes*, in a king's ancient phrase. He strolled through the arched entranceway and paused at the school announcements board. *The following have lost their personal possessions. They will call at the Prefect's Study by Thursday 4th June.*

No "please." No unnecessary softenings; simply a direct statement. Markham could imagine the brief conversation: "I'm sorry, you see—" "Standard punishment. Fifty lines, best handwriting. I'll have them tomorrow at break." And the student would grind out, *My carelessness with my personal property will cease.*

The fact that the student might well use one of the recent voice-writers for nearly all his school work didn't matter; the principle reigned.

Odd, how forms held on when everything else—buildings, politics, fame—fell away. Maybe that was the strength of this place. There was a timelessness here, too fragile for California's dry air to hold. Now that full summer had arrived with a flourish, the mannered ways of the schools and colleges seemed even older, a slice of worn time. He found his own spirits lifting at the release from the endless raw winter and the rainy spring.

He felt his mind veering away from the tachyon question, seeking refuge in this comfortable aura of the past. It was different for him here, he knew. Englishmen were fish swimming in this sea of the past. For them it was a palpable presence, a living extension, commenting on events like a half-heard stage whisper. Americans regarded the past as a parenthesis within the running sentences of the present, an aside, something out of the flow.

He walked back towards the colleges, letting this feel of the press of time seep into him. He and Jan had been to High Table at several of the colleges, the ultimate Anglophile experience. Memorial plate that gleamed like quicksilver, and crested goblets. In the after-dinner room of polished wood, gilt frames held glowering portraits of the college founders. In the great dining hall Jan had been surprised to find de facto segregation: Etonians at one table, Harrovians at another, the lesser public schools' alumni at a third, and, finally, state school graduates and everyone else at a motley last table. To an American in such a citadel of education, after the decades of ferocious equality-at-all-costs politics, it seemed strange. There persisted a reliance on inherited advantages, and even the idea that such a system was an inherited virtue as well. The past hung on. You could be quite up to the minute, quite knowing about the zack-o latin riffs of Lady Delicious, and yet sit quietly and comfortably in choir stalls of King's College chapel listening to cherubic lads in Elizabethan ruffs try to shatter the stained glass with treble attacks. It seemed that in a muzzy sense the past was still here, that they were all connected, and that the perception of the future as a tangible thing lived in the present, as well.

Markham relaxed a moment, letting the idea inside drift up from his subconscious. Walking was the gentle jog his mind needed; he had used the effect before. Something . . . something about the reality needing to be independent of the observer . . .

He glanced up. A swarming yellow cloud, moving fast and low over the gray towers, pressed shadows against the flanks of Great St. Mary's church. Bells pealed a cascade of sound through momentarily chilled air; the cloud seemed to suck heat from the breeze.

He watched the curling fingers of fog that dissolved overhead in the trail of the cloud. Then, abruptly, he had it. The nub of the problem was that observer, the guy who had to see things objectively. Who was *he?* In quantum mechanics, the equations themselves told you nothing about which way time should run. Once you made a measurement, an experiment had to be thought of from that moment on as a thing which generated probabilities. All the equations could tell you was how probable a "later" event was. That was the essence of the quantum. Schrödinger's equation could evolve things either forward in time, or backward. Only when the observer poked his finger in and made a measurement did something fix the direction of the flow of time. If the all-powerful observer measured a particle and found it at position x, then the particle had to be given a small push by the observer, in the very act of observing. That was Heisenberg's uncertainty principle. You could not tell precisely how much of a push the observer had given the wretched particle, so its future position was somewhat uncertain. Schrödinger's equation described the set of probabilities about where the particle would appear next. The probabilities were found by picturing a wave, moving forward in time and making it possible for the particle to appear in many different places in the future. A probability wave. The old billiard-ball picture, in which the particle moved with Newtonian certainty to its next point, was simply false, misleading. The particle's most probable location was, in fact, exactly the same as the Newtonian position—but other paths were possible. Less likely, yes, but possible. The problem came when the observer next poked his finger in and made a second measurement. He found the particle in *one* place, not spread out among a choice of spots. Why? Because the observer was always considered essentially Newtonian himself—a "classical measurer," as the tech chat went.

Markham grinned broadly as he turned up King's Parade. There was a trapdoor in that argument. The classical observer didn't exist. Everything in the world was quantum-mechanical. Everything moved according to waves of probability. So the massive, untouched experimenter himself got pushed back on. He received an uncertainly known push from the outraged particle, and that meant the observer, too, was quantum-mechanical. He was part of the system. The experiment was bigger, and more complex, than the simple ideas of the past. *Everything* was part of the experiment; nobody could stand apart from it. You could talk about a second observer, bigger than the first one, who was unaffected by the experiment—but that simply removed the problem one step further. The final fallback was to regard the whole *universe* as the "observer," so that it was a self-consistent system. But that meant you had to solve the entire problem of the motion of the universe *at once,* without breaking it up into convenient, separate experiments.

The essence of the problem was, what made the particle appear in only one spot? Why did it pick out one of the possible states and not another? It was as though the universe had many possible ways it could go, and something made it choose a particular one.

Markham stopped, studying the dizzy height of Great St. Mary's. A student peered over the edge, a knobby head against the steel blue.

What was the right analogy?

The tachyon beam brought up the same problem. If his ideas were right there was a kind of probability wave traveling back and forth in time. Setting up a paradox kept the wave going in a loop, setting the system into a kind of dumbfounded frenzy, unable to decide on what state it should be in. *Something* had to choose one. Was there some analogy here, a kind of unmoved observer, who set time flowing forward rather than backward?

If there was, then the paradox had an answer. Somehow the laws of physics had to provide an answer. But the equations stood mute, inscrutable. As was always the case, the basic question answered by the mathematics was *how*, not *why*. Did the unmoved mover have to step in? Who was he—God? He might as well be.

Markham shook his head in frustration. The ideas swarmed like bees, but he could not pin them. Abruptly he growled and swerved across a lane of bicycling students, into Bowes & Bowes.

•

The selection was getting thin; the publishing business was in trouble, retreating before the TV tide. A woman tending the register caught his eye; quite sexy. Beyond his age range, though, he thought ruefully. He was getting to the stage where ambitions nearly always exceeded his region of probable success.

The tachyon thing troubled him as he walked home, across the Cav and through the bathing grounds. A greensward, named Lammas Land for some ancient reason, lay beneath a moist, warm afternoon. There was a stillness, as though the year were poised motionless at the top of a long slope up which it had climbed out of winter's grip, and from which it must soon descend. He turned south, towards Grantchester, where the nuclear reactor was still a-building. It seemed that with all the delays they would never finish the squashed ping-pong ball that would cup the simmering core. The meadows around it were a pocket of rural peace. Cows standing in the inky shade of trees swished their tails to banish flies. There were drowsy sounds, murmurs of wood pigeons, a drone of a plane, buzzings and clickings. The air was layered with scents of thistles, yarrow, ragwort, tansy. Colors leaped in ambush from the lush grass: yellow camomile, blue harebells, the scarlet pimpernel of literary fame.

Jan was reading when he arrived home. They made a lazy sort of love in the close upper bedroom, dampening the sheets. Afterward, the image of the woman in Bowes & Bowes flickered through his dozing mind. A musky fullness hung in the air.

The long day stretched on to ten in the evening, holding off the night. Markham was reminded, as he checked a calculation in the pale late light, that elsewhere on the planet someone else was paying for these longest of summer days in the hard coinage of frozen winter nights. *Debts mount,* he thought. And as he read that evening of the spreading bloom, it seemed a vast one was coming due.

chapter sixteen

APRIL 8, 1963

Gordon was late for a faculty senate committee meeting, and hurrying, when Bernard Carroway intersected his trajectory. "Oh, Gaw-dun, I need to speak with you." Something in Bernard's tone made Gordon stop.

"I heard about this thing you have on with Shriffer. Saw a diddle about it on the late news—one of my students rang me to have a look." Carroway clasped his hands behind his back, the gesture giving him a judicial appearance.

"Well . . . yes, I think Saul went a little overboard—"

"Glad to hear you say so!" Bernard was suddenly jovial. "I spotted it as a, well, Saul is given to excess in this sort of thing, you know." He peered at Gordon for confirmation.

"Sometimes."

"Couldn't imagine anything more unlikely, myself—nuclear magnetic resonance experiments, he said? Bloody odd way to communicate."

"Saul thinks part of it, ah, the message, is astronomical coordinates. You'll remember when I came to you—"

"That's the basis of it, then? Merely some coordinates?"

"Well, he did break down the pulses into that picture," Gordon admitted lamely.

"Oh, that. Looks for all the world like a child's scrawling to me."

"No, there's structure there. As for the content, we don't—"

"I think you have to be careful in this, Gaw-dun. Understand, I *like* some of Shriffer's work. But I and others in the astronomical community feel he's, well, perhaps rather overstepped himself in this radio communication thing. And now this!—finding messages in nuclear resonance experiments! I think Shriffer's quite exceeded the bounds."

Bernard nodded seriously and peered down at his feet. Gordon wondered what to say. Bernard had a gravity about him that warded off direct contradiction. He carried his excess weight with an aggressive energy that seemed to dare anyone to make anything of it. He was short with the kind of barrel chest which, when he relaxed, would suddenly reveal itself to be merely an elevated stomach, held aloft with resolve. It sagged now as Gordon watched; Bernard had forgotten it in his concentration on the sins of Shriffer. His herringbone jacket bulged, the buttons strained. Gordon imagined he could hear Bernard's belt creak with the sudden new pressure. This torture of his wardrobe was redeemed by the unconscious flush of pleasure which spread across Bernard's serious face as his belly descended.

"It puts a black eye on the whole game, you know," Bernard said abruptly, looking up. "Black eye."

"I think until we get to the bottom—"

"The bottom is that Shriffer's foxed you in with him, Gawdun. I'm sure none of it was your idea. I'm sorry our department has to be mixed in with his foolery. You'll put paid to it, if you're wise."

This advice delivered, Bernard nodded and walked on.

●

Cooper glanced up as Gordon came into the laboratory. "Mornin', how are you?" Cooper said.

Gordon reflected sourly that people routinely asked you how you were, as a formal greeting, when in fact they had not the slightest interest. "I feel like crap on a soda cracker," Gordon muttered. Cooper frowned, puzzled. "You saw the TV last night?" Gordon asked.

Cooper pursed his lips. "Yes," he said, as though he were giving a good deal away.

"I didn't mean to let it get out of our hands like that. Shriffer took the ball and ran with it."

"Well, maybe he scored a touchdown."

"You think so?"

"No," Cooper admitted. He leaned over and adjusted a setting on an oscilloscope, rather obviously having said all he wanted to. Gordon shrugged his shoulders as though they had weights attached. He would not try to puncture Cooper's blithe goyische brass, so well concealed beneath the cloak of unconcern.

"Any new data?" Gordon asked, cramming his fists into his pants pockets and pacing around the lab, inspecting, feeling a certain private pleasure at the thought that here, at least, he knew what was happening and what mattered.

"I've got some good resonance lines. I'm carrying on with the measurements we agreed I should make."

"Ah, good." *See, I'm only doing what we agreed I should. You won't catch* me *with an unexpected result, nossir.*

Gordon paced some more, checking the instruments. The nitrogen dewar popped with its brittle cold, transformers hummed, pumps chugged bovinely. Gordon read through Cooper's lab notebook, looking for possible sources of error. He wrote out from memory the simple theoretical expressions which Cooper's data should confirm. The numbers fell reassuringly close to the theoretical mark. Beside Cooper's schoolboy neatness Gordon's sprawling handwriting seemed a raffishly human intrusion on the neat, remorseless rectangularity of the gridded pages. Cooper worked in precise ballpoint; Gordon used a Parker fountain pen, even for quick calculations such as this. He preferred the elegant slick slide and sudden choking death of pens, and the touch of importance their broad blue lines gave to a page. One of the reasons he had switched from white shirts to blue was the doomed hope that ink stains on the left breast pocket would be easier to conceal.

Working this way, standing up amid the careless tangle of the ongoing experiment and scribbling in a notebook, calmed him. For a moment he was again back at Columbia, a son of Israel loyal to Newton's cause. But then he had checked the last of Cooper's numbers and there was nothing more to do. The moment passed. He sank back into the world.

"Do you have the summary I asked you to write up for your candidacy exam?" he asked Cooper.

"Oh, yeah. Almost done. I'll get it to you tomorrow."

"Good. Good." He hesitated, not wanting to leave. "Say, ah —you haven't got anything but conventional resonance curves? No—"

"Message?" Cooper smiled very slightly. "No, no message."

Gordon nodded, looked around absently, and left.

●

He did not return to his office, but instead took a roundabout route to the Physical Sciences Library. It was on the ground floor of Building B and had a diffused, temporary air. Everything at UCLJ felt that way, compared to Columbia's hallowed corridors, and now there was talk that even the campus name would change. La Jolla was being annexed by the jumble of San Diego. The city council spoke of the savings in fire and police protection, but to Gordon it seemed one more step in the steady homogenizing, the Losangelization of what had before been pleasant and charming distinctions. So UCLJ would become UCSD and something more than a mere name would be lost.

He spent an hour browsing through the new crop of physics journals and then looked up a few references relating to a back-burner idea he had let fall by the wayside. After a while he had no more real business and lunch was still an hour away. Somewhat reluctantly he returned to his office, not going up to the third floor to collect the morning mail but instead walking between the Physics and Chemistry buildings, passing under the architect's wet dream of a connecting bridge. The graceful pattern of linked hexagons caught the eye, he had to give it that. Somehow, though, it looked uncomfortably like the scaffolding for some enormous insect's burrow, a design pattern for a future wasp nest.

He was unsurprised to see his office door open, for he usually left it that way. The one distinction he had noted in the behavior pattern of humanists vs. scientists was the matter of doors: humanists closed them, discouraging casual encounters. Gordon wondered if this had a deep psychological significance, or, more likely, was meant by the humanists to conceal when they were on campus. As nearly as Gordon could tell, the answer was: seldom. They all seemed to work at home.

Isaac Lakin was standing in Gordon's office, back to the door, studying the wasp's scaffolding that loomed above. "Oh, Gordon," he murmured, turning, "I've been looking for you."

"I can imagine why."

Lakin sat on the edge of Gordon's desk; Gordon remained standing. "Oh?"

"The Shriffer thing."

"Yes." Lakin gazed up at the fluorescents and pursed his lips, as though carefully selecting the right words.

"It got out of hand," Gordon said helpfully.

"Yes, I'm afraid so."

"Shriffer said he would keep me and UCLJ out of the news. The sole aim was to circulate that drawing."

"Well, it's done more than that."

"How so?"

"I've had a number of calls. So would you, if you stayed in your office."

"Who from?"

"Colleagues. People working in the nuclear resonance community. They all want to know what's going on. So, I might add, do I."

"Well—" Gordon summarized the second message and how

Shriffer got involved. "I'm afraid Saul took things further than they should properly have gone, but—"

"I would say so. Our contract monitor called, as well."

"So what?"

"So *what?* True, he does not have very much real power. But our colleagues do. They pass judgment."

"Again, so what?"

Lakin shrugged. "You will have to deny Shriffer's conclusions."

"Huh? Why?"

"Because they are false."

"I don't *know* that."

"You should not make statements you cannot prove to be true."

"But to deny them is also untrue."

"You consider his hypothesis likely?"

"No." Gordon shuffled uneasily. He had hoped he would not have to say anything, one way or the other.

"Then refuse to go along with it."

"I can't deny we got that message. It came through loud and clear."

Lakin raised his eyebrows with a European disdain, as though to say, *How can I reason with a person such as this?* In response, Gordon unconsciously hitched at his pants and hooked his thumbs into his belt at his hips, flexing his shoulders. Absurdly, he had a sudden image of Marlon Brando in the same pose, squinting at some thug who had just crossed him. Gordon blinked and tried to think of what to say next.

"You realize," Lakin said carefully, "that talk of a message will—aside from making you appear a fool—cast doubt on the spontaneous resonance effect?"

"Maybe."

"Some of my telephone calls were specifically about precisely this point."

"Maybe."

Lakin glanced at Gordon sharply. "I believe you should reflect upon it."

Gordon murmured impishly, "To shine is better than to reflect."

Lakin stiffened. "What are you—"

The telephone rang. Gordon seized it with relief. He answered the caller in monosyllables. "Fine. Three o'clock, then. My office number is 118."

When he hung up he looked levelly at Lakin and said, "*San Diego Union.*"

"A dreadful paper."

"Granted. They want some background on the story."

"You're *seeing* them?"

"Sure."

Lakin sighed. "What will you say?"

"I'll tell them I don't know where the hell the stuff is coming from."

"Unwise. Unwise."

●

After Lakin had left Gordon wondered at the sudden phrase that had forced its way into his mouth: *To shine is better than to reflect.* Where had he heard it before? Penny, probably; it sounded like some literary remark. But did he mean it? Was he after fame, like Shriffer? He was conditioned to accept a certain amount of guilt over something like that—that was the cliché, wasn't it, Jews feel guilty, their mothers train them to? But guilt wasn't it, no; his intuition told him that. His instinct was that something lurked in the message, it *was* real. He had been over this ground a hundred times and still he had to trust his own judgment, his own data. And if to Lakin the subject was foolish, if Gordon appeared to be a fraud—well, tough; so be it.

He hitched his thumbs into his belt and gazed out at the California insect engineering and felt good, pretty damn good.

●

After the *San Diego Union* reporter went away Gordon still felt confident, though with some effort. The reporter asked a lot of dumb questions, but that was par for the course. Gordon stressed the uncertainties; the *Union* wanted clear answers to cosmic questions, preferably in one quotable sentence. To Gordon the important point was how science was done, how answers were always provisional, always awaiting the outcome of future experiments. The *Union* expected adventure and excitement and more evidence of a university on its way to greatness. Across this gulf some information flowed, but not much.

He was sorting his mail, putting some into his briefcase for reading in the evening, when Ramsey came by.

After a few preliminaries—Ramsey seemed earnestly interested in the weather—he slipped a page from an envelope and said, "This the picture Shriffer showed last night?"

Gordon studied it. "Where did you get it?"

"From your student, Cooper."

"And where did *he* get one?"

"He says, from Shriffer."

"When?"

"A few weeks back. Shriffer came to him to check the dots and dashes, he says."

"Um." Gordon supposed he should have known Shriffer would check it. That was a reasonable precaution. "Okay, it's a small point. What about it?"

"Well, I don't think it makes any sense, but then I haven't really had any time to—look, what I mean is, what's this Shriffer guy doing?"

"He decoded a second message. He thinks it comes from a star called 99 Hercules that—"

"Yeah, yeah, I know. Point is, why's he going on TV?"

"To figure out that picture."

"He doesn't know about the first message, the one I'm working on?"

"Sure he does."

"Well, cripes—this stuff on the TV, it's garbage, right?"

Gordon shrugged. "I'm an agnostic. I don't know what it means, that's what I just told a reporter."

Ramsey looked worried. "You think this is the straight scoop, though? The stuff I'm working on is okay?"

"It's okay."

"Shriffer's just an asshole?"

"I'm an agnostic," Gordon said, suddenly tired. Everybody was asking him for the eternal, fixed Truth and he had none for sale.

"Geez. Some of the biochem is starting to make some sense, y'know? The li'l experiment I put one of my students on is panning out some, is how I know. Then this comes along . . ."

"Don't worry about it. The Shriffer message may be pure bullshit for all I know. Look, I've been rushed and—" Gordon wiped his brow—"it's just plain gotten away from me. Keep on with the experiments, okay?"

"Yeah, okay. Rushed why?"

"Shriffer. He thinks he's decoded something and all of a sudden he's on TV. Wasn't my idea."

"Oh. Oh, yeah. Makes it different." Ramsey seemed mollified. Then his face clouded again. "What about the first message?"

"What about it?"

"You releasing it?"

"No. No plans to."

"Good. Good."

"You can have all the time to work on it you want."

"Fine." Ramsey held out his hand as though a deal had just been concluded. "I'll be in touch."

Gordon shook the hand solemnly.

●

The bit of playacting with Ramsey had bothered him at first, but he realized it was part of dealing with people: you had to adopt their voice, see things from their point of view, if you wanted to communicate at all. Ramsey saw all this as a game with the first message as privileged information, and Shriffer as simply an interloper. Well, for the purposes of Ramsey's universe, so be it. At one time when he was younger Gordon would have been rudely cynical about striking a stance purely to convince someone. Now matters seemed different. He wasn't lying to Ramsey. He wasn't withholding information. He was merely tailoring the way he described the events. Adolescent clichés about truth and beauty and bird thou never wert were just crap, simplistic categories. When you had to get something done you talked the talk. That was the way it was. Ramsey would keep on with the experiments without fretting over unknowables, and, with luck, they might find out something.

He was walking away from the Physics building, toward Torrey Pines Road where his Chevy was parked, when a slight figure raised a hand in salutation. Gordon turned and recognized Maria Goeppert Mayer, the only woman in the department. She had suffered a stroke some time before and now appeared seldom, moving ghostlike through the hallways, one side partially impaired, her speech slurred. Her face sagged and she seemed tired, but in the eyes Gordon could see a dancing intelligence that let nothing slip by.

"Do you believe your . . . re . . . results?" she asked.

Gordon hesitated. Under her penetrating gaze he felt himself beneath the microscope of history; this woman had come out of Poland, passed through the war years, worked on the separation of uranium isotopes for the Manhattan Project at Columbia, done research with Fermi just before cancer caught him. She had come through all that and more: her husband, Joe, was a brilliant chemist and held a full professorship at Chicago, while she was denied a faculty position and had to be content with a research associate position. He wondered suddenly if she had been irritated at that while she did the work on the shell model of the nucleus that made her famous. Compared to what she faced, his troubles were nothing. He bit his lip.

"Yes. Yes, I think so. Something . . . something is trying to reach us. I don't know what."

She nodded. There was a serene confidence in the way she did it, despite her numbed side, that clutched at something in Gordon. He blinked in sunset's lancing light, and the glow turned to warm water in his eyes. "Good. Good," she murmured with a halting tongue, and moved away, still smiling at him.

•

He arrived home just after Penny, and found her changing clothes. He dumped his briefcase, carrying the cares of the day, into a corner. "Where to?" he asked.

"Surf's up."

"Christ, it's getting dark."

"Waves don't know that."

He sagged against the wall. Her energy staggered him. This was the facet of California he found hardest: the sheer physicality of it, the momentum.

"Come with me," she said, pulling on a French bikini brief and a T-shirt. "I'll show you how. You can body surf."

"Uh," he said, not wanting to mention that he had looked forward to a glass of white wine and the evening news. After all, he thought—and suddenly not quite liking the thought—there might be a followup on the Shriffer story.

"Come *on*."

•

At Wind 'n Sea beach he watched her carve a path down the slope of a descending wave and wondered at it: a frail girl, mastering a blunt board and harnessing the blind momentum of the ocean, suspended in air as though by some miracle of Newtonian dynamics. It seemed a liquid mystery, and yet he felt he should be unsurprised; it was, after all, classical dynamics. The gang from around the pump house was out in full force, riding their boards as they awaited the perfect oncoming toppling ton of water, brown bodies deft on the white boards. Gordon sweated through the remorseless routine of the Royal Canadian Air Force exercises, assuring himself that this was just as good as the obvious pleasure the surfers took in their splitting of the waves. The required situps and pushups done, he ran over the swaths of sand, puffing to himself and in a muzzy way trying to unscramble the events of the day. They refused his simple tug: the day would not break down into simple paradigm. He halted, gasping in the salt air, eyebrows dark and beaded with sweat. Penny walked forward on her board, perched in the thick air, and waved to him. Behind her the ocean cupped itself upright and caught her board in a smooth hand, tilting it forward. She teetered, wobbled, arms fanned the air: she fell. The soapy churn engulfed her. The slick white board tumbled forward, end over end, driven by momentum's grasp. Penny's head appeared, hair plastered like a cap to her head, blinking, teeth white and bared. She laughed.

●

As they dressed he said, "What's for supper?"

"Whatever you want."

"Artichoke salad, then pheasant, then a brandy trifle."

"I hope you can make all that."

"Okay, what do *you* want?"

"I'm going out. I'm not hungry."

"Huh?" A dull dawning of surprise. *He* was hungry.

"I'm going to a meeting."

"What for?"

"A meeting. A rally, I guess."

"For what?" he persisted.

"For Goldwater."

"*What?*"

"You may have heard of him. He's running for President."

"You're kidding." He stopped, foot in midair, halfway into his jockey shorts. Then, realizing how comical he must look, he stepped in and pulled them up. "He's a simple-minded—"

"Babbitt?"

No, Sinclair Lewis wouldn't have occurred to him. "Just leave it at simple-minded."

"Ever read *The Conscience of a Conservative?* He has a lot of things to say in there."

"No, I didn't. But look, when you have Kennedy, with the test ban treaty and some really *new* ideas in foreign policy, the Alliance for Progress—"

"Plus the Bay of Pigs, the Berlin Wall, that pig-eyed little brother of his—"

"Oh, come on. Goldwater is just a pawn of big business."

"He'll stand up to the communists."

Gordon sat down on their bed. "You don't *believe* that stuff, do you?"

Penny wrinkled her nose, a gesture Gordon knew meant her mind was set. "Who sent our men into South Vietnam? What about what happened to Cliff and Bernie?"

"If Goldwater gets in there'll be a million Cliffs and Bernies over there."

"Goldwater will *win* over there, not just fool around."

169

"Penny, the thing to do over there is *cut our losses*. Why support a dictator like Diem?"

"All I know is, friends of mine are getting killed."

"And Big Barry will change all that."

"Sure. I think he's solid. He'll stop socialism in our country."

Gordon lay back on the bed, spouting a resigned *whoosh* of disbelief. "Penny, I know you think I'm some sort of New York communist, but I fail to see—"

"I'm late already. Linda invited me to this cocktail party for Goldwater, and I'm going. You want to go?"

"Good God, no."

"Okay, I'm going."

"You're a literature student who's for Goldwater? Come *on*."

"I know I don't fit your stereotypes, but that's *your* problem, Gordon."

"Jeezus."

"I'll be back in a few hours." She combed back her hair and checked her pleated skirt and walked out of the bedroom, stiff and energetic. Gordon lay on the bed watching her leave, unable to tell whether she was serious or not. She slammed the front door so hard it rattled, and he decided that she was.

•

It was an unlikely match from the start. They had met at a wine and chips party in a beach cottage on Prospect Street, a hundred yards from the La Jolla Art Museum. (The first time Gordon went to the Museum he hadn't noticed the sign and assumed it was simply another gallery, somewhat better than most; to call it and the Met both museums seemed a deliberate joke.) His first impression was of her assembled order: neat teeth; scrupulously clear skin; effortless hair. A contrast with the thin, conflicted women of New York he had seen, "encountered"—a favorite word, then—and finally been daunted by. Penny seemed luminous and open, capable of genuinely breezy talk, uncluttered with the delivered opinions of *The New York Times* or the latest graduate seminar on What Is Important. In a flowered cocktail dress with a square neckline, the straight lines mitigated by a curving string of pearls, her glowing tan emitted warm yellow radiations that seeped through him in the wan light, life from a distant star. He was well into a bottle of some rotgut red by that time and probably overestimated the magic of the occasion, but she did seem to loom in the shadowed babble of the room. In better lit circumstances they might not have hit it off. This time, though, she was quick and artful and unlike any woman he had ever met before. Her flat California vowels were a relief from the congested accents of the east, and her sentences rolled out with an easy perfection he found entrancing. Here was the real thing: a naturalness, a womanly fervor, a clarity of vision. And anyway, she had ample, athletic thighs that moved under the silky dress as though her whole body were constrained by the cloth, capable of joyful escape. He didn't know much about women—Columbia's notorious deficiency—and as he knocked back more wine and made more conversation he wondered at himself, at her, at what was happening. It was uncomfortably like a cherished fantasy. When they left together, climbed into a Volkswagen and stuttered away from the still-buzzing party, his breath quickened at the implications—which promptly came true. From there the times spent together, the restaurants mutually enjoyed, the records and books rediscovered, seemed inevitable. This was the canonical It. The one thing he had always known about women was that there had to be magic, and now here it was, unannounced, even rather shy. He seized it.

And now in the metaphorical morning after, she had friends named Cliff and parents in Oakland and a liking for Goldwater. All right, he thought, so the details were not perfect. But maybe, in a sense, that was part of the magic, too.

chapter seventeen

APRIL 15, 1963

Gordon had breakfast at Harry's Coffee Shop on Girard, trying to read over his lecture notes and invent some problems for a homework set. It was difficult to work. The clatter of dishes kept intruding and a tinny radio played Kingston Trio songs, which he disliked. The only recent item in pop music he could tolerate was "Dominique," an odd hit recorded by an angel-voiced Belgian nun. He was not in the mood for concentration on things academic, anyway. The *San Diego Union* writeup of Saul's PR blitz had been worse than he'd expected, sensational beyond the bounds of reason. Several people in the department had tut-tutted him about it.

He mulled this over as he drove up Torrey Pines, without reaching any conclusion. He was distracted by a weaving Cadillac with its headlights burning on high. The driver was the typical fortyish man wearing a porkpie hat and a dazed expression. Back in the late '50s, he remembered, the National Safety Council had made a big thing of that. On one of the national holidays they publicized the practice of driving with headlights on during the day, to remind everyone to drive safely. Somehow the idea caught on with the slow-is-safe drivers and now, years later, you would still see them meandering through traffic, certain that their slowness bestowed invulnerability, lights burning uselessly. There was something about such reflex stupidity that never failed to irritate him.

Cooper was in the lab already. *Showing more industry as his candidacy exam approaches,* Gordon thought, but then felt guilty for being cynical. Cooper did seem genuinely more interested now, quite possibly because the whole message riddle had been elevated out of his thesis.

"Trying out the new samples?" Gordon asked with a friendliness fueled by the residue of guilt.

"Yeah. Getting nice stuff. Looks to me like the added indium impurities did the trick."

Gordon nodded. He had been developing a method of doping the samples to achieve the right concentration of impurities and this was the first confirmation that several months of effort were going to pan out. "No messages?"

"No messages," Cooper said with obvious relief.

A voice from the doorway began, "Say, uh, I was told . . ."

"Yes?" Gordon said, turning. The man was dressed in droopy slacks and an Eisenhower jacket. He looked to be over fifty and his face was deeply tanned, as though he worked out of doors.

"You Perfesser Bernstein?"

"Yes." Gordon was tempted to add one of his father's old jokes, "Yes, I have that honor," but the man's earnest expression told him it wouldn't go over.

"I, I'm Jacob Edwards, from San Diego? I've done some work I think you might be interested in?" He turned every sentence into a question.

"What kind of work?"

"Well, your experiments and the message and all? Say, is this where you get the signals?"

"Ah, yes."

Edwards ambled into the laboratory, touching some of the equipment wonderingly. "Impressive. Real impressive." He studied some of the new samples laid out on the working counter.

"Hey," Cooper said, looking up from the x-y recorder. "Hey, those samples are coated with—shit!"

"Oh, that's okay, my hands were dirty anyway. You fellas got a lot of fine equipment in here? How you pay for it all?"

"We have a grant from—but look, Mr. Edwards, what can I do for you?"

"Well, I solved your problem, you know? I have, yeah." Edwards ignored Cooper's glare.

"How, Mr. Edwards?"

"The secret," he said, looking secretive, "is *magnetism*."

"Oh."

"Our sun's magnetism, that's what they're after?"

"Who?" Gordon began to rummage through his mind for some way to get Edwards away from the equipment.

"The people who're sending you those letters? They're coming here to steal our magnetism. It's all that keeps the Earth going around the sun—that's what I've proved."

"Look, I don't think magnetism has anything to do—"

"You e*xper*iment here—" he patted the large field coils—"uses *magnets,* doesn't it?"

Gordon saw no reason to deny that. Before he could say anything Edwards went on, "They were drawn to your *mag-*

netism, Perfesser Bernstein. They're exploring for more magnetism and now that they've found *yours,* they're going to come and *get* it.''

''I see.''

''*And* they're going to take the *sun's* magnetism, too.'' He waved his hands and stared off at the ceiling, as though confronting a vision. ''*All* of it. We'll fall into the *sun?*''

''I don't think—''

''I can prove all this, you know,'' the man said calmly in an I'm-being-perfectly-reasonable tone. ''I stand before you as the man who has cracked—*cracked*—the unified field riddle. You know? Where all the particles come from, and where these messages come from? I've done it?''

''Jee-zus,'' Cooper said sourly.

Edwards turned on him. ''Whacha mean by that, boy?''

Cooper shot back, ''Tell me, are they coming in flying saucers?''

Edwards' face clouded. ''Who tole you that?''

''Just a guess,'' Cooper said mildly.

''You got somethin' you're not tellin' the newspapers?''

''No,'' Gordon cut in. ''No, we don't.''

Edwards poked a finger at Cooper. ''Then why'd he say— Ah!'' He froze, looking at Cooper. ''You're not *gonna* tell the newspapers, are you?''

''There is nothing—''

''Not gonna tell about the magnetism at *all*, are you?''

''We don't—''

''Well, you're not keeping it for yourself! The unified magnetism theory is *mine* and you, you educated—'' he struggled for the word he wanted, gave up and went on—''in your universities, aren't gonna keep me from—''

''There is no—''

''—from goin' to the newspapers and tellin' *my* side of it. *I've* had some education, too, y'know, an'—''

''Where did you study?'' Cooper said sarcastically. ''The Close Cover Before Striking Institute?''

''You—'' Edwards seemed suddenly congested with words, so many words he could not get them out one at a time. ''You—''

Cooper stood up casually, looking muscular and on guard. ''Come on, fella. Move it.''

''What?''

''Out.''

''You can't have my ideas!''

''We don't want them,'' Gordon said.

"Wait'll you see it in the *news*papers. Just you wait."

"Out," Cooper said.

"You won't get a peep at my magnetism motor, either. I was going to show you—"

Gordon put his hands on his hips and walked toward the man, boxing him in with Cooper on one side and the only escape leading to the laboratory doorway. Edwards backed away, still talking. He glared at them and struggled for a last phrase to hurl, but his imagination failed him. Edwards turned, grumbling, and shouldered his way into the corridor outside.

Gordon and Cooper looked at each other. "One of the laws of nature," Gordon said, "is that half the people have got to be below average."

"For a Gaussian distribution, yeah," Cooper said. "Sad, though." He shook his head and smiled. Then he went back to work.

•

Edwards was the first, but not the last. They turned up at a steady rate, once the *San Diego Union* story was picked up by other newspapers. Some drove in from Fresno or Eugene, intent on unraveling the riddle of the messages, each sure he knew the answer before he saw the evidence. Some brought manuscripts they had written on their ideas about the universe in general, or a particular scientific theory—Einstein was a favorite, and refuting him the common theme—or, occasionally, on Gordon's experiments. The notion of writing a supposedly learned treatise, using only a vague newspaper article as the sole source, bemused Gordon. Some of the visitors had even published their theses, using the private presses beloved of amateurs. They would present them to him, lovingly handing over bound bundles with lurid covers. Inside, a jumble of terms elbowed each other for room in sentences that led nowhere. Equations appeared by sleight of hand, festooned with new symbols like fresh Christmas tree decorations. The theories, when Gordon took the time to listen, would begin and end in midair; they had no connection with anything else known in physics, and always violated the first rule of a scientific model: they were uncheckable. Most of the cranks seemed to think constructing a new theory involved only the invention of new terms. Along with "energy," "field," "neutrino," and other common terms would appear "macron," "superon," and "fluxforce"—all undefined, all surrounded with the magic aura of the Believer.

Gordon came to recognize them easily. They would come to

175

his office or laboratory, or call him at home, and within a minute he could tell them from ordinary folk. The cranks always had certain buzz words that appeared early on. They would claim to have solved everything—to have wrapped up all known problems in one grand synthesis. "Unified theory" was a dead giveaway. Another was the sudden, unexplained appearance of the Believer Words such as "superon." At first Gordon would laugh when this happened, joshing the crank with a casual manner, sometimes making a joke. But a third hallmark of the crank was his humorlessness. They never laughed, never backed down from their ramparts. Indeed, open display of ridicule would bring out the worst in them. They were uniformly sure that every working scientist was out to steal their ideas. Several warned him that they had already applied for a patent. (The fact that you can patent an invention but not an idea had passed them by.) At this point Gordon would try to contrive a graceful exit from the conversation; on the telephone this was easy; he just hung up. Cranks in person were not so simple. Resistance to their groundbreaking ideas inevitably led to open threats that they would—here there came the grim look, the reluctant decision that they must use the final, ultimate weapon—go immediately to the newspapers. Somehow, to them, the press was always the judge of things scientific. Since Gordon had been elevated to their attention by the *San Diego Union,* he would of course fear deeply any attack on his position in the same hallowed pages.

Finally, Gordon developed defenses. On the telephone he was quick to hang up—so quick that he cut off his own mother once, when he did not recognize her voice and could not make out anything intelligible over the transcontinental static. Crank manuscripts and letters were equally easy. He wrote a note saying that while the person's ideas were "interesting" (a suitably nonjudgmental term), they were beyond his competence, so he was unable to comment on them. This worked; they never replied. On-the-spot cranks were the worst. He learned to be abrupt, even rude. This got rid of most of them. The harder, persistent sort—such as Edwards—Gordon learned to derail, to gently deflect onto other matters. Then he would edge them toward the door, murmuring reassuring phrases—but never a promise to read a manuscript, attend a lecture, or vouch for a theory. That way lay further involvement and more wasted time. He would edge them toward the door and they would go —grudgingly, sometimes, but they would go.

A side effect of this crank traffic came to light in casual remarks from other members of the department. They noted the cranks with interest at first. Amusement followed, and Gordon provided them with anecdotes of strange theories and even stranger behavior. But in time the mood changed. Other faculty disliked having the department known for its garbled image in the *San Diego Union*. They stopped asking him, at the afternoon coffee break, what new crank had come by. Gordon noticed the change.

chapter eighteen

MAY 24, 1963

The San Diego area was growing and spreading. Rather than pattern itself on the jumble of Los Angeles, the younger city to the south chose to encourage white-collar employers, "clean" industries, and think tanks. The largest such tank in the area was General Atomic, scarcely a mile from the fledgling University. Quite considerable fish were to be seen swimming in its waters, puzzling at government-sponsored problems. Noted names from Berkeley and Caltech spent pleasant months scribbling on blackboards while outside, the General Atomic squirrels and rabbits lazily foraged for their handouts. The animals were part of a psychologist's deliberate plan to evoke rest, quiet, and deep thought; the resemblance to a Disney film may have been accidental. The architect's remorselessly circular motif for the central General Atomic offices, with the eagerly cooperative library at its center, had a similar aim. The ringed roads and buildings recalled Oriental notions of completeness, of serenity, of rest. The curved hallways would increase contact between researchers. In fact, though, the inescapable geometry meant that no one could see further than thirty feet along the curving corridors. This tended to prevent the accidental meetings as scientists came and went; they passed out of view before they could be noticed. To go home or to the library meant moving radially, and thus seeing nobody. As Freeman Dyson said that summer, "The mean interaction distance around here is no bigger than a soccer goal." Yet often it was enough; these were exciting times. Only six months before, *Mariner II* had surveyed Venus close up for the first time. Gell-Mann and others were plumbing new depths in particle theory. In April, J. Robert Oppenheimer was named winner of the Atomic Energy Commission's 1963 Fermi award. Oppenheimer had been, in the eyes of many scientists, the public whipping boy of the McCarthy era; he had been declared a security risk in 1954. Now at last the government seemed to be serving some penance for its stupidity. Hard feelings against Edward Teller, who had not spoken out strongly for Oppenheimer, in turn began to wane.

The feeling of opening, of fresh starts, was on the political scene already a cliché. The Kennedy ambience was a canon of media hype. Vaughn Meader's "The First Family" album, which mocked the Kennedy clan, sold briskly; the public sensed that the derision was all in good fun. Scientists were a more skeptical lot, however, mostly liberal or radical, and bothered by Bobby Kennedy's generally perceived ruthlessness and neglect of the legal niceties of wire-tapping. But the rise of support for scientific research was now coming to seem like a permanent feature, beginning with a sudden rush after *Sputnik* and rising linearly. Everyone knew it would plateau out, but not soon; there was much to be done, and few to do it.

Freeman Dyson came to California on leave from Princeton's Institute for Advanced Study, to work on the Orion project. Dyson had an immense reputation as a theoretical physicist and thus was invited to give one of the last spring Colloquia in the UCLJ Physics Department. Gordon was pleased. He was to give the very last Colloquium of the year, and to have Dyson speak beforehand about some speculative ideas might defuse some of the reaction to Gordon.

Dyson was slim and humorous, moving gracefully before the blackboard as though in a light trance, thinking hard about what he wanted to say and bending each sentence to strike a precise point. He had been very careful earlier to correct George Feher when he was referred to as "Doctor." Dyson had never finished his doctorate and now seemed slightly proud of it, with the Englishman's pride at being, at least in the formal sense, an amateur. But there was nothing amateurish about Dyson's Colloquium. His slides were neat, with clear graphics, some in color. They had the professional aerospace finish that to Gordon underlined the pleasant perks of prosperity; in his undergraduate days at Columbia, rough sketches and hand-lettered slides were universal.

Dyson described his years of work on Project Orion, a plan to propel huge spacecraft by exploding nuclear bombs behind them. The blast would strike a "pusher plate," which would transfer the muted kick through shock absorbers to the ship itself. The idea at first seemed like a Rube Goldberg design, but as Dyson spoke it became plausible. The only way to ferry truly large payloads around the solar system was through nuclear drives of some kind. Orion was basically simple and used what we were already good at: making efficient bombs. Why not use man's destructive capability for something useful? Dyson thought that a strong effort would not simply put men on the moon by 1970—Kennedy's goal—but beyond, all the way to Mars. The principles involved had been tried in small-scale experiments and they worked. The problem, of course, was the first stage: lifting the craft from the earth's surface on a stuttering trail of nuclear blasts.

"Won't you plaster us with radioactive debris?" a voice from the Colloquium audience called.

Dyson pursed his lips. He was a compact man and his sharp features seemed to pin the problem like a butterfly. "Much less so than the atmospheric tests we and the Soviet Union are now conducting. We calculate Orion would add no more than one percent to the level of radiation that politics—" he pronounced the word carefully—"already sets for us."

At this point Dyson became wistful, as though he could sense Orion slipping from him. The newspapers brought daily reports of agreements on the Nuclar Test Ban; Washington rumor said it would be signed within months. If so, even Orion's small dose of radioactives would be ruled out. Toward the end of the hour, after the equations and graphs, there came a bittersweet quality. History would pass Orion by. It might someday fly above the atmosphere, once men had a safe way to get it into orbit with chemical rockets. But even then, much of the debris would eventually find its way down into the air. Maybe there was no completely safe way to harness our gift for making bombs. Maybe there were no shortcuts to the planets.

The applause which greeted Dyson's somber conclusion was prolonged. He bowed tentatively toward his audience, smiling with sad eyes.

●

Gordon gave the last Colloquium of the year. The audience was even larger than Dyson's of the week before, and noisier. Gordon opened with details of the experiment, history of the field, slides of the normal resonance lines. He had compiled all Cooper's conventional results to date, and showed how these confirmed the usual theory. It was a satisfactory but relatively unexciting discussion. Gordon had considered leaving matters at that—no reference to the messages, no risks. But something made him cut short the parade of slides. He murmured, "However, there are some unusual features in the noise observed in our work"—and he was off, describing the interruptions of Cooper's resonance curves, their suspicion that a pattern lay underneath, then the first decoding. Gordon used the viewgraph projector, sliding the transparent sheets into view as he spoke, his sentences coming quicker now, the words more clipped, a certain momentum coming into his voice. He showed the breakdown of the first message. He discussed the chances that such a message could be a fluke, an accident. From the crowded room there arose a sustained murmur. He described their efforts to track down a local source for the noise, their failure, and then the second message. Gordon made no mention of Saul and the 29-by-53 grid; he simply displayed the data. The RA 18 5 36 DEC 30 29.2 chart filled an entire viewgraph. Only then did Gordon mention "spontaneous resonance," giving Isaac Lakin full credit for the term and the idea. He kept his face blank and his voice flat and calm as he described "spontaneous resonance," gave the statistical probability of such an effect arising from random noise, and left the rows of RA 18 5 36 DEC 30 29.2 on the viewgraph as mute testimony. In dry, precise tones he told of their precautions against outside signals, of the waxing and waning of the "spontaneous resonance"—now he used the term archly, pausing before and after the words as if to put verbal quotation marks around them, smiling very slightly—and he paced back and forth before the blackboards, trying to remember the measured way Dyson had done it, head tilted down.

The voice came out of the audience. Before the first sentence was finished, heads turned to see the speaker. It was Freeman Dyson. "You realize, I suppose, that Saul Shriffer has made much of this? Of 99 Hercules?"

"Ah, yes," Gordon said, stunned. He had not seen Dyson in the crowd. "I, I did not authorize him to . . ."

"And that no one at 99 Hercules could possibly be responding to our commercial radio stations yet? It is too far away."

"Well, yes."

"So if this *is* a message from there, they must be using communication faster than light?"

The auditorium was silent. "Yes." Gordon hesitated. Should he back up Saul's idea? Or stand pat?

Dyson shook his head. "I spoke last week about a dream. It is good to dream—but be sure to wake up."

A wave of laughter came down from the crowd and broke over Gordon. He stepped backward two paces without thinking. Dyson himself looked surprised at the reaction, and then smiled down from his position halfway up the bowl-shaped auditorium, his face softening as he looked at Gordon, as though to blunt the edge of his remark. Around Dyson others were slapping their knees and rocking back and forth in their seats, as though something had unleashed a tension in them and now, with a sign from Dyson, they were sure of how to react.

"I don't propose . . ." Gordon began, but was drowned out by the continuing laughter. "I don't . . ." He noticed Isaac Lakin standing, a few seats from the front and to the left. Eyes in the audience turned from Gordon to Lakin. The laughter died.

"I would like to make a statement," Lakin said, voice booming. "I invented the idea of spontaneous resonance to explain unusual data. I did so completely honestly. I think there *is* something happening in these experiments. But this message thing—" he waved a hand in dismissal. "No. No. It is nonsense. I now disclaim any association with it. I do not want my name linked with such, such claims. Let Bernstein and Shriffer make what they want—*I* do not cooperate."

Lakin sat down decisively. There was applause.

"I don't propose to decide what this means," Gordon began. His voice was thin and it was hard getting the words out. He peered at Dyson. Someone was whispering to Dyson and smiling broadly. Lakin, Gordon noticed, was sitting with arms folded across his chest, glaring down at the RA and DEC. Gordon spun and looked at the coordinates looming above him, large and flat and remorseless.

"But I think it's there." He turned back to the crowd. "I know it sounds funny, but . . ." The buzzing in the audience kept on. He coughed, and could not seem to summon up the booming confidence that Lakin had used. The crowd noise got louder.

"Ah, Gordon . . ." He was surprised to find the Department Chairman at his elbow. Professor Glyer held up a palm toward the audience and the murmuring died. "We have already run over our allotted time, and another lecture is scheduled to begin here. Further, ah, further questions can be asked at the coffee to follow, served upstairs in the foyer." The chairman led a muted ritual applause. It was all but drowned out in a babble of voices as the crowd spilled out of the room. Someone passed near Gordon, saying to his companion, "Well, maybe Cronkite believes it, but . . ." and the companion laughed. Gordon stood with his back to the blackboard, watching them leave. Nobody came up to ask a question. Around Lakin a knot of people buzzed. Dyson appeared at Gordon's side. "Sorry they took it that way," he said. "I didn't mean it as . . ."

"I know," Gordon murmured. "I know."

"It simply seems so damned unlikely . . ."

"Shriffer thinks . . ." Gordon began, but decided to let the subject alone. "What did you think of the rest of the message?"

"Well, frankly, I don't believe there *is* a message. It makes no sense."

Gordon nodded.

"Uh, the press coverage hasn't helped you any, you realize."

Gordon nodded.

"Well, uh, some coffee, then?" Dyson bowed goodbye uneasily and moved away with the exiting crowd. The Colloquium had trickled away to the coffee and cookies upstairs and Gordon felt the tension drain out of him, to be replaced by the familar day-end numbness. As he collected his viewgraphs his hands shook. *I should get more exercise,* he thought. *I'm out of shape.* Abruptly he decided to skip the coffee hour. The hell with them. The hell with the whole damned bunch.

chapter nineteen

MAY 29, 1963

The maitre d'hotel at the Top of the Cove restaurant said, "Dinner, sir, *s'il vous plaît?*"

"Uh, yes."

He led them to a spot with a commanding view of the La Jolla Cove below. Waves broke into foamy white sprays beneath the floodlights. "Ees zees taab-le hokay?" Gordon nodded while Penny rolled up her eyes. After the man had bestowed the huge menus and gone away she said, "God, I wish they'd cut out the accent business."

"Vat ees eet, madame? You no like zee phony talk?" Gordon said.

"My French isn't great, but—" she stopped as the waiter approached. Gordon did the wine ritual, selecting something he recognized from the fat book. When he looked around he saw the Carroways sitting some distance away, laughing and having a good time. He pointed them out to Penny; she duly entered the fresh datum in their running tally. But they did not go over to report the latest figures. The Colloquium lay five days in the past, but Gordon felt uneasy in the department now. Tonight's splurge at the Top of the Cove was Penny's suggestion, to lift him out of his moody withdrawal.

Something thumped at his elbow. "I open it now," the waiter said, working at the bottle. "Muss lettit breed."

"What?" Gordon said, surprised.

"Open ta da air, y'know—breed."

"Oh."

"Yes suh." The waiter gave him a slightly condescending smile.

After he had left Gordon said, "At least he has the smile down pat. Are all the high-class restaurants around here like this?"

Penny shrugged. "We don't have the old world culture of New York. We didn't get mugged walking over here, either."

Gordon would normally have sidestepped the now-what-you-New-Yorkers-ought-to-do conversation, but this time he murmured "Don't *krechtz* about what you don't know," and without thinking about it he was talking about the days after he moved away from his parents and was living in a cramped apartment, studying hard and for the first time really sensing the city, breathing it in. His mother had assigned Uncle Herb to look in on him now and then, since after all he was living in the same neighborhood. Uncle Herb was a lean and intense man who was always landing big deals in the clothing business. He had a practical man's disdain for physics. "How much they pay you?" he would say abruptly, in the middle of discussing something else. "Enough, if I scrimp." His uncle's face would twist up in the act of weighing this and he would inevitably say, "Plus all the physics you can eat? Eh?" and slap his thigh. But he was not a simple man. Using your intelligence for judging discounts or weighing the marketability of crew neck sweaters —that was smart. His only hobby he had turned into a little business, too. On Saturdays and Sundays he would take the IRT down to Washington Park Square early, to get a seat at one of the concrete chess tables near MacDougal and West Fourth streets. He was a weekend chess hustler. He played for a quarter a game against all comers, sometimes making as much as two dollars in an hour. At dusk he would switch tables to get one near the street light. In winter he would play in one of the Village coffeehouses, sipping lukewarm tea with an audible slurp, making it last so his expenses didn't run too high. His only hustle was to make his opponents think they were better than he was. Since any chess player old enough to have quarters to spare inevitably also had an advanced case of chess player's ego, this wasn't hard. Uncle Herb called them "potzers"—weak players with inflated self-images. His game was no marvel, either. It was strategically unsound, flashy but built out of pseudo traps tailored to snare potzers who thought they saw an unsuspected opening suitable for a quick kill. The traps gave him fast wins, to maximize the take per hour. Uncle Herb's view of the world was simple: the potzers and the mensch. He, of course, was a *mensch*.

"You know what was the last thing he said to me when I left?" Gordon said abruptly. "He said, 'Don't be a *potzer* out there.' And he gave me ten dollars."

"Nice uncle," Penny said diplomatically.

"And you know last Friday, the Colloquium? I started to feel like a potzer."

"Why?" Penny asked with genuine surprise.

"I've been standing firm on the strength of my data. But when you look at it—Christ, Dyson would've given me a break, would've backed me up, if there'd been any sense to it. I trust his judgment. I'm starting to think I've made some dumb mistake along the way, screwed up the experiment so bad *nobody* can find what's wrong."

"You should trust your *own*—"

"That's what marks the potzer, see? Inability to learn from experience. I've been bulling ahead—"

"Zee compote, surrh," the waiter said smoothly.

"Oh *God*," Gordon said with such irritation that the waiter stepped back, his composure gone. Penny laughed out loud, which made the waiter even more uncertain. Even Gordon smiled, and his mood was broken.

Penny's forced merriment got them through most of the meal. She produced a book from her handbag and pressed it on him. "It's the new Phil Dick."

He glanced at the lurid cover. *The Man in the High Castle*. "Haven't got time."

"*Make* the time. It's really good. You've read his other stuff, haven't you?"

Gordon shrugged off the subject. He still wanted to talk about New York, for reasons he could not pin down. He compromised by relating to Penny the contents of his mother's latest letter. That distant figure seemed to be getting used to the idea of him living "in flagrant sin." But there was a curious vagueness about her letters that bothered him. When he first came to California the letters had been long, packed with chatter about her daily routine, the neighborhood, the slings and arrows of Manhattan life. Now she told him very little about what she was doing. He felt the void left by those details, sensed his New York life slipping away from him. He had been more sure of himself then, the world had looked bigger.

"Hey, c'mon, Gordon. Stop *brooding*. Here, I brought you some more things."

He saw that she had planned a methodically joyous evening, complete with door prizes. Penny produced a handsome Cross pen and pencil set, a western-style string tie, and then a bumper sticker: $Au + H_2O$. Gordon held it between thumb and index finger, suspending it delicately in the air over their table as though it might contaminate the veal piccata.

"What's this crap?"

"Oh, c'mon. Just a joke."

"Next you'll be giving me copies of *The Conscience of a Conservative*. Christ."

"Don't be so afraid of new ideas."

"*New?* Penny, these are *cobwebbed*—"

"They're new to *you*."

"Look, Goldwater might make a good neighbor—good fences make good neighbors, isn't that what Frost said? Little lit'rary touch for you, there. But Penny, he's a *simpleton*."

She said stiffly, "Not so simple he gave away Cuba."

"Huh?" He was honestly mystified.

"Last October Kennedy signed it *away*. Just like that." She snapped her fingers energetically. "Agreed not to do *anything* about Cuba if the Russians took their missiles out."

"By 'anything' you mean another Bay of Pigs."

"Maybe." She nodded sternly. "Maybe."

"Kennedy's already helped out quite enough fascists. The Cuban exiles, Franco, and now Diem in Viet Nam. I think—"

"You don't think at all, Gordon. Really. You've got all these eastern ideas about the way the world works and they're all *wrong*. JFK was weak on Cuba and you just watch—the Russians will give them the guns and they'll infiltrate everywhere, all over South America. They're a real *threat*, Gordon. What's to stop them from sending troops into Africa, even? Into the Congo?"

"Nonsense."

"Is it nonsense that Kennedy's chipping away at our freedoms here, too? Forcing the steel companies to back down, when all they did was raise prices? Whatever happened to free enterprise?"

Gordon raised a palm in the air. "Look, can we have a truce?"

"I'm just trying to shake you loose from those ideas of yours. You people from the east don't understand how this country really works."

He said sarcastically, "There might be a few guys on *The New York Times* who mull it over."

"Left-wing Democrats," she began, "who don't—"

"Hey, *hey*." He raised his palm toward her again. "I thought we had a truce."

"Well . . . All right. Sorry."

Gordon studied his plate for a moment, distracted, and then said with dawning perception, "What's this?"

"An artichoke salad."

"Did I order this?"

"I heard you."

"After the veal? What was I thinking of?"

"I'm sure I don't know."

"I don't need this. I'll flag one of those funny waiters."

"They're not 'funny,' Gordon. They're *queer*."

"What?" he asked blankly.

"You know. Homosexual."

"Fags?" Gordon felt as though he had been deceived all evening. He dropped his signaling hand, suddenly shy. "You should've told me."

"Why? It doesn't matter. I mean, they're all over La Jolla— haven't you noticed?"

"Uh, no."

"Most of the waiters in *any* restaurant are. It's a convenient job. You can travel around and live in the best spots. They don't have family obligations, most of the time their family wants nothing to do with them, so . . ." She shrugged. Gordon saw in this gesture an unaffected sophistication, an ease with the world, which he suddenly envied very much. The way their conversation had shifted from topic to topic this evening bothered him, had kept him off balance. He realized that he still could not get a grip on the real Penny, the woman behind so many different faces. The comic Goldwaterite lived right along-side the literature and arts major, who in turn blended into the casual sexual sophisticate. He remembered opening the bath-room door at a faculty party last year to find her seated on the toilet, her blue gown crescenting the bowl like a wreath of flowers. They had both been startled; she held a square of yel-low tissue in an upraised hand. Her heels dug into the grouting between the triangular brown tiles of the floor, so her toes canted cockily into the air. The low seat made her seem bottom-heavy. Between pale thighs he saw the unending oval yawn. A dark sheath of hose swallowed most of her legs, yielding only to the descending tongues of her garter belt. His jaw had sagged open with indecision and then he stepped in, mouth closing on the possibility of faux pas. The mirror on the far wall showed a startled stranger, puzzled. He shut the door behind him, drawn to her. "You can see this at home," she said impishly. With a studious deliberation she patted herself, unmindful of him, and let the yellow paper flutter into the mouth of water below. She half-turned on the seat, pressed the chipped ceramic handle. An answering gurgle took away her business from his prying eyes before she arose. Standing, smoothing her dress, she was taller and somehow challenging, an exotic problem. In the bleached, tiled pocket she appeared luminous with purpose, a Penny he had not known. "I couldn't wait," he said with a warmth that sounded strange to himself, considering that it wasn't true. He edged by her, unzipped. The mildly pleasurable gush: release. "Getting domestic, aren't we?" Penny raised one edge of her lipsticked mouth in the lyric curve of a half-smile, seeing the mood in him. "I guess so," he said lazily. Outside, his colleagues were discussing superconductivity while their wives made shrewd observations on local real estate; the women seemed to have a better grip on what was real. Penny's smile broadened and he concluded with a quick spurt that narrowly missed the seat. He gave himself a wobbly drying shake, tucked himself in and dried the seat with more of the yellow tissues. He had never felt this simple and open with a woman before, in such a rich, enameled air. Not wanting to hang on to the moment for fear that it would burst, he kissed her lightly and popped open the door. Outside, Isaac Lakin leaned against the wall, studying the Breughel prints in the shadowed hallway and awaiting entrance to the bathroom. "Ah," he said as they emerged together. "Up to something." A simple deduction. Lakin's eyes moved from one to the other as though he could glimpse the secret, as though he had just seen a new facet of Gordon. Well, maybe he had. Maybe they both had.

"*Gor*-don," Penny urged him back into the present. "You've been going off like that all *evening*." She looked concerned. He felt a sudden spurt of irritation. The dream Penny was soft and womanly; the one before him was a nag. "If you're going to do that, why not just *talk* about it?"

He nodded. Her programmed night out, full of forced gaiety, had begun to wear on him. And the sudden shifts in his emotions bothered him as well. He normally thought of himself as rock-steady, unmoved by passing notions.

"Got a call from Saul today," he said stonily, fleeing his own thoughts. "He and Frank Drake are going to get time on the big radio telescope in Green Bank, West Virginia. They want to study 99 Hercules."

"If they receive a signal, it will prove your case?"

"Right. It makes no sense, but—right."

"Why no sense?"

"Look, I mean—" Gordon waved a hand in exasperation. One of the waiters took this as a signal and began to advance. Hurriedly Gordon motioned him away. "Even if you bought the story whole, the tachyons and everything—why think there should be radio signals? Why *both*? The whole *point* of using tachyons is that radio's too slow."

"Well, at least they're doing *some*thing."

"Were you a cheerleader in high school, too?"

"God, you're a nasty bastard sometimes."

"Wrong time of the month."

"Look, Saul is trying to help."

"I don't think that's the way to solve the problem."

"What *is?*" When he waved away the question with a faintly disgusted look on his face, she persisted: "Really, Gordon, what is?"

"Forget it. That's the best way. Just hope everybody else will forget it, too."

"You don't really—"

"Sure I do. You should've been at that Colloquium."

She let him cool for a moment and then murmured, "You were confident a week ago."

"That was a week ago."

"At least you could work on it."

"Cooper's candidacy exam is two days away. I'm going to concentrate on helping him prepare, and then on getting him out. That's my *job*." Gordon nodded abruptly, as though having a job to do resolved all issues.

"Maybe you should try something like what Saul's doing."

"No point."

"How can you be so sure?" She folded her arms, sitting back in the rattan chair and looking squarely at him. "Have you ever thought about the rigid way scientists work? It's like military training."

"Bullshit."

"What do they teach you? Write down everything you know about a problem. Set it up in some equations. Most of the time, that's enough in itself, right? You just push the equations around a little and you've got the answer."

"Not that simple," Gordon said, shaking his head. But to himself he had to grudgingly admit that there was some truth to what she said. Assign symbols, making the x's and y's and z's the unknowns, then rearrange. Made-to-order thinking. They were all used to it and maybe it hid some elements of the problem, if you weren't careful. Dyson, for all his wisdom, could be dead wrong, simply because of habits of mind.

"Let's have chocolate mousse," Penny said brightly.

He looked up at her. She was going to make this evening end right, one way or the other. He remembered her perched on the toilet and felt a warmth steal over him. She had been both vulnerable and serene sitting there, performing an animal function amid a gauzy gown. Pert, and oddly elegant.

"Vas you-are dinner ex-see-lant, sir?"

Gordon peered at the waiter, trying to estimate if he was queer. "Ah . . . yes. Yes." He paused. "Lots better than Chef Boy-Ar-Dee."

The expression on the waiter's face was worth the price of the meal.

chapter twenty

MAY 31, 1963

Albert Cooper's candidacy examination began well enough. Gates, a high-energy physicist, started off with a standard problem. "Mr. Cooper, consider two electrons in a one-dimensional box. Can you write down for us the wave function for this state?" Gates smiled in a friendly way, trying to defuse the tension that oral examinations always had. The student nearly always balked somewhere along the line, unable to summon up some simple piece of physics purely because of his own skittering nervousness.

Cooper worked his way through an opening piece of the problem, sketching the lowest energy state. Then he stalled. Gordon could not tell if this was simple funk or a calculated delaying tactic. Lately, students had hit upon the frowning, silent stall as a method for extracting hints from their committee. Often it worked. After a moment Gates said, "Well then . . . should the spatial part of the wave function be symmetric?" Cooper responded eventually, "Ah . . . no . . . I don't think so. The spins should be . . ." and then, halting now and then, he successfully got through the rest.

Gordon felt uneasy as Gates led Cooper through a series of routine questions, all designed to find out if the candidate knew the general background of the thesis problem he proposed to attack. The air conditioning hummed with vacant energy; Cooper's chalk scratched and squeaked on the board. Gordon eyed Bernard Carroway, the astrophysicist. No trouble there. Carroway looked bored, impatient to be done with this ritual and get back to his calculations. The fourth and last member of the committee was the only problem: Isaac Lakin. As senior professor in the field of Cooper's thesis, his presence was unavoidable.

Gates finished his simple questions and Carroway, blinking sleepily, passed to Lakin. *Here it comes,* Gordon thought.

But Lakin was not so direct. He took Cooper through a discussion of Cooper's own experiment—usually safe ground for the student, since that was what he knew best. Lakin stressed the theoretical underpinning for the nuclear resonance effects. Cooper wrote down the scaling equations, working quickly. When Lakin probed deeper, Cooper slowed, then stopped. He tried the stalling tactic. Lakin saw through this and refused to give Cooper any meaningful hints. Carroway began to take an interest, sitting up straight for the first time during the examination. Gordon wondered why a student in difficulty always provoked more attention from a committee; was it the hunting instinct? Or a proper professorial concern that the student, presumed to be accomplished until he proved otherwise, had suddenly betrayed a fatal ignorance? Either answer was too simple, Gordon concluded.

By now Lakin had Cooper on the run. Lakin made him frame a clear picture of the theoretical model and describe the underlying assumptions. Then Lakin cut Cooper's explanation to ribbons. His statements were vague, his reasoning sloppy. He had neglected two important effects. Gordon sat absolutely still, not wanting to interrupt because he still clung to the hope that Cooper would right himself after being blown over in this quick storm, and begin to answer correctly. That hope faded. Gordon remembered Lakin relating a comment he had written on a thesis some years ago: "Young man, there is much in this work which is original and much which is correct. Unfortunately, what is correct is not original, and what is original is not correct."

Carroway joined in with a few incisive questions. Cooper seemed to make headway, then reverted back to his withdrawal mode, stalling for time. But in a two-hour examination there is more than enough time to uncover weaknesses. Carroway listened to Cooper's floundering replies, eyes still half-closed, but now obviously alert, a sour expression spreading across his face. Gates peered at Cooper as if to understand how a student who had appeared bright only moments before could now be in such trouble. When Cooper turned to answer a sally from Lakin, Gates shook his head.

Gordon decided to step in. It was not a good idea to defend your student very much in the candidacy examination precisely because it was so obvious, and it implied that you, too, conceded the student's defects. Gordon spoke up, interrupting the flow of Carroway's probes. He pointed out that in the time remaining the committee had to consider the form and details of Cooper's experiment, and they hadn't touched on that yet. This worked. Gates nodded. Cooper, who had been standing with his back pressed to the blackboard, smiled with evident relief. The committee room filled with the small sounds of hands riffling through papers, bodies shifting position in uncomfortable chairs: the earlier mood was broken. Cooper could repair some of the damage.

Five minutes passed smoothly. Cooper explained his experimental setup, elaborated details of the rig. He passed around samples of his early results.

Lakin gave these papers scarcely a glance. Instead, he slipped some pages of his own into the set of data and passed them to Cooper. "My concern here, Mr. Cooper, is not only with the easy-to-understand results. I am sure the committee will find them unsurprising. What I wish to know is whether they are *correct*."

"Sir?" Cooper said in a thin voice.

"We all know there are . . . odd . . . features in your work."

"Uh, I . . ."

"Could you explain these things to us?"

Lakin pointed at his pages, face up on the table. They were traces showing the sudden interruption of smooth resonance curves. Gordon peered at them with a sinking feeling.

The rest of the examination seemed to go by very quickly. Cooper lost a certain calm distance he had successfully kept through the earlier questioning. He explained the spontaneous resonance effect in halting sentences. He would rush forward through an explanation he knew and, reaching the end of it, back away from its implications. He tried to edge around the question of what caused the effect. Carroway, now visibly interested, drew him back to it. Gordon's interjections did nothing to stem the flow. Gates began to second Carroway's skepticism, so that Cooper spun from Lakin to Carroway to Gates, meeting fresh objections as he turned from right to left. "This issue is at the heart of the thesis," Lakin said, and the others nodded. "It must be settled. Only Mr. Cooper knows the truth of the matter." Everyone in the room knew they were talking about the messages and Gordon and Saul Shriffer, not merely about the correctness of Cooper's electronics. But this examination was a way for the faculty to express their professional judgment of the issue, and on this ground the battle had to be fought.

Gordon let it go as long as he dared, eating into the two hours. Finally he said, "This is all very well, but are we keeping to the point? You have seen the data—"

"Of course," Lakin shot back. "But are they right?"

"I submit that this question is *not* what we are considering. This is a candidacy examination. We pass on the *suitability* of a topic—not on the final outcome."

Gates nodded. Then, to Gordon's surprise, Carroway did, too. Lakin was silent. As though the question had been settled, Gates asked Cooper an innocuous question about his setup. The examination wound down. Carroway slumped in his chair, eyes half-closed to his own interior world, the spark gone out of him. Gordon thought wryly of what the taxpayers would think of their half-awake public servant, and then recalled that Carroway followed what were, for theoreticians, standard working hours. He would arrive at noon, ready to substitute lunch for breakfast. Seminars and discussions with students took him into evening. By then he was ready to begin calculations—that is, real work. This early afternoon exam was, for him, a waking-up exercise.

Gordon's real work began as Cooper left the room. This was when the thesis professor listened carefully to the comments and criticisms of his colleagues, ostensibly for future use in directing the thesis research of the candidate. A subtle tug of war.

Lakin opened by doubting Cooper's understanding of the problem. True, Gordon conceded, Cooper was weak on the overall theory. But experimental students were traditionally more concerned with their detailed lab work—"stroking their apparatus," Gordon called it, to provoke some much-needed mirth—than with the fine points of theory. Gates bought this; Carroway frowned.

Lakin shrugged, conceding it as a tied point. He paused while Carroway, and then Gates in turn, expressed some misgivings over Cooper's occasionally sloppy work on basic physics problems—the two electrons in a box, for example. Gordon agreed. He pointed out, though, that the Physics Department could only require students to take the relevant courses and then hope that the knowledge sank in. Cooper had already passed the department's Qualifying Examination—three days of written problems, followed by a two-hour oral examination. The fact that Cooper's grasp of some points was still slippery was, of course, regrettable. But what could this candidacy committee do? Gordon promised to press Cooper on these subjects, to—in effect—browbeat the student into making up the deficiency. The committee accepted this rather standard reply with nods.

So far Gordon had skated on relatively firm ice. Now Lakin tapped his pen reflectively on the table, *tick,* and slowly, almost languidly, reviewed Cooper's data. The true test of an experimenter, he said, was his data. The crux of Cooper's thesis was the spontaneous resonance effect. And this was precisely what was in question. "The thesis is an argument, let us remember, not a stack of pages," Lakin said with dreamy ease.

Gordon countered as best he could. The spontaneous resonance phenomenon was important, yes, but Cooper was not primarily concerned with it. His topic was much more conventional. The committee should look at the spontaneous resonances as a kind of overlay, occasionally obscuring the more conventional data Cooper was trying to get.

Lakin countered in earnest. He brought up the *Physical Review Letters* paper, which carried the names of Lakin, Bernstein, and Cooper. The final thesis would *have* to mention it. "And this, of course"—a sad, weary glance toward Gordon—"means that we must bring up the entire issue of the . . . interpretation . . . which has been placed upon these . . . interruptions . . . of the resonance curves."

"I disagree," Gordon snapped.

"The committee must consider all the facts," Lakin said mildly.

"The *fact* is that Cooper is going for a standard problem here."

"It has not been so advertised."

"Look, Isaac, what *I* do has no connection with *this* thesis and *this* committee."

"I really rather believe," Gates broke in, "we should focus on the possibilities of the experiment itself."

"Quite so," Carroway muttered, rising from his half-sleep.

"Cooper will probably not deal with the, ah, message theory at all," Gordon said.

"But he must," Lakin said with quiet energy.

"Why?" Gordon said.

"How can we be sure his electronics gear is functioning right?" Gates put in.

"Exactly," Lakin said.

"Look, there's nothing that special about his equipment."

"Who can say?" Lakin said. "It contains a few modifications above and beyond the usual resonance rig. These—if I understand them correctly—" a slight note of sarcasm here, Gordon saw "—were designed to increase sensitivity. But is that *all* they do? Is there not some unforeseen effect? Something which makes this experiment, this apparatus, pick up *new* effects in the solid in question—indium antimonide? How can we say?"

"Good point," Gates murmured.

"What sort of effect are you thinking of, Isaac?" Carroway said, genuinely perplexed.

"I do not know," Lakin conceded. "But that is the issue. *Precisely* the issue."

"I disagree," Gordon said.

"No, I think Isaac is dead right," Carroway murmured.

"There's some justice to it," Gates said, reflecting. "How can we be sure this is a good thesis topic until we know the equipment will do what Cooper says it will? I mean, there's Isaac here, who has doubts. You, Gordon—you think it's okay. But I feel we ought to have more info before we go ahead."

"That's not the purpose of this exam," Gordon said flatly.

"I believe it to be a legitimate issue," Carroway said.

Gates added, "So do I."

Lakin nodded. Gordon saw that they were all uncomfortable, not wanting to broach the issue buried under the detail of Cooper's apparatus and the niceties of theory. Still, Gates and Carroway and Lakin thought the message hypothesis was bullshit, pure and simple. They weren't going to let the issue slide by. Cooper couldn't explain all his data, not the interesting parts, anyway. As long as that riddle hung in the air, this committee wasn't going to pass on a thesis. Also, it was not simply a question of conflicting theories. Cooper was weak in some important areas. He needed more study, more time peering at textbooks. He had never been a particularly brilliant classroom student, and here it showed up in spades. That, plus the muddy issue of the messages, was enough.

"I move that we fail Mr. Cooper on this first try at the candidacy examination," Lakin said mildly. "He needs more preparation. Also, this matter of the spontaneous resonances—" a glance at Gordon—"should be resolved."

"Right," Gates said.

"Um," Carroway said drowsily, already picking up his scattered papers.

"But *look*—"

"Gordon," Lakin murmured with a kind of tired friendliness, "that is a majority of the committee. Could we have the form?"

Gordon stiffly handed over the University form for the examination, on which faculty could sign and write out either "yes" or "no" to the question of whether Cooper had passed. The form came back across the table with three *no*s. Gordon stared at it, still off balance, still not sure the whole thing was over. It was the first time he had shepherded a student through this examination and now the student had failed—a rather uncommon event. The candidacy was supposed to be a *putz* of an exam, for Chrissakes. Gordon thought suddenly of the conventional theory of scientific revolutions, where paradigms overtook each other, old replacing new. In a way the message theory and the spontaneous resonance theory were paradigms, erected to explain one bunch of mysterious data. Two paradigms, arguing over a scrap of experimental bread. It almost made him laugh.

The scraping of chairs and shuffle of papers roused him. He muttered something to each of the men as they left, still dazed with the outcome. Lakin even gave him a handshake and a lightly delivered, "We do have to straighten this out, you know," before leaving. As Gordon watched Lakin's retreating back he saw that to the other man this was a regrettable incident involving a junior faculty member who had gone off on a tangent. Lakin had abandoned the softer ways of persuasion. He could no longer come to Gordon and gently urge him to give up his notions. That kind of conversation would lead nowhere— *had* led nowhere. Their personalities didn't match, and maybe that was in the end the most important thing in research. Crick and Watson hadn't got on with Rosalind Franklin, and that prevented their collaboration on the DNA helix riddle. Together they might have cracked the problem earlier. Science abounded with fierce conflicts, many of which blocked progress. There were great missed opportunities—if Oppenheimer had broken through Einstein's hardening isolation, perhaps the two of them could have gone beyond Oppenheimer's 1939 work on neutron stars to consider the whole general relativistic problem of collapsed matter. But they hadn't, in part because Einstein stopped listening to others, cut himself off with his own drowsy dreams of a complete unified field theory . . .

Gordon realized he was sitting alone in the bleak room. Downstairs, Cooper was waiting for the result. There were joys to teaching, but Gordon suddenly wondered whether they were worth the bad moments. You spent three-quarters of your time on the bottom quarter of the students; the really good ones gave you no trouble. Now he had to go down and tell Cooper.

He shuffled his papers together and left. Sunlight streamed in yellow blades through the corridor windows. The days were getting longer. Classes were over. For a moment Gordon forgot Cooper and Lakin and the messages and let a single thought wash over him: the blessed long summer was beginning.

chapter twenty-one

AUGUST, 1998

By the time Marjorie heard a car crunch on the gravel of their driveway, she had everything ready. There was ice in the freezer, carefully hoarded through the power-off hours. She was looking forward to company after a dull week. John's description of Peterson had quite prepared her to dislike him; Council members were remote, forbidding figures. Having one in her own home carried the threat of committing some enormous social gaffe and the compensating thrill of contact with someone more important than a Cambridge don.

John had given her two hours' notice, the classic unthinking husband's trick. Luckily the house was reasonably tidy, and anyway men never noticed things like that. The problem was dinner. She felt that she would have to invite him to stay, out of politeness, though with any luck he would refuse. She had a roast in the battery-assisted freezer. She had been saving it for a special occasion, but there was no time to defrost it. She knew it was important to put on a good show for Peterson; John was not inviting him home out of friendship. A soufflé, perhaps. She had searched through her kitchen cupboards and found a tin of shrimp. Yes, that would do it. A shrimp soufflé and a salad and French bread. Followed by strawberries from the garden, and cream. Bloody elegant, considering. It would exhaust a good fraction of her weekly grocery budget, but economy be damned on such short notice. She had fetched up a bottle of their expensive California Chablis and put it in the tiny freezer, the only way to chill it in time. Might as well make the occasion festive, she thought. For days she had hardly seen John, as he worked late every night at the lab. She had got into the habit of fixing a quick and easy dinner for the kids and herself, keeping a pot of soup to heat up for John whenever he came home.

Outside, car doors clapped. Marjorie stood up as the two men came into the living room. John looked his usual teddy bear self, she thought affectionately. Seeing him in daylight for the first time that week, she also noticed how tired he was.

Peterson was goodlooking in a smooth sort of way, Marjorie decided, but his mouth was too thin, making him look hard.

"This is my wife, Marjorie," John was saying as she held out her hand to Peterson. Their eyes met as they shook hands. A sudden prickly feeling ran through her. Then he looked away again and they moved into the room.

"I hope this isn't inconveniencing you too much," Peterson said. "Your husband assured me it was all right, and we still have some business to discuss."

"No, not at all. I'm glad to have some company for a change. It can be pretty dull being the wife of a physicist when he's working on an experiment."

"I imagine it can." He gave her a brief dissecting glance and strolled over to the window. "You have a charming place here."

"What can I get you to drink, Peterson?" John asked.

"I'll take a whisky and soda, please. Yes, this is charming. I'm very fond of the country. Your roses look especially good." He gestured towards the garden and followed this up with precise comments on soil conditions.

"You live in London, I suppose, Mr. Peterson?"

"Yes, I do. Thank you." He accepted a drink from John.

"Have you got a weekend cottage in the country too?" Marjorie asked.

She thought she saw something flicker for a second in his eyes before he answered. "No, unfortunately. I wish I did. But I probably wouldn't have time to use it. My work requires a lot of travel."

She nodded sympathetically and turned to her husband. "I'm one ahead of you on the drinks, but I'd like another one, please, John," she said, holding out her glass.

"Sherry, is it?" From the deliberately light way he spoke Marjorie saw at once the effort he was making to get on with Peterson. She had felt the tension between the two men from the first instant. John crossed to the sideboard and said in a strained, jolly voice, "It's Ian's job to see we aren't forced to sop up too much of this stuff in order to face the world."

This remark made no visible impression whatever on Peterson, who murmured, "Unfortunate, that previous sots hadn't the excuse of a World Council to blame their reality-avoiding on."

"Reality-avoidance?" Marjorie broke in. "Isn't that the new therapy theory?"

"A disease masquerading as a cure, I'll wager." John chuckled.

Peterson confined himself to a "Hmmmm," and turned towards Marjorie. Before he could change the subject, as he obviously intended, she said, in part to keep him off balance, "What's the reality behind these odd clouds we're seeing? I heard a bit on the news about a Frenchman saying they were a new type, something—"

"Can't say," Peterson said abruptly. "Can't really say. I get awfully behind, you know."

Marjorie thought, quite an artful dodger, yes. "Brazil, then. What can the World Council tell us about that?"

"The bloom is spreading and we are doing what we can." Peterson seemed to warm to this subject, perhaps because it was already public.

"Is it out of your hands, then?" she asked.

"Largely. The Council identifies problems and directs research, integrating them with political considerations. We pounce on technology-related sore spots as soon as they become visible. Most of our function is integrating the satellite ecoprofiles. We sift through the data for telltale changes. Once a supernational riddle appears, it's really up to the technical types—"

"—to solve it," John finished, returning with the sherry. "It's that putting-out-fires psychology that makes untangling a riddle so sodding hard, though, y'see. With no continuity in the research—"

"Oh, John, we've heard that speech before," Marjorie said with a gay lilt in her voice she did not feel. "Surely Mr. Peterson knows your views by now."

"Right, I'll pack it in," John agreed mildly, as if remembering where he was. "Wanted to focus on the equipment thing, anyway. I'm trying to convince Ian here to get on the phone and get me help from the Brookhaven people. It takes clout, as the Americans say, and—"

"More than I have, regrettably," Peterson broke in. "You have a mistaken notion of how much, or rather what kind of influence I have. The scientific types don't like Council people moving them about like pawns."

Marjorie said, "I've noticed that myself."

John smiled fondly. "No point in being a prima donna if you don't get in the occasional aria, is there? But no—" turning back to Peterson "—I merely meant that some of Brookhaven's advanced equipment would cut through our noise problem. If you—"

Peterson compressed his lips and said quickly, "Look, I'll press from this end. You know what that's like—memos and committees and review panels and the like. Bar a miracle, it will take weeks."

Marjorie put in loyally, "But surely you can exert some, some . . ."

"Markham's the one who can do that best," Peterson said, turning to her. "I'll lay the groundwork by telephone. He can go and see the chaps in Washington and then Brookhaven."

"Yes," John murmured, "yes, that would do it. Greg has connections, I think."

"He does?" Marjorie said doubtfully. "He seems, well . . ."

Peterson smiled with amusement. "A bit off? A bit in bad taste? A bit not quite the thing? But he's an American, remember."

Marjorie laughed. "Yes, isn't he? Jan seems much nicer."

"Predictable, you mean," John said.

"Is that what I mean?"

"I think," Peterson said, "that is what we usually intend. Doesn't rock the boat."

Marjorie was struck by the agreement between the two men. It had a certain wry, sad quality to it. She hesitated for a moment as they both, almost as if on signal, stared into their glasses. Each tilted his glass and ice cubes tinkled against the sides. The amber fluid swayed and turned. She looked up at the silent, hovering room. On the dining room table the polished wood reflected the bouquet of flowers she had arranged, and the glossy vision of the vase seemed a cupped hand, upholding the world.

Had Peterson told John something earlier, some bit of news? She searched for a way to break the mood. "John, more sherry?"

"Right," he said, and got up to fetch it. He seemed vexed. "What was that earlier in the car, about the woman from Caltech?" he called to Peterson.

"Catherine Wickham," Peterson said with a flat voice. "She's the one working on those microuniverses."

"The papers you showed Markham?"

"Yes. If it explains your noise level, it's important."

"So that's what you put the call in about?" John asked, pouring sherry. "Like another?" He held up the whisky.

"Would, yes. I got through to her, and then Thorne, the fellow who's running that group. She's coming over on the next flight."

John stopped halfway through pouring. "*Well.* You must've pushed the right buttons."

"I know Thorne's contract monitor."

"Oh." Pause. "Quite."

"Well, let's not bore your wife by talking about business," Peterson said. "I'd like to see your garden, if I may. I spend most of my time in London or traveling and I must say it's delightful to see a real one-family home like this."

He glanced sideways at her as they got up. A deliberate play for her sympathy, she wondered?

"Does your wife travel with you?"

"No, she doesn't."

"No, I suppose she couldn't, with her business. She must be doing very well with it."

"Yes, I believe it's flourishing. Sarah usually does well with anything she undertakes." His voice gave nothing away.

"Do you know his wife, Marjorie?" John asked, puzzled. They were out on the terrace, at the head of the steps to the lawn. The sun was still high.

"No, not personally, but I know of her. She used to be Lady Sarah Lindsay-Stuart-Buttle, you know."

John looked blank.

"Oh, you wouldn't know. Anyway, she designs these marvelous little dresses now. Sarah Lindsay. You don't have any children, do you, Mr. Peterson?"

"No, I don't."

They walked across the lawn. Somewhere off to the right a cock crowed.

"Your chickens?" Peterson asked her.

"Yes, we keep half a dozen for eggs. Sometimes for eating too, though I hate killing the silly things."

"What kind do you raise? Orpingtons or Leghorns, I suppose, if they're mainly for eggs."

She looked at him in surprise. "You know something about hens, then, do you? Yes, we've got some Orpingtons. No Leghorns. They're good layers, but I like the brown-shelled eggs better than white."

"Right. And Leghorns are highly strung, too. They tend to cause chaos in a small run, which is what I suppose you have. How about Rhode Island Reds? They lay nice brown eggs."

"I've got a couple of pullets right now. They haven't started laying yet."

"You're going to crossbreed, are you? That rooster didn't sound like a Rhode Island Red."

"I'm surprised you know so much about them."

He smiled at her. "I know a lot of things that surprise people."

She smiled back politely, but tried to keep her eyes cold. She was one woman who was not so easily charmed. The man was despicable, she told herself. He had no interest in her at all. He automatically flirted with her just because she was a woman.

"Would you care to have dinner with us this evening, Mr. Peterson?" she asked, rather formally.

"That's very kind of you, Mrs. Renfrew. Thank you, but I already have a dinner engagement. As a matter of fact," he added, looking at his watch, "I should probably be going. I'm supposed to meet someone at 7:30 back in Cambridge."

"I'm afraid I'm going to have to go back to work this evening, too," John said.

"Oh, no," she protested. "That's too bad of you." She was feeling rather tipsy now and in the mood for company. She also felt full of energy, almost twitchy, as if she had drunk too much coffee. "I haven't seen anything of you for ages and I was going to make a shrimp soufflé for dinner. I absolutely *refuse* to be left all alone again this evening."

"Sounds like a tempting offer. I wouldn't hesitate for a moment if I were you, John," Peterson said with another of his insinuating smiles.

John looked embarrassed at her outburst before a stranger. "Well, all right, if it's that important, I'll stay for dinner. I'll probably have to go in for a couple of hours afterwards."

They went back into the house. Peterson put his glass down. "Thank you for the drink. I'll let you know when I next have to go to California. Mrs. Renfrew, thank you for this pleasant interlude."

She let John see him to the door and got herself another drink while they were in the hall. It was rather disappointing that Peterson was not staying to dinner. She might even have enjoyed a mild flirtation with him—although he was, she supposed, a totally unprincipled and unlikable character.

John came back into the room, rubbing his hands. "Well, that gets rid of him. I'm glad he couldn't stay, aren't you? What did you think of him?"

"Reptilian," she said promptly. "Smooth and slimy. *I* wouldn't trust him an inch. Of course, he's very attractive."

"Is he? He looks pretty ordinary to me. I was surprised that you knew all that about his wife. You never mentioned it before."

"Oh but heavens, John, it all came back to me while he was here. Don't you remember? There was that frightful scandal about her and Prince Andrew. Let me see, I was twenty-five, so it must have been 1985. Prince Andrew's the same age as me and she was—oh, I don't know—about thirty, I should think.

Anyway, I can remember how we all talked about it. Randy Andy, we called him."

"I don't remember it at all."

"Oh, but you *must*. It was in all the papers. Not just the gossip columns, either. Lots of letters about the public expecting higher standards of the Royal Family and all that stuff. And the Queen had Peterson made an ambassador to—well, I don't remember where, but it was a long way off. Africa."

"You mean they were married, then?"

"Well, of *course* they were. That was what made it such *scandal*. They'd had a big Society wedding only about a year before that. He wasn't actually made an ambassador. You know, first secretary or some such post. Yes, we used to think Prince Andrew was rather super. It was quite an exciting affair. I think the last straw was when they got a bit smashed one evening and he took her back to a room in Buckingham Palace and hung a Do Not Disturb sign on the door, a sign they'd pinched from some hotel. And then she told the reporters, when the story got out, that she'd always wanted to do it in the Palace but the beds were hard and lumpy!"

"Good heavens, Marjorie!"

She giggled at his expression. "Well, it is rather funny, when you come to think of it."

"She sounds completely irresponsible. It's almost enough to make me feel sorry for Peterson, although I dare say they deserve each other. I suppose he only stayed with her because she could further his career."

"Very probably. I must say I didn't care for him at all." Now that she had said it that seemed right. It helped explain some of the odd tension and confusion. He seemed interesting, but perhaps that was due to the three drinks. "Well, I'll get that soufflé into the oven. Could you set the table, love?"

"Um, yes," he murmured absentmindedly, moving across the room. "Thought we could catch the news, too . . ."

Marjorie turned back. "*News*, that's it. You and Peterson had this funny moment earlier—what were you thinking of?"

John stopped. "Oh, yes. He had the same look on his face as this afternoon, when he got a telephone call at the lab. It reminded me. I overheard part . . ."

He paused, thinking. "Well?" Marjorie said severely. "What *about?*"

"The clouds. A report on their composition. And when he sidestepped your question, I knew something was up."

"Do you think the news will have anything?"

"If Peterson's keeping mum, I doubt it. Still . . ."

The children had been watching ITV. John switched it back to BBC I. Marjorie stood in the doorway, watching. There was only one major news broadcast each day; the rest was entertainment, mostly situation comedies, with the occasional Western and old movie. Few wanted to see anything serious these days.

"—rioting in London, too, today, though there were no casualties. Cornish protest groups demonstrating in Trafalgar Square became involved in a scuffle with the police. A police spokesman says the group ignored an injunction to clear the streets and let traffic proceed, so the authorities were obliged to dispel the gathering by force and arrest those who resisted. Hugh Caradoc, leader of the Cornish Movement for Independence, claims that the demonstration was an orderly one and that the police attacked without provocation." The screen showed a wild-eyed man with one fist upraised being dragged away by two policemen. The announcer paused again and looked more cheerful. "Preparations for the Coronation are going forward. The King and Queen visited Westminster Abbey today and were received by the Right Reverend Gerald Hawker, Dean of the Abbey. They remained for a little under an hour." The familiar façade of Westminster Abbey appeared on the screen and, dwarfed by the portals, a couple emerged, waved briefly to some bystanders and ducked into a waiting limousine with the Royal Standard fluttering over it. "Invitations for the November ceremony have now been sent out to heads of state all over the world. At the Royal Mews, work has started on refurbishing the State coach traditionally used for Coronations. It is to be entirely regilded at an estimated cost of £500,000. Mr. Alan Harmon, M.P. for Huddersfield, said in the House of Commons today that it was 'an outrageous burden on the British taxpayer.' A Palace communique today confirmed that fourteen-year-old Prince David is suffering from chicken-pox and is in isolation at Gordonstoun School. The heir to the throne is reported to be whiling away his time reading science fiction comic books. And now for the sports news of the day. At the close of play, Kent were all out for 245 in their match against Surrey . . ."

Marjorie left the room to prepare the dinner. John Renfrew remained in front of the TV set, waiting for the Yorkshire score. He never had time for sports any more, but he still followed the county cricket matches and the Tests and supported Yorkshire.

In the kitchen, Marjorie bustled about. She felt jittery. Dull old cricket. Why did he sit there and watch that stuff? He could be helping her or at least talking to her, since he was planning

206

to go out again. She wondered about the wine and decided against it. It was a waste to drink it when she was going to spend the evening alone and she felt lightheaded anyway. She tossed the salad, got out bread and butter. The soufflé was just ready. She went back to the living room. John was still in front of the television.

"I thought you were going to set the table, then," she said sharply.

He looked up vaguely. "Oh, is dinner ready? I'll do it in just a minute."

"No, not in just a minute. The soufflé's done and won't wait. Jolly well do it *now*."

She flounced out of the room and he stared after her in surprise. He ambled over to the sideboard and pulled out some forks and mats and put them on the table. Marjorie came back with the soufflé.

"Do you call that setting the table? Where are the napkins? And the glasses? And call the children, too. I'm going to serve this before it falls." She sat down at the table.

"What's the matter, luv?" he asked innocently.

"What do you mean, matter? Nothing's the matter," she snapped back.

"You sound cross," he ventured.

"Well, it's jolly irritating. All I ask you to do is set the table and I get everything else ready and then find you haven't done a thing. I'm fed up with working hard all day and what's the *point* of it? I clean the house and we never entertain any more so no one sees it anyway. I make a nice dinner and you just eat and run. I might as well have opened a tin of baked beans for all you'd notice. And I'm sick of spending the evening alone and half the night, for that matter." She rose to her feet, confronting him.

"Marjorie, I'm sorry, my dear. I hadn't realized . . . Look, I'll stay home tonight, if you feel that strongly about it. I thought . . . I mean, I know I've neglected you of late but this work means an awful lot to me—it's vitally important, Marjorie, but I couldn't do it without knowing you're there behind me. You're the most stable element in my life. I don't tell you so because I take it for granted that you know it. I just count on you. I couldn't concentrate on my work at all if I knew anything were wrong with you."

She smiled wryly. "Now you're making me feel guilty. I've let you down, haven't I? You want me to keep the home fires burning, be your support system, behind every great man and so on and so forth. Well, mostly I'm happy to do it, but this evening I feel a little selfish. It's not just your being out all the time. It's been a long hard day, one thing after another. I had to queue up for hours, they were out of meat everywhere, I can't get anyone to come and fix the loo for a whole bloody fortnight, and someone broke the lock on the garage today and stole a bunch of tools.''

"They did? You didn't tell me."

"You gave me no chance. I can never reach you at the bloody lab. And Nicky came home from school in tears because Miss Crenshaw, of all people, has up and gone off to Tristan da Cunha with no notice or anything, and you know how devoted Nicky was to her. I thought the government was going to *stop* emigration of needed workers. I suppose Miss C. didn't qualify as needed. Anyway I had to console Nicky. And then you phoned and said you were bringing Peterson home. Honestly, sometimes I feel just like a football for other people to kick around.''

"Why don't you take a day off? Go into London shopping? Buy yourself a dress. Go to the theater."

"Alone?"

"You choose the day and I promise I'll come up in the evening and meet you for a play. How about that? So long as it's not one of those new-style gloom-and-doom pieces. The world's in bad enough shape already without that.''

She laughed, mollified. "Oh, things are not as bad as everyone makes out. The world's been through worse times. Think of the Black Death. Or the Second World War. We'll survive all this too. Yes, I think a day in London is a good idea. I haven't bought any new clothes for ages. Oh, John, I feel a lot better now. And you know, you don't really have to stay this evening. I know you're dying to get back to your work.''

"I'll stay," he said firmly. "Tell me more about what was taken from the garage. You know, it's high time we had an alarm system installed. Do you think it was those squatters up at the old farm?''

"Oh my God, John," she wailed suddenly, "look at the soufflé! It's flat as a pancake!" She sat down heavily and stared at it. Then she started to laugh. Her laughter merged gradually into sobbing. John stood behind her, patting her shoulder awkwardly.

"Don't take on so, luv," he kept saying.

Finally she dried her eyes and sat up. "Well, I'm not hungry anymore anyway. I don't want to eat the beastly thing. I'm exhausted. But the kids haven't had dinner. I suppose I'll have to get them something."

She started to get up, but John pushed her back into her seat. "No, you don't. I'll open a tin of soup for them or something. You go off to bed. You look all in. Don't worry about a thing. I'm staying home this evening and I'll take care of everything."

"Thanks, John, you're a dear. Yes, I really think I will go to bed."

She watched him go into the kitchen and stood up wearily. Then she almost started to laugh again. Just an hour or two ago, she had been feeling starved of sex because John was so seldom home. Now he was home for the evening and she was so tired she could hardly keep her eyes open long enough to get to bed. Bloody marvelous, wasn't it?

chapter twenty-two

She appeared on time at their agreed-upon meeting place, the low stone wall in front of King's. Peterson hesitated for only an instant, rummaging for the phrase that would call up her name. Ah, yes, Laura-at-Bowes. "Hope I haven't kept you waiting," she said, smoothing her dress with dainty hands.

He murmured something in automatic reply, struck again by how pretty she was. He noticed with amusement that she was wearing a simple dress that was a copy of one of Sarah's models. A good copy. It would have fooled almost anyone.

Laura was impressed with the car, a late model custom-modified for him. She looked wonderingly at the bossed wood and understated dash, yet said nothing. *Trying to appear blasé,* he judged. Even Sarah, who must have been sophisticated at age five, had exclaimed over the interior. Come to think of it, the only person he could recall who had not been impressed was Renfrew. He wondered what that meant.

When they entered the restaurant, some miles outside Cambridge, the head waiter apparently recognised him. The other male diners didn't; it was Laura who drew the stares. Gin-and-tonics, opulent linen napkins, the usual. Laura looked round the room in a way suggesting that she was taking mental notes for her friends. Impressive, he supposed, but stylistically a hodge-podge. Basically an English country inn with touches of French elegance that didn't fit. The chintz, the large stone fire-place filled now with plants for the summer, the beamed ceiling, the low round oak tables—all were comfortably familiar, solid. The chandeliers and tinted mirrors were wrong. Doubly so for the flatplate TV giving a not-quite-right view of a French court-yard, with distant moving figures in the fields, farmers apparently gathering hay. And the fake Louis XVI half-round side table with its bowed gilt legs was simply a monstrosity.

"Frangers!" Laura exclaimed.

"Yes," he said.

She remarked very precisely, "I wonder what the *rognons de veau flambé* is like? And the *côtes d'agneau à l'ail?*"

"The first, probably so-so. They're big on flaming here. The second, more likely adolescent mutton than real lamb. Your French is quite good." Might as well get that in. He phrased a longer compliment in French.

"Sorry, I only speak food."

He laughed, pleased to find a touch of wit in her.

They discussed shoplifting in Bowes & Bowes; Peterson had deflected most of her questions about Council matters. "Why not a guard at the door, searching briefcases?" he asked.

"Mr. Smythe wants ours to remain a gentlemen's establishment, where the customers don't feel they're under suspicion."

Peterson recalled a time when one could count on having rooms in college, and was given sherry when one went round to one's tutor, and wore a white dinner jacket for the May Balls. Now all the colleges admitted women, and women shared rooms with the men if they liked, and there was even an all-gay college, and academic gowns weren't required anywhere.

She went on about how rude the students were today. He nodded, guessing that this was the sort of thing she expected he would like to hear. Not far wrong, actually. But it was her charm that interested him, not her opinions.

He brought his mind to bear on the situation. It seemed like a straightforward problem in the timeless sexual game. Perhaps it was the predictability of it that explained his inattention to detail; he had to force himself to follow the thread of her talk. She wanted to get into films or maybe acting, check. A flat in London if she could only find some way to move, right. Cambridge was dull, unless you liked the dreadful academic sort of amusements. She felt something really did need fixing in the current political situation, but had no suggestions as to what that might be. No surprises, but she was awfully pretty and had a graceful way of moving.

She accepted all of the vegetables that arrived in silver dishes, each in its own sauce. Probably didn't get much variety at home, particularly since the French crop failures. He speculated for a moment about whether the Council should have stepped in on that one, ruling out the new techniques, and then pushed the subject back into place; no point in dwelling on past issues.

Since he was having trouble focusing, he began directing the flow of talk. It was easy enough to work in a recent state function, slide a few names past at the right speed to be understood, but not so slowly that she would suspect he was dropping them in deliberately. Then he slipped in a reference to Charles and she blurted, "Do you really know the King?" Actually he was on respectful and professional terms with Charles, but had no hesitation in exaggerating the relationship as far as believable. He felt confident that she did not even notice the discreet gesture with which he ordered another half bottle from the wine waiter. She was getting slightly giggly now. He took advantage of it to try rather more risqué stories on her. At one point she covered her glass with her hand, protesting that she had had enough. He set the bottle down and started to tell her the salacious details behind the Duke of Shropshire's recent divorce. He quickly got to the scene in court when the famous "headless" photo was produced. Lady Pringle had sworn it was the Duke, she would recognize him anywhere. The judge had asked to see the photo. He found it to be essentially a close-up of a man's genitalia, though his companion's face was clearly identifiable. Laura was giggling so helplessly that he felt sure she did not see him refill her glass. As he went on with how the judge had asked Lady Pringle how she could be so sure it was the Duke, he raised his glass and Laura imitated him unthinkingly. He let her swallow her wine before he told her Lady Pringle's reply, which had so convulsed the court that the judge had had to order it cleared.

He sat back and watched her. Things were going splendidly. She had abandoned her affected flirtatious attitude and, momentarily, her refined accent.

"Oh, go on with you," she said, her vowels sliding obliquely through a range of East Anglian diphthongs.

The waiter had pushed a trolley of sickeningly elaborate French pastries to their table. As he expected, she chose the creamiest and attacked it with the unabashed eagerness of a schoolgirl.

Over coffee she became earnest again, watching her vowels and pressing him about politics. She repeated the common newspaper cant about irresponsible corporations pushing questionable new products into the world without a thought for social impact. Peterson resigned himself to sitting through this standard lecture and then, without quite realizing it, found himself thinking aloud about matters he had shelved for a long time. "No, no, you've got it wrong," he said suddenly. "The wrong turning came when we started going for the socially relevant research in the first place. We accepted the idea that science was like other areas, where you make a product and the whole thing can be run from the top down."

"Well, surely it can," Laura said. "If the right people are at the top—"

"There *are* no right people," he said with energy. "That's

what I'm just now learning. See, we went to the senior scientists and asked them to pick the most promising fields. Then we supported those and cut the rest, to 'focus our efforts.' But the real diversity in science comes from below, not from innovative managers above. We narrowed the compass of science until nobody saw anything but the approved problems, the conventional wisdom. To save money we stifled imagination and verve."

"It seems to me what we have is *too much* science."

"Too much applied work without really understanding it, yes. Without pursuing the basics, you get a generation of technicians. That's what we have now."

"More checking to see the unforeseen side effects—"

"To see you must have vision," he said earnestly. "I'm just beginning to catch on to that fact. All this talk of bloody 'socially relevant' work assumes a bureaucrat somewhere is the best judge of what's useful. So now the problems are outstripping the can-do types, the folks with limited horizons, and, and . . ."

He stopped, puzzled with himself at this outburst. It had altered the carefully cultivated tone of the evening, perhaps fatally. Maybe spending the day with Renfrew had done it. For a moment there he had been arguing fervently against the very point of view that had brought him so rapidly to the top.

He took a long pull of coffee and chuckled warmly. "I rather got off the beam on that one, didn't I? Must be the wine." Properly played, the momentary outburst could be used to show that he was passionate about the world, involved, independent thinker, etc., all of which might well appeal. He set to work insuring that they did.

●

The moon was high above the trees. An owl swooped silently across the patch of sky above the clearing. Cautiously he slid his arm out from under her head and looked at his watch. Past midnight. Goddamn. He stood up and started dressing. She lay still, sprawled quite unself-consciously, legs flung wide as he had left her.

She was lying on his jacket. He stooped to retrieve it and in the moonlight saw tears on her cheeks. Oh, shit. Surely he wasn't going to have to cope with that too.

"Better put your clothes on," he said. "It's getting late."

She sat up and fumbled with her dress. "Ian," she began in a small voice, "that's never happened to me before."

"Come on," he said, not believing her. "You can't tell me you were a virgin."

"I didn't mean that."

He searched for her meaning. "You never—?"

"I—not with a man—not like that—I never had—" She stumbled over her words, trailing off, embarrassed.

So that was it. He didn't help her out. He felt weary and impatient, unmoved by her implied compliment. It was a point of honor to satisfy them, no more. God knows she had taken long enough over it. Still, it had been a better job than that Japanese nymphomaniac in La Jolla, Kiefer's wife. There was now an unpleasant twinge when he thought of her. He had done the usual—indeed, more. She had come again and again and seemed insatiable. There had been a kind of feverish clutching to her, a thing he had noticed in many women lately. But that was their problem, not his. He sighed and pushed away the memory.

He shook out his jacket, brushing away blades of grass. She was silent now, still fiddling with the tie on her dress, probably trying to make it into the same bow she'd left home with. He led the way from the clearing, empty of any further desire to touch her. When she slipped a hand into his he thought it politic to let it stay there; he would be coming to Cambridge again, after all. Absent-mindedly he scratched a midge bite on his neck that he'd collected while tussling in the grass. Tomorrow was going to be another long one. He flexed his shoulders. A cold ache had settled into the muscles at the base of his neck. Let's see, there was the subcommittee meeting tomorrow, and some backup reading on the Sacred Cow War still sputtering along in India . . . He realized with a start that he was living slightly in the future these days, as an ingrained habit. At Renfrew's he'd been distracted by thoughts of dinner and wine. At the restaurant he had watched Laura's hair and thought how it might look fanned out across a crisp white pillow. Then, immediately after the act, his mind had drifted on to the next day and what he had to do. Christ, a donkey driven by the carrot.

He was faintly surprised when they emerged from the damp woods into the moonlight and he remembered he was still in Cambridge.

chapter twenty-three

Gregory Markham was surprised when Ian Peterson appeared in the laboratory, striding purposefully down the lanes of electronic gear. After the usual greeting Greg said, "I would have imagined you didn't have much time these days for secondary efforts like this."

Peterson looked around the bay. "I was in the neighborhood. I saw Renfrew a few days ago and have been busy since. Wanted to talk to you and see this new Wickham woman."

"Oh, about that. I don't see the necessity of my going Stateside right away. There's—"

Peterson's face hardened. "I've cleared your way with NSF and Brookhaven. I've done all I can from my end. I should think you'd no objection to running interference for Renfrew back there."

"Well, I *don't*, but . . ."

"Good. I'll expect you on the flight tomorrow, as planned."

"I've got a lot of interesting theory to go over here, things Cathy brought—"

"Take it with you."

Markham sighed. Peterson was not the easy-going breed of administrator popular in the US, open to suggestion even after a decision had been made. "Well, it will hold things up, but . . ."

"Where's Wickham?"

"Ah, down that way. She came in yesterday and John's still showing her around."

A slim, rather bony woman approached. "Just finished the tour," she said to Markham. "Pretty impressive. I haven't met you, I think," she continued, turning her large brown eyes to Peterson.

"No, but I know of you. Ian Peterson."

"So you're the guy who got me strong-armed out here."

"More or less. You're needed."

"I was needed in Pasadena, too," she said grimly. "You must've lit a fire under some big honcho upstairs."

"I wanted to hear about these tachyons from subuniverses and so on."

"My, you must be used to getting what you want pretty damn fast."

"At times," Peterson murmured lightly.

"Well, I've got the lowdown from Greg and John here, and I think that noise just might have, well, cosmological origins. Maybe microuniverses, maybe distant Seyfert galaxies in our own universe. Hard to tell. Quasar cores can't produce this much noise, that's for sure. The data coming into Caltech and Kitt Peak seems to suggest there's a lot of dark matter in our own. Enough to imply there are microuniverses, maybe."

"Enough to close off our geometry?" Greg put in. "I mean, above the critical density?"

"Could be." To Peterson she added, "If the density of dark matter is high enough, our universe will eventually collapse back in on itself. Cyclic cosmos and so on."

"Then there's no way to avoid the noise in Renfrew's experiment?" Peterson asked.

"Probably not. It's a serious problem for John, who's trying to focus a beam in spite of all the spontaneous emission this tachyon noise causes. But it'll be no worry for 1963 or whatever. They're just receiving; that's a lot easier."

Peterson murmured a neutral, conversation-breaking reply and said that he had to make some calls. He departed quickly, seeming rather distracted. "Funny guy," Cathy said.

Markham leaned against the computer console. "He's the man who opens the cash register. Humor him."

She smiled. "I'm amazed you got funding for all this—" a sweep of the arm. Her eyes moved, studying his face. "Do you really think you can change the past?"

Markham said reflectively, "Well, I *think* Renfrew started out simply to get funding. You know, a practical icing on a cake that's really fundamental and 'useless.' He never expected it to work. I thought it was good physics, too, and we were both surprised at Peterson's interest. Now I'm coming to think that John was earnest from the first. Look, *you*'ve seen the equations. If an experiment doesn't produce a causal loop, it's allowed. That's open and shut."

Cathy sat in a lab chair and rocked back, putting her feet up on the console. The skin seemed stretched thin across her cheekbones, dry and papery, lined by sun and fatigue. Jet-lag shadows made crescents under her eyes. "Yeah, but those heating-up experiments you did first . . . That's one thing, simple stuff. With people involved, though—"

"You're thinking about paradoxes again," Markham said sympathetically. "Having people in the experiment introduces free will, and that leads to the problem of who's the observer in this pseudo-quantum-mechanical experiment, and so on."

"Yeah."

"And this experiment *works*. Remember Peterson's bank message."

"Yeah. But sending this ocean stuff—what would success be like? We wake up one day and that bloom is gone?"

"We're thinking in paradox-making channels again. You're separating yourself from the experiment. The old classical observer, sort of. See, things don't have to be causal, they only have to be self-consistent."

She sighed. "I don't know what the new field equations say about that. Here's a copy of my paper on the coupled solutions, maybe you . . ."

"Combining quantum-mechanical supersymmetry and general relativity? With tachyons in?"

"Yeah."

"Hey, that's worth looking at." Markham brightened.

"A lot of the old features are still in these equations, I can tell that much. Every quantum-mechanical event—that is, involving tachyons in a paradox-producing loop—still leads to a kind of scattering into a family of event-probabilities."

"A wave pattern between past and future. The light switch hung up between 'on' and 'off.' "

"Yes."

"So we still get probabilistic predictions. No certainties."

"I think so. Or at least, the formalism has that part in it. But there's something else . . . I haven't had time to figure it out."

"If there were time to think . . ." Markham puzzled over the neatly typed pages of equations. "Interpreting this is the hard part. The mathematics is so new . . ."

"Yeah, I sure as hell wish that guy Peterson hadn't yanked me away from Caltech. Thorne and I were on the verge—" Her head jerked up. "Say, how did Peterson know about me? You tell him?"

"No. I didn't know you were working on this."

"Ummmm." Her eyes narrowed. Then she shrugged. "He's got some power, that much I can tell. Seems like a typical English prig."

Markham looked uncomfortable. "Well, I don't know . . ."

"Okay, okay, put that down to my jet lag. The flight was packed, too. Jesus, I wish Peterson had held off a week or so."

Markham saw Peterson emerge from where Renfrew was working, and signaled to Cathy. She put on a bland, faintly comical face. Markham hoped Peterson wouldn't notice.

"Just talked to my staff," Peterson said, hitching thumbs into his waistcoat as he approached. "I had them look into the people who were working at NMR at Columbia, Moscow, and La Jolla around 1963. Biographies and so on."

Markham said, "Yes, that's an obvious thing to check, isn't it? Trust Ian to cut through all this physics and try something simple."

"Ummmm." Peterson glanced at Markham, eyebrow lifting microscopically. "Staff haven't much time, with all that's going on. They turned up nothing obvious, like papers in the scientific journals. There was something about 'spontaneous resonance' that never reappeared—seems to have been a red herring—but nothing about tachyons or messages. One chap did stumble on a piece in *New Scientist* about messages from space, though, and credited an NMR chap named Bernstein. There's a reference to some television appearance, along with a life-in-the-universe type."

"Can your staff dig that out?" Cathy asked.

"Perhaps. A lot was lost with the Central Park nuke, I'm told. The network files were in Manhattan. News programs 35 years old aren't kept in multiple copies, either. I've put a woman to searching, but Sir Martin's got a crash program going on this—" He broke off suddenly.

"You think it was this Bernstein who left that note in the bank?" Markham asked.

"Possibly. But if that is all the effect Renfrew's beams have had, the ocean information hasn't got through."

Markham shook his head. "Wrong tense. We can still keep transmitting; if one message made it, others can."

"Free will again," Cathy said.

"Or free won't," Peterson said mildly. "Look here, I've got to go into Cambridge, see to a few matters. Could you give me a briefing on your work, Cathy, before I go?"

She nodded. Markham said, "Renfrew's having a little party tonight. He means to invite you, I know."

"Well . . ." Peterson looked at Cathy. "I'll try to come round. Don't absolutely have to be back in London until tomorrow."

He and Cathy Wickham went into Renfrew's small office, to use the blackboard. Markham watched them talking through the clear glass paneling of the door. Peterson seemed caught up in the physics of the tachyons, and had largely forgotten the supposed usefulness of them. The two figures moved back and forth before the board, Cathy making diagrams and symbols with quick swoops of the chalk. Peterson studied them, frowning. He seemed to be watching her more than the board.

chapter twenty-four

Markham gestured with the hand that held his drink, spilling a little on the Renfrews' gray carpet. Absent-mindedly he dabbed at it with his foot, as if uncertain whether it was due to him, and went on talking to Cathy Wickham. "Those new equations of yours have some funny solutions. There's the old probability wave for the causal loops, yes, but . . ." He kept on in a dreamy, thoughtful way, at the same time in the back of his mind hoping Jan would arrive soon. He had called her from the lab when Renfrew told him that this gathering was to be a sort of informal bon voyage party for him. Renfrew was pinning hopes of overcoming the noise problem on the Brookhaven equipment, and Markham's dexterity at talking them out of it. "Pissing down out, isn't it?" Renfrew remarked, peering out a window. It was. A brooding gloom had followed the sudden, thundering rain. Peterson, driving in from Cambridge, had had to roll his window down and lean out to see the gate. Markham walked to the window and caught the heavy scent of damp earth and sodden leaves. Winged sycamore seeds spiraled down into the wet hedgerows. A soaked world.

Marjorie Renfrew hovered at the edge of the Peterson-Wickham-Markham triangle, unable to join in the casual science chat. John Renfrew prowled the room, pushing little plates of finger food a centimeter nearer the true center of the little tables. His face was flushed and he seemed to have drunk quite a lot already.

The doorbell rang. None of them had heard an approaching car in the hammering rain. Marjorie dashed to answer, looking relieved. Markham heard her voice in the hall, running on with no pause for an answer. "What a terrible evening! Isn't it absolutely awful? Come in, haven't you got a raincoat? Oh, you must to live here, no matter what, I'm glad Greg reached you. It was at the last minute, yes, but I am quite surrounded by scientists here and need *some*one to talk to."

He saw rain dripping steadily from the edges of the porch roof behind Jan, before Marjorie closed the door, bucking it with her shoulder to get it into the jamb. "Hi, hon." He kissed her with a casual warmth. "Let's get you dry." He ignored Marjorie's fluttering and tugged Jan into the living room.

"A real wood fire! How lovely," Jan said.

"I thought it would cheer things up," Marjorie confided, "but actually in a way it's depressing. It makes it seem like autumn and it's still only August, for goodness sake. The weather seems to have gone haywire."

"Do you know everyone?" Greg asked. "Let's see, this is Cathy Wickham."

Cathy, now sitting on the sofa with John Renfrew, nodded to her.

"Oh, to be in California, now that August's here, eh?"

"And this is Ian Peterson. Ian, my wife, Jan."

Peterson shook hands with her.

"Well, how did the experiment go?" Jan asked the company at large.

"Oh heavens, don't start them on that," Marjorie said quickly. "I was hoping we could talk about something else now you're here."

"Both good and bad," Greg said, ignoring Marjorie. "We got a lot of noise, but Cathy's detailed explanation of the noise level and spectrum sounds good, so with better electronics John here can sidestep some of the problem."

"I'm surprised Peterson can't get it for you with a telephone lift of his finger," Cathy said sharply. Heads turned towards her. She wagged her jaw back and forth, the sidewise swaying intense and unconscious.

"My omnipotence is overrated," Peterson said mildly.

"It's impressive to see the scientific tail wagging the CIA dog."

"I'm sure I don't know what you mean."

"People ought to put files back the way they found them."

"I'm sure I have no idea what you are—"

"Are you going to hide behind that memorized sentence forever?"

Marjorie stared at the two in horror, caught by the spark of tension. "Won't you have something to drink, Jan?" she broke in desperately, her voice a little too loud. Peterson's brittle retort drowned Jan's quiet reply.

"Here in England we still rather think discretion and civility oil the wheels of social intercourse, Miss Wickham."

"*Doctor* Wickham, if we're going to be formal, *Mister* Peterson."

"*Doctor* Wickham, of course." He made the word an insult. Cathy straightened, her shoulders rigid with fury.

"Your sort can't bear to see a woman as anything but a mindless lay, can you?"

"I assure you that is not the case in relation to yourself," Peterson said silkily. He turned to Renfrew, who looked as though he wished himself a thousand miles away. Markham sipped his drink, looking from one to the other with alert interest. Better than the usual party small talk . . .

"Funny, that wasn't the impression I got this afternoon," Cathy continued doggedly. "But then you haven't learned to take rejection very well, have you?"

Peterson's hand clenched on the stem of his glass, knuckles bleached white. He turned slowly. Marjorie said feebly, "Oh my goodness."

"You must have misunderstood something I said, Dr. Wickham," he said at last. "I would hardly raise the subject with a woman of your—ah—persuasion."

For a moment no one else moved or spoke. Then John Renfrew walked to the fireplace and stood in front of it, legs planted firmly apart, holding his mug of beer. He frowned, looking every inch the solid English squire.

"Look," he said, "this is my house and I expect my guests to behave civilly to each other in it."

"You're quite right, Renfrew," Peterson replied promptly. "I apologize. Put it down to intolerable provocation." It had the effect of making Cathy seem ungracious.

"Oh, God," she said ruefully. "John, I'm sorry that I had to get carried away in your house. But I did enjoy being rude to him—"

"That's *it*," Renfrew declared. "No more." He waved his mug in dismissal.

"Well done, John," Jan said. "Stand on your rights. Now, if I might have that drink—" She moved towards him, smiling. The rigid circle broke, tension dissipating. He took her elbow and they crossed to the sideboard. Peterson went to talk to Marjorie. Greg sat down on the sofa next to Cathy Wickham.

"Well, I think I took a fall in that round," she said cheerfully. "But it was worth it for a minute or two there."

"Did he actually proposition you?" Greg asked. "I was right there and never noticed a thing." Jan joined them, perching on the edge of the sofa.

"You kidding?" Cathy laughed. "Of course he did."

"Familiarity breeds attempt, or something. But to come right out and—"

"Oh, he was very subtle and discreet about it. Left room for a gracious refusal, save his ego and all. Self-satisfied bastard. But Jan disapproves of my actions, don't you, Jan?"

"Well, yes. I think you made things too uncomfortable for John and Marjorie. Frankly, I have the same opinion of him that you do, but . . ."

"This is fascinating," Greg said. "Let's hear you two get your claws into the poor guy."

"*Poor* guy? He's a highly successful, confident, slimy toad who despises women. You going to take his side as a man against two catty females?"

"He despises women?" Greg asked, startled. "I would have thought the opposite was true." Jan and Cathy exchanged glances.

"He loathes us, every one. And he can't stand rejection by an inferior being. Why do you think he implied I was gay?"

"Are you?"

She shrugged. "I'm bi, actually. But, yeah, I tend to prefer women. Don't look now, but old Ian is putting the make on our dear hostess. She's blushing like crazy." Markham twisted in his seat and stared across the room, curious.

"Christ, I can't imagine that. She doesn't strike me as sexy at all. Besides, she'd probably talk all the time."

"Now who's being catty? At least she's obviously heterosexual—that's all Peterson needs to soothe his wounded ego. It'll be Jan's turn next."

Jan raised an eyebrow. "Oh, come now. With Greg right here in the room? Anyway, he must know that I don't particularly care for him."

"You think either of those facts would bother him? Go talk to him—I'll bet it won't take five minutes before he makes a pass at you. Then you can cut him down to size."

Jan shook her head. "I'd rather avoid the experience."

"God, that's too much," Greg said. "I can't believe he's that bad."

Cathy made a face at him. "Well, bugger you. I'm going to talk to John about his experiment." She got up and left them.

"Well?" Greg asked.

"Well, what?"

"Don't you think she's overdoing it on Peterson? Do you think he really made a pass at her?"

"I'm quite sure he did. But I think what bothers her is being pulled away from her own work by someone who won't treat her like a scientist. And it can't be pleasant knowing one's personal papers have been gone through."

"Oh, the hell with it. Peterson seems quite reasonable to me, compared to the rest of the company. Renfrew's dull outside of the lab, Marjorie's a nit, and Cathy's abrasive. Jesus. There's only thee and me that's normal."

"And even thee's a bit queer," she supplied wryly. "I thought you were feeling good about the experiment. Why is everyone in such a terrible mood?"

"You're right—we're all edgy, aren't we? It's not the experiment. Personally, I'm not looking forward to flying to Washington."

"You're what?"

"Oh, God, of course—I haven't had a chance to tell you yet. Here, let me get you another drink and I'll explain."

"But we're planning—"

"I know, but this will only take a few days, and . . . ."

•

The other guests studiously avoided the sofa while Jan and Greg settled their family logistics. Then the Markhams sat for a while listening to the flow of English conversation around them, the long a's, the rising inflections.

Cathy had wandered out to the patio, announcing that the rain had passed, unnoticed in the tension of the living room. A stretched, artificial good humor seemed to tighten the throats of Peterson and Renfrew as they talked. Their words became clipped and slightly higher in tone. Marjorie's rushed sentences wove between theirs in a kind of birdlike counterpoint. Peterson was describing the immense paperwork boondoggle surrounding the saving of the Sumatran and Javan species of rhinoceros. The World Council had decided to redirect money for the Javan dieback into isolating the rhino. Ecoinventory had dictated that as part of the stabilization plan, aimed at saving species. The one species in excess was, of course, humans. The Council's policies had been applauded by the environmental types, politely not mentioning that in the zero-sum game of resources, this meant less available land and money for people. "Matter of choices," Peterson said distantly, swirling the amber fluid in his glass. Wise nods.

•

Greg Markham said to Marjorie Renfrew, "No, no, forget that scene between Cathy and Ian. Means nothing. We're *all* edgy lately."

They were standing on the patio, at the edge of the orange glow from inside.

"But scientists are less emotional, I thought, and to have them *at* each other . . ."

"First, Peterson's not a scientist. Second, all that about suppressing emotion is mostly a convenient legend. When Newton and Hooke were having their famous dispute over who discovered the inverse square law, I'm sure they were livid with rage. But it took two weeks to get a letter back and forth. Newton had time to consider his reply. Kept the discussion on a high plane, y'see. These days, if a scientist writes a letter, he publishes the damn thing. The interaction time is very low and the tempers flare higher. Still . . ."

"You don't think that explains the irritability of the times?" Marjorie observed shrewdly.

"No, there's something more, a feeling . . ." Greg shook his head. "Oh, rat'sass, I should stick to physics. Even there, of course, we don't really know much that's basic."

"Really? Why?"

"Well, take the bare fact that all electrons have the same mass and charge. So do their antiparticles, the positrons. Why? You can talk about fields and vacuum fluctuations and so on, but I like the old Wheeler idea—they have the same mass because they're all the same particle."

Marjorie smiled. "How can that be?"

"There's only one electron in the universe, see. An electron traveling backwards in time looks like its antiparticle, the positron. So you bounce one electron back and forth through time. Make *every*thing out of that one particle—dogs and dinosaurs, stones and stars."

"But why would it travel back in time?"

"Tachyon collision? I don't know." Greg's levity evaporated. "My point is, the foundation of everything is shaky. Even logic itself has holes in it. Theories are based on pictures of the world—human pictures." He looked upward and Marjorie's eyes followed. Constellations hung like blazing chandeliers. A distant airplane droned. A green light winked at its tail.

"I rather like the old, certain things," she began shyly.

"So we can have archaic and eat it, too?" Greg asked impishly. "Nonsense! We have to go on. Let's get back inside."

•

Markham went to the window and gazed up at the clearing skies. "Makes you wonder what sort of clouds dropped this water, doesn't it?" he mused, half to himself. His head turned, looking idly around the yard, and suddenly stopped. "Say, who're they?"

John Renfrew came over to the window and peered out into the gloom. "Who—I say, they're into our garage!"

Markham turned from the window, thinking of the man at the bus stop the other day. "What've you got in there?"

Renfrew hesitated, studying the shadowy figures who now had the garage door swung open. "Tools, old things, I—"

"Food!" Marjorie exclaimed. "My preserves, some are stored there. And tinned things."

"That's what they're after," Markham said decisively.

"The squatters down the way," Renfrew muttered to himself. "Call the police, Marjorie."

"Oh my," she said, unmoving.

"Go *on*." John gave her a push.

"I'll do it," Jan said briskly. She ran into the hall.

"Let's head 'em off," Markham said. He picked up a poker from the hearth almost casually.

"No," John said, "the police will—"

"These guys'll be long gone by that time," Markham said. He strode quickly to the front door and opened it. "Let's go!"

"They may be armed," Peterson's voice called after him.

Markham sprinted out the door and onto the lawn. Renfrew followed.

" 'ey!" a voice from the garage cried. "Scarper!"

"Come on!" Markham called.

He ran towards the dark maw of the open garage. He could make out a man stooped over, picking up a carton. Two others were carrying things. They hesitated as Markham came down on them. He raised the poker and called out towards the house, "Hey, John! Got your gun?"

The men unfroze. Two bolted down the drive. Greg charged forward and got between them and the gate. He swung the poker. It made a loud *swoosh*. The men stopped. They backed away, looking at the hedges to each side of the yard.

Renfrew ran at the third man. The dark figure sidestepped and slipped past him. At that moment Cathy Wickham came down the steps of the porch. Renfrew slipped on the wet grass. "Christ!" The man picked up speed, looking back at Renfrew. Cathy Wickham, trying to make out the shadows on the lawn, stopped dead in the path. The figure smashed into her. They sprawled on the stones.

Markham swung the poker back and forth in front of him. The men seemed paralyzed by the sound of it. In the gloom they could not tell how close it came. Markham could not judge the distance either. *Ignorant armies clash by night*, he thought giddily. Should he charge them?

"Your friend's bought his," he called out clearly.

They both turned to look. The yellow rectangle of the doorway sent a blade of light out onto the glistening lawn. In the beam John Renfrew yanked the fallen man to his feet and said, "What're you—"

Markham stepped quietly forward and swung the poker *crack* into the nearest man's leg.

"Awrrr!" The struck man collapsed. His partner saw Markham rearing up out of the shadows and backed away. Suddenly he turned and ran diagonally across the lawn. Markham tried to keep both men in sight. Two down, one to go.

"Look out, Greg, he's got a knife!" Cathy Wickham shouted.

The man turned, transfixed by the yellow light in the center of the lawn. Metal glinted in his hand. "Naw, you just leave off," he said roughly.

Markham walked towards him. *Swoosh, swoosh.* The sound caught the man's attention. Ian Peterson came trotting forward. "Let him go," he called to Markham.

"Hell no!" Markham answered with gusto.

"No point in risking—"

"We've got 'em," Markham insisted.

"That one's getting away!" Cathy Wickham cried. The man lying in the drive had moved at a crouch towards the gate. As she spoke he ran with a limp to the gate and vaulted over it.

"Damn!" Markham said with chagrin. "Should've covered him."

"No need for melodramatics," Peterson called mildly. "The police will be here shortly." Markham glanced back at Renfrew.

"Eric!" the man with the knife shouted. "Switch!"

Abruptly, before Markham could understand the signal, the two men moved. Renfrew's captive wrenched away from him and dashed back towards the garage. Markham followed. The man ran into the dark of the garage. Markham hesitated. He could see nothing. Suddenly the man reappeared, a shadow. Markham could make out that he had something long in his hand. Markham backed away warily. He saw the man with the knife moving towards the gate. An elementary maneuver to distract him. The shadow stepped further into the light and swung a rake at Markham's head. Markham ducked and jumped backward. "Christ, somebody—" Both men suddenly ran for the gate. One turned and threw the rake directly at Markham. He dodged aside. "Bastards!" he shouted and hurled the poker after them into the darkness. He listened to their footsteps fade away.

"No use going after them," Renfrew said at his side.

Cathy Wickham agreed, "Leave them to the police, Greg."

"Yeah, okay," he mumbled.

They trailed back into the house. There was a moment of silence and then everyone began chattering about the incident. Markham noted that those who had stayed inside and watched from the door had a different view of the details. They thought Renfrew had subdued his man, when in fact the fellow had simply been waiting for a proper opening for escape. *The relativity of experience,* Markham thought. He was still puffing from the exertion, adrenalin singing in him.

From the distance came the two-tone hooting of a siren.

"The police," Peterson said swiftly. "Late, as usual. Look, I'm going to cut and run before they get here. I don't want to have to answer questions for the rest of the night. You fellows are the heroes, anyway. Thanks for the drinks and goodbye, everyone."

He left hastily. Markham watched him go. He reflected on the fact that their first unthinking response had been to assume the shadowy figures were thieves. There was no hesitation, no one suggesting it was some mistake, people who'd got the wrong house. Twenty years ago that might have been the case. Now . . .

The others, standing in the center of the living room, drank a toast to each other. The siren drew nearer.

chapter twenty-five

JULY, 1963

Gordon saw that he would have to spend a lot of the summer working with Cooper. The candidacy exam had been a blow. Cooper took weeks to recover his self-confidence. Gordon finally had to sit him down and give him a Dutch uncle talk. They decided on a routine. Cooper would study fundamentals each morning, to prepare for a second try at the exam. Afternoons and evenings he would take data. By autumn he would have enough to analyze in detail. By that time, with coaching from Gordon, Cooper could take the exam again with some confidence. With luck, winter would find him with most of his thesis data complete.

Cooper listened, nodded, said little. At times he seemed moody. His new data came out smooth, unblemished: no signals.

Gordon felt a letdown whenever he looked over Cooper's lab books and saw the bland, ordinary curves. Could the effect come and go like that? Why? How? Or was Cooper simply discarding all the resonances which didn't fit his thesis? If you were damned certain you weren't looking for something, there was a very good chance you wouldn't see it.

But Cooper kept everything in his notebooks, as a good experimenter should. The books were messy but they were always complete. Gordon thumbed through them daily, looking for unexplained blank spots or scratched-out entries. Nothing seemed wrong.

Still, he remembered the physicists in the 1930s who had bombarded substances with neutrons. They had carefully rigged their Geiger counters so that, once the neutron barrage stopped, the counters shut off, too—to avoid some sources of experimental error. If they had left the counters on they would have discovered that some substances emitted high-energy particles for a long time afterward—artificially induced radioactivity. By being careful they missed the unexpected, and lost a Nobel prize.

•

The July issue of *Physics Today* carried a piece in the Search and Discovery section dealing with spontaneous resonance. There was a sample of the data, taken from the *Physical Review Letters* paper. Lakin was quoted extensively. The effect, he said, "promises to show us a new kind of interaction which can occur in Type III-V compounds such as indium antimonide—and perhaps in *all* compounds, if the experiments are sensitive enough to pick up this effect." There was no mention of the apparent correlations between the times when the spontaneous resonances appeared.

Gordon decided to attack the "spontaneous resonance" phenomenon afresh. The message idea made sense to him—at least, *something* was there—but the rebuffs from his colleagues could not be ignored. Okay, maybe they were right. Maybe a series of bizarre coincidences led him to believe there were coded words in the scope traces. In that case, what *was* the explanation? Lakin was afraid the concentration on the message idea would obscure the true problem. Okay, say Lakin was right. Say they were *all* right. What other explanation was possible?

He worked for several weeks on alternatives. The theory governing Cooper's original experiment was not particularly deep; Gordon labored through it, pondering the assumptions, redoing the integrals, checking each step. Some fresh ideas cropped up. He studied each one in turn, running it to ground with equations and order-of-magnitude estimates. The earlier theory dropped some mathematical terms; he investigated them, looking for ways they could suddenly stop being negligible and upset the theory. Nothing seemed to fit his needs. He reread the original papers, hoping for an offhand clue. Pake, Korringa, Overhauser, Feher, Clark . . . the papers were classics, unassailable. There were no visible escape hatches from the canonical theory.

He was pursuing a calculation at his desk, waiting for Cooper to show up for a conference, when his telephone rang. "Dr. Bernstein?" the voice of the department secretary asked.

"Um," he said, distracted.

"Professor Tulare would like to see you."

"Oh, okay." Tulare was Chairman. "When, Joyce?"

"Now, if it's convenient."

When Joyce ushered him into the long, spare room, the chairman was reading what Gordon recognized as a personnel folder. Events soon confirmed that it was his.

"Briefly," Tulare said, "I have to tell you that your Merit Increase has been, uh, subject to controversy."

"I thought it was a standard thing. I mean—"

"Ordinarily, it is. The department meets only to consider promotions from Assistant Professor to Associate Professor—that is, getting tenure—or from Associate Professor to full Professor."

"Uh huh."

"A Merit Increase, as in your case, from Assistant Professor Step II to Assistant Professor Step III, does not require the entire department vote. We usually ask the senior men in the candidate's group—in your case, the spin resonance and solid state group—to give an opinion. I am afraid . . ."

"Lakin vetoed it, huh?"

Tulare looked up in alarm. "I did not say that."

"But you meant it."

"I will not discuss individual comments." Tulare looked worried for a moment and then sat back, studying the tip of his pencil as though a solution lay there. "However, you realize the . . . events . . . of the last few months have not inspired a great deal of confidence in your fellow faculty members."

"So I had guessed."

Tulare began a series of reflections on scientific credibility, keeping the discussion safely vague. Gordon listened, hoping there would be something in it he could learn from. Tulare was not the standard administrator sort, in love with his own voice, and this little lecture was more a defense mechanism than an oration. Despite his earlier bravado, Gordon began to feel a sinking sensation steal into his legs. This was serious. A Merit Increase was routine; only really questionable cases had trouble. The big test was the leap from Assistant Professor to Associate Professor, which spelled tenure. Gordon had started out as Assistant Professor I and been advanced to II within a year, which was speedy; most faculty spent two years at each step. Once he reached Assistant III he could be promoted to Associate I, although the typical route was to go to Assistant IV before making the jump to tenure. But now he wasn't going to make the standard step from II to III on schedule. That didn't bode well for his prospects when he came up for tenure review.

A coldness had reached up from his legs into his chest when Tulare said, "Of course, you have to be careful of what you do in *any* field, Gordon," and discussed the necessary wariness a scientist had to have, the quality of being skeptical about his own findings. Then, incredibly, Tulare launched into a recital of the story of Einstein and the notebook for writing down thoughts, ending in the line, "So Einstein said, 'I doubt it. I have only had two or three good ideas in my life.' " Tulare slapped the desk with genuine mirth, relieved at being able to turn a difficult interview into something lighter. "So you see, Gordon—not *every* idea is a good one."

Gordon made a weak smile. He had told that story to Boyle and the Carroways and they had sat there and laughed. Undoubtedly they had heard it before. They were simply humoring a junior faculty member who must have appeared to be a buffoon.

He stood up. His legs were strangely weak. He found that he was breathing quickly, but there was no discernible cause. Gordon murmured something to Tulare and turned away. He knew he should be most concerned about the Merit Increase but for the moment all he could think of was the Carroways and their smiles and his own vast stupidity.

chapter twenty-six

JULY 7, 1963

During the summer the rhythm of their days changed. Penny began to sleep later and Gordon found himself waking before her. He resolved that he would stick to his Canadian Air Force exercise program religiously, and the best time to do it was in the early hours, on the deserted stretches of Wind 'n Sea beach. He never liked doing them at home, particularly if Penny was there. He liked going down to the white sands which had been cleaned by the night tides and working his way through the exercises as the sunlight brimmed above Mount Soledad to the east. Then he would run as far as possible along the beach. Each cove was a scooped-out world of its own, the shadows shortening as the sun rose. His sheen of sweat cooled in the blue shadows and the thick ocean air had a tangible watery weight as he sucked it in, puffing, legs setting a *thump thump thump* that came up through the bones, a curious sound in this air, like chunks of wood falling on an oak floor. He had run like this when he was a kid, on the scruffy beaches of New Jersey. His Uncle Herb took him there often, just after his father started with the sickness. When Jersey crowded in summertime, Uncle Herb took him for rides in a yellow Studebaker, out to Long Island. His mother had always spoken of the people who lived out there, of People Who Actually Owned Beach Front Property, as though they were another race. The first time Uncle Herb took him, Gordon asked if they were going to visit relatives, hoping he had some thread of connection with those mythical folk. Uncle Herb laughed in his quick, barking, not altogether friendly way, and wheezed, "Yeah, I'm going to visit a Mister Gatsby, doncha know," and slapped the side of the big yellow car, making a solid metallic *thump*. Gordon had sat with his arm out the window for the whole trip, the summer breeze of their passage caressing the black hair on his arm. The hair was more apparent that summer; Gordon compared his to Uncle Herb's and found that he had made remarkable progress in just a year. It took six more years before he understood the enigmatic remark about Gatsby. By the time he had read the book—ignoring the proffered Malamud from his mother—he could no longer remember much about the big houses on Long Island, or whether any of them had a green light on the end of a dock, or any of the other stuff. The beaches there, he remembered, were thin and stony, a bleak margin begrudged by the big inland estates. There wasn't much to do. Children built sand castles which their parents periodically approved, peering into the yellow-blue sun haze over the tops of their paperback books. He remembered thinking that if Long Island was typical, goyische life was dull. By contrast, Uncle Herb took him to some actual prizefights that summer, fights as big and real as he'd ever thought life could be. *Thump thump* his legs pounded on, and before him he saw again the white square of the ring, the two figures dancing and punching, a head jerking back when hit, the ref waltzing around the men, shouts and whistles and a hot, close, salty smell from the liquid crowd. "Didja see that guy Alberts in the fifth round," Uncle Herb said at the intermission, "feet like sandbags? Like a guy looking for a collar button he dropped. Sheesh!" And after the decision: "Those refs! Giving him two rounds, using what for eyes? I wouldn't want to go on hunting trips with *them*." *Thump thump thump* and the salty smell of the crowd went away and Gordon was running into a rising sun, the tang in his nostrils was a sea breeze thousands of miles from Long Island and he was throwing his fists out as he ran, uppercuts and cross punches and jabs with their own rhythm, his feet connected to his fists, panting hard, a face muddy and formless in front of him, now resolving into Lakin as Gordon wondered at it the same instant that he gave it two of his best, a fake and a belly punch and then the jab, fast and easy, then some more as he thought about Lakin and began to self-consciously erase the swimming face, but held it for three quick jabs, his knuckles sailing through the milky image and the head rocking back one, two, three times *thump thump thump* yeah Uncle Herb taking him places that whole long summer while his father was hanging on, keeping the boy's mind occupied—Gordon threw two more punches at the air, aiming at he didn't know what—mind filled yeah with fights and beaches and books while his father said nothing, smiled when you talked to him, never complained, just crawled away from everyone to die, the way they did it in the Bernstein family, just quietly, no fuss, nobody beating the drum for you, not for a Bernstein *thump thump thump* the beach sand now warming under his feet, sweat trickling into his eyes, stinging, blurring the morning, his throat raw. Jesus, he had run a long way. The cliffs were high here. He had slogged past Scripps pier and down to Black's Beach, a long deserted stretch below the Torrey Pines Park. He was running in shadow now and as he brushed the sweat from his eyes he suddenly saw that he was about to stumble on something. He leaped, thinking it was a sleeping dog, ran on by reflex and looked back. A couple. Legs akimbo. Woman's heels pointed at the sky. The whites of four eyes. *Jesus* he thought, but somehow it didn't disturb him that much. The idea was logical: lonely beach, horny couple, beautiful sunrise, salty smell. But it did mean he had to run even farther. Give them time to finish their *thump thump thump*. Certainly it was a better vision to end a run with than Lakin's creamy face, Gordon thought muzzily. Lakin was a problem he couldn't solve and maybe, he saw, that was why he was running so far, wearing himself out so a real fist wouldn't smack into a real face. Maybe, yeah, and maybe not. He had Uncle Herb's contempt for too much analysis. One way to be a potzer was to worry about things like that too much, yeah. Gordon smiled and licked his lips and threw two more punches, slicing the forgiving air.

•

Saul Shriffer called in mid-July. He had finished up the observations of 99 Hercules, using the Green Bank radio telescope. Results were negative. No coherent signal rose up out of the interstellar sputter. Gordon suggested using higher frequencies and narrower bandwidths. Saul said he had tried some. Without more to show for their efforts, though, he wasn't going to be able to get any more time on the instrument. Conventional research projects had precedence. They talked for a few minutes about alternatives, but there weren't any. The Cavendish group had turned down Saul's request for telescope time. Saul said a few reassuring things, and Gordon mechanically agreed. When Saul hung up Gordon felt an unexpected letdown. He saw that, without admitting it to himself, he had been pinning hope on the radio-listening idea. That evening, when he met Penny for dinner at Buzzy's, he did not mention the call. The next day he wrote Saul a letter asking that he not publish any summary of the radio search. Let's wait until something positive comes along, he argued. But more than that, Gordon wanted to keep quiet. Maybe it would all go away. Maybe it would be forgotten.

•

When Penny went board surfing at Scripps Beach, Gordon sat on the sand and watched. He had been doing a lot of that recently—sitting, thinking, letting others play out the summer. He liked running on the beach and knew he should try riding the waves, now that he had someone to teach him, but something held him back. He watched the La Jolla ladies work on their expensive tans, and came to know the types: People who worked outdoors were pale behind the knees, whereas beach loungers were a uniform chocolate, a consummation carefully arrived at.

Penny came out of the tumbling waters, board perched on a hip, straggly hair dripping. She sagged down beside him, wrung out her hair, flicked a glance at his set expression. "Okay," she said finally, "time to 'fess up."

"Fess who?"

"Fess *Parker*. Gordon, come *on*. You're doing your zombie imitation."

Gordon had always prided himself on getting right to the point; now he found himself rummaging for something to say. "Y'know . . . I've been looking through the journals in the library. Astronomy journals, I mean. *Nature, Scientific American, Science News*. Most of them are flat out *ignoring* Saul's PR work. Even if they mention it, they don't reproduce the picture. And not a one gave the Hercules coordinates."

"Publish them yourself."

Gordon shook his head. "Won't do any good."

"When did you start feeling so inadequate?"

"At tcn," Gordon said, hoping for some way to deflect this conversation, "when I began to suspect I wasn't Mozart."

"Uh huh."

"I was that American myth, the 98-pound weakling. Those Charles Atlas ads, remember. When I went to the beach, bullies didn't kick sand in my face—they'd kick *me* in the face. Eliminate the middle man."

"Uh huh." She studied him, face compressed. "You know that was the first thing you've told me about the Saul business in, what, a month?"

He shrugged.

"You never tell me *any*thing anymore."

"I don't want to get you so involved that people will ask you about it. So you'll have to defend me to friends." He paused. "Or deal with cranks."

"Gordon, I'd rather know what's going on. Really. If I'm to talk to UCLJ people I can't very well gloss over it."

He shrugged again. "Big deal. I might be leaving UCLJ anyway."

"*What?*"

So he told her about not getting the Merit Increase. "Look," he concluded, "being appointed an Assistant Professor is always risky. You may have to move on if things don't work out. I outlined all that to you. We talked it over."

"Well, sure, *eventually* . . ." She stared off toward La Jolla Point, face blank. "I mean, in the long run, if you didn't publish . . ."

"I've published," he murmured in a half-breath, defensively.

"Then why?"

"The business with Lakin. I can't do research in a group with two guys I like, Feher and Schultz, and one I rub the wrong way, Lakin. Personalities are—"

"I thought scientists rose above mere squabbling. You told me that once."

"This is more than a squabble, can't you see that?"

"Ha."

"Lakin is kind of out of the old school. Skeptical. Thinks I'm trying to deliberately make trouble for him." He ticked off motivations on his fingers. "Getting older and feeling a little shaky, maybe. Hell, *I* dunno. But I can't work in a group dominated by a guy like that. I've told you that before."

"Ah." Her voice had a brittle edge. "So, in effect, we talked that one out, too?"

"Oh, Christ."

"I'm glad you're conferring with me on all these problems. On *your* problems."

"Look—" he spread his hands, a wide gesture—"I don't know what I'll do. I was just talking."

"It'll mean leaving La Jolla. Leaving California, where I lived all my life? If that comes up, give me a few minutes to mull it over, okay?"

"Sure. Sure."

"You can still stay on here, though? It's your choice?"

"Yeah. We'll decide it together."

"Good. Fair and square? Open? No holding yourself aloof?"

"One man, one vote."

"That's what I'm afraid of."

"One *person*, one vote."

"Zappo."

Gordon lay down and opened a wrinkled *Time* magazine against the hovering sun. He tried to dismiss the boiling alternatives in his head and concentrate on a piece in the Science section on the planned Apollo moon shots. He made progress slowly; a decade of reading the close-packed language of physics had robbed him of speed. On the other hand, it did make him more conscious of style. He was gradually coming to feel that the breezy simplicities of *Time* hid more than they revealed. He was mulling this point when a shadow fell over him.

"Thought I recognized you," a gruff man's voice said.

Gordon blinked up into the hazy sunshine. It was Cliff, in a bathing suit and carrying a sixpack of beer.

Gordon became very still. "I thought you lived in northern California."

"*Hey!* Cliffie!" Penny had rolled over and seen him. "Whacha doin' here?" She sat up.

Cliff squatted on the sand, eyeing Gordon. "Jest walkin' along. My day off. Got a job in Oceanside."

"And you saw us here?" Penny said happily. "How long have you been down this way? You should've called me."

"Yes," Gordon said dryly, "a remarkable coincidence."

"Little over a week. Got me a job in two days flat."

Cliff hunkered down, not sitting on the sand but resting with the beer in both hands between his legs and his buttocks only an inch from the beach. Gordon remembered seeing Japanese perched like that for hours, in a movie somewhere. It was a curious pose, as though Cliff did not wish to commit himself to fully sitting with them.

Penny burbled on, but Gordon was not listening. He studied Cliff's sun-baked ease and looked for something behind the eyes, something that explained this improbable coincidence. He did not believe it for an instant, of course. Cliff knew that Penny surfed and that this was the nearest good beach. The only interesting question was whether Penny had known this was going to happen as well.

There was no sign between them, no small inexplicable smiles, no gestures, no false notes that Gordon could see. But that was just it—he wasn't good at that sort of thing. And as he watched them talking with their slow and easy grace they seemed so alike, so familiar from a thousand movies and cigarette ads, and so strange. Gordon sat, white as the underbelly of a fish in comparison, a flabby dirty alabaster with black swirls of hair. He felt a slow flush of emotion, a wash of feeling he could not quite name. He did not know if this was some elaborate, cute game they were playing, but if it was—

Gordon surged up, lurched to his feet. Penny watched him. Her lips parted in surprise at his stony expression. He struggled for the words, for something to fill the ground between knowledge and suspicion, something just right, and finally mumbled, "Don't, don't mind me."

"Hey, sport, I—"

"Goy games." Gordon waved a hand in dismissal, face hot. It had come out more bitter than he planned.

"Gordon, come on, really—" Penny began, but he turned away and broke into a trot. The rhythm picked him up instantly. He heard her voice, raised above the crunch of breakers, but it was thin and fading as she called to him. *Okay,* he thought, *no Great Gatsby finish, but it got me out of that, that—*

Not ending the sentence, not wanting to think about any of it any more, he ran toward the distant carved hills.

chapter twenty-seven

AUGUST 6, 1963

"I'm thinking of going into industry," he said to Penny one evening over supper. They had shared their small talk already, in what had become a thin ritual. Gordon refused to discuss the meeting on the beach, refused to have Cliff over for a drink, and felt his withdrawal would, ultimately, settle the matter. Only dimly did it occur to him that the refusals were the cause of the curiously stale conversations they now had together.

"What's that mean?"

"Work in a company research lab. GE, Bell Labs—" He launched into an advertisement for the virtues of working where results counted, where ideas evolved swiftly into hardware. He did not, in fact, believe the industrial labs were superior to university groups, but they did have an aura. Things got done faster there. Helpers and technicians abounded. Salaries were higher. Then too, he enjoyed the unavoidable smugness of the scientist, who knew he could always have a life beyond academe. Not merely a *job*, but a *pursuit*. Genuine research, and for decent pay, too. Maybe something beyond the laboratory, as well—look at Herb York with his consulting on "defense posture" and the cloudy theories of disarmament. The government could use some clear scientific thinking there, he argued.

"Gordon, this is just plain old bullshit."

"Huh?" It stalled him for a moment.

"You don't want to go work for a company."

"I'm thinking very seriously—"

"You want to be a professor. Do research. Have students. Give lectures. You lap it up."

"I do?"

"Of *course* you do. When everything's going okay you get up humming in the morning and you're humming when you come home at night."

"You overestimate the pleasures of the job."

"I'm not *estimating* at all. I see what professoring does to *you*."

"Uh." His momentum blunted, he ruefully admitted to himself that she knew him pretty well.

"So instead of talking up some temporary escape hatch like industry, you ought to be *doing* something."

"Like what?"

"Something *different*. Move your x's and y's and z's around. Try—"

"Another approach," he finished for her.

"Exactly. Thinking about problems from a different angle is—" She broke off, hesitated, then plunged ahead. "Gordon, I could tell what was going on there with Cliff. I could reassure you and do a whole routine, but I'm not sure any more that you'd believe me."

"Uh."

"Remember this," she said firmly. "You don't own me, Gordon. We're not even married, for Chrissake."

"Is that what's bothering you?"

"Bothering *me*? God, it's *you* that's—"

"—'cause if it is, maybe we ought to talk about that and see if—"

"Gordon, wait. When we started out, moved in together, we agreed we were going to try it out, that's all."

"Sure. Sure." He nodded vigorously, his food forgotten. "But I'm willing, if it's making you play games like this thing with Cliff—and that was really childish, Penny, arranging that meeting, just childish—I'm willing to talk about it, you know, ah, getting—"

Penny held out her hand, palm toward him. "No. Wait. Two points, Gordon." She ticked them off. "One, I didn't arrange any meeting. Maybe Cliff was looking for us, but I didn't know about it. Hell, I didn't even know he was *around* here. Two— Gordon, do you think our getting married will solve anything?"

"Well, I feel that—"

"Because I don't want to, Gordon. I don't want to marry you at all."

•

He came up out of the muggy press of late summer in the subway and emerged into the only slightly less compacted heat of 116th Street. This entrance and exit were relatively new. He dimly remembered an old cast-iron kiosk which, until the early '50s, ushered students into the rumbling depths. It stood between two swift lanes of traffic, providing a neat Darwinian selection pressure against undue mental concentration. Here, students with their minds stuffed chock full of Einstein and Mendel and Hawthorne often had their trajectories abruptly altered by Hudsons and DeSotos and Fords.

Gordon walked along 116th Street, glancing at his watch. He had refused to give a seminar on this, his first return to his Alma Mater since receiving his doctorate; still, he did not want to be late for his appointment with Claudia Zinnes. She was a kindly woman who had barely escaped Warsaw as the Nazis were entering it, but he remembered her impatience with late students. He hurried by South Field. To his left students clustered on the shallow steps of Low Library. Gordon headed for the physics building, perspiring from the effort of carrying his big brown suitcase. Among a knot of students he thought he saw a familiar face.

"David! Hey, David!" he called. But the man turned away quickly and walked in the opposite direction. Gordon shrugged. Maybe Selig didn't want to see an old classmate; he always had been an odd bird.

Come to think of it, everything here now seemed a little bit odd, like a photograph of a friend with something retouched. In the yellow summer light the buildings looked a little more scruffy, the people wan and pale, the gutters slightly deeper in trash. A block away a drunk lounged on a doorstep, drinking from something in a brown paper bag. Gordon picked up his pace and hurried inside. Maybe he had been in California too long; everything that wasn't crisp and new struck him as used up.

Claudia Zinnes was unchanged. Behind her warm eyes lurked a glinting intelligence, distant and amused. Gordon spent the afternoon with her, describing his experiments, comparing his apparatus and techniques with her laboratory. She knew of spontaneous resonance and Saul Shriffer and the rest. She found it "interesting," she said, the standard word that committed you to nothing. When Gordon asked her to try to duplicate the experiment with Cooper, at first she brushed aside the idea. She was busy, there were many students, the time on the big nuclear resonance magnets was all booked up, there was no money. Gordon pointed out how similar one of her present setups was to his own; simple modifications would make it identical. She argued that she didn't have a sample of indium antimonide good enough. He produced five good samples, little slabs of gray: here, use them any way you want. She arched an eyebrow. He found himself slipping into a persona he had forgotten—pushy *yid* schoolboy, hustling the teacher for a better grade. Claudia Zinnes knew these routines as well as anybody living, but gradually his pressure piqued her interest. Maybe there was something to the spontaneous resonance effect after all. Who could tell, now that the waters around it had been muddied so? She gazed at him with the warm brown eyes and said, "It's not for that you want me to check. Not to clear up this mish-mosh," and he nodded, yes, he hoped she would find something else. But—a warning finger—let the curves speak for themselves. He smiled and made little jokes and felt a little eerie, living in his student persona again, but somehow it all came together and worked. Claudia Zinnes slipped from "maybe" and "if" to "when" and then, seemingly without noticing the transition, she was scheduling some time on the NMR rig in September and October. She asked after some of his classmates, where they were, what sort of jobs. He saw suddenly that she had a true affection for the young people who passed through her hands and out into the world. As she left she patted his arm, brushed some lint from his damp summer jacket.

As he walked away across South Field he remembered the undergraduate awe that ran through him in those first four long, hard years. Columbia was impressive. Its faculty was world famous, the buildings and laboratories imposing. Never had he suspected that the place might be a mill grinding out intelligent trolls willing and able to wire the circuits, draw the diagrams, to spin the humming wheels of industry. Never had he thought that institutions could stand or fall because of the vagaries of a few individuals, a few uninspected biases. Never. Religions do not teach doubt.

•

He took a taxi crosstown. The cab banged into potholes on some of the side streets, a jarring contrast with California's smooth boulevards. He was just as glad Penny had refused to come; the city wasn't at its best on the grill of August.

They had been tense with each other since the marriage thing came up. Maybe a short separation would help. Let the whole subject drift downstream into the past. Gordon watched the blur of faces going by outside. There was an earthen hum here, like the sound the IRT made going under Broadway. The hollow, heavy rumble seemed to him strangely threatening with its casual reminder of other people going about their other lives, totally ignorant of nuclear magnetic resonance and enigmatic suntanned Californians. His obsessions were merely his, not universal. And he realized that every time he tried to focus on Penny his mind skittered away, into the safe recesses of the spontaneous resonance muddle. So much for being captain of his fate.

He got out of the cab into the street where he grew up, blinking in the watery sunlight. Same beat-up trash cans adding their perfume, same grillwork, same Grundweiss grocery down the corner. Dark-eyed young housewives toting bags, herding their chattering children. The women were conservatively dressed, the only hint of undercurrents being their broad, lip-sticked, sensuous mouths. Men in gray business suits hurrying by, black hair cropped short.

His mother was on the landing, arms spread wide, as he came up. He gave her a good-son kiss. When he came into the old living room with its funny, close flavors—"It's in the furniture, the stuffing, it's with us for life," she said, as though the stuffing was immortal—it washed over him. He decided to just let everything go. Let her tell him the months of carefully stored gossip, show the engagement pictures of distant relatives, cook him "a good home meal, for once"—chopped liver and *kugel* and *flanken*. They listened to calypso rhythms on the ancient brown Motorola in the corner. Later they went down to see the Grundweisses—"He tells me three times, bring that boy down, I'll give him an apple like before"—and around the block, hailing friends, discussing seriously the statistics of earthquakes, heaving a softball into the waning summer light for a bunch of kids playing in a lot. The next day, just from that one throw— "Can you believe it?"—his arm was sore.

He stayed two days. His sister came over, cheerful and busy and oddly calm. Her dark eyebrows moved with each arch of a sentence, each surge of her face, making dancing parentheses. Friends dropped by. Gordon went all the way over to 70th Street to get some California wine for these occasions, but he was the only one who drank more than a glass. Still, they talked and joked with as much animation as any La Jolla cocktail party, proving alcohol an unnecessary lubricant.

Except his mother. She ran out of neighborhood news soon enough and then relied on his friends or his sister to carry the conversation. Alone with him, she said little. He found himself slowly drawn into this vacuum. The apartment had been thick with talk as he grew up, except in the last times of his father, and a silence here unnerved him. Gordon told his mother about the battle over his work. Of Saul Shriffer. (No, she had not seen the TV news, but she heard. She wrote him, remember?) Of spontaneous resonance. Of Tulare's warning. And finally, of Penny. His mother didn't, wouldn't, couldn't believe a girl would turn down a man like her son. What could she be thinking of, to do that? Gordon found this response unexpectedly pleasing; he had forgotten the ability of mothers to shore up sons' egos. He confessed to her that somehow he had gotten into the habit of thinking he and Penny would settle into something more conventional ("respectable," his mother corrected). It had come as a surprise that Penny wasn't thinking in parallel. Something had happened to him then. He tried to explain it to his mother. She made the familiar, encouraging sounds. "Maybe, I don't know, it was . . . Penny I wanted to hold on to, now that everything else is going kaput . . ." But that wasn't quite what he meant, either. He knew the words were false as soon as they were out. His mother picked up on them, though. "So she doesn't know what's what, this is a surprise? I tried to tell you that." Gordon shook his head, sipping tea, confused. It was no use, he saw. He was all jumbled up inside and he suddenly didn't want to talk about Penny any more. He started on the physics again and his mother clattered the spoons and teapot with fresh energy, smiling, "Good work, yes, that's good for you now. Show *her* what she's lost by—" and on she went, longer than Gordon wanted. He felt a momentum building in him, an urgency. He veered from these muddy matters of women. As his mother's voice droned in the heavy air he thought about Claudia Zinnes. He shuffled numbers and equipment in his head. He was making some plans when her phrases gradually penetrated: she thought he was leaving Penny. "Huh?" he sputtered, and she said blankly, "Well, after that girl re*jec*ted you—" An argument followed. It reminded him far too much of the debates over when he had to be home from dates, and what he wore, and all the other small things that finally drove him to an apartment of his own. It ended with the same sad shaking of the head, the "You are *fartootst,* Gordon, *fartootst* . . ." He changed the subject, wanted to call up Uncle Herb. "He is in Massachusetts. He bought a consignment of hats cheap, now goes up there to spread them around. The market fell *kapoosh* when Kennedy wouldn't wear one, you know, but your uncle figures in New England the men, their heads are cold." She made more tea, they went for a walk. The silences widened between them. Gordon made no attempt to bridge them. His mother was aboil over Penny, he could see that, but he'd had enough. He could stay longer, but the spreading silences promised more trouble. He stayed overnight, took her to an off-Broadway play and topped it off with crêpes at Henry VIII's. The next morning he caught the 8:28 United for the coast.

chapter twenty-eight

AUGUST 12, 1963

Cooper looked doubtful. "You think this is enough?"

"For now, yeah. Who knows?"—Gordon shrugged—"Maybe for good, too."

"I at least ought to fill in some of the high field observations."

"Not that important."

"After what that committee did to me, I want to be sure—"

"More data isn't the answer. You need more background reading, more analysis of your data, things like that. Not more numbers churning out of the lab."

"You sure?"

"You can close out your run by tomorrow."

"Umm. Well, okay."

●

In reality, Cooper probably could strengthen his case with more data. Gordon had always disliked the practice of overmeasuring every effect, though, mostly because he suspected it deadened the imagination. After a while you saw only what you expected to see. How could he be sure Cooper was really taking all the data as it came?

This was a justifiable reason for bumping Cooper off the NMR rig, but that wasn't why Gordon did it. Claudia Zinnes would be starting up in September. If she found anything anomalous, Gordon wanted to be running simultaneously.

Gordon came home from the lab hungry. Penny had already eaten and was watching the 11 o'clock news. "Want anything?" he called from the kitchen.

"No."

"What's that you're watching?"

"March on Washington."

"Uh?"

"Martin Luther King. You know."

He hadn't been paying any attention to the news. He asked nothing more; discussing politics with Penny would only set her off. She had been elaborately casual since he had returned. There was an odd truce between them, not a peace.

"Hey," he called, coming into the living room, which was lit only by the pale electric glow of the TV. "Dishwasher won't go on."

"Uh huh." She didn't turn her head.

"Did you call?"

"No. *You*, for once."

"I did last."

"Well, *I*'m not. Hate that. Let it be broke."

"You spend more time with it than me."

"That'll change, too."

"What?"

"Not busting ass to fix meals any more."

"Didn't think you had."

"How'd *you* know. You couldn't fry butter."

"Two points off for credibility," he said lightly. "You know I can cook some things, anyway."

"Come on."

"I'm serious," he said sharply. "I'm going to be in the lab a lot and—"

"Loud and prolonged applause."

"For Chris*sake*."

"I won't be here much, so."

"Neither will I except in and out."

"Least you're *doing* something now."

"Crap, that's not what you're on the rag about."

"Metaphorical rag?"

"Real rag, metawhatever rag—how do I know?"

"I thought you thought maybe real rag. Otherwise maybe you would've touched me since you got back."

"Oh."

"Didn't notice, huh?"

Grimly: "I noticed."

"Okay, why?"

"Wasn't thinking about it, I guess."

"Think about it."

"You know, busy."

"Think I don't know? Come on, Gordon. I saw your face when you got off that plane. We were going to have a drink at the El Cortez, look at the city. Lunch."

"Okay. Look, I need dinner."

"You dinner, I'll watch the speech."

"Good. Wine?"

"Sure. Enough for later?"

"Later?"

"My mother should've taught me to be more direct. Later, when we fuck."

"Oh, yes. Fuck we will."

They did. It wasn't very good.

●

Gordon broke Cooper's experiment down to the basic components. Then he rebuilt it. He checked each piece for shielding, looking for any way an unsuspected signal could get into the circuitry. He had most of it reassembled when Saul Shriffer appeared, unannounced, in the lab.

"Gordon! I was just at UCLA and thought I'd drop by."

"Oh, hi," Gordon murmured, wiping his hands on an oily cloth. A man with a camera followed Saul into the lab.

"This is Alex Paturski, from *Life*. They're doing a piece on exobiology."

"I'd appreciate a few shots," Paturski said. Gordon murmured yeah, sure, and Paturski quickly brought in reflecting screens and camera gear. Saul talked about the reaction to his announcement. "Dreadful example of closed minds," Saul said. "*No*body is following up our lead. I can't get anyone in the astronomical community to give the idea five seconds." Gordon concurred, and decided not to tell Saul about Claudia Zinnes. Paturski circled them, clicking and bobbing. "Turn this way a little more, eh?" and Saul would do as directed. Gordon followed suit, wishing he wore something more than a T-shirt and jeans. This was, of course, the one day he had not worn his usual slacks and Oxford broadcloth.

"Great, gentlemen, just great," Paturski said in conclusion. Saul inspected the experiment a moment. Gordon showed him some preliminary warmup traces he'd taken. Sensitivity was low but the curves were obviously clean resonance lines.

"Too bad. More results could open this whole thing up again, you know." Saul studied him. "Let me know if you see anything, okay?"

"Don't hold your breath."

"No, I suppose not." Saul appeared momentarily dejected. "I really thought there was something to it, too."

"Maybe there is."

"Yes. Yes, of course, perhaps there is." He brightened. "Don't get the idea that it's all over, eh? When it's died out a little, and people have stopped hooting with laughter at the very idea—well, it'll make a good article. Maybe something for *Science* titled 'Tilting at Orthodox Windmills.' That might go over."

"Uh huh."

"Well, Alex and I have to be off. We're going up through Escondido to Palomar."

"Doing some observing there?" Gordon asked casually.

"No. No, I don't do the observations, you know. I'm more an idea man. Alex wants to take some pictures, that's all. It's an awesome place."

"Oh yes."

In a moment they were gone and he could get back to his experiment.

•

The first day Gordon got the NMR rig back on the air there were signal-to-noise problems. On the second day stray leakage waves clouded the results. One of the indium antimonide samples acted funny and he had to cycle the rig down, dump the cold bath and pull the defective sample. That took hours. Only on the third day did the resonance curves begin to look right. They were reassuringly accurate. They fit theory quite well, within the crossbars of experimental error. *Beautiful,* Gordon thought. *Beautiful and dull.* He kept the rig running all day, in part to be sure the electronics stayed stable. He found he could take care of ordinary business—coaching Cooper; making up lecture notes for the coming semester; cutting the tiny gray indium antimonide bars on the hot-wire, oil-immersion setup—and duck into the lab for a quick NMR measurement every hour or two. He settled into a routine. Things got done. The curves remained normal.

•

"Professor Bernstein?" the woman said, her voice pitched high and grating. He wondered idly if her accent was midwestern. "Yes," he said into the telephone.

"This is Adele Morrison with *Senior Scholastic Magazine.* We are doing a major piece on the, uh, claim you and Professor Shriffer have made. We are treating it as an example of controversy in science. I wondered—"

"Why?"

"Pardon?"

"Why bring it up? I'd prefer you just forgot about it."

"Well, Professor Bernstein, I don't know, I . . . Professor

Shriffer was most cooperative. He said he thought our readership—which is high school seniors, you know—would learn a great deal from such a study.''

"I'm not so sure of that."

"Well, Professor, I'm afraid I'm only an assistant editor here, I don't make policy. I believe the article is—yes, here, it's already in galley form. It's mostly an interview with your colleague, Professor Shriffer."

"Uh huh."

The voice rose higher. "I was asked to see if you had any final comment on the, uh, status of the, uh, controversy. We could add it to the galleys now if—"

"No. Nothing to say."

"You're sure? The editor asked me to—"

"I'm sure. Let it go as is."

"Well, all right. We have several other professors quoted in the article and they make some very critical comments. I thought you should know that."

For a moment it tempted him. He could ask their names and listen to the quotations and frame some reply. The woman was waiting, the phone spitting that faint hiss of long distance. He blinked. She was good; she'd almost hooked him into it. "No, they can say what they like. Let Saul carry this one." He hung up. Let the scholastic seniors of this great nation think whatever they wanted. He only hoped the article wouldn't increase the rate of crank visits.

●

The summer sun bleached everything into a flatness stripped of perspective. Penny came in from surfing and plopped down beside Gordon. "Too many wipeouts," she explained. "Rip tide, too. Kept sucking me into the pilings."

"Running is a lot safer," he observed.

"And boring."

"But not worthless."

"Maybe. Oh, that reminds me—I'm going up to see my parents some time soon. I'd go before classes, but Dad is off on some business trip."

"What reminded you of that?"

"Huh? Oh. Well, you said running wasn't worthless, and I remembered that I had a student last semester who used the longest word in the English language, deliberately, in a paper I was grading. It's 'floccinaucinihilipilification.' It means 'the act of estimating as worthless.'"

"Um. Really."

"Yeah, and I had to look the damn thing up. It isn't in any American dictionary, but I found it in the Oxford English."

"And?"

"That's the dictionary my Daddy gave me."

Gordon smiled and lay back on the sand, hoisting an *Esquire* up to blot out the sun. "You're a highly nonlinear lady."

"Whatever that means."

"It's a compliment, believe me."

"Well?"

"Well what?"

"Do you want to go up to Oakland with me or not?"

"That's what this is about?"

"Despite your attempts to avoid it, yes."

"Attempts to—? Penny, you've been reading too much Kafka. Yes, sure, I'll go."

"When?"

"How should I know? It's *your* trip, *your* parents."

She nodded. An odd, pinched expression appeared on her face, then vanished. Gordon wondered what she was feeling but he knew no simple way to ask. He opened his mouth to begin a fumbling approach, and then gave up. Was going to Oakland part of the courtship dance, taking the boy home to be viewed? Maybe that was only an east coast phenomenon; he wasn't sure. After announcing that she didn't want to marry him, and then staying on and living with him as though things would just keep going that way, Penny had become an utter mystery to him. Gordon sighed to himself, giving up on the whole subject.

He read for a few minutes and then said, "Hey, it says here the Test Ban Treaty is in effect."

"Sure," Penny murmured, rolling over from her drowsy sleep in the sun. "Kennedy signed it months ago."

"I must've missed it." Gordon thought of Dyson and Orion, a strangely appealing dream that was now dead. Nobody was going to get out to the planets right away; the space program would limp along on liquid fuel rockets. It struck Gordon that the times were pressing in now. New ideas and new people were coming into the old La Jolla of Chandler's day. The same Kennedy who had pushed the Test Ban and killed Orion was also federalizing the Alabama National Guard, to stop George Wallace from using them against the desegregation program. Medgar Evers had been killed just a few months before. There was a feeling running through the country now, that things had to change.

Gordon tossed the magazine aside. He rolled over beneath

the sun's broiling and began to doze off. A sea breeze brought a sour reek of the rotting kelp bank farther down the beach. He wrinkled his nose. The hell with the press of the times. *Politics is for the moment,* Einstein said once. *An equation is for eternity.* If he had to choose sides, Gordon was on the side of the equations.

•

That evening he took Penny out to dinner and then dancing at the El Cortez. It wasn't the sort of thing he usually did, but the strange, stretching tension between them needed attention. They talked during dinner. Over drinks afterward, he began, "Penny, the thing between us, it's complicated . . ." She replied, "No, it's complex." He hesitated and murmured, "Well, okay, but . . ." She said sharply, "There's a difference." And for some reason that made him angry. He decided to shut up, let the evening go on in the mindless, evening-out-with-the-wifey way she seemed to like. It was odd how she could be a very intelligent, uncompromising literature student one moment, and then in the next come on as ordinary, middle-America, relentlessly oatmeal. Maybe she was part of this time, of things changing.

They danced only to the slow numbers. She moved deftly, lightly, in a slim pink dress. He wore heavy black shoes left over from New York and now and then would miss the beat. The male vocalist sang, in a bluesy voice, "People stay, just a little bit longer. We wanna play, just a little bit more." Penny suddenly hugged him to her with remarkably strong arms. "Sam Cooke," she murmured into his ear. He didn't know what she meant. The idea of knowing who had composed a certain pop song seemed, well, faintly incredible.

chapter twenty-nine

AUGUST 28, 1963

The noise level in the NMR measurements began to rise. Each day it was a little higher. Usually Gordon would notice the change in the first data-taking of the morning. He attributed it at first to the slow failure of a component. Repeated checking of the obvious points in the circuitry turned up nothing. Testing of the nonobvious didn't help, either. Each day the noise was worse. At first Gordon thought this might be a new sort of "spontaneous resonance" effect. The signal was too choppy to tell, though. He spent more time trying to lower the signal/noise ratio. Gradually it came to take up most of his working day. He began to come in nights. He would sit before the on-line oscilloscope and watch the traces. Once, when he had a meeting early the next morning, he slept overnight in the lab. A Fourier decomposition of the noise spectrum showed certain harmonic components, but this clue led nowhere. Meanwhile, the phase-averaged noise level rose.

•

"Gordon? This is Claudia Zinnes."

"Oh, hello. I hadn't expected to hear from you so soon."

"We have had some delays. This's and thats's. Nothing fundamental, but I wanted you to know we should be on the air within a week."

"Good. I hope . . ."

"Yes. Yes."

•

A Santa Ana wind was blowing outside. It pushed with a dry, heavy hand through the low coastal mountain passes, bringing the desert's prickly touch. Brush fires broke out in the hills. The red wind, some natives called it. To Gordon, sealed in his air-conditioned lab, it was a mild surprise as he left for home late at night; the air seemed thick and layered, ruffling his hair.

He remembered this hot, dry touch the next day as he walked

across to the chemistry building. Ramsey, unable to reach him in his office, had left a message with Joyce, the department secretary. Gordon crossed between the buildings on the ornate hexagonal tiered bridge. Entering the land of chemistry brought a sweet-sour aroma, too strong and many-flavored for the air system's whine to banish. He found Ramsey in a forest of flasks and tubes, talking quickly and precisely to a graduate student. Ramsey titrated a solution as he spoke, pointing out color shifts, adding a drop of milky stuff at a crucial moment. Gordon found a welcome chair and sagged into it. This jungle of clamps and slides and retorts seemed possessed of more life than a physics lab; the knocking of pumps and ticking of timers was a complicated heart, pacing Ramsey's earnest search. On the wall hung a chart of the gigantic molecular chain that carbon dioxide descends to become carbohydrate; a ladder forged by photons. A liquid scintillation counter muttered, tocktocking through a series of isotopically labeled flasks. Gordon shifted, finding a ledge to lean on, and toppled a Lily cup. Nothing spilled. He inspected it and found a sludge of coffee, thick as glue and mottled by mold. All things here were alive. He had a sudden vision of this glassy palace as a wilderness of nucleic acids, responding to the dry brush of red wind outside. His NMR lab seemed silent and sterile by comparison. His experiments were insulated from the pulse of the world. For the biochemists, though, life cooperated in the study of itself. Ramsey himself looked more vital, squinting and hovering and talking, an animal padding through the lanes of this chemical jungle.

"Sorry, Gordon, had to finish that—say, you look kinda worn out. This weather got you down, fella?"

Gordon shook his head and rose, following Ramsey to a side office. A slight giddiness swarmed through him. *Must be the air in here,* he thought. That, and the Santa Ana, and his shallow, momentary sleep of the night before.

Ramsey was already several sentences ahead of him before Gordon registered the fact. "What?" he said, his voice a croak from the dryness.

"I said, the clues were all there. I was just too blind to see them."

"Clues?"

"At first I was just looking for preliminary data. You know, something to kick off a grant, get the funding agencies interested. Defense, I guess. But that's the point, Gordon—this is bigger than DOD now. NSF should go for it."

"Why?"

"It's *big,* that's why. That line, 'enters molecular simulation regime begins imitating host'—that's the giveaway. I took a solution like the one that message described. You know, land runoff stuff, pesticides, some heavy metals—cadmium, nickel, mercury. Threw in some long-chain molecules, too. Had a grad student make them up. Lattitine chain, like the message said. Got a friend at DuPont to loan me some of their experimental long-chain samples.''

"Could you find the labeling numbers the message gave?"

Ramsey frowned. "Nope, that's the puzzler. This buddy of mine says they don't have anything called that. And Springfield claims they don't have an AD45 pesticide, either. Your signal must've got messed up there.''

"So you couldn't duplicate it.''

"Not exactly—but who needs exactly? What these long-chain babies are is *versatile*.''

"How can you be—"

"Look, I took the batches down to Scripps. Took Hussinger out to lunch, talked up the project. Got him to give me some sea water testing troughs. They're first class—constant temperature and salinity, steady monitoring, the works. Lots of sunlight, too. And—" he paused, compressing a smile—"the whole damn thing came true. Every bit.''

"The diatom bloom part, you mean?"

"Sure, only that's a later stage. Those long-chain bastards go like Poncho, I tell ya. That sea water started out ordinary, supersaturated with oxygen. After two months we started getting funny readings on the oxygen column. That's a measurement of the oxygen budget in a vertical column of water, maybe thirty meters high. Then the plankton started to go. Just crapped out on us—dead, or funny new forms.''

"How?"

Ramsey shrugged. "Your message says 'virus imprinting.' Mumbo-jumbo, I think. What's virus got to do with sea water?''

"What has a pesticide got to do with plankton?"

"Yeah, good point. We don't know. That other phrase you had—'can then convert plankton neuro jacket into its own chemical form using ambient oxygen content until level falls to values fatal to most of the higher food chain'—sounds like *some*body knows, right?"

"Apparently.''

"Yeah, 'cause that's smack on what we found.''

"It scavenges the oxygen?"

"And how." He cocked an eyebrow. "Spreads like a son-ofabitch, too. That mixture turns the plankton into *itself*, seems like. Makes some pretty lethal side products, too—chlorinated benzenes, polychlorinated biphenyls, all kinds of crap. Have a squint at this."

A photograph, produced with a flourish from a folder. A lean fish on a concrete slab, eyes glazed. Its lips bulged, green and laced with filaments of blue. A pale sore beneath the gills.

"Lip cancers, asymmetries, tumors—Hussinger turned white when he saw what it did to his sample stock. See, he usually doesn't worry about pathogens getting into the troughs. Sea water is cold and salty. It kills disease-carriers, all except some . . ."

Gordon noticed the pause. "Except what?"

"Except some viruses, Hussinger said."

"Uh huh. 'Virus imprinting.' And these fish—"

"Hussinger isolated my troughs and stopped it. All my sample fish died."

The two men stared at each other. "I wonder who's using it down in the Amazon," Ramsey said softly.

"Russians?" The possibility now seemed quite real to Gordon.

"Where's the strategic advantage?"

"Maybe it's some kind of accident."

"I dunno . . . You still don't know why you're getting this over your NMR rig?"

"No."

"That Saul Shriffer crap—"

Gordon waved it away. "Not my idea. Forget it."

"We can't forget *this*." Ramsey held up the fish photo.

"No, we can't."

"Hussinger wants to publish right away."

"Go ahead."

"You sure this isn't a DOD thing you're working on?"

"No, look—that was *your* idea."

"You didn't knock it down."

"Let's say I didn't want to expose my source. You can see what happened when Shriffer got hold of it."

"Yeah." Ramsey peered at him, a distant and assessing look. "You're pretty sly."

Gordon thought this was unfair. "*You* brought up the DOD angle. I said *nothing*."

"Okay, okay. Tricky, though."

Gordon wondered if Ramsey was thinking to himself, *Shifty Jew*. But he caught himself as he thought it. Christ, what paranoia. He was getting to sound like his mother, always sure the goyim were out to get you.

"Sorry about that," Gordon said. "I was afraid you wouldn't work on it if I didn't, well . . ."

"Hey, that's okay. No big deal. Hell, you put me onto a fantastic thing. Really important."

Ramsey tapped the photograph. Both men stared at it, reflecting. A silence fell between them. The fish's lips were swollen balloons, the colors horribly out of place. In the quiet Gordon heard the lab outside the small office. The regular chugging and ticking went on unmindful of the two men, rhythms and forces, voices. Nucleic acids sought each other in the capillaries of glass. An acid smell cut the air. Enameled light descended. *Ticktock ticktock.*

●

Saul Shriffer gazed out from the cover of *Life* with a casual self-confidence, arm draped over a Palomar telescope mount. Inside, the story was titled BATTLING EXOBIOLO-GIST. There were pictures of Saul peering at a photograph of Venus, Saul inspecting a model of Mars, Saul at the control panel of the Green Bank radio telescope. One paragraph dealt with the NMR message. Beside the big magnets stood Saul, with Gordon in the background. Gordon was looking into the space between the magnet poles, apparently doing nothing. Saul's hand hovered near some wiring, about to fix it. The NMR signals were described as "controversial" and "strongly doubted by most astronomers." Saul was quoted: "You take some chances in this field. Sometimes you lose. Them's the breaks."

●

"Gordon, your name is in here *once*. That's all," Penny said.

"The article's about Saul, remember."

"But that's why he's *in* here. He's riding on your . . ."

Mocking: "My success."

"Well, no, but . . ."

●

Gordon tossed the drawing on Ramsey's desk. "Did I give you a copy of this?"

Ramsey picked it up and wrinkled his brow. "No. What is it?"

"Another part of the signal."

"Oh yeah, I remember. It was on TV."

"Right. Shriffer showed it."

Ramsey studied the interweaving curves. "Y'know, I didn't think anything of this at the time. But . . . ."

"Yes?"

"Well, it looks like some sort of molecular chain to me. These dots . . . ."

"The ones I connected up?"

"Yeah, I guess. You drew this first?"

"No, Saul unscrambled it from a coded sequence. What about them?"

"Well, maybe it's not a bunch of curves. Maybe the points are molecules. Or atoms. Nitrogen, hydrogen, phosphorus."

"Like in DNA."

"Well, this isn't DNA. More complicated."

"More complicated, or more complex?"

"Crap, I don't know. What's the difference?"

"You think it has some relation to those long-chain molecules?"

"Could be."

"Those in-house names. DuPont and Springsomething."

"Dupont Analagan 58. Springfield AD45."

"Could this be one of those?"

"Those products don't exist, I told you."

"Okay, okay. But could they be that kind of thing?"

"Maybe. Maybe. Look, why don't I see if I can figure this thing out."

"How?"

"Well, try assigning atoms to the sites in the chains. See what works."

"The way Crick and Watson did DNA?"

"Well, yeah, something like that."

"Great. Maybe that'll unravel some of—"

"Don't count on it. Look, the important thing is the experiment. The oxygen loss, the fish. Hussinger and I are going to publish that right away."

"Good, fine, and—"

"You don't mind?"

"Huh? Why?"

"I mean, Hussinger says he thinks we should publish it together. If you and I want to do a paper on the message and its content, Hussinger says, that's another—"

"Oh, I see." Gordon rocked back in his chair. He felt worn down.

"I mean, I don't go along with him on that one, but . . . ."

"No, never mind. I don't care. Publish it, for Chrissakes."

"You don't mind?"

"All I did was say, look into it. So you looked and you found something. Good."

"It wasn't my idea, this Hussinger thing."

"I know that."

"Well, thanks. Really. Look, I'll follow up on this chain picture you got here."

"If it *is* a chain."

"Yeah. But I mean, maybe we can publish that. Together."

"Fine. Fine."

•

The resonance curves remained smooth. However, the noise level continued to rise. Gordon spent more of his time in the laboratory, trying to suppress the electromagnetic sputter. He had most of his lecture notes for the graduate course in Classical Electromagnetism finished, so he was free to pursue research. He abandoned his sample preparation, however, in favor of more time on the NMR rig. Cooper was still digesting his own data. The noise would not go away.

chapter thirty

1998

He banged the outer office door shut and thumped across the old broad-boarded flooring. He had a respectably ancient office, just off Naval Row, but at times he would just as soon have had less oiled wood and more modern air-conditioning. Ian Peterson, returning from a morning-long meeting, dumped a file of papers on his desk. His sinuses had a stuffed, cottony feel. Meetings invariably did that. He had felt a thin haze descend on his mind as the meeting progressed, sealing him off from much of the tedious detail and bickering. He knew the effect from years of experience; fatigue at so much talk, so many qualified phrases, so many experts covering their asses with carefully impersonal judgments.

He shook off the mood and thumbed into his desktop Sek. First, a list of incoming calls, arranged by priority. Peterson had carefully sorted out names into lists, so the answering Sek computer would know whether to alert him. The list changed weekly, as he moved from problem to problem. People who had once worked with him on a project had an annoying tendency to assume that they could then ring him up about continuing secondary issues, even months or years later.

Second, incoming memos, flagged with deadlines for reply.

Third, personal messages. Nothing there this time except a note from Sarah about her bloody party.

Fourth, news items of interest, broken down into abstracts. Last, minor unclassifiable items. No time for that today. He reviewed category One.

Hanschman, probably wailing about the metals problem. Peterson deflected that one to an assistant by typing in a three-letter symbol. Ellehlouh, the North African, with a last-gasp plea for more fly-ins to the new drought region. That he routed up to Opuktu. He was the officer in charge of selecting who got the grain and molasses shipments; let him take the flak. Call from that Kiefer in La Jolla, flagged urgent. Peterson picked up his telephone and punched through. Busy. He stabbed Repeat Call and said "Dr. Kiefer" so the tape could add it to the "Mr.

Peterson of the World Council is urgently trying to reach'' message which now would try Kiefer's number every twenty seconds.

Peterson turned to the memos and brightened. He punched for a screening of his own memo, dictated while riding to work this morning and machine-typed. He had never tried the system before.

—are you certain you—oh, yes, I { see / sea } the light go on { fore / for / four } autorite God why { cant / can't } they spell anything out correctly { there / their } certainly is space { fore / for / four } another letter all { write / right } here goes paragraph ah have { two / to / too } hit the button I { see / sea } isn't { their / there } a oh contextual option key, right

Summary for Sir Martin on Coriolis Proposal

Committee agrees the logical { sight / site } uh s-i-t-e for the fully deployed system is in the Gulf Stream hope I've got those capitalizations right off the Atlantic coast of Miami period yes. There is a four not oh special spelling button I suppose k-n-o-t, there, a four knot current steady and reliable. Those currents rotate the giant turbine fans, producing enough electricity for all Florida. The turbines are admittedly huge, 500 meters in diameter. However, I would paraphrase the technical discussion as saying they are basically Victorian engineering. Large and simple. Their floating hull is 345 meters long and they hang fully 25 meters below the surface. That's enough for passing ships to run safely over. The anchoring cables have to go down { to / two } that's t-w-o miles in some places. That is minor compared to the cables carrying power to land, but technical branch says that probably has no bad side effects either.

Our projections are that the nearest candidates—natural gas from seaweed and ocean thermal energy conversion—are hopelessly behind Coriolis. The name, as you undoubtedly know and I didn't, springs from a French mathematician who had a hand in showing why ocean currents go as they do. Effects of the earth's rotation and so on.

The snags are obvious. Having 400 of these slowing the Gulf Stream might be dicey. The weather pattern for much of the Atlantic Ocean hinges on that current, which sweeps by the US and Canada and then out to sea and back to the Caribbean is that the spelling must be. A full-scale numerical simulation on the omni all caps OMNI computer shows a measurable effect of one percent. Safe enough, by current guidelines.

Negative political impact is minimal. Introducing 40 gigawatts to that area will silence criticism of our halt to fishing, I should believe. I therefore advise prompt approval. Yours sincerely et cetera.

Peterson grinned. Remarkable. They even assigned the most probable homonym. He corrected the piece and sent it off through the electronic labyrinth to Sir Martin. Committee flotsam and jetsam was for the assistants; Sir Martin saved his time for judgments, the delicate balancing act above the flood of information. He had taught Peterson a good deal, all the way down to such fine points as how to speak on a committee where your opponents are lying in wait. Sir Martin would pause and breathe in the middle of his sentences, then rush past the period at the end and on for a clause or two into the next sentence. No one knew when to make a smooth interruption.

Peterson asked for his Sek for an update. He found the Kiefer call still facing the blank buzzing of a busy signal, and two underlings leaving recorded messages he would check later.

He reclined in his armchair and studied his office wall. Quite an array, yes. Pseudoparchment citations for bureaucratic excellence. Photos of himself beside various charismatic sloganeers with their buzzword bibles. Practitioners of leaderbiz, smiling at the camera.

The committee meeting this morning had its share of those, along with earnest biochemists and numerical meteorologists. Their reports on the distribution of the clouds were unsettling but vague. The clouds were further examples of "biological cross function," an all-purpose term meaning interrelations nobody had thought of yet. Apparently the circumpolar wind vortex, which had shifted towards the equator in recent years, was picking up something from the region near the bloom. The unknown biological agents being carried by the clouds had caused withering of the Green Revolution crop strains. Besides giving uniform high yields, the Green Revolution plants also had uniform weaknesses. If one became diseased, they all did. How devastating the strange yellow-tan clouds might be was unknown. Something odd was in the biocycle, but research had not pieced together the puzzle as yet. The meeting had broken up into rivulets of indecision. Belgian biologists argued with plump disasterologists, neither with any hard evidence.

Peterson pondered what it might mean, while leafing through some reports. Inventories, assessments, speculative calculations, order-of-magnitude truths. Some were in the clunky gingerbread of Cyrillic, or the swoops of Arabic script, or Asia's ant squiggles, or the squared-off machine type of ModEng. A tract on *Erdwissenschaft* made man a minor statistical nuisance, a bug skittering over a world reduced to nouns and numbers. Peterson was at times entranced by the mix of minds in the World Council, the encyclopedic power they tapped. Voices, a babble of voices. There was the furious energy of the Germans; the austere and finally constricting logic of *la belle France;* the Japanese, smothered now in industrial excess; strangely sad Americans, still strong but like an aging boxer, swinging at sparring partners no longer there; the Brazilians, wandering now onto the world stage, blinking into the spotlight, dazed. Several years ago he had gone on a tour of Ethiopia with a clucking band of international future-seers and watched their calculus collide with life. In dusty red-rocked gorges he had seen men attacking and scattering ant hills to snatch away the crumbs of wheat stored there. Naked women, colored like mud and with thin sacks for breasts, climbed mimosa trees to clip the green shoots of fresh growth, for soup. Children gathered stuff like briars, to chew for moisture. Trees were stripped bare of bark, gnawed at the roots. Skeletons baked white and luminous near brackish water holes.

The forecasting methodologists had paled and turned away.

When he was a boy he had watched the *National Geographic* programs on TV and come to think of the almost mythic beasts in Africa as distant friends, playing on the horizon of the world. Lions, vast and lazy. Giraffes, their stiff-necked lope taking them teetering into the distance. He'd had a boy's dreamy love of them. Now they were nearly gone. He had learned a lesson there, in Africa. Soon there would be nothing bigger than a man on the planet that was not already a client, a housepet. Without the giants mankind would be alone with the rats and the cockroaches. Worse, perhaps, he would be alone with himself. This fuzzy issue had not occupied the futurologists. They cluck-clucked over butter mountains here versus starvation there, and supplied their own recipes. They loved their theories more than the world. Forrester, rattling his numerical fantasies like beads; Heilbroner, urging mankind into a jail so they all could be sure of eating; Tinbergen, who thought one good crisis would shape us up; Kosolapov, whose Marxist optimism sat waiting patiently for the hacksaw of history to cut away capitalism, as though poverty were civilization's headcold, not a disease; his opposites, the followers of Kahn, with cocky assurance that a few wars and some starving wouldn't get in the way of higher per capita income; Schumacher's disciple, with his shy faith that the hydrocarbon cartels would decide cottage industries were best after all; and Remuloto, the Third Industrial Revolutionist, seeing salvation in our starry satellites.

Peterson remembered with a smile that the US Department of the Interior had made a thorough prediction of trends in 1937, and had missed atomic energy, computers, radar, antibiotics, and World War II. Yet they all kept on, with their simpleminded linear extrapolation that was, despite a bank of computers to refine the numbers, still merely a new way to be stupid in an expensive fashion. And they were filled with recipes. Order up more fellow-feeling, y'see, and we'll do better. To survive now Man had to be more patient, preferring long-range rational solutions to global problems, while suspending his nasty old irrational demands for short-range local fixes. They all wished some Lockeian dream of the future, a natural law which set forth human rights and human obligations simultaneously. An unwritten law, but reachable by reason. A mythology of stoic endurance would do the job, get us through the pinch. But who had one for sale? The secular faith in the technological fix had trickled away into astrology and worse. Jefferson's descendants were sucking up whatever liberties they could and leaving for posterity a used-up garbage dump. *Au revoir, Etats-Unis!* Check your beclouded vision at the door. Peterson glanced at the one item on his wall that was out of place, a century-old sampler:

> *All nature is but art, unknown to thee;*
> *All chance, direction, which thou canst not see;*
> *All discord, harmony not understood;*
> *All partial evil, universal good;*
> *And spite of pride, in erring reason's spite*
> *One truth is clear: whatever is, is right.*

He laughed as the telephone rang.

"Hello, Ian?" Kiefer's voice was thin and reedy.

"Happy to hear from you," he said with artificial friendliness.

"I don't think you'll be so happy in a minute."

"Oh?" Kiefer had not responded with the expected jovial banter that usually opened executive conversations.

"We've turned up the underlying process in that diatom bloom."

"Good, then you can rectify it."

"Eventually, yeah. Problem is, it's a runaway. The process enters a phase where it can take the jacket of the plankton and change that material into the original pesticide-based molecules."

Peterson sat very still and thought. "Like a religious movement," he said to have something to say.

"Huh?"

"Turns heathen into apostles."

"Well . . . yeah. Point is, that's what makes it spread so fast. Never seen anything like it. It's got a lot of the lab guys worried."

"Can't they find an . . . antidote?"

"In time, probably. Trouble is, we haven't *got* much time. This is an exponential process."

"How much time?"

"Months. Months to spread to the other oceans."

"Christ."

"Yeah. Look, I don't know how much pull you've got there, but I'd like this result taken right to the top."

"I'll do that, certainly."

"Good. I've got a technical report on LogEx right now. I'll transmit it on key, okay?"

"Right. Here, I'm receiving."

"Good. Here it comes."

•

It was Sir Martin who saw the connection. There was very little transfer of vapor from the ocean's surface into cloud formation. But suppose the impurity in the bloom could convert the cellular jackets of living microorganisms into itself. Then a trivial amount of the stuff, given time, could spread through a cloud. Transport through the air was quick. Certainly it was much faster than through contact at the biological interface, at the working surface between the bloom and the living sea.

•

Peterson made his way into the twilight that prevailed inside the restaurant. Or at least it called itself a restaurant; all he could see was people sitting on the floor. Incense curled into his nostrils, making him want to sneeze.

"Ian! Over here!"

Laura's voice came from somewhere to the left. He felt his way along until he could make her out, sitting on pillows and sucking something milky through a straw. Oriental music drifted through the room. He'd known as soon as he set out that it was a mistake to meet some girl he'd had it off with, simply because she was going through some sort of crisis. The

California news and the stir it was causing in the Council had kept him pinned to his desk throughout the night. The technical types were hysterical. Some senior people wrote off that fact, on the grounds that the technical people had been fairly alarmed before, and were proved wrong. This time Peterson was not so sure that that easy logic made sense.

"Hello. I really would have preferred to meet you at my club. I mean, this is quite all right, but—"

"Oh no, Ian, I wanted to see you in a place *I* knew. Not some stuffy men's club."

"It's really very pleasant, not stuffy at all. We can go round and have a light supper—"

"I wanted to show you where I'm working, though."

"You work here?" He looked round incredulously.

"It's my day off, of course. But it's a job, and a blow for independence!"

"Oh. Independence."

"Yes, it's exactly what you told me to do. Remember? I've moved out on my parents. Quit Bowes & Bowes, and come to London. *And* got a job. Next week, I'll start acting classes."

"Oh. Oh, that's very good."

A waiter materialized out of the gloom. "Would you like to order, sir?"

"Ah, yes. Whisky. And some food, I suppose."

"They have great curries."

"Beef, then."

"I am sorry, sir, we have no meat dishes."

"No bloody *meat?*"

"This is a vegetarian restaurant, Ian. Really tasty. It's fresh, brought in every day. Do try it."

"Oh, Christ. A biryani, then. Egg."

"Ian, I want to tell you all about my, my escape from my parents, and my plans. And I want your advice on getting into acting, I'm sure you know many, many people who know how to do it."

"Not really. I'm in government, you know."

"Oh, but you must, I'm sure you do. If you'll just think a bit, I'm sure . . ." and as she rattled on Peterson saw he had indeed made a mistake. He had felt he needed a break from the tension at the Council center, and Laura's telephoning had come at precisely the right moment to lure him. He had let the moment dominate his better judgment. Now he had to eat some dreadful meal in a restaurant kept dark because they didn't want you to see the dirt, and into the bargain he had to be hustled by this shopgirl. Peterson grimaced, certain she wouldn't see him in this light. Well, at least he was going to get a meal out of it; fuel for the work that was certain to come. And he did need a break from Sir Martin. "Do you have a place nearby?" he asked.

"Yes, in Banbury Road. A closet, nearly, I'm afraid."

"I'm sure I won't mind it." He smiled in the darkness.

chapter thirty-one

Markham spread his working papers out on the narrow little drop tray the airline provided. He had hours of boring Atlantic crossing ahead, jammed in next to the window. Cathy Wickham's equations swam before him, tensor indices beckoning to be turned this way and that, a dense notation compacted with promise.

"Lunch, sir," the professionally blank-faced steward muttered. This echo of politeness was to put a gloss on his casual dumping of a cardboard package on the drop table. Markham pried open the wedged boards. A rain of packets thumped down among his papers. They were the now-universal, easy-for-them modular units of food. He unwrapped one and found it to be the obligatory rubber chicken. He bit in reluctantly. Pasty, sour stuff. The only saving grace in this was the absence of plastic packaging, he thought. The bombing of the Saudi fields several years ago had brought an abrupt end to that, and a return to humble cardboard. The pulpy gray surface of the package recalled his boyhood, before hydrocarbons ruled the world. The humanizing side of paper containers was the simple fact that they accepted the touch of a pen, would carry a message; plastic's sheen rejected the imprint of its temporary users. Idly, he jotted the new quantum field equations on the lunchbox. The elegant epsilons and deltas made their stately march across the UNITED AIRLINES block letters. He chewed absently. Time passed. Markham saw a way to separate the tensor elements into several reduced equations. With descending strokes he paired off field components. He jotted side calculations to check himself. Other passengers moved in the distance. In a while the five new equations lay aslant on the ribbing of cardboard. Three he suspected were old friends: the Einstein equations, with modifications for quantum effects when the length scale became small enough. These were well known. The other two seemed to imply more. A deeper sense of the quantum effects added a fresh term here, a tangle of tensors there. There seemed no way to reduce the system further. Markham tapped idly at them with his pen, frowning.

"Say, give-a!" the man next to him cried out. Markham peered out his window. An immense cloud, sulfurous yellow and veined with orange, hung ahead of them. "First I've seen," the man said excitedly. Markham wondered if the pilot would fly through it. In seconds the window was hazed by strands of cloud and Markham realized that they were already passing through a lower segment of the yellow mass ahead. Fresh weight tugged him down; the plane tilted to rise.

"Right ahead of us, folks, is one of those clouds we've been hearing about. I'm taking us over it, for a better look."

This explanation seemed transparently false to Markham. Pilots didn't change altitude for a lark. The cloud seemed gravid and somehow more solid than the fluffy white cumulus around it. Threads of a coiling, dark blue wound through its cap, giving it a domed profile.

Markham murmured something and went back to his papers. He copied the new equations off the cardboard and studied them, trying to screen out the thin, high wail of the engines. An engineer had once told him the new generation of superfast engines screamed at unbearable levels. Rockwell International had had to go into cost overrun to blunt the jagged spikes of sound. Six months had been spent to bury the screech in a reassuring bass blanket, so the warm, ticketed bodies carried inside would remain woozy and complacent in the metallic grasp. Well, it didn't work for him. He had always been noise-sensitive. He found the earplugs in the flap compartment in front of him and inserted them. A blanket sealed him in. The only remnant of the engine scream was an acoustic tremor that came up through his legs and settled in his teeth.

He spent an hour testing the new equations. They gave sensible solutions to limiting-case problems he knew. Taking the scale length small and neglecting the gravitational effects, he got the standard equations of relativistic particle theory. Einstein's work emerged easily, with a few fluid strokes of the pen. But when Wickham's equations were taken face on, with no side-stepping onto familiar ground, they became opaque.

He squinted at the short, stubby notation. If he sliced through this knot of terms here, just dropped them—but no, that wasn't right. There was more than remorseless crank-turning to be done here. The work had to have the right deft feel, to glide forward on its own momentum. Beyond the logical standards, there were aesthetic questions. New developments in physics

269

always gave you, first, a logical structure that was more elegant. Second, once you understood it, the structure was not only elegant, it was simpler. Third, from the structure came consequences that were more complex than before. The ever-present trap in seeking a new path was to invert the steps. It was hard to express this to a philosopher; there was something in the art of mathematics that eluded you, unless you watched for it. Plato had been a great philosopher, and he had decided he wanted the planets to move in sets of circles, all compounded together to give the observed orbits. But as Ptolemy found out, the laws that were needed to give those stacked circles were horrendously complex. That would mean complex laws leading to simple consequences, the wrong way round. So all of Ptolemy's labors gave forth a theory that clanked and groaned, crystalline spheres grinding around, sprockets and wheels and rachets whirring in a doomed machine.

On the other hand, Einstein's theory was logically more elegant than Newton's. Subtle, but simple. Its consequences were much harder to work out, which was the right way round. Markham scratched his beard absently. If you kept that in mind, you could discard many approaches before you began, knowing they would ultimately fail. There was no choice between beauty and truth, really. You had to wind up with both. In art, elegance was a whore of a word, bent a different way by each generation of critics. In physics, though, there was some fragile lesson to be learned from past millennia. Theories were more elegant if they could be transformed mathematically to other frames, other observers. A theory that remained invariant under the most general transformation was the most deft, the nearest to a universal form. Gell-Mann's SU(3) symmetry had arrayed particles into universal ranks. The Lorentz group; isospin; the catalogue of properties labeled Strangeness and Color and Charm—they all cooked gauzy Number into concrete Thing. So to proceed beyond Einstein, one should follow the symmetries.

Markham scratched equations across a yellow pad, searching. He had intended to spend this time plotting his tactics with the NSF, but politics was dross compared with the actual doing of science. He tried different approaches, twisting the compacted tensor notation, peering into the maze of mathematics. He had a guiding principle: nature seemed to like equations stated in covariant differential forms. To find the right expressions—

He worked out the equations governing tachyons in a flat space-time, doing the exercise as a limited case. He nodded.

Here were the familiar quantum-mechanical wave equations, yes. He knew where they led. The tachyons could cause a probability wave to reflect back and forth in time. The equations told how this wave function would shuttle, past to future, future to past, a befuddled commuter. Making a paradox meant the wave had no ending, but instead formed some sort of standing wave pattern, like the rippling patterns around an ocean jetty, shifting their troughs and peaks but always returning, an ordering imposed on the blank face of the churning sea. The only way to resolve the paradox was to step in, break up the pattern, like a ship cutting across the troughs, leaving a swirl of sea behind. The ship was the classical observer. But now Markham added the Wickham terms, making the equations symmetric under interchange of tachyons. He rummaged through his briefcase for the paper by Gott that Cathy had given him. Here: *A Time-Symmetric, Matter and Anti-Matter Tachyon Cosmology.* Quite a piece of territory to bite off, indeed. But Gott's solutions were there, luminous on the page. The Wheeler-Feynman forces were there, mixing advanced and retarded tachyon solutions together with non-Euclidean sums. Markham blinked. In his cottony silence he sat very still, eyes racing, imagination leaping ahead to see where the equations would fold and part to yield up fresh effects.

The waves still stood, mutely confused. But there was no role left for the ship, for the classical observer. The old idea in conventional quantum mechanics had been to let the rest of the universe be the observer, let *it* force the waves to collapse. In these new tensor terms, though, there was no way to regress, no way to let the universe as a whole be a stable spot from which all things were measured. No, the universe was coupled in firmly. The tachyon field wired each fragment of matter to every other. Hooking more particles into the network only worsened things. The old quantum theorists, from Heisenberg and Bohr on, had let in some metaphysics at this point, Markham remembered. The wave function collapsed and that was the irreducible fact. The probability of getting a certain solution was proportional to the amplitude of that solution inside the total wave, so in the end you got only a statistical weighting of what would come out of an experiment. But with tachyons that dab of metaphysics had to go. The Wickham terms—

Sudden motion caught his eye. A passenger in the next row was clutching at a steward, eyes glassy. His face was laced with pain. A stretched mouth, pale lips, brown teeth. Mottled pink splotched his cheeks. Markham pulled his earplugs. A brittle scream startled him. The steward got the man down on the floor in the middle of the aisle and pinned his frantically clawing hands. "I can't—can't—breathe!" A steward murmured something comforting. The man shook with a seizure, eyes rolling. Two stewards carried him past Markham. He noticed an acrid smell coming from the sick man and wrinkled his nose, forcing his glasses upward. The man panted in the enameled light. Markham replaced his plugs.

He settled again into the embalming quiet, conscious only of the reassuring hum of the engines. Without peaks and valleys of sound the world had a stuffed, spongy feel, as though Maxwell's classical ether were a reality, could be sensed at the fingertips. Markham relaxed for a moment, reflecting on how much he loved this state. Concentration on an intricate problem could loft you into an insulated, fine-grained perspective. There were many things you could see only from a distance. Since childhood he had sought that feeling of slipping free, of being smoothly remote from the compromised churn of the world. He had used his oblique humor to distance people, yes, keep them safely away from the center of where he lived. Even Jan, sometimes. You had to form for yourself a lucid language for the world, to overcome the battering of experience, to replace everyday life's pain and harshness and wretched dreariness with—no, not with certainty, but with an ignorance you could live with. Deep ignorance, but still a kind that knew its limits. The limits were crucial. Galileo's blocks gliding across the marble Italian foyers, their slick slide obeying inertia's steady hand —they were cartoons of the world, really. Aristotle had understood in his gut the awful fact that friction ruled, all things groaned to a stop. *That* was the world of man. Only the childlike game of infinite planes and smooth bodies, reality unwrinkled, cast a web of consoling order, infinite trajectories, harmonic life. From that cartoon world it was always necessary to slip back, cloaking exhilarating flights in a respectable, deductive style. But that did not mean, when the papers appeared in their disguise of abstracts and Germanic mannerisms, that you had not been to that other place, the place you seldom spoke of.

He paused in the impacted hush, and then went on.

He wondered distantly if his first guess was right: these new Wickham equations allowed no way out of the paradox, because the whole universe was swept into the experiment. The consequence of setting up the standing wave was to send tachyons forward and backward in time, yes, but also to spray them at superlight speeds throughout the entire universe. Within an instant, every piece of matter in the universe learned of the paradox. The whole structure of space-time became woven into one piece, instantly. That was the new element with tachyons; until their discovery, physics assumed that disturbances in the space-time metric had to propagate outward at light speed.

Markham realized he had been hunched forward, scribbling mathematical statements of these ideas. His back stabbed him with small, hot knives. His writing hand protested with a sweet ache. He leaned backward, reclining the seat. Below he saw the slate-gray plain of the sea like a giant blackboard for God's idle equations. A freighter plowed a wake that curved with the currents, silver in the sun. They were descending toward Dulles International on a gentle long parabola.

Markham smiled with serene fatigue. The problems caught you up and carried you along, unminding currents. Was there any way to resolve the paradox? He knew intuitively that here lay the heart of the physics, the way of showing whether you could reach the past in a rigorous way. Peterson's laconic bank vault note proved something had happened, but what?

Markham twisted uncomfortably, irked by the narrow, cramped seat. Air travel was getting to be a rich man's route again, only this time without the perks. Then he fetched his mind back from these passing reminders of the relentlessly real world. The problem was not solved, and time remained.

But is the paradox decidable at all? he thought. The German mathematician Gödel had shown that even simple systems of arithmetic contained things which were true, but unprovable. In fact, you couldn't even show that arithmetic itself was consistent—that is, didn't contain paradoxes. Gödel had forced arithmetic into describing itself in its own language. He had trapped it into its own box, deprived it of ever proving itself by reference to things outside itself. And that was for arithmetic, the simplest logical system known! What of the universe itself, with tachyons lancing through it, threading the cloth of space-time? How could all the squiggles on all the yellow pads in the world ever trap that vast weave into the old boxes of yes/no, true/false, past/future? Markham relaxed in his brimming warmth. The plane went *clunk* and tilted earthward.

The point that continued to puzzle him was whether Renfrew needed to send a message at all, to make a paradox. Tachyons were constantly being produced by natural collisions of high-energy particles—that's how they had been discovered. Why didn't those natural tachyons produce a paradox somehow? He frowned. The plane nosed further, giving the illusion of hanging over the lip of a pit, legs dangling. *Natural tachyons . . .* The answer had to be that it took some minimum impulse to trigger a paradox. Some critical volume of space-time had to be tweaked, and then the disturbance would propagate outward instantaneously, with enough amplitude to matter. You could change the past at will, yes, so long as you didn't make paradoxes that had large amplitude. Once you exceeded the threshold, the tachyon wave would have a significant impact on the whole universe. But if so, how could you tell that that had happened? What was the signature? How did the universe pick a way to resolve the paradox? They knew they had reached the past—Peterson proved that. But what more could happen?

Markham felt a sudden stab of perception. If the universe was a wholly linked system with no mythical classical observer to collapse the wave function, then the wave function did not *have* to collapse at all. It—

A wrenching thump. Markham looked out in surprise and saw the ground veer suddenly. Ahead were the patient green fields of Maryland. A clump of forest swarmed beneath the wings. In the cabin, a babble of voices. Shouts. A rasping buzz. The forest went whipping by. The trees were sharp, precise, with the clarity of good ideas. He watched them flick past as the airplane became light, airy, a gossamer webbing of metal that fell with him, mute matter tugged by gravity's curved geometry. *Skreeeeeee*. The trees were pale rods in the slanting light, each with a ball of green exploding at the top. They rushed by faster and faster and Markham thought of a universe with one wave function, scattering into the new states of being as a paradox formed inside it like the kernel of an idea.—If the wave function did not collapse . . .Worlds lay ahead of him, and worlds lay behind. There was a sharp *crack* and he saw suddenly what should have been.

chapter thirty-two

Peterson woke slowly. He kept his eyes closed. His body told him not to move but he couldn't remember why. There was a murmur of movement around him, subdued voices, somewhere in the distance a metallic clash. He opened his eyes briefly, saw white walls, a chrome rail. A whirling dizziness. He remembered where he was now. Gingerly he tested his body. A dull, cottony feel. Seeping, cold ache. The rail down the side of a bed came into fuzzy focus. He rolled his head, wincing, and saw a bottle suspended above him. He tried to follow the tubes with his eyes but couldn't. Something was plugged into his nose. A tube taped to his arm pricked him as he moved. He tried to call the nurse. It came out a rattling croak.

She had heard him anyway. A round face with glasses and a white cap leaped into his field of vision.

"Waking up, are we? That's right. You'll be all right now."

"Cold . . ." He closed his eyes. Felt blankets being tucked in around him. The plug was removed from his nose.

"Can you hold a thermometer in your mouth?" the bright brisk voice asked. "Or should we try the other end?"

He squinted at her, loathing her.

"Mouth . . ." His tongue felt furry and enormous. Something cold slipped into his mouth. Cool fingers clamped his wrist.

"Well, coming down nicely. You're one of the lucky ones, you are. Got you some Infalaithin-G before it got to you."

He frowned. "Others?"

"Oh, yes," she said cheerfully. "We're overrun with them. No more beds at all. They're putting them in Emergency now. That'll be full soon, I'll warrant. You've got a private room, but you should hear them moanin' and groanin' in Ward E. Sixty beds, they've got in there. All this funny food thing, like you. Though mostly worse cases. Like I said, you're one of the lucky ones. Now, time to get some food into you."

"Food?" he said in horror. The memory of his last dinner with Laura engulfed him in nausea. "Nurse!"

"Going to upchuck, are you?" She sounded as cheerful as ever. Deftly she fitted a kidney-shaped basin under his chin and supported his head. He retched miserably. Greenish slime trailed down his chin and left a bitter taste in his mouth. His stomach hurt like hell.

"Nothing in you, see. Just lie still now and don't go getting excited again."

"You said food," he rasped accusingly.

She laughed merrily. "Well, so I did, but I didn't mean *food*. Time to change your IV bottle, that's all."

He closed his eyes again. His head throbbed. He heard her bustling around. Presently the door closed. Distantly, through double windows, he heard the hum of London's traffic. Where was he, anyway? Guy's Hospital, perhaps? He remembered more clearly now. It had come on him very suddenly. He had felt fine going home. He had waked after an hour's sleep, feeling vaguely nauseated, and had got out of bed. The clenching paralysis seized him after a few steps. He remembered lying curled on the bedroom floor, unable to call out, hardly daring to breathe. Sarah, of course, was out. He supposed he might have died if it had been the housekeeper's night off, too.

When he woke, he felt more lucid. His head pulsed with a slow ache. He rang for the nurse. It was a different one, an Indian girl this time. He knew he was better when he found himself trying to gauge the size of her breasts under the starched uniform.

"How are you feeling now, Mr. Peterson?" she asked in a singsong voice, bending over him.

"Better. What time is it?"

"It's half-past five now."

"I'd like my watch back. And I'm hungry. I could manage something very light."

"I'll see what's allowed," she said and left the room silently.

He struggled into a sitting position. The nurse trotted in again with a radio and a note.

"You had a visitor, Mr. Peterson," she said, smiling. "She wouldn't stay, but she left this. And you can have some broth. It'll be up presently."

He recognized Sarah's large graceful loops and flourishes on the envelope and opened the note.

Ian—What a terrible bore for you. Can't stand hospitals so I won't visit, but I thought you could use this radio. I'm leaving for Cannes Friday. Hope to see you before then. If not, give me a ring. I'll probably be home Wednesday evening. Bye bye. Sarah.

He screwed it up and dropped it in the wastepaper basket. He turned on the radio, a neat little battery one. There seemed to be nothing but music anywhere. He looked automatically at his watch and realized he wasn't wearing it. What time had the nurse said it was? His stomach gurgled loudly. Three pips suddenly interrupted the music.

"This is the BBC Radio Four," a woman's voice announced, "and here is the 6 o'clock news. First, the headlines: Fifty people are dead tonight after violent rioting in the streets of Paris. A United Airlines flight from London to Washington crashed early this morning, killing everyone on board. The bloom spreading across the Atlantic Ocean has advanced miles in a day. The World Council has approved an Energy Plan despite a veto by the OPEC countries. Power failures lasting over six hours caused factories to shut down in the Midlands today. The Test match at Lord's cricket ground was canceled today as ten members of the Australian team have been hospitalized with food poisoning. Tomorrow's weather: sunny in patches, increased chance of storms." A pause. "Rioting French students were joined by workers today in Paris . . ."

Peterson did not listen. He felt light and unsteady. The nurse came in with a tray. He signaled her to leave it on the bedside table. Something in the news had disturbed him and he wasn't quite sure what it was. It must be the news of the bloom. And yet he felt no reaction as he ran that past again.

"United Airlines flight 347, London to Washington, D.C., encountered turbulence on its approach to Dulles airport and crashed in late afternoon. Transmissions from the pilot were garbled. There seem to have been seizures of both pilot and copilot in the moments before the crash. Witnesses said the plane appeared to explode as it struck the trees. There were no survivors. This latest in a series of airline disasters has—"

Jesus! His palms were sweating. He pressed the buzzer for the nurse. She did not come at once. He held the button down and shouted "Nurse!"

She came in hurriedly, leaving the door open.

"What's the matter now? Why, you haven't even touched your broth."

"Damn the broth. What day is this? Is it Wednesday?"

"Yes, it is. But are you—"

"I want a phone. Why isn't there a phone in here?"

"It was taken out so you wouldn't be disturbed."

"Well, get it back."

"I don't know if I'm supposed to do that . . ."

"What's going on here?" The first nurse bustled in again.

"Sister, Mr. Peterson is asking for a phone in here."

"Oh no, we don't need that. Don't want you to be disturbed, do we?"

"I'm being disturbed now," he shouted. "Get me a phone!"

"Now, now, Mr. Peterson, we can't have that . . ."

"Listen, you stupid cunt," he said clearly and tensely, "I want a phone in here right now or I'll have you fired!"

There was a shocked silence and the two women backed from the room, eyeing him warily. He lay back, shaking. Through the door, which they had left open, he could hear moaning.

Presently an orderly brought in a phone and plugged it in. Peterson took a sip of water and fought the rising nausea. He dialed his secretary's number.

chapter thirty-three

SEPTEMBER 25, 1963

Gordon was walking down the hallway, on his way back to the lab, when he overheard the remark. Two full professors were talking in low voices. "—and as Pauli said, it isn't even wrong!" one finished as Gordon approached. They saw him and instantly fell silent. Gordon knew the story. Pauli was a prominent, highly critical physicist in the first half of the century. He had remarked, about a scientific paper, "This work is so bad it's not even wrong." Meaning, it began and ended in midair; it was so badly formulated it could not be tested. Gordon knew instantly they were talking about him. The *Life* article had done its work. When he reached the end of the hallway there was more murmured talk behind him and then a final bark of laughter.

●

Penny brought home a copy of *National Enquirer* and left it out for him to see when he came in late. On the front page was a headline, NUCLEAR CALL FROM OUTER SPACE and beneath it, *Prominent Scientists Contact Other World*. There were two photographs of Saul and Gordon, evidently by the *Life* photographer. Gordon threw it in the trash without reading it.

●

At the beginning of classes there was a party for the physical sciences faculty, to mark the opening of the new Institute for Geophysics building. The staff sterilized the bowl of a fountain on the lawn outside. Hugh Bradner and Harold Urey filled it with a potent mix of vodka and fruit juices. Gordon had thrown his invitation away with the usual university news notices; Penny discovered it and insisted they go. He wanted to get some rest, but her nagging made him pull on his lightest jacket and, for the first time, skip wearing a tie. In California such details were unimportant. Penny sported a floppy tan straw hat—"For dress-up," she said. Behind it she could hide a fraction of her face. This sense of added mystery rekindled in him an interest in her. He realized that he had been going through the motions these last few weeks, saddled with lecture preparations and spending most of his time with the NMR rig. This knowledge shocked him. The zest of their beginnings was seeping away. The abrasions between them were rubbing off the cosmetic illusions.

He spoke to several members of the Physics Department, but struck up no interesting conversations. Penny found some literary types but he was unmoored, wandering from one knot of academics to another. The English Department people already seemed drunk, quoting modern poets and ancient movies. There were bright, airy people there he'd never seen, goy princes, blond and unbearably self-assured, the sort of people who had refrigerators full of yogurt and champagne. He saw a visitor from Berkeley in the crowd, tall and well dressed, a Nobel winner of some years back. Gordon had met him before. He wedged himself into the crescent of people around the man and, when the Nobel laureate's eyes shifted to him, he nodded. The eyes passed on. No nod, nothing. Gordon stood, plastic cup in hand, glassy smile on his face. The eyes came by again. No pause, no flicker of recognition. Gordon backed out of the chattering crescent, face reddening. *Maybe he didn't recognize me,* Gordon thought, walking away. He got himself another cup of the vodka. *On the other hand, maybe he did.*

"Good booze, eh?" a man said at his elbow. "Try to say 'spectroscopy' three times, real fast." Gordon tried the exercise, and failed. The man turned out to be named Book, and indeed, he did look bookish. He was from General Atomic and proved to be far friendlier than the university people. They stood under a sign that proclaimed, IF YOU CAN READ THIS, THANK A TEACHER. None of Book's levity penetrated Gordon's mood. Vodka, however, began to relieve the world of its awful concreteness. He began to see the point in goys drinking so much. Book went off somewhere and Gordon drifted into conversation with a visiting particle physicist, Steingruber. Both of them shared a deepening appreciation for the vodka. They began to discuss the ageless topic, women. Gordon made several pronouncements about Penny. In a curious way he did not quite understand, Gordon inverted their roles, so that Penny had been the sexual student initiated into the adult world by himself, the sophisticate from New York. Steingruber accepted this as only reasonable. Gordon came to see that Steingruber was indeed a fine fellow, capable of profound insight. They had another drink together. Steingruber pointed to a blonde standing a short distance away and asked, "What is your opinion of that one there?" Gordon peered at her and pronounced, "Pretty cheap looking. Yeah." Steingruber looked at Gordon sharply. "She's my wife." In a moment, before Gordon could frame a suitable reply, he was gone.

Lakin came by, smiling amiably. He was with Bernard Carroway. "I have heard that you are repeating Cooper's experiment," Lakin said without preamble.

"Who did you hear that from?"

"I could see for myself."

Gordon took his time. He had a swallow from his cup and discovered it was empty. Then he looked at Lakin. "Fuck off," he said very clearly. Then he walked away.

He found Penny in a crowd gathered around Marcuse. "The newly appointed Communist-in-Residence?" Gordon asked when he was introduced. To his surprise, Marcuse laughed. A black woman graduate student standing nearby did not think anything was amusing. It developed that her name was Angela and that the revolution was not going to be brought about by people at cocktail parties; this was all Gordon could get out of the conversation, or at least all he could remember. He took Penny's hand and wandered away.

Jonas Salk was off in a corner. Gordon debated trying to meet him. Maybe he could find out how Salk felt about Sabin —who had really developed the vaccine? An interesting question, indeed. "A parable of science," Gordon muttered to himself. "What?" Penny asked. He steered her instead toward a pack of physicists. Some nagging voice within bid him to shut up, so he let Penny carry their fraction of the conversation. People around him seemed distant and vague. He tried to decide if this was due to him or due to them. The eternal relativistic problem. Maybe Marcuse knew the answer. Some Frenchmen asked Gordon about his experiments and he tried to sum up what he believed. It proved surprisingly difficult. The odd thickness of his tongue had gone away, but there remained the problem of what he himself thought was true. The Frenchmen asked about Saul. Gordon sidestepped the question. He tried to keep discussion focused on the results of his experiments. "As Newton said, 'I frame no hypotheses'—at least, not yet. Ask me only about data." He went off in search of more vodka, but the fountain bowl was empty. Sadly, he took the last of the crackers and pâté. When he returned, Penny was standing a little distance away from the Frenchmen, staring out at the view of La Jolla and the satiny glow of the sea. The Frenchmen were speaking French. Penny seemed angry. He tugged at her and she came along, glancing back.

She insisted on driving them home, though Gordon could see no reason why he should not. Going past the beach clubs and rambling private homes, Penny said, "Those *bastards*," with sudden vehemence. "Huh? What?" She grimaced. "After you wandered off they said you were a bungler."

Gordon frowned. "They said that to you?"

"No, silly. They started speaking French. They assumed that of course no American understands another language."

"Oh."

"They called you a fake. A fraud."

"Oh."

"They said everybody was saying that about you."

"Everybody?"

"Yeah," she said sourly.

chapter thirty-four

OCTOBER 7, 1963

It came up out of the noise, suddenly. One minute the scope showed hash and Gordon was tinkering with a new band-pass filter, a recent circuit he'd breadboarded to cut through the noise. Then, abruptly, the NMR curves began to warp and change. He stared at the scope, unmoving. It was 11 p.m.

He brought his hand up to his lips, as if to mask a cry. The jiggling lines went on. It occurred to Gordon that he might be hallucinating. He bit his finger. No, the ragged lines remained. Quickly, suppressing his excitement beneath the urge to be precise, he began to take data.

●

ACTION OF ULTRAVIOAMSLDUZ SUNEYDUFK OM CHAINS APPEARS TO RETARD DIFFUSION IN SURFACE LAYERS OF AMSUWLDOP BUT GROWTH
RA 18 5 36 DEC 30 29.2
RA 18 5 FGDUEL 30 29.2
RA 18 5 36 DEC 30 29.2
EFFECTS DIATOM ENZYME INHIBITED B NETWORK CHAIN REPRO ATTEMPT TO CONTACT YOU WITH T CHYONIC BEAM WREDOPRL AL POINT SOURCE CAN VERIFY RA 18 5 3MCDU DEC 30 29.2 RDUTFKIGLP ASLDURMFU CAMBRIDOLR CAMBRIDG DIATOM BLOOM GHTUPDM ASANATH DEC 30 29.2 THIS VIOLATES NO CAUSAL POSTULATE UNDER WHEELER-FEYNMAN FORMULATION AS LONG AS FEEDBACK IN CAUSAL LOOP PERMITS EXPERIMENT TO CONTINUE IMPERATIVE YOU PERFORM EXPTS TO CHECK MOLECULAR CHAIN XCDEURDL 18 5 36 DEC 30 29.2 TIME DIFFERENTIAL AUSMP

●

"Claudia? Is that you?" It was the first time he had ever called her by her first name.

"Yes, yes, is this Gordon?"

"Right. I've been running in parallel with you. Were you people on last night?"

"What?"

"Were you running last night?"

"I . . . no, I don't . . . my student was making some measurements. I believe he finished about 6 o'clock."

"Shit."

"What? I'm sorry, I don't believe I can hear you correctly—"

"Sorry, never mind. I, ah, I was running last night around 11 p.m. and I got some anomalous resonance effects."

"I see. Well, that would be 2 a.m. here."

"Oh yes. Of course."

"How long did the effect last?"

"Over two hours."

"Well, let me see, the student should be in soon; it is a little after eight. Gordon, you are up at 5 a.m.?"

"Ah, yes. I was waiting for you to get in."

"Have you slept?"

"No, I . . . I was seeing if there was any more of the—the effect."

"Gordon, go to sleep. I will talk to the student. We will run some experiments today. But you get some sleep."

"Sure, sure."

"I promise you we will do the measurements. But get some sleep, eh?"

"Good. Good. That's all I want."

●

"Gordon, Mrs. Evelstein, she brought over the *Life* magazine. Why didn't you *tell* me? There was my son's name, big as life—as *Life!*—and he doesn't tell me. Weeks ago, it was, and—"

"Mom, look, I'm sorry I didn't tell you. I—"

"And the *National Enquirer* thing, she had that, too. That one I didn't like so good."

He breathed sourly into the telephone receiver. What time was it? Christ, 5 p.m. What was the Zinnes group getting?

"Look, Mom, I was asleep, I—"

"Asleep? At this hour?"

"I was working in the lab overnight."

"You shouldn't, you'll ruin your health."

"I'm okay."

"But I wanted to say, about the *Life*, it was such a surprise—"

"Mom, I've got to go back to sleep. I'm worn out."

"Well, all right. I wanted to hear your voice again, though, Gordon. I don't hear your voice so much any more."

"I know, Mom. Look, I'll call you in a few days."

"All right, Gordon."

He hung up and went back to sleep.

•

The Zinnes group found nothing. Gordon could not pick up the signal again. He kept checking as the week wore on. On Friday there was a department Colloquium on plasma physics, given by Norman Rostoker. Gordon went and sat well in the back. Rostoker's first slide was:

Seven Phases of the Thermonuclear Fusion Program
I   Exultation
II   Confusion
III Disenchantment
IV   Search for the Guilty
V   Punishment of the Innocent
VI   Distinction for the Uninvolved
VII Burying the Bodies/Scattering the Ashes

The audience laughed. Gordon did, too. He wondered at which stage he was. But no, the whole message thing wasn't a directed research project, it was a discovery. The fact that he was the only person in the world who believed it made no difference. "Search for the Guilty," though, seemed to fit. He thought about it for a moment and then, in the middle of Rostoker's talk, fell asleep.

•

He answered the call from Ramsey's office and found Ramsey in the lab. The chemist had broken down the interweaving chain into a plausible configuration. Phosphorus, hydrogen, oxygen, carbon. It made sense. What was more, it fit into a class that resembled the pesticides. More sophisticated, yes—but a clear lineal descendant. Gordon smiled, still sleepy from the Colloquium. "Good work," he murmured. Ramsey beamed. On his way out Gordon passed through the glass forest of the laboratory. He had come to enjoy its rhythms. The biologists down the hall had pens of animals for their tests and Gordon wandered down that way, feeling obscurely happy. On a cart in the hallway there were trays. In them were heaps of gutted brown hamsters, like burst potatoes. Life in the service of life. He walked away quickly.

•

His telephone rang at 6 p.m., as he was putting papers and books in his briefcase for the weekend. The physics building was nearly deserted and the ringing echoed.

"Gordon, this is Claudia Zinnes."

"Oh, hello. Have you—?"

"We have something. Interruptions." She went on to describe them.

"Look, ah, do me a favor? Try to break them down into patterns. I mean, I know it's late and it's, what, 9 o'clock there, but if you—"

"I think I understand you."

Exhaling: "See if it fits Morse code."

A quiet laugh. "I'll see, Gordon."

He asked her to call him at home and gave her the number.

•

"I told you last *week*," Penny said. "We're going Air Cal to Oakland Saturday morning at ten, out of Lindbergh."

"I don't remember it."

"Oh, crap. I *told* you."

"Penny, I have a lot to do this weekend. A lot to think about."

"Think about it in Oakland."

"No, I can't, you can tell your parents we—"

The telephone rang.

"Claudia?"

"Gordon? I checked and, and, you were right."

A sudden hot dizziness swarmed over him. "What does it say?"

"Those astronomical coordinates you told me about. That's all I have. They go on for pages."

"Great. That's just great."

"What *is* it, Gordon?"

"I don't know."

They spoke for a few more moments. Claudia would keep their experiment running constantly. Signal strength seemed to come and go irregularly. Gordon listened, nodded, agreed. But his mind was not on the details. Instead, an odd sensation had begun to creep up through his legs and into his chest. He put down the telephone after saying good night and felt the hair rise on the back of his neck. It was real. All along he had reserved a certain possibility that he was a potzer, that the experiment was wrong, that he was finding books in babbling brooks, as Penny once joked about it. But now he knew: *someone was trying to reach him.*

"Gordon? Gordon, what is it?"

"Zinnes. New York." He looked up, dazed. "They found it."

She kissed him and together they did a little jig. No potzer, he. Gordon lurched around the living room, barking jubilantly *ha* and *right!* After a moment he felt dizzy and sat down. He was suddenly tired. *Scratch one hypothesis, mark up one fact.* But what should he do next?

"Penny, you're right—we go to Oakland."

chapter thirty-five

1998

A babble of conversation met Peterson as he opened the front door. Through the entrance to the drawing room, across the stone hallway, he could see people talking rapidly. A burst of laughter, glasses clinking, a sugary swelling of the new Latin rhythms.

He paused only an instant. Without looking to either side he crossed the black and white squares of marble and went up the wide curved staircase. It was generally true that people would not intercept you if you passed by quickly, not letting anyone catch your eye. It was perfectly reasonable that he should be there, after all; it was his town house. A guest would assume he and Sarah together were putting on this bloody party which he had forgotten, and that Peterson was tending to some domestic chore upstairs.

He moved silently on the deep carpet and crossed the landing. The hall bathroom door showed a crack of light at the floor; probably someone inside. He would be in the bedroom long enough for it to clear, but he should keep in mind the flow of traffic to and fro when he made his exit. He would have to go out the way he came in; to reach the rear exit through the kitchen he would have to pass through the party.

He closed the bedroom door and went to the closet. A rank of overcoats effectively concealed the two suitcases from anything short of a spring housecleaning. He pulled them out. A bit heavy, but manageable. He got them into position by the doorway and then gazed round. Opposite, the three long Georgian windows looked out onto a series of peaked roofs. Most buildings had dim rows of windows lit; it was the brownout hour, he recalled. Others were black. Zealous conservation, he wondered, or people who had left town already? No matter—he wasn't going to concern himself with such things any longer. Between the windows were full-length mirrors, framed in brown velvet which was in turn edged in black; Sarah's latest notion. Peterson hesitated, studying his reflection. Still a bit drawn, white around the eyes, but basically recovered. He had bluffed his way out of the hospital as soon as he felt able to move about. He had gone directly to his office. The Council was in a full crisis state, and no one noticed him clearing certain documents from his files, placing a few last-minute orders by telephone, and giving certain instructions to his solicitor. Sir Martin had him in for an overview conference, and there Peterson saw his preparations were none too soon. The clouds were definitely carrying the bloom material far and wide. The cloud form was slightly different from the ocean form, but they shared the neurojacket effect Kiefer had found only a few days ago. Kiefer's data were of great use, but effective countermeasures were still a problem for the laboratories. The clouds dumped the stuff wherever they rained. Land plants generally resisted the neurojacket mechanism, but not always. Plant cellulose remained intact, but the more complex portions were vulnerable. Quick tests had turned up a method of cleansing certain plants, to cut off the process before the stuff could diffuse through the plant skin. Washing the harvested crops in some solutions seemed feasible, and promised a 70 percent success rate. Peterson thought wryly of Laura's "Oh, the vegetables and everything are perfectly fresh. The finest. They're brought in from the country each day." Yes, and that's where he'd got the damned stuff. In the human digestive tract it played hob with all sorts of metabolic processes—often fatally, if untreated.

No one knew what the more subtle, secondary effects on the food chain might be. There were some decidedly dark projections by the biologists.

What's more, the cloud mechanism was spreading the bloom faster. Reddish dots were appearing in the North Atlantic now.

With amazing energy Sir Martin was marshaling the Council resources, but even he seemed worried. They were dealing with an exponential process and no one could say where the effect would saturate.

Peterson looked round the room for one last time. Every feature in it was tailored for his habits, from the elegant accordionlike shoe rack to the artfully arranged bookshelf, with its concealed communications center. A pity to leave it, really. But the whole point was to leave before the rush, and yet have a plausible reason to be absent from the Council for a few days. Recovering at some country hospital would do nicely. Sir Martin had studied him for a long moment when Peterson announced his departure, but that was an unavoidable risk. The two men probably understood each other quite well. A pity things couldn't have worked out better between them, Peterson thought, and edged open the bedroom door.

A departing back, going down the stairs after a trip to the loo. Peterson waited until the man had vanished across the marble foyer. He shouldered open the door and carried the bags to the head of the stairs. Christ, they were heavy. He'd never allowed for the possibility that he might be ill when he had to make his move.

He went down the stairs with soft thumps, taking the weight solidly and checking his balance before attempting the next step. He had to watch the footing intently. The stairway was immensely long. He began puffing. Latin music started abruptly, brassy and rich, flooding his ears and throwing off his concentration. Out of the corner of his eye he sensed movement. A man and a woman, approaching from the drawing room. He took the last three steps rapidly and nearly slipped on the slick floor.

"Ian! My, don't you look the traveler. I thought Sarah said you were in hospital."

He thought rapidly. Smile, that was it. "I still am, actually," he began, at the same time walking round the corner to a small tucked-in closet. He had to get the bags out of the way before anyone else came along. "It's filling up, however, so I thought it best I get out of the public's way. Go to a suburban place to recuperate, you know."

"Oh Christ yes," the man said. "City hospitals are the worst. Can I help you with those?"

"No no, just a few clothes." He had scooted them into the closet and now closed the door firmly.

"I say, we were looking for a place to, you know, be private for a time." The woman looked at him expectantly. She was one of Sarah's friends, one of the sort he could never remember from one time to the next. She turned to gesture upstairs, no doubt thinking he had a thin imagination and needed a diagram. Her eye caught the door of his bedroom, standing open. "Oh, that would be perfect! It has a lock, hasn't it?"

Peterson felt a cold anger. "I'd rather think there might be—"

"I shouldn't think we'd be long. You don't mind, do you? Yes, you do mind. He minds, Jeremy." She put one foot on the lower stair and looked at the man with her, clearly turning this difficult chap over to him.

"I, it really would be most, most obliging of you if you would give us some help here, Ian."

Peterson felt suddenly hot and weak. He had to cut through all this, get free. He had reacted automatically to the idea of anyone using his bedroom for some stupid rutting, but now he saw that was pointless. He had just now kissed the place good-bye, after all. "Yes, I see, go right ahead. I don't mind." He was able to say it almost cheerfully.

The couple thanked him and moved up the staircase with what seemed to Peterson deliberate slowness. He glanced at the drawing room and took several deep, clearing breaths. He could get the bags and be gone without arousing comment, if only—

Sarah. She had seen him as she passed by a knot of chattering people. She tugged at a man, nodded towards Peterson. They crossed the squares of the foyer, like chess pieces advancing. Knight errant and queen to the attack, he thought. He noted remotely that she was wearing one of her own sleek dresses, a jungle-print creation with a matching silk scarf tied round her head and hanging artfully to the left. He looked at the man with her and felt a cold shock. It was Prince Andrew. Jesus, she couldn't be starting that up again, could she? Well, it would hardly matter now.

"Ian! You're out already? *Squisito!*" Sarah exclaimed, taking his hand.

"Just getting some things. They're transferring me to a place in the country." He extended a hand to Andrew. "Good evening, sir."

"For heaven's sake, Ian, you don't have to call me sir here."

"Andy's getting us invites to the Coronation Ball—the *small* one. Isn't that lovely of him?"

"Yes, very. How is your brother faring, Andrew?"

"Oh, I haven't seen him for a week myself. He's always busy now. Glad I don't have that job. He's better suited to it than the rest of us, anyway."

"Oh, I'm sure you could do magnificently," Sarah murmured.

Andrew shook his head in a wobbly way. "No, I doubt it. I've often wondered whether it was just luck that the heir turned out that way or whether he turned out that way precisely because he *was* the heir."

Peterson suppressed a fidgeting motion with his hands and tried to think of something to say. Was this conversation unreal or was it just him? "He takes his work very seriously," he said blandly. "The times I've consulted with him, he's gone right to the point."

"Got a sense of humor, though, you know," Andrew replied, as though apologizing for his brother's seriousness. He blinked owlishly.

Peterson realized that Andrew was drunk, in precisely the

291

degree that royalty can get drunk without arousing comment. That was to say, quite a bit. Sarah tugged at Peterson's sleeve, beckoning him into the party. He considered for an instant and then followed. He wanted no one to notice the size or weight of the cases he carried as he left. Best to get Sarah and Andrew back into the mob and slip away later. He allowed Sarah to parade him around, introducing him to a few new people he could spot as being potentially useful to her. He smiled, nodded, said little. Gradually it dawned on him that everyone there was addled in some way—drunk, high on drugs, or simply hysterical with frenetic energy. And they were all talking the most superficial rubbish, as well. He had expected a barrage of questions on the bloom or the clouds, but absolutely no one asked. He found himself watching them from a distance. As elegant and ignorant as swans. Yet he knew some of them must have doubts. Again, the sensation of unreality.

It took well over an hour before he saw his chance. He wanted to be damned sure Andrew didn't see the bags, so he waited until Sarah was clinging to Andrew's arm and had just set into one of her stock outrageous stories. Then Peterson slipped through several babbling groups, seeming to be among them but in fact listening to nothing, watching only to see if anyone important saw his exit. At the right moment he moved quickly into the foyer. Out came the bags. As he turned, his own bedroom door opened and a bleary, reddened face appeared. Before the woman could hail him he wrenched open the outer door and fled. Not the smooth departure he had envisioned, but good enough. Ahead lay Cambridge and then, by God, he could rest.

chapter thirty-six

Marjorie sat in the Markhams' small rented house and watched Jan. She had come expecting to play the gentle, efficient helper to a distraught and grieving friend, but found their roles almost reversed. Jan was packing systematically. Marjorie had offered to do it for her. She felt that Jan should properly have the freedom to sprawl face down on her bed, face into her pillow, if she felt like it. Jan had refused her help, saying she wouldn't be able to find things if she didn't pack them herself. Marjorie had offered to make her some tea. Strong sweet tea soothed anyone. But Jan hadn't wanted that either. She went on working. Marjorie, slightly offended, thought she might even start humming a tune as she worked. Marjorie wished Jan would offer a drink. Abruptly she clamped down on that thought. God, it was still only the morning.

"Isn't there *anything* I can do?" she asked with a thin tone of desperation.

Jan stopped and pushed a strand of hair back from her eyes.

"Well, come to think of it, you could pack up Greg's clothes. Why don't you take this big box and go upstairs? Just his clothes and shoes. I'm going to try to sell them to the second-hand shop on Petty Cury. Oh, and check the hall closet. I think his raincoat is in there. And his robe is on the back of the bathroom door." She gave a sideways smile. "You may as well check all the rooms. I never broke him of the habit of dropping his things wherever he happened to be."

Marjorie stared at her, disbelieving. She herself had carefully avoided mentioning Greg's name.

"How can you be so *calm?*" she burst out.

Jan considered. "I think it's because there's so much to do. I haven't time to break down. Don't worry, Marjorie, it will hit me sooner or later. I suppose I haven't really taken it in yet."

Marjorie noticed that Jan packed her clothing in a strict ritual. Skirts first, folded carefully lengthwise and then at the hip. Hose in neat little balls. Jan concentrated on her task with absolute energy. She laid out blouses with precisely defined movements, the sleeves in stiff parallels. She fastened the buttons at the collars and down the front, fingers working rhythmically. The arms folded over. She deftly set the creases, smoothed wrinkles. The soft cloth made neat rectangles, each a package. Jan lined them up in a suitcase, tucking in corners. The lid closed snug and tight.

"Would you like to stay with us until you can get a flight? I don't feel you should be alone here."

"I'll be all right. I'm going to London to line up for a flight. There's evidence that Greg's flight picked up some virulent form of the cloud stuff—they think that's what happened to the pilot. No telling, of course. But it means the airlines are scheduling very little until the Council lifts that limitation on flights. They've canceled everything that might cross the really thick clouds." Jan shrugged.

"You're sure you should go home? To California?"

"Might as well." A wan fatigue crept into Jan's face. "I'm no use here."

"I still think you should stay with us a bit. The children are home—the schools closed, you know—and we could have picnics and—"

"No, I'm sorry, no. Thanks, though." Jan picked up the box. She stared into it for a moment. "I hope I make it."

●

Renfrew paced the lab floor, smacking one fist into the other palm. His assistant Jason leaned against a gray cabinet, staring moodily at the floor.

"Where's George?" Renfrew asked suddenly.

"Home, sick."

"Well, I suppose it doesn't matter. There's nothing we can do anyway. Damn power failures. And I still haven't been able to reach Peterson. His secretary says he's ill. What a time to choose to be ill!"

He paced some more. The roughing pumps stood silent around him. The lab was gloomy, lit only by a skylight. Late afternoon sunlight slanted in.

"God, Markham would have been back here tomorrow and we'd have had the Brookhaven backing. Who's going to speak for us now?"

"Mr. Peterson said he was prepared to help, the last time he was here."

"I don't trust the fellow. But if I could at least get in *touch* with him, God damn it!"

He went over to the water fountain and pressed the button. Nothing happened. He kicked it.

"I never thought I'd live to see water rationing in England," he said, "and it's raining cats and dogs, too. 'Water, water everywhere and not a drop to drink.' I remember learning that one at school. 'And slimy things did crawl with legs upon the slimy sea,' yes." He snorted. "It'll be the red cliffs of Dover soon."

"Why don't you go home?" Jason suggested. "I'll stick here in case there's a call from London."

"Home?" Renfrew said vaguely. Once, Marjorie had been the first person to turn to in times of stress. Her capable motherly presence and simple optimism had always reassured him. But now she was edgy and nervous all the time. He suspected she was drinking too much. He had mentioned as much to her once, but she had flown off the handle, so he hadn't brought it up again. Her innate good sense would pull her through, he was sure. And the kids. He hadn't even seen them, except briefly, for a month. They got up late, since there was no school, so he didn't even see them at breakfast. Yes, perhaps he should go home. Try to make contact with his family again.

Leaving the lab, he found that someone had cut through the chain and stolen his bicycle.

•

It was evening and dark by the time he got home. He stood wearily on the porch and shook the rain off his coat. His key turned in the lock but the door was chained on the inside. He rattled it, but no one came. He pressed the bell, realizing as he did so that there were no lights on in the house so the bell wouldn't work either. Turning up his coat collar, he left the shelter of the porch and squished round to the back. The kitchen door was locked, too. Peering through the window, he saw Marjorie sitting at the table in flickering candlelight. He rapped on the window pane. She looked up, screamed. The candle went out and there was a crash.

"Marjorie!" he shouted. "Marjorie! It's me, John."

A thumping. The chain rattled. She opened the back door.

"Don't *do* that," she complained. "My God, you almost gave me a heart attack. Now I can't find the damn candle. It fell on the floor somewhere." She locked the door behind him. "I'll get another one."

In the dark he heard her fumbling round, banging cupboard doors. His feet crunched on what sounded like broken glass on

the floor. He smelled whisky. *She never used to drink whisky.*
A match burst orange; wan candlelight sent their shadows leaping up the kitchen walls.

"Why in heaven's name don't you use more than one candle?" he asked.

"Because you can be sure that will be the next thing the country will run out of."

"Where are the kids?"

"Good heavens, John, they're at my *brother's.* I *told* you that. They were just trailing around here twiddling their thumbs so I thought they'd have more fun with their cousins. They can help with the harvest. If the rain doesn't *completely* wipe it out."

She bent to pick up the pieces of broken glass from the floor.

He started to ask if there was anything for dinner, then tactfully reworded it. "Have you eaten yet?"

"No." She gave a little giggle. "I drank my dinner instead. It saves trouble."

The giggle reminded him of the old bouncy Marjorie. With a strange surge of feeling he reached out and took her hands.

"Damn!" He jerked back, sucking his thumb where a splinter of glass had cut him.

"You silly bugger," she said unsympathetically. "You could see what I was doing." She threw the pieces of glass into the trash and wiped the floor with a sponge.

"You never used to drink whisky," he said, watching her.

"It's quicker. I know what you're thinking. You're afraid I'm becoming an alcoholic. But *I* know when to stop. I just drink enough to take the edge off things."

"How about some food then?"

"Help yourself," she shrugged. "You could open a tin of beans and heat it on the gas ring. Or there's some cheese in the larder."

"You know, it's not a whole lot of fun to come home on a rainy night to a cold dark house and not even any dinner."

"I don't see how you can blame me because it's cold and dark. What am I supposed to do, burn the furniture? And it's the first time you've come home this early in God knows how long and since you *didn't* let me know, you could hardly expect to find *dinner* ready. John, you have no idea how awful it is to shop for food these days. You have to queue up for hours—literally—and then there's practically nothing to be had anyway."

"I don't know, Marjorie. You always used to be so resourceful. We ought to be better off than most people. We could kill a chicken, and then there's your vegetable garden.''

''God, John, sometimes I feel as if you'd been away for months. The chickens were stolen *weeks* ago. All of them. And I *know* I told you. As for the vegetables, am I supposed to go slopping around there in the rain looking for a leftover potato or two? It's the end of *September*. The garden's a swamp now anyway.''

The lights came back on suddenly. The refrigerator whirred. They blinked, two people confronted with each other without the shadowy softenings. A silence fell. John fidgeted.

''Heather's mother died,'' she said abruptly. ''Well, it's a happy release. Not like Greg Markham. God, that was a shock. It's hard to believe he's dead. He seemed so—well, so *alive*. And Heather and James lost their jobs, you know.''

''Don't tell me any more bad news,'' he said gruffly and disappeared into the larder.

chapter thirty-seven

Marjorie hoped John would be home soon. He had worked past midnight every night this week. She ran a hand through her hair, eyed her empty glass. Better not. She'd had three already. Was this how one became an alcoholic? She got up suddenly, turned on the radio and the stereo at high volume. A cacophony of sound blared through the room, a jazz band clashing against a trio of Latin singers, bringing a kind of life. She went through the ground floor again, turning on all the lights. Conservation be damned. Her nerves were jumping and she was having a little difficulty focusing her eyes. After all, what was there to stay sober for? She picked up her glass and headed for the sideboard.

Halfway across the room she stopped, catching some half-heard sound. Lottie was barking furiously, shut up in the laundry room. She hesitated, then turned down the radio and stereo. This time it was unmistakably the front doorbell. She stood in the middle of the room. *Who would . . . ?* The bell rang again. Then a knock. How silly of her! As if a prowler would knock at the door. It was probably a friend. Yes, thank God, someone to talk to, spend the evening with. She hurried to the hall, turned on the porch light. Through the stained glass window to the left of the door she saw the silhouette of a man. Panic seized her again. Distant thunder growled. She took a deep breath, then leaned against the door and called out as calmly as she could manage, "Who is it?"

"Ian Peterson."

She stared blankly at the door for a moment, mind a blur. She slowly slid back the chain and the two bolts and opened the door a crack. His hair was ruffled. His jacket showed wrinkles and he wore no tie. A wave of embarrassment ran over her as she realized what a sight she must present, too, with her hair awry, clutching an empty glass in one hand and dressed, for God's sake, in a tatty old sundress because it was so hot. She smoothed her dress with one sticky hand and tried to hide the glass behind her with the other.

298

"Oh, Mr. Peterson. Um, I'm afraid John isn't here. He's, um, working at the lab this evening."

"Oh? I was hoping to catch him here."

"Well, I'm sure you could go round—"

A sudden wind howled across the yard, blowing leaves over Peterson's shoulders. "Oh!" Marjorie exclaimed. Peterson automatically stepped inside. She slammed the door. "My word, what a gust," she said.

"Storm coming."

"How was it on the road?"

"Difficult. I've been laid up, actually, in a hotel south of here for several days. After I recovered I decided to take a run by here to see if John has anything new."

"Well, I think not, Mr. Peterson. He—"

"Ian. Please."

"Well, Ian, John's been scrounging fuel for the power supply the laboratory has. He says he can't rely on commercial service any longer. That's been taking his time. He is continuing to transmit, I can tell you that."

Peterson nodded. "Good. I suppose that is all anyone can expect. It was an interesting experiment." He smiled. "I suppose I half-believed it could be done, you know."

"But can't it still? I mean . . ."

"I think there's something we don't understand about the process. I must admit I was for the most part interested in the work simply because it was a good bit of science in its own right. A last indulgence of mine, I suppose. Playing cards on the Titanic. I've had a chance to think this over the last few days. I left London, thinking I was all right, and then the illness hit me again. I tried to get into a hospital and was rejected. No room. So I stayed in a hotel, riding out the last side effects. Take no food, that's the cure. So I thought about the experiment to distract myself."

"My *word*. Do come and sit." Marjorie saw as he moved into the light that Peterson was pale and thinner. There was a sunken, hollow look about his eyes. "This illness, was it . . ."

"Yes, the cloud-carried thing. Even after they clear it from your system, there are residual metabolic irregularities."

"We've been eating tinned food. The radio says that's best."

Peterson grimaced. "Yes, they would say that. It means they haven't the treating fluids they need to save the present crop. I telephoned my Sek today and learned quite a few little gems I suppose they haven't told the public."

"Is it bad?"

"Bad? No, disastrous." He sank wearily onto the sofa. "No

matter how much you plan for it, the real thing seems curiously, well, unreal."

"I thought we *hadn't* planned for this."

He blinked, as if orienting himself. "Well, no, I meant . . . the endless projections . . . so mathematical . . . not this way . . ." He shook his head and went on. "I'd advise you to eat as little as possible. I have a suspicion—and so do the experts, sod them for all they know—the effects of this will change our lives utterly. There's a shortage of the system-flushing drugs we need, and . . . some think the biosphere's going to be permanently altered."

"Well, yes," she said worriedly, feeling a strange sensation wash through her. "If you fellows can't . . . ."

Peterson seemed to pull himself back from the mood that had struck him. "Let's not dwell on it, shall we, Marjorie? I may call you Marjorie?"

"Of course."

"And how are you feeling?"

"To tell you the truth, I'm just a bit squiffy. I was nervous here on my own and I had a couple of drinks. I'm afraid they go to my head rather."

"Well, that's probably the best way to be. May I get myself a drink and catch up a bit?"

"Please do. Can you help yourself? I hardly even know what we've got. I'm drinking Pernod."

She watched him cross the room. While his back was turned, she felt free to stare at him. He squatted lightly before the sideboard, tilting the bottles to read their labels. She leaned her head in her hand. She was aware of him coming back across the room, stopping by her, crouching.

"Are you sure you're all right, Marjorie?"

She could not meet his eyes. She knew she was blushing. His hand rested on the arm of her chair. She looked at his gold watch, the slender wrist, the dark hair on the back of his pale hand. She felt unable to move. She stared at the hand.

"Marjorie?"

"I'm sorry. I feel terribly hot, Ian."

"Let me open a window. It *is* very stuffy in here."

The hand disappeared from view and presently she felt air cooling her damp forehead.

"Oh, that's better. Thank you."

She leaned back, was able to look at him. After all, he was not so very special. Goodlooking, but not strikingly so. She smiled back at him.

"I'm sorry. I'm a bit weird this evening. There's been this

cloud thing, and then Greg Markham, and . . . well, things can seem pointless. And yet one is . . . glad to be alive . . . I'm sorry, I'm not making much sense, am I? It's just that we're so powerless. I keep wanting to *do* something.''

"You're making a lot of sense, Marjorie."

Thunder crashed suddenly, shaking the house.

"Christ, that was close!" she exclaimed, and then was taken aback at herself. She mustn't be so excitable. A prickly wave rushed over her skin. "I wonder if more of those cloud organisms are coming down in this rain."

"Probably."

"There was a local woman, I heard, who kept a home for cats. She gave all her own tinned food to the cats, thinking the boxed food she had for them had been contaminated. I expect she'll starve."

"Mad." He took a substantial pull on his drink.

"Did you hear about the Coronation? They've canceled preparations."

Peterson said sarcastically, "My, I expect the country will be in an uproar over that."

Marjorie smiled. A flash, then a booming crash of thunder. Marjorie leaped up in fright. They looked at each other and abruptly burst out laughing.

"As long as you can hear it, you're safe," he said. "By that time the lightning's passed."

Suddenly she felt very good. She was glad to have him there, keeping loneliness and fear at bay.

"Are you hungry? Would you like something to eat?"

"No, I'm not. Relax. Don't play the hostess. If I want anything, I'll get it."

He smiled wanly at her. Was there a double entendre in his words? He must be used to getting anything he wanted. Tonight, though, he was less certain, more . . . "It's good to see you," she said. "It's been pretty lonely here recently with the children away and John working late."

"Yes, I imagine—" He didn't finish the sentence. The lights went out, dramatically accompanied by a roll of thunder.

"Now I'm *really* glad you're here. I'd be scared stiff on my own, thinking someone had cut the lines to the house or something."

"Oh, I'm sure it's just a power failure. Lines blown down by the wind, probably."

"That's been happening a lot recently. I've got some candles in the kitchen."

She crossed the room, skirting the furniture in the dark from long familiarity. In the kitchen she felt in the cupboard for candles and matches. Automatically she lit three and set them in candlesticks.

The mechanical clock on a shelf went *tick,* followed by a clacking as gears moved. She turned and found Ian in the doorway. He stepped inside. The clock made a sound like a rachet sticking. "Oh, I fetched that out of the garage, whilst straightening up," she said. "With the power always off, an old windup is better . . ." *Tick.* "Makes that odd sound, though, doesn't it?"

"Perhaps if you oiled it . . ."

"But I did, you see. There's something needs mending. It stays pretty near right, though."

He leaned against the counter and watched her put away the matches. She noticed that the pine shelving loomed up in the shadows cast by the candles. Things in the room waved and rippled, except for the straight shelves. *Tick.*

"Interesting," Ian murmured, "how we keep on wanting to know the time, in the midst of all that's going on."

"Yes."

"As if we still had appointments to keep."

"Yes."

A silence stretched between them, a chasm. She searched for something to say. *Tick.* The shelves seemed more substantial now than the walls. The clock nested in the middle of them, surrounded by preserves.

She looked at Ian. In this dim light his eyes were very dark. She leaned against the cupboard, less nervous now. She should take the candles into the living room, but for the moment it felt right to stay here, not hurry.

Ian moved across the small kitchen. Distantly she wondered if he was going to take a candle. *Tick.*

He reached up and touched her cheek.

Neither of them moved. She felt warm. She took a shallow breath. She breathed in and it seemed to take a long time to fill her lungs.

Very slowly he bent and kissed her. It was a light, almost casual touch.

She sagged against the cupboard. *Tick.* She breathed out. In the silence she wondered if he could hear the air flowing in and out of her. She watched as he picked up a candle. A hand touched her shoulder. He steered her out, away from the kitchen and shelves and clock, toward the living room.

chapter thirty-eight

OCTOBER 12, 1963

Penny's voice cut through to him: "As I was saying."

"Huh? Oh, yes, go on."

"Come *on*, you weren't listening at all." She swerved the rented Thunderbird around a curve. The Bay Area lay below and to the right, the twinkling of the bay hazed by fog. "Absent-minded prof."

"Okay, okay." But he slipped back into a fog of his own as she zoomed them around Grizzly Peak's hairpin turns above the Berkeley campus and then onto Skyline. He glimpsed Oakland's sprawl, green dots of islands in the blue-gray bay, and San Francisco in alabaster isolation. They flitted behind stands of pine and eucalyptus, the trees making black and green grids against the brown of the hillsides. Penny had the top down. Cool air made her hair stream and float behind her head. "Mount Tamalfuji!" she called, pointing at a short, blunted peak to the north across the bay. Then they were into the descent, brakes squealing and gears growling as she took them down Broadway Terrace. A forest musk enveloped them. They emerged from the tree-thick hillside and shot past a jumble of houses, a technicolor spattering. Traffic thinned as they neared her parents' house. Clearly, a ritzy section with an appropriately posh name: Piedmont. Gordon thought of Long Island and Gatsby and yellow sedans.

Her parents proved unmemorable. Gordon could not be sure whether this was due to them or to him. His mind kept drifting back to the experiment and the messages, rummaging for some fresh tool to pry up the lid of the mystery. *Come at it from a different angle,* Penny had said once. He couldn't get the phrase out of his mind. He found he could carry on conversation and smile and do the dance of guest and host, without ever really taking part in what was going on. Penny's father was big and reassuringly gruff, a man who knew how to turn money into more money. He had the standard graying temples and a certain sun-baked assurance. Her mother seemed serene, a joiner of clubs and charities, a scrupulous housekeeper. Gordon felt he had met them before but couldn't place them, like characters in a movie whose title won't spring to the lips.

The invitation had been to stay over at the house. Gordon insisted on their staying in a motel on University Avenue—to put them smack in the middle of town, he said, but in fact because he wanted to avoid the touchy question of whether they would share a room in her parents' castle. He wasn't ready for that issue, not this weekend.

Her father had heard about the Saul thing, of course, and wanted to talk about it. Gordon told him just enough to be polite and then deflected talk to the department, UCLJ, and gradually to topics further and further away. Her father—"Jack," he said with a warm, forthright handshake, "just call me plain Jack"—had bought some introductory astronomy books to learn more. This proved to be a handy time-filler, as Gordon sat back and let Jack regale him with facts about the stars, and the obligatory reverent awe at the scope of the universe. Jack had a sharp, inquiring mind. He asked penetrating questions. Gordon soon found his own rather elementary knowledge of astronomy was stretched thin. While the women cooked and chattered in the kitchen, Gordon struggled to explain the carbon cycle, supernova explosions, and the riddles of globular clusters. He summoned up smatterings of half-remembered lectures. Jack caught him in a few boners and Gordon began to feel uncomfortable. He thought of Cooper's exam.

At last they had a beer before lunch and Jack switched to other subjects. Linus Pauling had just won the Nobel Peace Prize: what did Gordon think of that? Wasn't this the first time anybody had won two Nobels? No, Gordon pointed out, Madame Curie had won one in physics and another in chemistry. Gordon was afraid this would launch them into politics. He was pretty sure Jack was a member of the disarmament-equals-Munich school, pushed locally by William Knowland of the Oakland *Trib*. But Jack adroitly side-stepped the point and ushered them into a steaming lunch of soup and well-marbled minute steaks. Jacaranda trees cloaked a portion of the view from the dining room. The rest of the windows gave a sweeping vista of bay and city and hills. The steak was perfect.

•

"See?" Penny called. "Ajax knows what you're going to do before you know yourself."

Gordon watched. The big horse shivered, snorted, blinked. She took Ajax from a standing position directly into a canter. Ajax bounded forward, puffing, ears pricked. She could get the animal to turn from either foot instantly, and make him walk sideways using only the pressure of her leg. She moved Ajax subtly, coasting around the corral.

Gordon slumped against the railings. *Come at it from a different angle.* Okay, Ramsey had the biochem part wrapped up. But that was a piece, not the whole puzzle. The only other hard data they had was good old RA 18 5 36 DEC 30 29.2, a drum beat that led nowhere. It had to mean *some*thing—

"Gordon! I'm taking Ajax out on a trail ride. Want to come?"

"Uh, okay. No riding, though."

"Come *on*."

He shook his head, distracted. All he could remember now from the previous hour of her instruction was how to avoid getting kicked. When you walked behind him you had to keep close to the rump, so the horse knew there wasn't room to get in a good healthy whack with his hoof. Brushing the tail apparently told the animal you were not a suitable target to relieve its minor irritations on, and it lost interest. This seemed doubtful to Gordon. It was an animal, after all, incapable of such foresight.

He hiked along the ridge line above her. RA 18 5 36 DEC 30 29.2. They were just below the lip of the Oakland hills. The rumpled brown landscape of Contra Costa County lay in the distance. The redwoods and pines around him were musty with a dry, swarming odor he could not place. 263 KEV PEAK. POINT SOURCE IN TACHYON SPECTRUM. A fine dust rose in puffs to greet his steps. It was late afternoon. Blue shadows lanced through the dusty clouds behind Ajax. Penny had come here every day when she was in high school, Jack told him. Gordon had considered making a wry joke about the Freudian implications of adolescent girls and horseback riding. He decided against it after a glance at Penny. CAN VERIFY WITH NMR. This horsy ambience was far away from the sandlot ball he remembered as his only sport. *Clop clop* of hooves, images of Gary Cooper or maybe Ida Lupino, a stately glide through aisles of looming redwoods: serene. Gordon felt heavy and conspicuous. He plodded through the woods in black street shoes his mother had bought in Macy's, unsuited for this distant continent. He felt surrounded here by a naturalness he found foreign. RA 18 5 36 DEC 30 29.2, RA 18 5 36 DEC 30 29.2. Yea verily.

•

That night, when he made love to her back at the motel, Penny seemed changed. Her hips had got harder. Angular patterns of bone spoke to him through the thin cloak of flesh. She was tough, western, a horsewoman. She knew that artichokes grew on a sort of bush, not on trees. She could cook over an open fire. He found her breasts more pointed, with pronounced nipples, rosy and soft, that puckered swiftly as he sucked on them. The east was east and the rest was west.

•

Jack took them out Sunday in late morning to watch some walnutting he had invested in. In the walnut groves near Alamo a mechanical tree-shaker chuffed and wheezed. Its hydraulic arm yanked at the tree trunks, bringing showers of nuts bursting from the sky. Men shepherded a contraption down the lanes between the trees, coaxing its engine. It flicked rubber flippers to the side, herding the nuts into ragged rows. A picker followed after. The walnuts were still in their dappled green husks and the picker scooped them up, leaving behind the twigs and dirt and snapped branches. Jack explained that this new method would pay off in no time. A trailer carried the nuts to a gauntlet of brushes and wire nets, where the hulls were rubbed off. A natural gas oven baked off any hulls that stuck. "Going to revolutionize the industry," Jack pronounced. Gordon watched the huffing machines and the gangs of men tending them. They worked even on Sunday; it was harvest. The walnut groves were soothing after the bleak scrub desert of Southern California. The long shadowed ranks of green reminded him of upper New York State. The clanking arm that strangled trees for their nuts was disturbing, though: a new, robot west.

"Can I borrow some of those astronomy books of yours this afternoon?" he asked Jack abruptly.

Jack nodded, surprised, covering it with a baffled grin. Penny rolled her eyes and grimaced: *Won't you ever stop working, even for a weekend?* Gordon shrugged, daunted for a moment by her silent condemnation. He saw that she wanted this weekend to work, in some sense. Perhaps he and just plain Jack were supposed to strike up some sudden comradeship. Well, maybe they would, given the right occasion. But this weekend wasn't it. Gordon knew he had been drifting through it in a daze, distracted by the problem. Yet knowing the fact didn't change it. And whenever he did join in, he found himself misreading Penny's parents. He was acutely conscious of sleeping with their daughter. *Sticking it to the shiksa, yeah.* What was the agreed-upon California way to deal with that fact? Politely ignoring the sleeping arrangements? He supposed so, and yet he still felt uncomfortable.

306

The tree-shaker grunted and yanked, bringing him out of his ruminations. He had been standing with his hands behind his back, his usual lecturer pose, staring at a clod of earth. Gordon looked up at the others, who had moved off toward the car. Penny gave her father a wry, resigned look, gesturing at Gordon: family signals.

●

There was nothing in the indexes of Jack's books about Hercules. Gordon paged through them, looking for something about the constellations. There were star charts, seasonal views of Ursa Major and Orion and the Southern Cross. Students who had been reared under city lights needed a simple guide to the stars. Gordon was no different. He studied the lines connecting the stellar dots, trying to understand why anybody thought these looked like hunters or swans or bulls. Then a passage caught his eye.

Our own sun is in motion, just as all stars are. We revolve about the center of our galaxy at a speed of about 150 miles per second. In addition, the sun is moving at about 12 miles per second toward a point near the star Vega, in the Hercules cluster. Many thousands of years from now, the constellations will appear different, because of such motions of stars relative to each other. In Figure 8 the constellation . . .

Penny drove him over to the Berkeley campus. She had liked the idea of going for a drive around the area again, even though it meant seeing a little less of her parents. Her attitude changed when she saw that he did not want to stroll around the campus at all, and instead headed directly for the Physics Department library. The library was in a building next to the campanile but Gordon refused to ride the elevator up and look at the view. He waved goodbye to her and went inside.

Solar motion, discounting the rotation about galactic center, can be adequately described as a cosine θ distribution. We are moving away from the *solar antapex* and toward the *solar apex*. Since the position of the solar apex represents an average over many local stellar motions, there are significant uncertainties. RA can be specified only to 18 hr, 5 min ± 1 min; DEC to 30 degrees, ± 40 min.

Gordon blinked at the clotted sentences, doing arithmetic in his head. The musty library air carried a heavy, solemn silence. He found a worn copy of *Astrophysical Quantities* and checked the coordinates again.

RA 18 5(±1)   DEC 30 ±40

He plucked a pencil from his shirt pocket and scribbled beneath it, ignoring the scornful look of a librarian.

RA 18 5 36   DEC 30 29.2

He walked out into a cooling autumn afternoon.

        •

        On the Air Cal flight to San Diego he said, "The coordinates in the message match the solar apex, that's the point. To within the uncertainties in the present measurements, I mean."

"That's what the plus and minus signs on top of each other mean?" Penny said doubtfully.

"Right. Right."

"I don't get it."

"That's the direction the sun—and the earth with it—is heading toward."

"Well, *oy veh.*"

"Huh?"

"That's what you say. Indicates surprise. *Oy veh.*"

"No, it means—well, dismay. Anyway, I don't say that."

"Sure you do."

"No I don't."

"Okay, okay. Look, what's this mean, Gordon?"

"I haven't got any idea," he lied.

chapter thirty-nine

OCTOBER 14, 1963

"Gordon, this is Claudia Zinnes. I wanted to let you know we lost the anomalous effect this weekend. Did you?"

"I wasn't running. Sorry."

"Well, it would have been a waste, anyway. The funny stuff simply faded out."

"It comes and goes like that a lot."

"We will continue trying, however."

"Good, good. So will I."

•

Gordon spent an afternoon with star charts, plotting the motion of the point in Hercules. It fell beneath the horizon for a good portion of the day. If there were tachyons—whatever that name meant—they would come directly, on a line between his NMR rig and Hercules. When the earth was between him and Hercules, the particles would probably be absorbed. That meant, to get any signal, he had to run when Hercules was up above the horizon.

"Claudia?"

"Yes, yes, I haven't called you because we have not seen—"

"I know, I know. Look, those coordinates you and I got. They're in the constellation Hercules. I think we might have more luck if we only observed at certain times, so—say, have you got a pencil? I just worked these out. I figure between 6 p.m. and—"

•

But neither Columbia nor La Jolla could pick up any effect at the times he calculated. *Could there be some other interference?* It would further complicate things, but what was the cause? Gordon went back and estimated the times when he or Cooper had recorded signals. Most of them matched times when Hercules was in the sky. In some cases, though, there was no record of when the observations were made. A few others seemed to correspond to times when Hercules was definitely below the horizon. Gordon had always liked Occam's Razor: *Entities are not to be multiplied beyond necessity*. It meant that the simplest theory which explained the data was the best. The interference theory was simple, but it had to take care of the times when Hercules was below the horizon, somehow. Maybe those points were mistakes, and maybe not. Rather than reach any conclusion, Gordon decided to keep trying and let the data sort themselves out.

•

Gordon had been teaching Classical Electricity and Magnetism, using the standard Jackson text, for only a few weeks. Already his lecture notes were running out and he was behind in grading the problem sets he assigned. The familiar blizzard of demands fell on him: committees; office hours with students; reading over Cooper's work and talking to him about it; arranging seminars. The first-year graduate class looked good, as far as Gordon could tell from the problem sets they handed in. Burnett and More were sharp. The middle of the pack—Sweedler, Coon, Littenberg particularly—had promise. There were the twins from Oklahoma who did uneven work and had an irritating way of cross-examining him. Maybe he was a little touchy these days, but they—

"Hey, got a minute?"

Gordon looked up from his grading. It was Ramsey. "Sure."

"Look, I wanted to talk to you about this press conference Hussinger and I are doing."

"Press conference?"

"Yeah, we're, ah, going to announce our conclusions. It looks pretty big." Ramsey stood quietly by the doorway, without his usual animation.

"Well, good. Good."

"We wanted to use that chain configuration I figured out. You know, the one I thought you and I would publish together."

"You need to use that?"

"It makes the case stronger, yeah."

"How will you explain where it comes from?"

Ramsey looked pained. "Yeah, that's the catch, isn't it? If I claim it's from your experiments, some people are going to think the whole idea is bullshit."

"I'm afraid so."

"But still, look—" Ramsey spread his hands. "It makes the argument more convincing, to see the structure—"

"No." Gordon shook his head vigorously. "I'm sure you'll be believed, solely on the basis of the experiments. It's not necessary to drag me into it."

Ramsey looked doubtful. "It's a nice piece of work, though."

Gordon smiled. "Leave it out. Leave *me* out, okay?"

"If you say so, sure. Sure," Ramsey said, and left.

●

To Gordon the conversation with Ramsey was amusing, a distant reminder of the real world. To Ramsey and Hussinger, publishing first was the crucial step. Holding a press conference put their seal on the work even more strongly. But Ramsey knew nothing would have happened without Gordon, and the thought bothered the man. Proper procedure was to first get Gordon's consent to separate publication, and then to write a warm acknowledgement at the end of their paper. Gordon told Penny about the conversation that evening, and about how strange the whole process seemed to him now. It was getting the result that made science worth doing; the accolades were a thin, secondary pleasure. People became scientists because they liked solving riddles, not because they would win prizes. Penny nodded, and remarked that she understood Lakin a little better. He was a man past the point of finding anything truly fundamental; scientific invention normally trickles away past the age of forty. So now Lakin clung to the accolades, the visible talismans of accomplishment. Gordon nodded. "Yeah," he said, "Lakin's an operator without real eigenvalues." It was an obscure physicist's joke, and Penny didn't understand it, but Gordon laughed for the first time in days.

●

"Hey, gee, you're still here?" Cooper said from the laboratory doorway.

Gordon looked up from an oscilloscope face. "Trying to take some new data, yeah."

"Crap, it's *late*. I mean, I just dropped in after a date to pick up some books and saw the light. You been here since I left for dinner?"

"Uh, yes. I got something out of the vending machines."

"Geez, that's terrible food."

"Right," Gordon said, turning back to the equipment.

Cooper ambled over and noticed the resonance traces scattered on the lab bench. "Looks like my stuff."

"Close, yeah."

"You're doing indium antimonide? Y'know, Lakin asked me

about your taking so much time on the rig here. Wants to know what you're doin'."

"Why doesn't he come ask me?"

A shrug. "Look, I don't want to get—"

"I know."

After a few neutral comments, Cooper left. Gordon had been carrying out his normal duties for the last week and then spending the evenings taking data, listening, waiting. There were random yellow jitterings among the traces, but no signal. All eroded into noise. The pumps coughed, the electronics gear gave an occasional hot *ping*. *Tachyons,* he thought. Things faster than light. It made no sense. He had taken up the idea with Wong, the particle physicist, and got the conventional reply: they violated special relativity, and anyway, there was no evidence for them. Tachyons, gliding across the universe in less time than Gordon's eye took to absorb a photon of the pale, watery laboratory light—these things went against reason.

Then there came a flutter of interrupted resonances. Gordon had worked out a faster way of compiling the curves and he could extract the Morse coded portions almost immediately.

THREATEN OCEAN

A few moments later, another sputter of interruptions:

CAMBRIDGE CAVENDISH LABO

and then a blur of noise. Gordon nodded to himself. He felt comfortable, working here alone, monklike. Penny didn't like his long hours here, but that was a secondary issue. She didn't understand that sometimes you had to press on, that the world would yield if you just kept at it.

When the scope face cleared he took a break. He walked the silent corridors of the physics building to shake off a sleepy daze. Outside Grundkind's lab was a big sheet of computer paper with a disheartened graduate student's scrawl at the top:

An experiment may be considered a success if no more than 50% of the observed measurements must be discarded to obtain a correspondence with theory.

Gordon smiled. The public thought of science as an absolute, sure thing, money in the bank. They never knew how some slight error could give you wildly wrong results. Below the top scrawl were penciled-in contributions from other students:

Mother nature is a bitch.

> *The probability of a given event
> occurring is inversely
> proportional to its desirability.*

*If you fool around with something long
enough it will eventually break.*

> *One fudged curve is worth a thousand
>   weasel words.*

*No analysis is a complete failure—
      it can always serve as a bad example.*

> *Experience varies directly
> with the equipment ruined.*

He got himself a Hershey bar and went back to the lab.

•

"Jesus," Penny said in the morning, "you look like something somebody took out of an old trunk."

"Yeah, yeah. Got a class next hour. What's in the larder?"

"Lard, that's what the fuck's in the larder—fucking lard."

"As you're always putting it, come *on*."

"Cereal, then."

"I'm *hungry*."

"Two bowls, then."

"Look, I had to work."

"Not getting promoted really shook you up, didn't it?"

"Bull, just bull."

"Bull, right."

"I've got to find out."

"That woman, Zinnes. That's all you needed."

"For confirmation, yes. But we don't *understand* it."

Gordon rummaged for shredded wheat. He put the toasted rolls into a bowl and threw the packet into the trash. At the bottom of the trash container was an empty half-gallon of Brookside burgundy.

"You staying there tonight?" Penny said.

"Uh, yeah."

"I got a letter from my mother."

"Uh huh."

"They thought you were really pretty weird."

"They're right."

"You might've tried."

"I was trying to do it cool and WASP."

"Cool and dopey."

"I didn't know it was that important."

"It wasn't. I just thought."

"Look, there'll be other times."

"You got a call."

"I mean, maybe around Thanksgiving."

"Uh huh."

"San Francisco, we didn't see much of it."

"It was from New York."

He stopped slurping shredded wheat. "What?"

"The call. I gave him your office number."

"I wasn't in my office much. Who was it?"

"Didn't say."

"You ask?"

"No."

"Next time, ask."

"Yessir."

"Oh crap."

•

The *San Diego Union* headlined VIET REGIME TOP-PLED. Gordon looked at the pictures of corpses in the streets and thought about Cliff. The *Union* said it was a straightforward military coup d'etat. Somebody had caught Ngo Dinh Diem and shot him in the head and that was the end of it. The Kennedy administration said they had nothing to do with it. They deplored the whole thing. On the other hand, they said, maybe this cleared the way for some true progress in the war there. *Maybe so*, Gordon thought dimly, and threw the paper in the lab trash can.

•

Claudia Zinnes had picked up some of the same fragments, but not all. The noise level came and went. Gordon wondered if there were some other effect at work, beyond the matter of Hercules being visible. Maybe the beaming of the tachyons was inaccurate. That would explain why the signal came and went. He held these ideas in his head, together with suspicions and hunches. During the long evenings of watching the scope he turned them like pieces of a jigsaw puzzle, fitting edges together. His hunch was based on the solar apex number, and it led to a conclusion about the messages that he found difficult to believe. He tried to steer clear of the conclusion. There might easily be another explanation, after all. On the other hand, Wong had mentioned the causality argument against tachyons, so there was at least some crude connection. Occam's Razor did not seem to be of much use here. The whole thing had an Alice-in-Wonderland quality about it. Which meant, he reminded himself, that it was even more important to stick to the facts, the digits, the hard data. *Give me a solid set of numbers and I shall rule the world,* he thought to himself, and laughed out loud.

●

He had dozed. He shook himself and rubbed his eyes. Halfway through the gesture he jerked his hands away and stared at the chart recorder.

Jagged lines. The lyric curves of the resonances were shot through with sudden interruptions.

He fished backward through the spool of tape. If he had missed the key-in point—

But no; there it was. He began to decode.

NEUROM I OL AJ WRITE QUOTE MESSAGE RECEIVED LA JOLLA UNQUOTE ON PAPER PLACE IN SAFETY DEPOSIT VAULT SAN DIEGO FIRST FEDERAL SAVINGS IN NAME OF IAN PETERSON MUST GUARANTEE BOX HELD THIRTY SIX YEARS SENDING THIS TO CHECK RECEIPT OF TRANSWRSODRMCJ RESULTING DINO-FLAGELLATES AND PLANKTONIC AVSDLDU AHXNDUROPFLM

●

The clerk peered at him. "Yes, it's true, we do have free safety deposit boxes. But until the end of the century—!" He raised his eyebrows.

"You offer that, don't you?"

"Well, yes, but—"

"In a public advertisement."

"Certainly. However, the intent—"

"Your ad says I get a safety deposit box if I maintain a minimum balance of twenty-five dollars, right?"

"Indeed. But as I was beginning to say, we intend this as an *initial* offering to encourage clients to set up accounts. The firm certainly does not mean for customers to hold these indefinitely, solely on the strength—"

"Your ad doesn't quibble the way you do."

"I don't think your—"

"I'm right and you know it. You want I should ask for the manager? You're just starting out here, aren't you?"

The clerk's face gave away nothing as he thought. "Well . . . you do seem to have uncovered an aspect we had not anticipated . . ."

Gordon grinned. He took the yellow sheet of paper out of an envelope and put it on the desk.

chapter forty

NOVEMBER 3, 1963

"Hello."

"Gordon? Gordon, is that you?"

"Uncle Herb, ah." Gordon hesitated and looked at his office telephone receiver in puzzlement, as though his uncle's voice were out of place here.

"You're working so hard, you can't go home at night?"

"Well, you know, some experiments."

"So the girl said."

Gordon smiled. Not *lady,* his usual term. No, Penny was a *girl.* And his mother had undoubtedly told Uncle Herb what kind of girl.

"I'm calling about your mother."

"What? Why?"

"She is *krank.*"

"What? Cronk?"

"*Krank,* sick. She has been sick for quite a while."

"Not when I was there."

"When you were here, too, yes. She was. But for your visit, she did not let on."

"Good grief. Look, what's wrong?"

"Something with the pancreas, they said. They're not sure. These doctors, they never are."

"She said something about pleurisy, a long time ago—"

"That was it. That was when it started up with her."

"How bad is it?"

"You know doctors, they don't say yet. But I think you ought to come home."

"Uncle Herb, look, I can't just now."

"She has started asking about you."

"Why didn't she *call?*"

"You know her, the trouble between you two."

"We weren't having any bad trouble."

"You can't fool your uncle, Gordon."

"No, really, I didn't think it was."

"She thinks so. I think so, too, but I know you don't listen to your old dummy uncle's advice."

"Look, you're no dummy. I—"

"Come see her."

"I have a *job,* Uncle Herb. Classes to teach. And these experiments now, they're very important."

"Your mother, you know she won't call you, but—"

"I would if I could, and I will, I *will* as soon as—"

"It's important to her, Gordon."

"Where is she now?"

"In the hospital, where else?"

"For what?"

"Some tests," he admitted.

"Okay, look, I really can't get away now. But soon. Yes, soon I'll come."

"Gordon, I think now."

"No, look, Uncle Herb, I know how you feel. And I will come. Soon."

"Soon means when?"

"I'll call you. Let you know as soon as I can."

"All right then. Soon. She hasn't heard from you much lately."

"Right, I know. Soon. Soon."

●

He called his mother, to explain. Her voice was thin and reedy, shrunken by the miles. She seemed in good spirits, though. The doctors were very nice, they treated you with consideration. No, she had no problem with the hospital bills, he was not to worry about that. She played down the idea that he should come see her. He was a professor, he had students, and why spend all that money for only a few days. Come home at Thanksgiving, that would be early enough, that would be fine. Uncle Herb was a little overconcerned, that was all. Gordon said abruptly into the telephone, "Tell him for me, I'm trying to not be a potzer, here. The work is at a crucial point." His mother paused. *Potzer* was not really a polite word, too close to *putzer.* But she let it go. "That he'll understand. So do I, Gordon. Do your work, yes."

●

The university had arranged the press conference for Ramsey and Hussinger. There was a three-man team from the local CBS station, and the journalist who did the *A University on Its Way to Greatness* feature, as well as *San Diego Union* and *Los Angeles Times* men. Gordon stood in the back of the hall. There were slides of the results, pictures of Hussinger beside the testing tanks, graphs of the breakdown in the ocean ecosystems. The audience was impressed. Ramsey fielded questions well. Hussinger—an overweight, balding man with quick, black eyes—spoke with rapid-fire intensity. A reporter asked Ramsey what led him to conjecture that such terrible things could come from such an obscure cause. Ramsey skirted the issue. He glanced at Gordon and then made a vague remark about hunches coming out of nowhere. People you knew or worked with said something and then you put them together, all without really knowing where the initial spark was from. Oh, the reporter asked, was someone else at UCLJ working on things like this? Ramsey looked uneasy. "I don't think I can say anything about that at this time," he murmured. Gordon slipped out the back before the conference broke up. Outside, the air seemed smoky. He breathed deeply, felt dizzy, and coughed harshly. The shafts of sunlight had a shifting, watery look.

•

Hercules fell below the horizon around 9 p.m. now, so Gordon could shut down the rig reasonably early. There was still decoding work to be done, though, if he found any interruptions of the NMR traces. He got home reasonably early most of the time, for about a week. Then the noise level began to rise again. He received sporadic signals. Hercules was in the sky from midmorning until night. He spent the day taking data. Then, after 9 o'clock, he would prepare his lectures and grade papers. He began to stay later and later. Once he slept in his office overnight.

•

Penny looked up with surprise as he unlocked their front door. "Well, well. Run out of electricity?"

"No. Just finished early, that's all."

"Jesus, you look terrible."

"A little tired."

"Want some wine?"

"Not Brookside, if that's what you're drinking."

"No, it's Krug."

"What was that Brookside doing around here?"

"For cooking."

"Uh huh."

He got some wine and some corn chips and sat down at the

kitchen table. Penny was grading essays. The radio was blaring AM music. *Don't know much about history.* Gordon frowned. *Don't know much biology.* "Christ, turn that off." *Don't know what a slide rule is for.* Penny tilted her head to listen. "That's one of my favorites, Gordon." *But I do know that I love you—*

He got up suddenly and savagely snapped the switch over. "Bunch of know-nothing bullshit."

"It's a pretty song."

Gordon made a dry laugh.

"Christ, what's with *you?*"

"I just don't like shit music played decibels too high."

"*I* think you're feeling screwed by the Ramsey and Hussinger thing."

"No, that's not it."

"Well, why not? You let them take all the credit."

"They deserved it."

"It wasn't their *idea.*"

"They can have it. What I'm working on is a lot bigger than that."

"*If* it works out."

"It'll work. The signal is coming through better."

"What does it say?"

"Some biochem stuff. More specs on tachyons."

"That's good? I mean, what can you use it for?"

"I'm sure it's going to fit together, as soon as I get enough pieces. I've got to find just one clear statement that confirms my hunch, my guess, and that'll lock it up."

"What's your hunch?"

Gordon shook his head silently.

"Come *on*. Look, you can tell *me*."

"No. Nobody. I'm telling nobody until I'm sure. This whole thing is going to be mine. I don't want word leaking out before I can nail it for sure."

"Christ, Gordon, I'm *Penny*. Remember me?"

"Look, I'm not saying."

"Goddamn, you're getting completely screwed up in the head, you know that?"

"If you don't like it, you can leave me alone."

"Yeah, well, maybe I will, Gordon. Maybe I will."

●

He found himself falling asleep in the day. He would jerk awake before the oscilloscope as though startled by some noise, instantly afraid that he had missed some data.

He taught his Classical Electricity and Magnetism class as though in a dream. He would drift from one blackboard to another, jotting down formulas in what he thought was a neat, readable print. He spoke facing the class, but he gave the impression of carrying on an internal debate with himself. Occasionally, after lecture, he would glance back at the boards before leaving, and be shocked at the cluttered lines of nearly unreadable scribbles.

•

Lakin avoided talking to Gordon about anything other than routine laboratory operations. Cooper, too, stayed in his small student's office and seldom sought out Gordon, even when he was blocked on a particular point. Gordon rarely went up to the Physics Department office on the third floor any more. Secretaries had to seek him out in the laboratory. He brought his own lunch in a bag and ate it there, tending the NMR apparatus, fighting the recurring signal/noise problems, watching the jiggling yellow lines of the resonance curves.

•

"Dr. Bernstein?"

"Huh?" Gordon had been dozing in front of the scope. His eyes darted to the resonance lines, but they were undisturbed. Good; he had missed nothing. Only then did he look up at the slender man who stood inside the laboratory door.

"I'm from UPS. I'm doing a background story on the Ramsey-Hussinger results. They've excited an enormous amount of concern, you know. I thought I would look into the contributions made by other faculty to—"

"Why come to me?"

"I could not help but notice that you were the man Professor Ramsey kept looking at during their press conference. I wondered if you might be the 'other sources' Professor Ramsey recently admitted—"

"When did he say that?"

"Just yesterday, while I was interviewing him."

"Shit."

"What was that, Doctor? You seem rather concerned."

"No, nothing. Look, I have nothing to say."

"Are you sure, Doctor?"

"I said I have nothing to say. Now leave, please."

The man opened his mouth. Gordon jerked his thumb toward the door. "Out, I said. *Out*."

●

Gordon worked each day, gradually collecting fragments of sentences. They came out of sequence. The technical information was repetitious, probably to be sure it came through correctly, despite transmission and receiving errors. *But why?* he thought. *This stuff fits my guesses, sure. But there must be an explanation in this text itself.* A rational explanation, clearly set out. One evening he had a dream in which Uncle Herb was watching him play chess in Washington Square. His uncle frowned as Gordon moved the pieces across the squares and said over and over, in a disapproving voice, "God forbid there should not be a rational explanation."

●

On the morning of Monday, November 5, he drove into work late. He had got into a pointless argument with Penny over minor domestic matters. He turned on the car radio to take his mind off it. The lead news item was that Maria Goeppert Mayer of UCLJ had won the Nobel Prize in physics. Gordon was so stunned by the news he barely recovered in time to make the turn at the top of Torrey Pines Road. A Lincoln blared its horn at him and the driver—a man in a hat driving with his lights on—glared. Mayer had won the prize for the shell model of the nucleus. She shared it with Eugene Wigner of Princeton and Hans Jensen, a German who had devised the shell model at about the same time as Maria.

The University held a press conference that afternoon. Maria Mayer was shy and soft-spoken beneath the barrage of questions. Gordon went to see. The questions asked were mostly dumb, but you expected that. The kindly woman who had stopped to inquire about his results, when the rest of the department was ignoring him, was now a Nobel Prize winner. The fact took a while to sink in. He had a sudden sense that things were converging at this place, this time. The research done here was important. There were the Carroways and their quasar riddle, Gell-Mann's arrays of particles, Dyson's visions, Marcuse and Maria Mayer and the news that Jonas Salk was coming to build an institute. La Jolla was a nexus. He was grateful to be here.

chapter forty-one

NOVEMBER 6, 1963

The signal strength got abruptly better. There were whole paragraphs about the Wheeler-Feynman theory. Gordon called Claudia Zinnes to see if the Columbia group was getting the same results.

"No, not for five days now," she said. "First we had some equipment failure. Then the graduate student got the flu—the one that's been going around. I think he was overtired. Those times you gave us—that's ten, twelve hours in the lab, Gordon."

"You mean you have *nothing?*"

"Not for those days, no."

"Can't you do some of the times yourself?"

"I will, starting tomorrow. I do have other things to do, you know."

"Sure, yes. I want to have some confirmation, that's all."

"We have that *now*, Gordon. Of the effect, I mean."

"It's not only the effect that's important. Claudia, look back over those signals. Think about what it means."

"Gordon, I don't think we know enough yet to—"

"Okay, I agree, basically. Most of my data is a jumble. Fragments. Pieces of sentences. Formulas. But there is a consistent feel to it."

Her voice took on the precise, professional clarity he remembered from graduate school. "First the data, Gordon. Then we indulge in some theory, maybe."

"Yeah, right." He knew better than to argue with her on the philosophy of experimental physics. She had rather rigid views.

"I promise you, I start up tomorrow."

"Okay, but it could fade by then. I mean—"

"Don't kvetch, Gordon. Tomorrow we start again."

●

It came less than three hours later, shortly after noon on Tuesday, November 6. Names, dates. The spreading bloom. The phrases describing this were clipped and tense. Parts were garbled. Letters were missing. One long passage, though, related how the experiments had begun and who was involved. These sentences were longer and more relaxed and almost conversational, as though someone were simply sending what came into his head.

—WITH MARKHAM GONE AND BLOODY DUMB RENFREW CARRYING ON THERE'S NO FUTURE IN OUR LITTLE PLAN NO PAST EITHER I SUPPOSE THE LANGUAGE CAN'T DEAL WITH IT BUT THE THING SHOULD HAVE WORKED IF—

There came a scramble of noise. The long passage disappeared and did not return. The terse biological information reappeared. There were missing words. The noise was rising like a tossing sea. Through the last staccato sentences there ran an unstated sense of desperation.

•

Penny saw something different in his face when he came into the kitchen. Her raised eyebrows asked a question.

"I got it today." He surprised himself at the easy, blank way he could say it.

"Got what?"

"The answer, for Chrissake."

"Oh. *Oh.*"

Gordon handed her a Xerox copy of his lab notebook. "So it really is the way you thought?"

"Apparently." There was a quiet assurance in him now. He felt no pressing need to say anything about the result, no tension, not even a hint of the manic elation he had expected. The facts were there at last and they could speak for themselves.

"My God, Gordon."

"Yeah. My God, indeed."

There was a moment of silence between them. She put the Xerox page on the kitchen table and turned back to deboning a chicken. "Well, that should take care of your promotion."

"It sure as hell should," Gordon said with some relish.

"And maybe—"she gave him a sidelong look—"maybe you'll be worth living with again." The sentence had started out all right but by the end a bitter tone came into it. Gordon pursed his lips, irked.

"You haven't made it any easier."

"There are *limits,* Gordon."

"Uh huh."

"I'm not your goddam little wifey."

"Yes, you made that brilliantly clear some time ago."

She sniffed, lips pressed so tight they grew pale, and wiped her hands on a paper towel. Penny reached over and clicked on the radio. It began playing a Chubby Checker tune. Gordon stepped forward and turned it off. She looked at him, saying nothing. Gordon picked up the Xeroxed page and put it in his jacket pocket, carefully folding it beforehand.

He said, "I think I'll go do some reading."

"You do that," she said.

●

All through the afternoon of November 7 the noise level rose. It blotted out the signal most of the time. Gordon got a few words here and there, and a very clear RA 18 5 36 DEC 30 29.2, and that was all. The coordinates made sense now. Up ahead in the future they would have a precise fix on where they would seem to be in the sky. The solar apex was an average of the sun's motion. Thirty-five years from now the earth would be in a location near the average motion. Gordon felt a certain relaxing in him as he watched the jittering noise. All the pieces fit now. Zinnes could confirm at least part of it. Now the question was how to present the data, how to build an airtight case that couldn't be dismissed out of hand. A straightforward paper in *The Physical Review?* That would be the standard approach. The lead time on *Phys Rev* was at least nine months, though. He could publish in *Physical Review Letters*, but letters had to be short. How could he pack in all the experimental detail, plus the messages? Gordon smiled ruefully. Here he had an enormous result and he was dithering over how to present it. Showbiz.

●

Penny carried knives and forks to the table; Gordon brought the plates. The slatted blinds let in yellow swords of sun. She moved gracefully in this light, her face pensive.

They ate silently for a moment, both hungry. "I thought about your experiments today," she began hesitantly.

"Yes?"

"I don't understand them. To think of time that way . . ."

"I don't see how it can make sense, either. It's a *fact*, though."

"And facts rule."

"Well, sure. I kind of feel we're looking at this the wrong way, though. Space-time must not work the way physicists think."

She nodded and pushed potatoes around her plate, still pensive. "Thomas Wolfe. 'Time, dark time, secret time, forever flowing like a river.' I remember that from *The Web and the Rock*."

"Haven't read it."

"I looked up a Dobson poem today, thinking about you." She took a paper from her books and handed it to him.

Time goes, you say? Ah, no!
Alas, time stays, we go.

He laughed. "Yeah, something like that." He cut into a frankfurter with enthusiasm.

"Do you think people like Lakin are going to keep on questioning your work?"

He chewed judiciously. "Well, in the best sense, I hope they do. Every result in science has to stand up to criticism every day. Results have to be checked and rethought."

"No, I meant—"

"I know, are they going to try to cut me off at the knees. I hope so." He grinned. "If they push things further than legitimate scientific skepticism, they'll have just that much farther to fall."

"Well, *I* hope not."

"Why?"

"Because—" her voice broke—"it'll be hard on you, and I can't *take* what it does to you any more."

"Honey . . ."

"I can't. You've been tight as a drum all summer and fall. And when I try to deal with it, I can't get through to you and I start snapping at you and . . ."

"Honey . . ."

"Things get so *impossible*. I just . . ."

"God, I know. It runs away with me."

She said quietly, "And me . . ."

"I start thinking about a problem and other things, other people, they just seem to get in the way."

"It's been my fault, too. I want a lot out of this, out of *us*, so much, and I'm not getting it."

"We've been clawing at each other."

She sighed. "Yeah."

"I . . . I think the physics stuff isn't going to be so bad from now on."

"That . . . that's what I hope. I mean, these last few days, they've been different. Better. It feels like a year ago, really. You're relaxed, I'm not bugging you all the time to . . . I feel better about us. For the first time in ages."

"Yeah. Me, too." He smiled tentatively.

They ate in a comfortable silence. In the moist sunset glow Penny swirled her glass of white wine and gazed at the ceiling, thinking. Gordon knew they had made an unspoken pledge.

Penny began to smile, her eyes hazed. She sipped more of the amber wine and plunged a fork into a frankfurter. Holding it aloft with a wise smile, she turned it this way and that, studying it critically. "Yours is bigger than this," she said judicially.

Gordon nodded solemnly. "Maybe. That's, what, about thirty centimeters? Yeah, I can beat that."

"In matters of this kind, the preferred unit system is inches. It's sort of traditional."

"So it is."

"Not that I'm a purist, you understand."

"Oh no, I wouldn't think that."

•

He awoke with an arm that had gone to sleep. He gently rolled her head off his bicep and lay still, feeling the tingling ebb away. Outside, the balmy fall night had descended. He sat up slowly and she snuggled to him, murmuring. He studied the rounded knuckles of her curved spine, knobbed hills amid the brown sweep of skin. He thought of time that could flow and loop back on itself, unlike any river, and his eyes followed the narrowing of her back. Then came the flaring into hips, a complex of smooth surfaces descending to the ripe swelling below, the tan fading into a startling pure white. Drowsy, she had solemnly informed him that Lawrence had called his a pillar of blood, a phrase that struck her as grotesque. But on the other hand, she added, it was sort of like that, wasn't it? "All in pursuit of *la petite mort,*" she murmured, and slid into sleep. Gordon knew she had been right about the tension between them. It was seeping away now. He saw that he had loved her all along, but there had been so much in the way . . .

He heard a distant siren. Something made him slowly untangle himself from her. He moved across the cold floor to the window. He could see people walking along La Jolla Boulevard under a bleached neon glow. A motorcycle cop raced by. The police here were jackbooted and military, with eggshell helmets, goggles, their square faces a frozen blank, like actors in a futuristic anticipation, a B-grade black and white. In New York the cops were soft, their uniforms a worn, neighborhood blue. The siren shrieked. A police car flashed by. Buildings, palms, turning heads, shops and signs—all pulsed red in response to the revolving hysterical light atop the streaking car.

Fragments of red ricocheted from store windows. Kinetic confusion swept by, wailing, its mechanical mouth announcing tumult. The Doppler death of this shriek stirred pedestrians, filling their steps with new energy. Heads pivoted to seek the crime or fire that had drawn the bulletlike car. Gordon thought of the messages and the thin thread of desperation that ran through them. A siren. It had come in speckled dabs, impulses, light reflected from random waves, visions from far across a river. It should be answered. For scientific reasons, yes, but for more than that.

●

"Uh, you busy?"

It was Cooper. "No, come on in." Gordon pushed the pile of papers he was grading to the corner of his desk. Then he leaned back in his chair and put his feet up on top of them. He clasped his hands behind his neck, elbows out, and grinned. "What can I do for you?"

"Well, I'm gonna take my exam again in three weeks, y'know. What do I say about those interruptions? I mean, Lakin and the others came down on me like a shitload of bricks last time."

"Right. If I were you, I would ignore the point."

"But I *can't*. They'll cream me again."

"I'll take care of them."

"Huh? How?"

"I'll have a little work of my own to present, by that time."

"Well, I dunno . . . Getting Lakin off my back is nontrivial. You saw the way he—"

"Why do you say 'nontrivial'? Why not 'hard' or 'difficult'?"

"Well, you know, it's physics talk . . ."

"Yes, 'physics talk.' We have a lot of jargon like that. I wonder if sometimes it doesn't disguise things, rather than making them clearer."

Cooper gave Gordon an odd look. "I guess."

"Don't look so uncertain," Gordon said jovially. "You're home free. I'm going to save your ass."

"Uh, okay." Cooper moved uncertainly to the door. "If you say so . . ."

"See you on the ramparts," Gordon said by way of dismissal.

●

He was about a quarter of the way through the first draft of his paper for *Science* when there was a knock on his door. He had decided on *Science* because it was big and prestigious and got things into print fairly quickly. They carried long articles, so he could tell the whole thing in one piece, stacking up the evidence in a pile so high no one could knock it down. He had already checked with Claudia Zinnes. She would publish a letter in the same issue, confirming some of his observations.

"Hello. Can we come in?" It was the twins, first-year graduate students.

"Well, look, I'm pretty busy—"

"It's your office hours."

"It is? Oh yes. Well, what did you want?"

"You graded some of our problems wrong," one of them said. The flat statement took Gordon aback. He was used to a little more humility from students. "Oh?" he countered.

"Yeah. Look—" One of them began to write rapidly on Gordon's blackboard, covering up some notes Gordon had put there while he was outlining his paper. Gordon tried to follow the argument the twin was making. "Careful of that stuff I have written there." The twin frowned at Gordon's intruding lines. "Okay," he said democratically, and began to write around them. Gordon focused his attention on the rapid-fire sentences about Bessel's functions and boundary conditions on the electric field. It took him five minutes to straighten out the twin's misconception. All through it he was never sure which one of the twins he was talking to. They were virtually carbon copies. As soon as one finished the other would leap to the attack with a new objection, usually phrased in a cryptic few words. Gordon found them exceptionally tiring. After ten more minutes, during which they began to interrogate him about his research and how much money a research assistant made, he finally got rid of them by pleading a headache. That, plus three significant glances at his watch, got them out the door. As he was closing it, another voice called, "Wait a sec! Dr. Bernstein!"

Gordon reluctantly opened it. The man from UPI stepped partway in. "I know you don't want to be bothered, Professor—"

"Right. So why are you bothering me?"

"Because Professor Ramsey blew the story to me, just now. That's why."

"What story?"

"About you and those chain molecules. Where you got the picture in the first place. How you wanted it kept secret. I've got it all, the works." The man beamed at him.

"Why did Ramsey tell you?"

"I worked out some of it. He didn't paper over the seams in his story very well. Not a very good liar, Ramsey."

"I suppose not."

"He wasn't going to tell me anything. But I remembered that thing you were involved in a while back."

Gordon said with sudden fatigue, "Saul Shriffer."

"Yeah, he's the guy. Me, I put two and two together. I went to see Ramsey for some more backgrounding and in the middle of it I popped him with that one."

"And he babbled like a brook."

"You got it."

Gordon sagged into his chair. He sat there, slumped down, staring at the man from United Press International.

"Well?" the man said. He took out a notebook. "You going to tell me, Professor?"

"I don't appreciate being grilled."

"Sorry if I offended you, Professor. I'm not grilling you. I just did a little sniffing around and—"

"Okay, okay, I'm sensitive about that."

"It's going to come out sometime, you know. The Ramsey-Hussinger thing hasn't got any real attention in the papers so far, I know. But it's going to be important. People are going to hear about it. Your part could be valuable."

In a dreamy way Gordon began to laugh softly. "Could be valuable . . ." he said, and laughed again.

The man frowned. "Hey, look, you are going to tell me, aren't you?"

Gordon felt an odd, seeping tiredness in himself. He sighed. "I . . . I suppose I am."

chapter forty-two

Gordon had not realized the lights would be so bright. There were banks of lamps to both sides of the small platform, to make his face shadow-free. A TV camera snout peered at him, an unwinking Cyclops. There were some chemists in the audience, and nearly all the Physics Department. The department draftsman had labored until midnight to get all the charts drawn. Gordon had found the staff a great help in hustling things together for this. He was beginning to realize that the hostility he had felt from them all was an illusion, a product of his own doubts. The last few days had been a revelation. Department members hailed him in the hall, listened intently to his descriptions of his data, and visited the lab.

He looked around for Penny. There—near the back, in a pink dress. She smiled wanly at his hand wave. The press men were murmuring to each other and finding seats. The TV crewmen were in place and a woman with a microphone gave last-minute instructions. Gordon counted the crowd. Incredibly, it was larger than the number who turned out for Maria Mayer's Nobel conference. But then, this one had a day or two of lead time. The UPI man got his exclusive story—picked up by the other wire services—and then the University had stepped in and set up this dog and pony show.

Gordon riffled through his notes with damp fingers. He had not really wanted any of this. The feel of it seemed somehow wrong to him—science carried on in public, science elbowing for time on the 6 o'clock news, science as a commodity. The momentum of it was immense. In the end there would remain the article in *Science*, where his results had to meet their tests, where no amount of bias for or against him could tip the scales—

"Dr. Bernstein? We're ready."

He wiped his brow one last time. "Okay, shoot." A green light winked on.

He looked into the camera and tried to smile.

chapter forty-three

1998

Peterson pulled the car into the brick garage and hauled out the suitcases. Puffing, he set them outside, on the path to the farmhouse. The garage doors locked with a reassuring *clank*. A biting wind was blowing off the North Sea, sweeping cleanly across the flat East Anglian landscape. He pulled up the collar of his sheepskin jacket.

No sign of movement from the house. Probably no one had heard the car's quiet purr. He decided to take a walk round, to survey and stretch his legs. His head buzzed. He needed the air. He had stayed in a Cambridge hotel overnight, when the sudden sinking feeling came over him again. He slept through most of the morning, and came down expecting lunch. The hotel was deserted. So were the streets outside. There were signs of life in the houses nearby, chimney smoke and an orange glow of lamps. Peterson did not stop to inquire. He drove out of a bleak and empty Cambridge and up through the flat, somber fen country. ,

He rubbed his hands together, more in satisfaction than to keep them warm. For a while there, when the illness first struck him again outside London, he had thought he would never make it this far. The roads had been clogged on the way from London, and then, next day, north of Cambridge, strangely empty. He had seen overturned lorries and burning barns north of Bury St. Edmunds. By Stowmarket a gang tried to hail him down. They had axes and hoes. He had ploughed straight through them, sending bodies into the air like bowling pins.

But here the farm lay quiet beneath the rolling gray clouds of East Anglia. Ranks of leafless trees marked the field boundaries. Black blobs hung in the latticework of bare twigs, rooks' nests framed against the sky. He tramped through the western field, legs weak, the black mud sticking to his boots. To his right, cows stood patiently by a gate, their breath steaming in the air, waiting to be led home to their shed. The harvest had been cut two weeks ago—he'd ordered that. The fields stood wide and empty now. Let them lie; there was time.

He circled round through the sugar beet acres to the old stone house. It looked deceptively run down. The only visible new note was a glass conservatory jutting to the south. The panes had cross-hatchings of wire imbedded, quite secure. Years ago, when he'd first begun, he'd decided on a system totally buried, completely isolated. The greenhouse had filtered water and fertilizers. Water tanks under the northern field held a year's supply. The greenhouse could produce a reasonable supply of vegetables for a long time. That, and the stores buried under the house and barn, would provide ample backup.

He had hired it done, of course, using laborers from distant towns. He'd had the vast coal bin filled from Cambridge, rather than nearby Dereham. The mines in the fields and along the one road—capable of being armed either on command or by the detection system—he'd had a mercenary install. Peterson had arranged that the man be hired on some Pacific operation soon after, and he had not returned. The electronic watchdogs that dotted the farm he had brought in from California and hired a technical type from London to do up. Thus no one person knew the extent of the operation.

Only his uncle knew it all, and he was the grimly silent sort. Bloody boring company, though. For a moment he regretted not bringing Sarah. But she would be the high-strung type out here, unable to bear the sameness of the long days. Of all the women he'd had in the past year, Marjorie Renfrew was the one most likely to fit in. She knew something of farming and had turned out to be unexpectedly lusty. She had seen the need in him when he stumbled in last night and had met it with an instinctive passion. Beyond that, though, he couldn't imagine living with her for even a week. She would talk and bustle about, fretting, alternately criticizing and mothering him.

No, the only companions he could imagine for what lay ahead were men. He thought of Greg Markham. There was someone you could have trusted not to trip and shoot you in the back in a deer hunt or run away from an adder. Intelligent conversation and companionable silence. Judgment and a certain perspective.

Still, it was going to be difficult without a woman. He probably should have spent more time on that, not dwelled in Sarah's butterfly crowd. No matter how the world struggled out of the present muck, with hard times attitudes would change. There would be no more of what the social science lot called "free sexuality," which to Peterson was simply getting what he'd always thought the world owed anybody. Women, women of all kinds and shapes and flavors. As people they varied, of course, but as tickets to a side of life beyond the brittle intellect, they were remarkably alike, sisters sharing the same magic. He had tried to understand his own attitude in terms of psychological theory, but had come away convinced the simple flat fact of living went beyond those categories. No convenient ideas worked. It wasn't ego-enforcing or disguised aggression. It wasn't a clever cover for some imagined homosexuality—he'd had a taste of that when young and found it thin gruel indeed, thanks. It was something beyond the analytical chat level. Women were part of that world-swallowing he had always sought, a way of keeping oneself sensual but not stupefied by glut.

So in the last year he had tried them all, pursued every possibility. He had known for a long while that something was coming. The fragile pyramid with him near the top would crumble. He had enjoyed what would soon pass, women and all the rest, and now felt no regrets. When you sail on the Titanic, there's no point in going steerage.

He wondered, idly, how many of the futurologists had got out. Few, he would guess. Their ethereal scenarios seldom talked about individual responses. They had looked away uncomfortably on that northern African field trip. The personal was, compared with the tides of great nations, a bothersome detail.

He approached the stone house, noting with approval how ordinary and even shabby it looked.

"You're back, m'lord!"

Peterson whirled. A man approached, pushing a bicycle. A man from the village, he noted quickly. Work trousers, faded jacket, high boots. "Yes, I've come home for good."

"Ar, good it is. Safe 'arbor in these days, eh? I've brought yor bacon an' dried beef, I 'as."

"Oh. Very good." Peterson accepted the cartons. "You'll just put them on the account, then?" He kept his voice as matter-of-fact as he could.

"Well, I was meanin' to speak to the house"—he nodded, pointing at the farmhouse—" 'bout that."

"You can deal with me."

"Right. Well, as things is happenin', I'd appreciate payment on the day, y'see."

"Well, I see no reason why not. We—"

"And I'd like payment in goods, if you please."

"Goods?"

"Money's no good now, is it? Some of yor vegetables, p'haps? Tinned goods is what we'd truly like."

334

"Oh." Peterson tried to judge the man, who was giving him a fixed smile, one that had other interpretations than simple friendliness. "I suppose we can do a bit of that, yes. We don't have many tinned goods, however."

"We'd like 'em, though, sir."

Was there an edge to his voice? "I'll see what we can do."

"That'd be fine, sir." The man sketched a brief gesture of touching a forelock, as though he were a retainer and Peterson the squire. Peterson stood still as the man swung onto his bicycle and pedaled off. There had been enough of parody in the gesture to give the entire conversation a different cast. He watched the man leave the property without looking back. Frowning, he turned towards the house.

He went round behind the hedge, avoiding the garden, and crossed the farmyard. From the henhouse came low contented cluckings. By the door he scraped his boots on the old iron scraper and then tossed them down in the passageway just inside the door. He slipped on some house shoes and hung up his jacket.

The large kitchen was warm and bright. He had put in modern appliances but left the flagged stone floor, worn smooth by centuries of use, and the huge fireplace and the old oak settle. His uncle and aunt sat on either side of the fire in comfortable highbacked wing chairs, as silent and motionless as iron firedogs. In its place at the head of the table, the big round teapot sat under its quilted cosy. Roland, the farmhouse factotum, silently set the plate of scones, pats of sweet butter, and a dish of homemade strawberry jam on the table.

He crossed to the fire to warm his hands. His aunt, seeing him, gave a start.

"Well, bless my soul, it's Ian!"

She leaned forward and tapped her husband on the knee.

"Henry! Look who's here. It's Ian, come to see us. Isn't that nice?"

"He's come to live with us, Dot," his uncle answered patiently.

"Oh?" she said, puzzling. "Oh. Where's that pretty gel of yours then, Ian? Where's Angela?"

"Sarah," he corrected automatically. "She stayed in London."

"Hmm. Pretty gel but flighty. Well, let's have tea." She threw back the rug from her legs.

Roland came forward and lifted her to her seat by the teapot. They all sat round the table. Roland was a big man, slow-moving. He had been with the family two decades.

"Look, Roland, here's Ian, come to visit." Peterson sighed. His aunt had been senile for years; only her husband and Roland had any continuity in her mind.

"Ian's come to live with us," his uncle repeated.

"Where are the children?" she asked. "They're late."

No one reminded her that both sons had drowned in a sailing accident some fifteen years before. They waited patiently for the daily ritual to be completed.

"Well, let's not wait for them." She picked up the heavy teapot and began to pour the strong steaming tea into the striped blue and white farmhouse cups.

They ate in silence. Outside, the rain that had threatened all day began to fall, tentatively at first, pattering against the windows, then more steadily. Distantly, the cows, disturbed by the drumming of the rain on the roof of their shed, lowed mournfully.

"It's raining," his uncle volunteered.

No one answered. He liked their silence. And when they spoke, their flat East Anglian vowels slid like balm into his ears, slow and soothing. His childhood nurse had been a Suffolk woman.

He finished his tea and went into the library. He fingered the cut glass decanter, decided against a drink. The steady sound of pouring rain was muted by the heavy oak shutters. They had been well made, concealing a panel of steel. He had turned the place into a fortress. It could withstand a lengthy siege. The cowsheds and barn were double-walled and connected by tunnels to the house. All doors were double, with heavy bolts. Every room was a miniature armory. He stroked a rifle on the library wall. He checked the chamber; oiled and loaded, as he had ordered.

He chose a cigar and dropped into his leather armchair. He picked up a book that lay waiting, a Maugham. He began to read. Roland came in and built a fire. Its rich crackling cut the edge of cold in the room. There would be time later to review the stock of provisions and lay out a dietary plan. No outside water, at least for a while. No more trips into the village. He settled further into the chair, aware that things needed doing, but not for the moment feeling up to it. His limbs were sore and the sudden flashes of weakness still came upon him. Here he was still Peterson of Peters Manor and he let the sense of that sweep through him, bringing a kind of inner rest. Was it Russell who had said that no man is truly comfortable far from the environment of his childhood? There was some truth in that. But the fellow from the village, just now . . . Peterson frowned.

They really couldn't use the bacon any longer; everything would be blighted with the cloud stuff, at least for a while. The village man probably knew that. And beneath the yes-m'lord manner there had been a clear threat. He had come to barter security, not bacon. Give them some tinned food and all would be well.

Peterson moved in the chair restlessly. All his life he had been in motion, he thought. He had moved up from this landed gentry role, through Cambridge, and into the government. He had used each level and then moved on. Sarah, he supposed, was the most recent clear case, not forgetting the Council itself. They had all helped. The government itself had, of course, followed much the same strategy. Modern economics and the welfare state borrowed heavily on the future.

Now he was in a place he could not leave. He had to depend on those around him. And suddenly he was uncomfortably aware that this small, easily managed band in the manor and village were free agents, too. Once society faltered, what became of the ordering that had kept Peters Manor calm and safe? Peterson sat in the waning light of day and thought, a finger tapping on the arm of his chair. He tried to begin again with his book, but it held no interest for him. Through the window he could see the cut fields that stretched to the horizon. A north wind stirred the crisp outline of the trees. Dusk fell. The fire popped.

chapter forty-four

NOVEMBER 22, 1963

Gordon wrote out the equation in full before commenting on it. The yellow chalk squeaked. "So we see that if we integrate Maxwell's equations over the volume, the flux—"

Movement at the back of the class caught his eye. He turned. A secretary from the department waved a hand hesitantly at him. "Yes?"

"Dr. Bernstein I hate to interrupt but we've just heard on the radio that the President has been shot." She said it in one long gasp. There was an answering rustle from the class. "I thought . . . you would want to know," she finished lamely.

Gordon stood unmoving. Speculations raced through his mind. Then he remembered where he was and firmly put them aside. There was a lecture to finish. "Very well. Thank you." He studied the upturned faces of the class. "I think, in view of how much more material there is to cover in this semester . . . Until something more is known, we should go on."

One of the twins said abruptly, "Where was he?"

The secretary answered meekly, "In Dallas."

"I hope somebody gets Goldwater, then," the twin said with sudden vehemence.

"Quiet, quiet," Gordon said mildly. "There is nothing we can do here, right? I propose to continue."

With that he returned to the equation. He got through most of the introductory discussion of the Poynting vector, ignoring the buzz of whispers at his back. He fell into the rhythm of the discussion. His stabs with the chalk made their clicking points, one by one. The equations unfolded their beauties. He conjured up electromagnetic waves and endowed them with momentum. He spoke of imaginary mathematical boxes brimming with light, their flux kept in precise balance by the unseen power of partial differentials.

Another stirring at the back of the room. Several students were leaving. Gordon put down his chalk. "I suppose you can't concentrate under the circumstances," he conceded. "We'll take it up next time."

One of the twins got up to leave and said to the other, "Lyndon Johnson. Jesus, we might end up with *him*."

Gordon made his way down to his office and put away his lecture notes. He was tired, but he supposed he should go hunt up a TV and watch. The last week had been a madhouse of interviews, challenges by other physicists, and an astonishing amount of attention from the networks. He was thoroughly weary of the whole process.

He remembered that the student center down by Scripps beach had a TV. The drive down in his Chevy took only moments. There seemed to be few people on the streets.

Students were ranked three deep around the set. As Gordon came in and stood at the back Walter Cronkite was saying, "I repeat, there is still no definite word from Parkland Memorial Hospital about the President. A priest who just left the operating room was heard to have said that the President was dying. However, that is not an official announcement. The priest did acknowledge that the last rites have been administered to the President."

Gordon asked a student next to him, "What happened?"

"Some guy shot him from a school book building, they said."

Cronkite accepted a piece of paper from off camera. "Governor John Connally is undergoing treatment in the operating room next to the President. The doctors working on the governor have said only that he is in serious condition. Meanwhile, Vice President Johnson is known to be in the hospital. He is apparently waiting in a small room down the corridor from where the President lies. The Secret Service has the area completely surrounded, with the help of the Dallas police."

Gordon noticed several of the students from his class gathered nearby. The recreation room was packed now. The crowd was absolutely still as Cronkite paused, listening to a small headset which he pressed to his ear. Through the glass sliding doors which led out onto a wooden porch Gordon could see the waves breaking into white and sliding up the beach. Outside, the world went on with its unending rhythm. In this small pocket, a flickering color screen held sway.

Cronkite glanced off camera and then back. "The Dallas police have just released the name of the man they suspect of the shooting. His name is Lee Oswald. Apparently he is an employee of the School Book Depository building. That's the building that the shots—some said rifle shots, but that has not been confirmed—came from. The Dallas police have not released any further information. There are many policemen around that building now and it is very difficult to get any information. However, we do have men on the scene and a television camera is being set up, I am told."

The recreation room was becoming hot. Fall sunlight streamed through the glass doors. Someone lit a cigarette. The plumes of smoke slowed and formed blue layers as Cronkite spoke on, repeating himself, waiting for more reports. Gordon began breathing more rapidly, as though the thickened air would not come freely into his lungs. The light became watery, weaving. The crowd around him caught the feeling and moved restlessly, human wheat beneath a strange wind.

"Some members of the crowd around Deeley Plaza say there were two shots fired at the Presidential motorcade. There are reports of three and four shots, however. One of our reporters on the scene says the shots came from a window on the sixth story of that School Book Depository—"

The scene suddenly shifted to a bleak fall landscape in black and white. Knots of people crowded the sidewalk before a brick building. Trees stood out in stark contrast to the bright sky. The camera panned to show a bleached, open plaza. Cars blocked the streets. People milled aimlessly.

"That is the site of the shooting you are seeing now," Cronkite continued. "There is still no definite word about the President. A nurse in the corridor outside has said that the doctor working on the President has carried out a tracheotomy—that is, a cut in the windpipe, to make another breathing path for the President. This seems to confirm reports that Mr. Kennedy was struck in the back of the neck."

Gordon felt ill. He wiped beads of sweat from his brow. He was the only person in the room wearing a jacket and tie. The air felt silky, moist. The odd sensation of a moment before was ebbing slowly away.

"There is a report that Mrs. Kennedy has been seen in the corridor outside the operating room. We have no indication of what this means." Cronkite was in shirt-sleeves. He looked uncertain and anxious.

"Back at Deeley Plaza—" Again the crowds, the brick building, police everywhere. "Yes, there is a police statement that Oswald has been removed from the area under heavy police guard. We did not see them leave the School Book Depository building, at least not from the front entrance. Apparently they left through the back. Oswald has been inside the building since he was captured there, moments after the shooting. Wait—wait—" On the screen the crowd parted. Men in overcoats and hats moved ahead of a double rank of police, pushing the crowd back.

"Someone else is leaving the Depository building, taken by the police. Our camera crew there tells me it is another person involved in the incident, in the capture of the suspect, Lee Oswald. I think I can see him now—"

Between the lines of policemen marched a teenager, a boy. He looked around at the press of bodies, appearing dazed. He wore a tan leather jacket and blue jeans. He was well over six feet in height and looked out over the heads of the policemen. His head swiveled around, taking it all in. He had brown hair and wore glasses that reflected the glaring, slanted sunlight. His head stopped when he saw the camera. A figure moved into the foreground, holding a microphone. The police surged to block him. Distantly: "If we could have just a statement, I—"

A plainclothesman leading the group shook his head. "Nothing until later, when—"

"Hey, hold on!" It was the teenager, in a loud, booming voice that stopped everyone. The plainsclothesman, a hand raised palm forward toward the camera, looked back over his shoulder.

"You cops have bugged me enough," the boy said. He shouldered his way forward. The policemen yielded before him and concentrated on keeping the crowd back. He reached the plainclothesman. "Look, am I under arrest or what?"

"Well, no, you're under protective custody—"

"Okay, that's what I thought. See that? What it is, is a TV camera, right? You guys don't have to protect me from *that,* do you?"

"No, look, Hayes—we wanna get you off the street. There could be—"

"I tell you that guy was alone up there. There isn't *anybody* else to worry about. And I'm gonna talk to these TV guys 'cause I'm a free citizen."

"You're a minor," the plainclothesman began hesitantly, "and we have to—"

"That's a lotta bull. Here—" He reached beyond the plainclothesman and grabbed the microphone. "See?—no trouble." Several people standing nearby applauded. The plainclothesman glanced uncertainly around. He began, "We don't want you giving—"

"What happened in there?" someone shouted.

"A lot!" Hayes shouted back.

"Didja see that guy shooting?"

"I saw it all, man. Cold-cocked the guy, I did." He peered at the camera. "I'm Bob Hayes and I saw it all, I'm here to tell ya. Bob Hayes from Thomas Jefferson High."

"How many shots were fired?" an off-camera voice asked, trying to get Hayes on the track of the story.

"Three. I was walkin' down the hall outside when I heard the first one. The guy downstairs was eatin' lunch and he sent me up to get some magazines they had stored up there. So I'm lookin' for them and I hear this loud noise."

Hayes paused, plainly enjoying this. "Yeah?" someone said.

"I knew it was a rifle right off. So I open this door where it came from. I see these chicken bones on a carton, like somebody's havin' lunch. Then I see this guy crouched down and pointin' this rifle out the window. He had it on the sill, to brace it. He was leaning on some cartons, too."

"That was Oswald?"

"That's what these guys said his name was. Me, I didn't ask." Hayes grinned. Someone laughed.

"I start over toward this guy and *boom* he fires again. I can hear somebody yelling outside. I didn't think about it, I just went for him. Dove over this crate and slammed into him. Just then the rifle goes off again, just as I hit him. I used to play some football, y'know, an' I know how to take a guy out."

"You got the rifle away from him?"

Hayes grinned again. "Hell no, man. I mashed him up against that window sill. Then I leaned back to get some room an' I gave him a good one up side the head. He forgot all about that rifle, right then. So I hit him again and he went all glassy-eyed. His number was *up*, man."

"He was out cold?"

"Sure was. I do good work, fella."

"Then the police arrived."

"Yeah, once this guy was out, I looked out the window. Saw all these cops lookin' up at me. Waved to 'em and called down to tell 'em where I was. They got up there right away."

"Could you see the President's Lincoln speeding away?"

"I didn't know there *was* any President. Just a lot of traffic, that's all. Some kind of parade, I thought. For Thanksgiving or somethin', y'know. I came down here because Mr. Aiken, our physics teacher, sent me on down."

The crowd around Hayes was utterly silent. The boy was a born performer, beaming straight into the camera and playing to the audience. The off-camera questioner asked, "You realize that you may have prevented a successful attempt on the life of the—"

"Yeah, that's amazin'. Great. But y'know, I didn't have any idea about that. Didn't even know he was in town. Woulda gone downstairs to see him and Jackie if I'd known."

342

"You had not seen Oswald before? You had no sign that he had a rifle and—"

"Look, like I said, I was down here to get some magazines. Mr. Aiken is doin' this special two-day extra-credit project in our college level physics course, the PST one. It was on the stuff in this magazine, *Senior Scholastic*. Mr. Aiken, he had me come down here to get 'em for the class this afternoon. There was somethin' about y'know this ah, signal from the future an'—"

"The shots—how many of them hit?"

"Hit what?"

"The President!"

"Hell, *I* dunno. He got off two of 'em okay. I socked him good just before the third."

Hayes grinned, looking around, beaming. The plainclothesman tugged at his arm. "I believe that's enough, Mr. Hayes," he said, using another tactic. "There will be a press conference later."

"Oh, yeah," Hayes said affably. His momentum was spent for the moment. He was still transfixed by being the center of attention. "Yeah, I'll tell it all later."

More shouted questions. A blur of motion as the police formed a wedge for Hayes. Clicking of cameras. Calls to clear the way. A rumble as a motorcycle started. Flickering images of men in overcoats pushing, mouths twisted.

Gordon blinked and for a moment he seemed to lose his balance. *Senior Scholastic*. The rec room swam in its pale, musty light.

Then Cronkite was talking again in that reedy voice. At Parkland Memorial Hospital a brief press conference had just concluded, while Hayes was speaking. Malcolm Kilduff, assistant press secretary to the President, had described the wound. A bullet had entered the lower back of the President's neck. It had passed through and left a small exit wound. The entry wound was larger and bled freely. The President had received several pints of O RH negative blood as well as 300 mg. hydrocortisone intravenously. At first the attending physicians had inserted a tube to clear the President's breathing passage. This failed. The senior physician, Michael Cosgrove, elected to perform a tracheotomy. This took five minutes. Lactated Ringer's solution—a modified saline solution—was fed into the right leg via catheter. The President began breathing well, though he was still in coma. His dilated eyes were open and staring directly into a glaring fluorescent lamp overhead. A nasogastric tube was thrust through Kennedy's nose and fitted behind his trachea, to clear away possible sources of nausea in his stomach. Bilateral chest tubes were placed in both chest pleural spaces to suck out damaged tissue and prevent lung collapse. The President's heartbeat was weak but regular. The exit wound was treated first, since the President was on his back. Three doctors then rolled the body onto its side. The entry wound gaped, larger than the exit wound by more than twice, and was the principal point of blood loss. It was treated without difficulty. Kennedy was still in Trauma Room No. 1 of Parkland as Kilduff spoke. His condition appeared stable. There was no apparent damage to the brain. His right lung was bruised. His windpipe was ripped apart. It appeared that, barring complications, he would live.

Mrs. Kennedy was not hit. Governor Connally was in critical condition. The Vice President was not hit. The attending physicians could make no comment on the number of shots fired. It was clear, however, that only one bullet had struck the President.

•

The crowd around the television murmured and stirred. The sensation of lightness and pressing heat had gone. Objects no longer swayed as though seen underwater, refracted. Gordon shouldered his way through the close-packed students. Speculations buzzed around him. He slid aside the glass door to the wooden deck and stepped through. Without thinking he vaulted over the railing and out onto the parking lot. He got his running gear out of the trunk of the Chevy. He changed in the nearby men's room. In shorts and tennis shoes he looked as young as many of the students still flocking to the rec room in search of news. He felt an airy sense of liberation and a humming, random energy, almost pleasurable. He did not want to think just now.

He began to run on the flat, watery sand. A steady breeze came in, blowing strands of black hair across his eyes. He ran with his head down, watching his feet strike. When his heel hit the sand a pale circle leaped into being as the water rushed out, driven by the impact. The beach hardened under each step, upholding him, and dissolved back to a gray slate sameness behind him. A helicopter passed *whump whump whump* overhead.

He skirted the town and ran through crescent coves, heading south, until he reached Nautilus Street. Penny was grading papers. He told her the news. She wanted to turn on the radio, learn more, but he tugged her away. Reluctantly she went with him. They went to the beach and walked south. Neither spoke. Penny fidgeted, face cloudy. The sea breeze scuffed the tops from the whitecaps and furled a banner of foam from each. Gordon looked at them and thought about them coming across the Pacific, driven by tides and winds. They were shallow out in the ocean and moved fast. As they neared the land the sea bed reared up beneath them and they deepened and slowed. Coming in, a wave moved faster at the top than at the bottom and they toppled forward, the energy from out of Asia churning into turbulence.

Penny called to him. She was already charging into the shallows. He followed. It was the first time he had tried this but that did not matter. They swam out beyond the waves and waited for the next big one to come in. It moved with stately slowness. The dark blue line thickened and rose and Gordon looked at it and estimated where it would break. He pulled forward, stroking fast and kicking. Penny was ahead. He felt something picking him up and the water ahead fell away. A rushing sound, and he moved faster. He flung out his arms and leaned to the left. Spray hazed his eyes. He blinked. He cut down the face of the wave, cupped in a wall of water, curling and churning toward the shore.

chapter forty-five

1998

John Renfrew worked through the night. He had the temporary power supply going and he was damned if he'd stop while the fuel held out. If he stopped he could not be sure of getting it started again. Better to go on and see what would happen. Then he could have no regrets.

He grimaced. See what *would* happen? Or *had* happened? Or *could* happen? Human language did not fit the physics. There was no tense of the verb *to be* that reflected the looping sense of time. No way to turn the language on the pivot of physics, to apply a torque that would make the paradoxes dissolve into an ordered cycle, endlessly turning.

He had let the technicians go. They were needed at home. Outside, on the Coton footpath, no bicycles, no movement. Families were home, tending the ill, or else had fled to the countryside. He felt a twinge of the dysentery that had come in the night. A brush with the gnawing stuff from the clouds, he guessed. He had been drinking from a store of bottled fruit drinks he'd found in the cafeteria, and eating packaged foods. For two days he'd been here, alone, not pausing to go home for a change of clothes. The world as he had lived in it was closing down, that much was clear from the windows of the lab. Since early morning a plume of oily smoke had furled upward in the distance; obviously no one was trying to put it out.

He tuned the apparatus gingerly. *Tap tap. Tap tap.* The tachyon noise level remained constant. He had been transmitting the new message about the neurojacket process for days now, mixing it with the RA and DEC monotony. Peterson had phoned new biological sentences in from his London office. The man had sounded strained and hurried. The content of the message, as nearly as Renfrew could understand it, explained why. If the California group was right, this thing could spread through the cloud-seed mechanism with blinding speed.

Renfrew tapped patiently on his Morse key, hoping he had the focusing right. It was so bloody difficult to know if you had the rig aimed. A slight error in targeting the beam put it at the wrong x, and thus at the wrong t. He had got through once, that they'd learned from Peterson's bank vault. But how could he check now, if the pulsing coils were a microsecond slow, or the fringing fields throwing the beam a degree to the left? He had only his sandy-eyed calibrations to trust. He was adrift here, in a world where t was time and tea was brine and x for space, x for the unknown floated in the air before him, a passing pattern.

He shook himself. The lab stool pinched his buttocks. He had less fat there, now; must have lost weight. Have to put on some extra ballast, yes.

Tap tap tap. Out went the Morse cadences. *Tap tap.*

Maybe the weight loss explained why the room rippled and stretched as he watched. Christ, he was tired. A wan anger welled up in him. He had been *taptaptap*ping out biological stuff and coordinates and the lot, all impersonal and—he was sure of it now—in the end, all useless. Bloody boring, it was. He reached over and took up the identifying passage he had been transmitting regularly, and began sending it again. But this time he added a few comments of his own, about how this whole thing got started, and Markham's ideas, and Peterson the stiff-faced bastard, and the lot, all the way up to Markham's crash. It felt good to get it all down, pushing the words out in Morse as he thought of them. He told it in ordinary sentences, not the clipped telegraph style they'd adopted for compressing the biological information. It was a relief to tell it, really. The whole sodding thing was pointless, the beam was pouring down some unsuspected cosmic rathole, anyway, so why not enjoy the last shot? *Tap tap.* Here's my life story, mate, written on the head of a pin. *Tap tap.* Into the void. *Tap tap.*

But after a while the momentum left him and he stopped. His shoulders sagged.

The scope screen rippled and the tachyon noise level rose. Renfrew peered at it. *Tap tap.* On impulse he flipped off the transmitting switch. The past be damned for a moment. He watched the scramble of curves arc and intersect, dancing. For brief snatches of time the noise resolved into these snakings across the screen. Signals, clearly. Someone else was transmitting.

Regular jolts of wave forms, evenly spaced. Renfrew copied them.

ATTEMPT CONTACT FROM 2349 IN TAC

and a blur of noise again, swallowing all.

English. Somebody sending in English. From the year 2349?

Perhaps. Or maybe with tachyons in the 234.9 kilovolt range. Or maybe it was a fluke, a sport.

Renfrew slurped cold coffee. He had made a thermos days ago and forgotten it. He hoped the water was okay. The coffee hadn't the dog's fur flavor he remembered; more like scorched earth. He shrugged and drank it without thinking further.

He felt his brow. Sweat. A fever. A strange, distant mutter came to him. Voices? He went to look, surprised at his weakness, at the lurking ache in his ankles and thighs. Should get more exercise, he thought automatically, and then laughed. Scuffling noises. Had they heard him? He lurched down a corridor. But there was no one about. Only the sound of the wind. That, and the gritty scraping of his own shoes on the bare concrete.

He went back and stared at the scope. His throat burned. He tried to think calmly and cleanly about what Markham had said so long ago. The microuniverses were not like black holes, not in the sense that inside them all matter was compressed into infinite densities. Instead, their average density was a reasonable number, though higher than ours. They had formed in the early moments of the universe and been forever isolated, living out microlives inside a folded geometry. Wickham's new field equations showed they were out there, between the clusters of galaxies. *An* x *and* t *we cannot see,* he thought, *apart from me and thee.* Now there was a literary flourish for you, worthy of the last edition of the *Times.* The very last edition.

Abruptly he sat, feeling dizzy. An ache behind his eyes, spreading. Matter was swallowed into the net of space-time, of differential geometries. *G* times *n*. A tachyon could wing out of the knots, a free phoenix, its flight ordained by the squiggles and jots of Markham and Wickham. Renfrew shivered as the cold seeped into him.

Another set of bursts. He scribbled them on a pad. The scratching pen cut the silence.

MENT ENHANCE RESONANCE STRUCTURE BY TUNING TO SIDE-BAND CARRIER

and then the sea of noise again, the waves lost.

This all meant something to someone, but who? Where? When? Another:

AMSK WEDLRUF XSMDOPRDHTU AS WTEU WEHRTU

Wrong language? A code from across the galaxy, from across

the universe? This apparatus opened up communication with everywhere, everywhen, instantly. Talk to the stars. Talk to the compressed beings inside a dot of space. A telegram from Andromeda would take less time than one from London. Tachyons sleeted through the laboratory, through Renfrew, bringing word. It was within their grasp, if only they had time . . .

He shook his head. All form and structure was eroded by the overlapping of many voices, a chorus. Everyone was talking at once and no one could hear.

The roughing pumps coughed. Tachyons of size 10^{-13} centimeters were flashing across whole universes, across 10^{28} centimeters of cooling matter, in less time than Renfrew's eye took to absorb a photon of the pale laboratory light. All distances and times were wound in upon each other, singularities sucking up the stuff of creation. Event horizons rippled and worlds coiled into worlds. There were voices in this room, voices clamoring, touching—

Renfrew stood up and suddenly clutched at a scope mount for support. Christ, the fever. It clawed at him, ran glowing smoke fingers through his mind.

ATTEMPT CONTACT FROM 2349. All thought of reaching the past was gone now, he realized, blinking. The room veered, then righted itself. With Markham gone and the Wickham woman missing for days, there was no longer even any hope of understanding what had happened. Causality's leaden hand would win out. The soothing human world of flowing time would go on, a Sphinx yielding none of her secrets. An infinite series of grandfathers would live out their lives safe from Renfrew.

ATTEMPT CONTACT, the scope sputtered again.

But unless he knew where and when they were, there was no hope of answering.

Hello, 2349. Hello out there. This is 1998, an x and t in your memory. Hello. ATTEMPT CONTACT.

Renfrew smiled with flinty irony. Whispers came flitting, embedding soft words of tomorrow in the indium. Someone was there. Someone brought hope.

The room was cold. Renfrew huddled by his instruments, perspiring, peering at the bursts of waves. He was like a South Sea islander, watching the airplanes draw their stately lines across the sky, unable to shout up to them. *I am here*. Hello, 2349. Hello.

He was trying a modification of the signal correlator when the lights winked out. Utter blackness rushed in. The distant generator rattled and chugged into silence.

It took a long time to feel his way out and into the light. It was a bleak, gray noon, but he did not notice; it was enough to be outside.

He could hear no sound from Cambridge at all. The breeze carried a sour tang. No birds. No aircraft.

He walked south, towards Grantchester. He looked back once at the low square profile of the Cav and in the diffused light he raised a hand to it. He thought of the nested universes, onion skin within onion skin. Leaning back, head swimming, he peered at the clouds, once so benign a sight. Above that cloak was the galaxy, a great swarm of colored lights, turning with majestic slowness in the great night. Then he looked down at the bumpy, worn footpath and felt a great weight lift from him. For so long now he had been transfixed by the past. It had deadened him to this real world around him. He knew, now, without knowing quite how he knew, that it was forever lost. Rather than feeling despair, he was elated, free.

Marjorie lay up ahead, no doubt frightened to be alone. He remembered her preserves on the uncompromising straight shelving, and smiled. They could eat those for some time. Have some easy meals together, as they did in the days before the children. They would soon have to go to the countryside and get Johnny and Nicky, of course.

Puffing slightly, his head clearing, he walked along the deserted path. There was really quite a lot ahead to do, when you thought about it.

chapter forty-six

OCTOBER 28, 1974

He walked from his hotel on Connecticut Avenue. The reception was to be a buffet lunch, the letter said, so Gordon had slept in until eleven. He had long ago learned that on short trips to the east it was best to grant nothing to the myth of time zones, and keep to his western schedule. Invariably this fit the demands on an out-of-town visitor anyway, since such occasions were excuses for lingering over sauce-drenched entrees in expensive restaurants, followed by earnest, now-that-we're-away-from-the-office-I-can-speak-frankly revelations over several cups of coffee, and then late night stumblings-to-bed. Arising at ten the next morning seldom got him to the NSF or AEC later than the executives themselves, since he ate no breakfast.

He tramped through the city zoo; it was more or less along the way. Yellow canine eyes followed him, contemplating the results if the bars were suddenly lifted. Chimps swung in pendulum strokes on an unending circuit of their cramped universe. The natural world was a pocket here amid distant honks and looming, square profiles of sour brown brick. Gordon savored the clammy fullness of the breeze that had tunneled its way up from the Potomac. He welcomed this traveler's brush with the seasons, punctuations to the extended sentences of the months, a welcome relief from California's monotonous excellence.

He had first come here with his mother and father. That tourist's orbit was now a dim set of memories from a corner of his preadolescence, the period of life that he supposed was everybody's golden age. He remembered being awed at the sleek white glow of the Washington Monument and the White House. For years afterward he was certain these solemn edifices were what was meant when his grammar school class sang "America" and chorused about alabaster majesties. "The country, it really begins in Washington," his mother had said, not forgetting to add the pedagogical "D.C.," so that her son would never confuse it with the state. And Gordon, towed through the list of historic shrines, saw what she meant. Beyond the Frenchified design of the city center lay a rural park, land that breathed of Jefferson and tree-traced boulevards. To him Washington had ever since been the entranceway to a vast republic where crops sprouted under a WASP sun. There, blue-eyed blondes drove yellow roadsters that left dust plumes on the open roads as they roared from one county fair to the next, women won prizes for strawberry preserves and men drank watery beer and kissed girls who had been struck from the template of Doris Day. He had gazed upward at the *Spirit of St. Louis* hanging like a paralyzed moth in the Smithsonian, and wondered how a cornhusker city—"without a single good college in it," his mother sniffed—could flap wings and scoot aloft.

Gordon thrust his hands into his pockets for warmth and walked. The corners of his mouth perked up in an airy mirth. He had learned a lot about the huge country beyond Washington, most of it from Penny. Their mutual abrasions had healed over in the aftermath of 1963 and they had found again the persistent chemistry that had first drawn them into their mutual bound orbits, circles centered on a point midway between them. The thing between them was not a geometric dot but rather a small sun, igniting between them a passion Gordon felt was deeper than anything that had happened to him before. They were married in late 1964. Her father, just plain Jack, put on a massive wedding, glittery and champagne-steeped. Penny wore the traditional white. She made a downward-turning leer whenever anyone mentioned it. She had come with him to Washington that winter, when he was making his first big presentation to the NSF for a major grant of his own. His talk went well and Penny fell in love with the National Gallery, going every day to see the Vermeers. Together they ate shellfish with luminaries from the NSF and strolled down from the Congressional dome to the Lincoln Monument. They did not mind the raw, cold damp then; it went with the scenery. Everything had seemed to go with everything else.

Gordon checked the address and found that he had another block to go. He had always been intrigued by the contrasts of Washington. This busy street brimmed with its own importance, yet intersecting it were thinner avenues of small shops, decaying houses, and corner grocery stores. Old black men leaned in doorways, their large brown eyes surveying the tax-funded bustle. Gordon waved to one and, turning a corner, discovered a mammoth courtyard. It had the austere French style of 1950s Government Classical, with conical evergreens standing like sentries at the abrupt, uncompromising corners. Regimented bushes led the eye, willing or not, into remorseless perspectives.

Well, he thought, blocky and self-important architecture or no, this was it. He teetered back on his heels to look. Granite facings led upward into a bland sky. He took his hands out of his pockets and brushed hair back from his eyes. Already there was the giveaway thinning at the crown, he knew, sure sign that his father's baldness would find echo in his own forties.

He pushed open a series of three glass doors. The spaces between seemed to serve as air locks, preserving inside a dry heat. Ahead were tables with luxuriant linen draped over them. In the center of the carpeted foyer, knots of suited men. Gordon pushed through the last air lock and into a hushed buzz of talk. Thick drapes swallowed sounds, giving the air of solemnity found in mortuaries. To the left, a band of receptionists. One detached herself and came toward him. She was wearing a long, cream-colored silky thing Gordon would have taken for an evening gown if it were not midday. She asked for his name. He gave it slowly. "Oh," she said, eyes round, and went to one of the draped tables. She returned with a name tag, not the usual plastic, but a sturdy wooden frame housing a stark white board with his name in calligraphy. She pinned it on him. "We do want our guests to look their best today," she said with abstract concern, and brushed imaginary lint from his coat sleeve. Gordon warmed at the attention and forgave her efficient gloss. Other men, all suited, most in basic bureaucratic black, were filling the foyer. The receptionists met them with a volley of name tags—plastic, he noted—and seating assignments and admission cards. In a corner a woman who looked like an executive secretary helped a frail white-haired man from his immense, weighty overcoat. He moved with delicate, hesitant gestures, and Gordon recognized him as Jules Chardaman, the nuclear physicist who had discovered some particle or other and received a Nobel for his trouble. *I thought he was dead,* Gordon mused.

"Gordon! Tried to call you last night," called a brisk voice behind him.

He turned, hesitated, and shook hands with Saul Shriffer. "I got in late and went out for a walk."

"In this town?"

"It seemed safe."

Saul shook his head. "Maybe they don't mug dreamers."

"I probably don't look prosperous enough."

Saul flashed his nationally known smile. "Naw, you're looking great. Hey, how's the wife? She with you?"

"Oh, she's fine. She's been visiting her parents—you know, showing off the kids. She's flying in this morning, though." He glanced at his watch. "Should be here soon."

"Hey, great, like to see her again. How about dinner tonight?"

"Sorry, we've got plans." Gordon realized he had said this too quickly and added, "Maybe tomorrow, though. How long will you be in town?"

"I have to zip over to New York by noon. I'll catch you next time I'm on the coast."

"Fine."

Saul unconsciously pursed his lips, as though considering how to put his next sentence. "You know, those parts of the old messages you kept to yourself . . ."

Gordon kept his face blank. "Just the names, that's all. My public statement is that they were lost in the noise. Which is partly true."

"Yeah." Saul studied his face. "Look, after all this much time, it seems to me—look, it would make a really interesting sidelight on the whole thing."

"No. Come on, Saul, we've had this discussion before."

"It's been *years*. I fail to see—"

"I'm not sure I got the names right. A letter here and there and you've got the wrong name and the wrong people."

"But look—"

"Forget it. I'm never going to release the parts I'm not sure about." Gordon smiled to take the edge off his voice. There were other reasons, too, but he wasn't going to go into that.

Saul shrugged goodnaturedly and fingered his newly grown moustache. "Okay, okay. Just thought I'd give it a try, catch you in a mellow mood. How're the experiments going?"

"We're still hammering away at the sensitivity. You know how it is."

"Getting any signals?"

"Can't say. The hash is unbelievable."

Saul frowned. "There should be *some*thing there."

"Oh, there is."

"No, I mean besides that stuff you got back in '67. I'll grant you that was a clear message. But it wasn't in any code or language we know."

"The universe is a big place."

"You think they were from a long way off?"

"Look, anything I say is pure guess. But it was a strong signal, tightly beamed. We were able to show that the fact that it lasted three days and then shut off was due to the earth passing through a tachyon beam. I'd say we just got in the way of somebody else's communications net."

"Ummm." Saul pondered this. "Y'know, if we could only be sure those messages we can't decode weren't from a human transmitter, far up in the future . . ."

Gordon grinned. Saul was one of the biggest names in science now, at least in the public eye. His popularizations made the bestseller lists, his television series ran in prime time. Gordon finished for him, "You mean, we'd have proof of an alien technology."

"Sure. Worth trying, isn't it?"

"Maybe so."

The big bronze doors at the end of the foyer swung back. The crowd shuffled toward the reception room beyond. Gordon had noted that people in groups move as though by a slow diffusion process, and this mob was no different. Many he knew—Chet Manahan, a methodical solid state physicist who always wore a vest with matching tie, spoke five languages, and made sure you knew this within a few minutes of meeting him; Sidney Roman, a swarthy, delicate, thin man whose precise equations led to outrageous conclusions, some of which had proved right; Louisa Schwartz, who, contrary to her name, had luminous white skin and a mind that catalogued everything in astrophysics, including most of the unprintable gossip; George Maklin, red-faced and loud, shoulders rippling with muscle, who carried out experiments suspended by whiskers into liquid helium, measuring wisps of momentum; Douglas Karp, a czar of a rabble of graduate students which cranked out two papers a month on the band structure of assorted solids, enabling him to lecture in sunny summer schools on the Mediterranean; Brian Nantes, with enormous, booming energy which in his papers squeezed into adroit, laconic equations, denuded of commentary or argument with his contemporaries, with a decidedly pearls-before-swine abstract to accompany the text—and many more, some casually met at conferences, others opposed in heated sessions of APS meetings, most of them dim faces associated with the stutter of initials beneath interesting papers, or met at a sandwich-and-beer faculty lunch just before delivering a seminar, or seen receiving polite applause at a meeting after they had mumbled an invited paper into a microphone. In this pack Saul drifted away, halfway through describing a plan to ferret out extraterrestrials by the squiggles and beeps in the tachyon spectrum. Gordon could do the observations, see, and Saul would look at the data and see what they meant.

Gordon wormed away diagonally, letting a rapidly talking clump of particle physicists come between him and Saul. The buffet lunch lay dead ahead of him. Characteristically, the scientists wasted no time politely hanging back from the self-serve table. Gordon piled beef on bread and escaped with a presentable sandwich. He bit in. The sting of the horseradish cleared his sinuses, watering his eyes. The punch was a superior grade of champagne diluted with pungent orange juice.

Shriffer was surrounded now by a crescent of approving faces. It was odd, how celebrity invaded science these days, so that appearing on the Johnny Carson show was more effective with the NSF than publishing a brilliant series of papers in *Physical Review*.

Yet in the end it was media fixation that had done it all, Gordon reflected. At the conclusion of the press conference of Ramsey and Hussinger, Gordon had felt the constricting heat flow through him and seem to wash through the air. Then, watching Cronkite talk grimly into the camera on November 22, he had felt it again. Was that the signature of a true, unavoidable paradox? Was that when the future had radically altered? There was no way to tell, at least not yet. He had pored over records of atmospheric phenomena, of cosmic ray counts, of radio noise and starlight fluence—and found nothing. There were no instruments yet designed which could measure the effect. Gordon felt, though, that he had a subjective perception of when it had happened. Perhaps because he was close to the site where the paradoxes were driven home? Or because he was already strung out, as Penny would've put it, that is, fine-tuned? He might never know.

A passing face nodded. "Quite a day," Isaac Lakin said formally, and moved on. Gordon nodded. The remark was suitably ambiguous. Lakin had become a director at the NSF, shepherding the magnetic resonance work. Gordon's controversial area, tachyon detection, was under another man. Lakin was now best known for his coauthorship of the "spontaneous resonance" paper in PRL. The refracted fame had lifted him, agreeably buoyant, into his present position.

The other coauthor, Cooper, had done reasonably well, too. His thesis went through the committee with slick speed, once stripped of the spontaneous resonance effects. He had gone off to Penn State with evident relief. There, postdoccing his way through some respectable electron spin work led to a faculty position. He was now safely worrying various III-V compounds into yielding up their transport coefficients. Gordon saw him at meetings and they had an occasional drink together, sharing wary conversation.

He eavesdropped on gossip about revival of the Orion spaceship idea, and new work by Dyson. Then, as Gordon was fetching another sandwich and talking to a reporter, a particle physicist approached. He wanted to talk over plans for a new accelerator which had a chance of producing a tachyon cascade. The energy required was enormous. Gordon listened politely. When a revealing skeptical smile began to spread over his face, he forced his lips back into an expression of professorial consideration. The high-energy types were struggling to make tachyons now, but most outside observers felt the effort was premature. Better theory was needed. Gordon had chaired several panels on the subject and had grown thick-skinned about new, big-money proposals. The particle physicists were addicted to their immense accelerators. The man who has only a hammer to work with finds that every new problem needs a nail.

Gordon nodded, looked sage, sipped champagne, said little. Though the evidence for tachyons was now overwhelming, they did not fit into the standard ongoing program of physics. They were more than simply a new species of particle. They couldn't be put on the shelf beside the mesons and hyperons and kaons. Before this physicists had, with the instincts of accountants, decomposed the world into a comfortable zoology. The other, simpler particles had only minor differences. They fit into the universe like marbles in a sack, filling but not altering the fabric. Tachyons didn't. They made new theories possible, kicking up the dust of cosmological questions by their mere existence. The implications were being worked out.

Beyond that, though, were the messages themselves. They had ceased in 1963, before Zinnes could get extensive confirmation. Some physicists thought they were real. Others, forever wary of sporadic phenomena, thought they must have been some fortuitous error. The situation had a lot in common with Joe Weber's detection of gravitational waves in 1969. Later experiments by others had found no waves. Did that mean Weber was wrong, or that the waves came in occasional bursts? It might be decades before another flurry could settle the question. Gordon had talked to Weber, and the wiry, silver-maned experimenter seemed to take the whole thing as a kind of inevitable comedy. In science you usually can't convert your opponents, he had said; you have to outlive them. For Weber there was hope; Gordon felt his own case was forever uncheckable.

The new theory by Tanninger certainly pointed the way. Tanninger had put tachyons into the general relativity theory in a highly original way. The old question that came up in quantum mechanics, of who the observer was, had finally been resolved. Tachyons were a new kind of wave phenomenon, causality waves looping between past and future, and the paradoxes they could produce gave a new kind of physics. The essence of paradox was the possibility of mutually contradictory outcomes, and Tanninger's picture of the causal loop was like that of the quantum-mechanical waves. The difference came in the interpretation of the experiment. In Tanninger's picture, a kind of wave function, resembling the old quantum function, gave the various outcomes of the paradox loop. But the new wave function did not describe probabilities—it spoke of different universes. When a loop was set up, the universe split into two new universes. If the loop was of the simple killing-your-grandfather type, then there would result one universe where the grandfather lived and the grandson disappeared. The grandson reappeared in a second universe, having traveled back in time, where he shot his grandfather and lived out his life, passing through the years which were forever altered by his act. No one in either universe thought the world was paradoxical.

All this came from using tachyons to produce the standing-wave kind of time loop. Without tachyons, no splitting into different universes occurred. Thus the future world that had sent Gordon the messages was gone, unreachable. They had separated sometime in the fall of 1963; Gordon was sure of that. Some event had made Renfrew's experiment impossible or unnecessary. It could have been the Ramsey-Hussinger press conference, or putting the message in the safety deposit box, or the Kennedy thing. One of those, yes. But which?

He moved among the crowd, greeting friends, letting his mind drift. He recalled that a human being, eating and moving around, gave off 200 watts of body heat. This room trapped most of it, bringing prickly perspiration to his brow. His Adam's apple snagged on the knot of his tie.

"Gordon!" a silvery voice called to him above the tangle of talk. He turned. Marsha threaded her way through the crowd. He bent and kissed her. She was toting an overnight case, swinging it with abandon as she turned to call hellos to people she knew. She told him about the crush of traffic getting into town after her shuttle flight from LaGuardia, eyebrows darting upward to underline a word, hands describing averted collisions with swooping arcs. The prospect of a few days of freedom from the children gave her a manic, gay air that spread to Gordon. He realized he had grown somber as this overheated, glittery reception went on, and Marsha had erased that in a moment. It was this quality in her, of swelling life, that he remembered best when he was away from her. "Oh, God, there's that Lakin," she said, eyes rolling up in a parody of panic. "Let's move the opposite way, I don't want to start off with *him*." Wifely loyalty. She tugged him to the shrimp salad, which he had passed over, probably following instinctively a genetically ingrained dietary axiom. Marsha snared a few of their friends along the way—to form a protective barrier against Lakin, she said. All this was done with comic exaggeration, drawing chuckles from the sober faces. A waiter sought them out and delivered glasses of champagne. "Ummm, I'll bet this isn't what's in the bowl over there," Marsha said, sipping, lips puckered in approval. The waiter hesitated, then agreed, "The Chairman said to bring out some of the private stock," and then was gone, fearing he had revealed too much. Marsha seemed to polarize the medium, Gordon noted, drawing friends out of corners of the large room to form a cloud around them. Carroway appeared, shaking hands, chuckling. Gordon basked in her compact energy. He had never been able to relax so with Penny, he remembered, and maybe that should have told him something from the start. In 1968, when they were in the thick of their last elaborate sparring, he and Penny had come to Washington in winter again. It was a veiled city. Fog rose from the Potomac's shifting currents. He had avoided dinner parties with physicists that trip, he recalled, mostly because Penny found them boring and he could not predict when she would get into one of her political arguments or, worse, descend into a swollen silence. They had areas they had silently agreed not to talk about, areas which expanded in time. Each had axes to grind—*you're an injustice collector*, Penny had accused, once —but, perversely, the good periods between the bad had become radiant with a released energy. He had oscillated in mood through 1967 and '68, not buying Penny's Freud-steeped recipes for repair, but discovering no alternative. *Isn't it a little obvious to be so hostile to analysis?* she said once, and he had realized it was so; he felt the clanky, machinelike language was a betrayal, a trap. Psychology had modeled itself after the hard sciences, with physics as the shining example. But they had taken the old Newtonian clockwork as their example. To modern physics there was no ticktock world independent of the observer, no untouched mechanism, no way of describing a system without being involved in it. His intuition told him that no such exterior analysis could capture what rubbed and chafed between them. And so, in the descending days of 1968 his personal nucleus had fissioned, and a year later he met Marsha Gould from the Bronx, Marsha, short and dusky, and some inevitable paradigm had come home. Remembering the events now, seeing them sealed in amber, he smiled as Marsha brimmed beside him.

The western windows of the long room now let in a light like beaten brass. Luminaries from the funding agencies were arriving, customarily late. Gordon nodded, shook hands, made appropriate small talk. Into Marsha's crescent of conversation came Ramsey, smoking a thin cigar. Gordon greeted him with a conspiratorial wink. Then a face said, "I wanted to meet you, so I'm afraid I just plain gatecrashed." Gordon smiled without interest, bound up in his own recollections, and then noticed the young man's self-lettered name badge: *Gregory Markham.* He froze, hand hanging in midair. The surrounding chatter faded and he could distinctly feel his heart thumping. He said stupidly, "I, ah, see."

"I did my thesis in plasma physics, but I've been reading Tanninger's papers, and yours of course, and, well, I think that's where the real physics is going to be done. I mean there's a whole set of cosmological consequences, don't you think? It seems to me—" and Markham, who Gordon saw was really only a decade or so younger than he, was off, sketching ideas he had about Tanninger's work. Markham had some interesting notions about the nonlinear solutions, ideas Gordon had not heard before. Despite his shock, he found himself following the technical parts with interest. He could tell Markham had the right feel for the work. Tanninger's use of the new calculus of exterior differential forms had made his ideas difficult for the older generation of physicists to approach, but to Markham it presented no problem; he was not hobbled by the more accepted, gnarled notation. The essential images conjured up in the mind's eye, of paradoxical curves descending with elliptic logic to the plane of physical reality, Markham had mastered. Gordon found himself becoming excited; he yearned for a place to sit down and scribble out some arguments of his own, to let the impacted symbols of mathematics speak for him. But then an aide approached, wearing white gloves, and intruded, nodding respectfully but firmly and saying, "Dr. Bernstein, Mrs. Bernstein, we require your presence now." Markham shrugged and grinned lopsidedly and in what seemed an instant was gone among the crowd. Gordon collected himself and took Marsha's arm. The aide cleared a path for them. Gordon had an impulse to call out to Markham, find him, ask him to dinner that evening, not let the man slip away. But something held him back. He wondered if this event itself, this chance meeting, could have been the thing that framed the paradoxes—but no, that made no sense, the break had come in 1963, of course, yes. This Markham was not the man who would calculate and argue in that distant Cambridge. The Markham he had just seen would not die in a plane accident. The future would be different.

A puzzled expression flickered across his face and he moved woodenly.

They met the Secretary for Health, Education & Welfare, a man with a tapered nose and a tight, pouting mouth, the two forming a fleshy exclamation point. The aide ushered them all into a small private elevator, where they stood uncomfortably close to each other—*inside our personal boundary spaces,* Gordon observed abstractedly—and the Secretary for HEW emitted boisterous one-liners, all shaped with a speech writer's gloss. Gordon recalled that this particular Cabinet appointment had been a highly political one. The elevator slid open to reveal a pinched passageway packed with unmoving people. Several men gave them an obvious once-over and then their eyes went neutral again, heads routinely swiveling back to assigned directions. Security, Gordon supposed. The Secretary led them through a narrow channel and into a larger room. A short woman came bustling over, dressed as though about to go to the opera. She looked like the sort who habitually put her hands up to her string of pearls and took a deep breath before speaking. As Gordon was framing this thought she did precisely that, saying, "The auditorium is *filled* already, we never thought there would be so many, so early. I don't think there is any point Mr. Secretary in staying back here just through that way everybody's out there already almost."

The Secretary moved forward. Marsha put a hand on Gordon's shoulder and reached up. "Your tie's too tight. You look like you're trying to strangle yourself." She loosened the knot with deft fingers, smoothed it out. Her teeth bit into her lower lip in her concentration, pressing until the red flesh was pale beneath the slick finish of lipstick. He remembered the way the beach turned white beneath his feet as he ran on it.

"Come. Come," the pearled lady urged them. They walked across a stark, marbled wedge of space and abruptly onto a stage. Spotlighted figures milled about. Chairs scraped. Another aide in the absurd white gloves took Marsha's arm. He let the two of them into the glare. There were three rows of chairs, most already occupied. Marsha was at the far end of the front row and Gordon next to her. The aide saw that Marsha negotiated a safe landing. Gordon plunked himself down. The aide evaporated. Marsha was wearing a dress of fashionable shortness. Her efforts to pull the hem down over the curve of her knees caught his attention. He was filled with an agreeable sense of ownership, that the luxuriant curve of thigh so concealed in public was his, could be his for the cost of a wordless gesture tonight.

He squinted to see past the battery of lights. A curving crowd of faces swam in the half-space beyond the stage. They rustled with anticipation—not for him, he knew—and to the left a TV camera peered in cyclopean stupor at the vacant dais. A sound engineer tested the mikes.

Gordon searched the faces he could see. Was Markham out there? He trolled for the right combination of features. It had struck him how alike most people were, despite their vaunted individuality, and yet how quickly the eye could cut through the similarities to pick out the small details that separated known from stranger. Someone caught his eye. He peered through the glare. No, it was Shriffer. Gordon wondered with amusement what Saul would think if he knew Markham was probably only meters away, an unknowing link to the lost world of the messages. Gordon would never reveal those distant names now. It would get into the press and confuse everything, prove nothing.

It was not only keeping the identities secret that made him slow to publish his full data. Most of what he had thought was noise in his earlier experiments was actually indecipherable signals. Those messages fled backward in time from some unfathomable future. They were scarcely absorbed at all by the present rather low-density distribution of matter in the universe. But as they ran backward, what was to men an expanding universe appeared to the tachyons as a contracting one. Galaxies drew together, packing into an ever-shrinking volume. This thicker matter absorbed tachyons better. As they flowed back into what was, to them, an imploding universe, increasing numbers of the tachyons were absorbed. Finally, at the last instant before it compressed to a point, the universe absorbed all tachyons from each point in its own future. Gordon's measurement of the tachyon flux, integrated back in time, showed that the energy absorbed from the tachyons was enough to heat the compressed mass. This energy fueled the universal expansion. So to the eyes of men, the universe exploded from a single point because of what *would* happen, not what had. Origin and destiny intertwined. The snake ate its tail.

Gordon wanted to be absolutely sure before he reported on the flux and his conclusions. He was sure it would not be well received.

The world did not want paradox. The reminder that time's vast movements were loops we could not perceive—the mind veered from that. At least part of the scientific opposition to the messages was based on precisely that flat fact, he was sure. Animals had evolved in such a way that the ways of nature seemed simple to them; that was a definite survival trait. The laws had shaped man, not the other way around. The cortex did not like a universe that fundamentally ran both forward and back.

So he would not smudge the issue with a few tattered names, not for Shriffer's spotlight. Perhaps he would tell Markham, just as he would inevitably publish the faint calls he had measured from Epsilon Eridani, eleven light years away. They were voices from an undated future, reporting shipboard maintenance details. No paradoxes there. Unless, of course, the information blunted the leap into rocketry now underway, aborted the upcoming space station by some contrary twist. That was always possible, he supposed. Then the universe would split again. The river would fork. But perhaps, when this was all understood and Tanninger's squiggles cut deeper into the riddle, they would know whether paradoxes should be avoided at all. Paradoxes did no true damage, after all. It was like having a dusky twin beyond the looking glass, identical but for his lefthandedness. And the nature of the tachyons made accidental paradox unlikely, anyway. A starship reporting back to its Earth would use tight beams. No fringing fields would by chance catch the present Earth on its helical whirl through space, intersect its gavotte around the galaxy.

Ramsey moved across his field of vision and jerked him back into this illuminated moment. Ramsey stubbed out his smoke, the slim cigar twisting like a dying insect. The man was nervous. Suddenly, a blare of recorded music. *Hail to the Chief.* Everyone on the stage stood, belying the fact that the man who entered from the right, smiling and waving a casual hand, was a public servant. President Scranton shook the Secretary's hand with media-sharpened warmth and took in the rest of the stage with a generalized smile. Despite himself, Gordon felt a certain zest. The President moved with a comfortable certainty, acknowledging the cheers and finally sitting beside the Secretary. Scranton had discredited Robert Kennedy, tripping the scowling younger brother in a tangle of Democratic wiretapping, and then the use of the intelligence community and the FBI against the Republicans. Gordon had found the charges difficult to believe at the time, particularly since Goldwater had uncovered the first hints. But in retrospect it was good to be rid of the Kennedy dynasty idea, and the Imperial Presidency along with it.

The Secretary was at the dais now, making the mechanical introductions and slipping in the obligatory puffing-up of the administration. Gordon leaned over to Marsha and whispered, "Christ, I didn't make up a speech."

She said merrily, "Tell them about the future, *Gordelah*."

He growled, "That future's only a dream now."

She replied laconically, "It's a poor sort of memory that works only backward."

Gordon grinned back at her. She had fetched that up from her reading to the kids, a line from the looking-glass, time-reversed scene, the White Queen. Gordon shook his head and sat back.

The Secretary had finished his prepared speech and now introduced the President to a solid round of applause. Scranton read the citation for Ramsey and Hussinger. The two men came forward, awkwardly managing to get in each other's way. The President handed over the two plaques amid applause. Ramsey glanced at his and then exchanged it with Hussinger's, to laughter from the audience. Polite hand clapping as they sat down. The Secretary came forward, shuffling papers, and handed some to the President. The next award was for some achievement in genetics which Gordon had never heard about. The recipient was a chunky Germanic woman who spread some pages before her on the dais and turned to the audience, plainly prepared for an extended history of her work. Scranton gave the Secretary a sidelong look and then moved back and sat down. He had been through such things before.

Gordon tried to concentrate on what she said, but lost interest when she launched into a salute to other workers in the field who regrettably could not be honored here today in such august surroundings.

He toyed with the question of what to say. He would never see the President again, never again even have the ear of so influential a person as the Secretary. Perhaps if he tried to convey something of what this all meant . . . His eyes strayed over the audience.

He had a sudden sense that time was *here*, not a relation between events, but a *thing*. What a specifically human comfort it was to see time as immutable, a weight you could not escape. Believing that, a man could give up swimming against this riverrun of seconds and simply drift, cease battering himself on time's flat face like an insect flapping against a blossom of light. If only—

He looked at Ramsey, reading his plaque, oblivious to the geneticist's ramble, and remembered the foaming waves at La Jolla, cupping forward out of Asia to break on the bare new land. Gordon shook his head, not knowing why, and reached for Marsha's hand. A warming press.

He thought of the names ahead, in that deflected future, who had tried to send a signal into the receding murk of history, and write it fresh again. It took courage to send firefly hopes through the dark, phosphorescent dartings across an infinite swallowing velvet. They would need courage; the calamity they spoke of could engulf the world.

Scattered, polite applause. The President gave the hefty woman her plaque—the check would come later, Gordon knew —and she sat. Then Scranton peered into his bifocals and began to read, in the squarish vowels of Pennsylvania, the citation to Gordon Bernstein.

"—for investigations in nuclear magnetic resonance which produced a startling new effect—"

Gordon reflected that Einstein won the Nobel prize for the photoelectric effect, which was considered reasonably safe by 1921, and not for the still controversial theory of relativity. Good company to be in.

"—which, in a series of definitive experiments in 1963 and 1964, he showed could only be explained by the existence of a new kind of particle. This strange particle, the tac—tac—"

The President stumbled over the pronunciation. Agreeing laughter rippled through the audience. Something pricked in Gordon's memory and he searched the dark bowl of faces. That laugh. Someone he knew?

"—tachyon, is capable of moving faster than the speed of light. This fact implies—"

The tight bun of hair, the lifted, almost jaunty chin. His mother was in the third row. She was wearing a dark coat and had come to see this day, see her son on the bright stage of history.

"—that the particles can themselves travel backward in time. The implications of this are of fundamental importance in many areas of modern science, from cosmology to—"

Gordon half rose, hands clenched. The proud energy in the way she beamed, head turned to the flow of words—

"—the structure of the subnuclear particles. This is truly an immense—"

But in the tangled rush of the months following November of 1963 she had died in Bellevue, before he ever saw her again.

"—scale, echoing the increasing connection—"

The woman in the third row was probably an aging secretary, called forth to see the President. Still, something in her alert gaze— The room wavered, light blurred into pools.

"—between the microscopic and the macroscopic, a theme—"

Moisture on his cheeks. Gordon peered through his fuzzed focus at the lanky outline of the President, seeing him as a darker blotch beneath the burning spotlights. Beyond him, no less real, were the names from Cambridge, each a figure, each knowing the others, but never wholly. The shadowy figures moved now beyond reach, bound for their own destinations just as he and Ramsey and Marsha and Lakin and Penny were. But they were all simply figures. A piercing light shone through them. They seemed frozen. It was the landscape itself which changed, Gordon saw at last, refracted by laws of its own. Time and space were themselves players, vast lands engulfing the figures, a weave of future and past. There was no riverrun of years. The abiding loops of causality ran both forward and back. The timescape rippled with waves, roiled and flexed, a great beast in the dark sea.

The President had finished. Gordon stood. He walked to the dais on wooden feet.

"The Enrico Fermi Prize for—"

He could not read the citation on it. The faces hung before him. Eyes. The glaring light—

He began to speak.

He saw the crowd and thought of the waves moving through them, breaking into white, swallowing foam. The small figures dimly sensed the eddies of the waves as paradox, as riddle, and heard the tick of time without knowing what they sensed, and clung to their linear illusions of past and future, of progression, of their opening births and yawning deaths to come. Words caught in his throat. He went on. And he thought of Markham and his mother and all these uncountable people, never loosening their grip on their hopes, and their strange human sense, their last illusion, that no matter how the days moved through them, there always remained the pulse of things coming, the sense that even now there was yet still time.

ON THE OTHER SIDE OF TIME AND SPACE

AND SPACE

Stories of
Fantastic, Futuristic Worlds
That Illuminate Universes

Pocket Books offers the best in Science Fiction—
a genre whose time has come.

_____	43684	**JUNIPER TIME** Kate Wilhelm	**$2.75**
_____	41593	**RUINS OF ISIS** Marion Zimmer Bradley	**$2.25**
_____	82917	**ROAD TO CORLAY** Richard Cowper	**$1.95**
_____	82876	**A WORLD BETWEEN** Norman Spinrad	**$2.25**
_____	81207	**JOURNEY** Marta Randall	**$1.95**
_____	42882	**COLONY** Ben Bova	**$2.95**
_____	82835	**EYES OF FIRE** Michael Bishop	**$2.25**
_____	43288	**THE DEMU TRILOGY** F. M. Busby	**$3.50**
_____	81130	**DYING OF THE LIGHT** George R. R. Martin	**$1.95**

POCKET BOOKS, Department SFT
1230 Avenue of the Americas, New York, N.Y. 10020

Please send me the books I have checked above. I am enclosing $_____
(please add 50¢ to cover postage and handling for each order, N.Y.S. and N.Y.C.
residents please add appropriate sales tax). Send check or money order—no
cash or C.O.D.s please. Allow up to six weeks for delivery.

NAME_____

ADDRESS_____

CITY_____ STATE/ZIP_____